PLENTY TO HIDE

BY
Moira Leigh MacLeod

Plenty to Hide

Copyright © 2018 by Moira Leigh MacLeod

This book is a work of fiction. Any resemblance to persons, places or events, living or dead, is purely coincidental.

All rights reserved. No part of this publication may be reproduced, distributed, or transmitted in any form or by any means, including photocopying, recording, or other electronic or mechanical methods, without the prior written permission of the author, except in the case of brief quotations embodied in critical reviews and certain other non-commercial uses permitted by copyright law.

Tellwell Talent
www.tellwell.ca

ISBN
978-0-2288-0400-0 (Hardcover)
978-0-2288-0399-7 (Paperback)
978-0-2288-0401-7 (eBook)

Table of Contents

Chapter 1: The Hand.. 1
Chapter 2: The Storm... 5
Chapter 3: Who Took My Smokes 15
Chapter 4: The Abdominal Snowman........................... 23
Chapter 5: Lipstick, Lies and the Long Wait 33
Chapter 6: The Silver Compact.................................... 67
Chapter 7: The Change Purse 75
Chapter 8: Dirty Politics 81
Chapter 9: The Post 85
Chapter 10: Heckles and a Handbag 89
Chapter 11: The Big Surprise....................................... 97
Chapter 12: The Meeting 101
Chapter 13: Messages, Mufflers and Michael's Surprise 109
Chapter 14: The Bus, The Break-in and The Backlash 113
Chapter 15: Doubts, Dick Tracy and a Dead Cat 133
Chapter 16: Mannie and the Man in the Camel Hair Coat 145
Chapter 17: Biscuits, Brisket and the Boys 149
Chapter 18: A Funeral, a Fight and a Flat Cap.................. 161
Chapter 19: The Mending, the Mounties and the Madonna 173
Chapter 20: Flying Coal, Alfalfa and Tuna 181
Chapter 21: Window Pains... 193
Chapter 22: Egg Nog, Tinsel and Cleavage 201

Chapter 23: Ho…Ho…Ho and Off You Go 207
Chapter 24: She Friggin Bit Me 225
Chapter 25: A Funeral, a Shoe Box and the Finger. 237
Chapter 26: Off By One 255
Chapter 27: Pit Socks, a Menorah and a Blue Angel. 259
Chapter 28: Life Goes On 265
Postscripts: Till Next Time… 268

The Hand

Monday, Nov. 18, 1948

Gladys Ferguson stood on her snowy steps, rummaging at the bottom of her purse. She found her key, held it up to her driver and waved him on. She pushed the door open, grateful for the warmth of her small, tidy bungalow and turned on the kitchen light. She placed her woolen coat over the back of a chair and sat to unzip her boots. "That's strange," she murmured, looking at the small pools of dirty water dotting her freshly-waxed floor and then up at the ceiling for any sign of a leaky roof. She stood in the doorway to her pitch black living room, ran her hand along the inside wall and flicked the switch.

Gladys tried to scream, but only managed a high-pitched squeak. Her once dead-to-the-world intruder stirred. She brought her trembling hand to her mouth. "Please! Please, don't hurt me!" she begged. "Take what want and get out!"

Her unwelcomed visitor opened his eyes, momentarily confused by his surroundings. He pulled the patchwork quilt away from his head and sat up. "Gladys," he said in a raspy voice.

She backed into the door frame. "Please! Please! I beg—"

"*What?*"

"Don't...don't hurt—"

"Aunt Gladys! *It's me. Dan. Danny!*"

She laid her hand over her pounding chest and peered at the unfamiliar figure staring back at her. "*Danny?*"

"Yes, *Danny*," he said, slowly standing.

She took in the balding, bearded man smiling and walking toward her. "You don't look like Dan," she said, still unconvinced.

He started to laugh. "It's me. I swear. Hell, what's it been, fifteen years? Anyway, sorry I scared you. I didn't mean to fall asleep. I just collapsed from exhaustion."

Gladys kept her eyes on him. "Ya don't look like anythin I remember."

"Well, you haven't changed a bit," he said, thinking she was as fat and ugly as ever.

"How d'ya get in?"

"Basement door. Sorry, needs a new latch. I'll fix it in the morning."

"Where d'ya come from?"

"Newfoundland. Took a freighter to North Sydney. Musta walked ten or more miles before I got a lift. Look, I'm kinda in a bad way. He held up his left hand."

Gladys gasped. His four fingers were reduced to knobby stubs.

"Fishing accident," he said. "Having a little trouble findin work. Hard enough to get a job with two hands, let alone one. Hopin I can stay in my old room for a while till I get things sorted out."

Gladys looked down at his duffle bag. "I pretty much gave you up fer dead, not hearin hide nor hair from ya for so long."

"*Yeah*, you know me, never been one to put pen to paper. What can I say? I shoulda called."

"Well then, yer here now. Take off that coat of yours and put yer boots in the porch. I'll fix us some tea. It'll help warm you up and settle my frayed nerves. Then ya can explain what you've been up to all this time, and why ya didn't even bother to check in on yer old aunt." She turned to re-enter the kitchen. "Are ya hungry?"

"Famished. I could eat the leg off the lamb of God," he said, pulling out a chair and kicking off his boots.

Gladys put the kettle on, removed a roll of waxed bologna from the fridge and cut four thick slices. She stabbed one and held it up to her nephew who eagerly wolfed it down. "Police have been by looking for you, ya know."

"*The police?*"

"Yeah, Captain Dunphy. Came by a few times askin if I heard from ya."

"What the hell does he want with me?"

"Said he had some questions about the MacIntyre boy goin missin."

"*MacIntyre boy?* Christ! That was what, two years ago? What the heck would I know about that! I was working the lakes."

"I know that! It's that pervert, the boy's father. Keeps goin round tellin folks you were involved in the kidnappin."

Her hungry nephew was about to reach for a second slab of bologna, but stopped. *Kidnapping? How'd they find the kid? Did Lenny and Sylvie rat him out?*

"Go ahead and help yerself," she said, nodding to the cutting board. "MacIntyre's a sick man. Even claimed you were back in town and robbed me! Don't worry, I gave him and the police a piece of my mind. Told em ya weren't home in years and that it was him who robbed me! Just tryin to cause you more trouble, that's all. Miserable *so-n-so* broke into my shed and stole a good amount of my savins. Thinks he can get away with murder." She turned to face him, waving her bread knife in the air. "He'll get his comeuppance. Mark my words, he'll pay for it one way or another...if not in this world, the next. Ya want mustard on yer sandwich?"

Dan's mouth was dry. "*Kidnappin?* Hell, I ran into a buddy from home and he told me the kid fell off a cliff."

"That's what folks thought. Heard they were even plannin a service. Turns out some crazy couple snatched him up. Brother and sister, I think. Yes, I'm sure of it. Anyways, boy's home safe and sound. Don't get me wrong, I'm happy no harm came to the child, just sorry MacIntyre and that miserable wife of his didn't get their due. Not right what they put you through. Not right at all. So do ya want mustard or not?"

"Yes." Dan was now thinking it was a huge mistake to come back to town. He had hoped to come home, lay low for a while, get some quick cash and head back out. News of the kidnapping and of the police wanting to question him threw him for a loop. "So the couple who took the boy, they're in the slammer?"

"No, they're in the ground. Both dead." Gladys put his sandwich on the table. "Sit and eat," she said, returning to the counter for their teacups. "Sister died of some sorta contractible disease. Scarlet fever, I think it was. Heard her brother was eaten by coyotes. *Can you imagine?*"

Dan was reeling and wondered what, exactly, the cops knew. "I don't get it. What the hell do the police want with me? I mean—"

"I'm sure it's nothin. Yer friend, Sergeant McEwan, told me they knew you were in Ontario when the boy went missin. They just wanted to talk to ya cause you and the kidnapper..." She looked up at the ceiling, then shook her head. "I can't recall his name…Anyway, you two spent time together in Dorchester."

Dan ran his hand over his head. "That's it! Our paths crossed, so they think I had something to do with it! That's crazy!" He reached for his sandwich, awkwardly balanced it on his mangled hand and tore into it. "Goddamn bastards! Just trying to railroad me again."

Gladys poured his tea. "Don't get yerself all worked up. Like I said, they just wanna ask ya some questions. You just need to march down to Dunphy's office first thing in the mornin and straighten this all out." She stepped back when he glared at her.

"I'm not goin anywhere near that fuckin place!" he shouted.

She closed her eyes and covered her ears. Dan immediately regretted his outburst. He needed to be kinder to the one person he could turn to. He softened his tone. "I'm sorry. I'm tired. And…it's just that I don't trust the cops. They're all dirty. They've had it in for me for years. That's why they forced me out…turned on me. I was one of the good ones." He held up his hand. "Look at me now," he said, tearing up.

Gladys poured his tea. "I know life's not been fair to ya. Losin yer parents at such a young age. What happened at work, then Dorchester…now this," she said. She hesitated, then patted his damaged hand. "But you'll get back on yer feet. I'll help ya. I don't have much to give, other than a roof over yer head and food in yer belly, but I'm here and I'll support ya in any way I can." She smiled. "That's what families do. You've always had a good head for numbers. I'm sure we can find some office work for ya somewhere. I do have connections, ya know. Now on my third term as treasurer of the Benevolent Society. Raised almost one hundred and forty dollars at today's tea and sale. Maybe we can find ya somethin with the coal company. Trust me, this will all work out. Just give it time."

Dan nodded and pulled his hand away. "All the same, I need to lay low for a bit. Probably best no one knows I'm stayin here, at least till I talk to McEwan and sort this nonsense out. I don't need the cops breathin down my neck on top of everythin else I'm dealin with."

"The neighbours are bound to see you? What am I gonna tell them?"

"Tell em to mind their own goddamn business."

The Storm

Tuesday, Nov. 19

Alice stood in front of the mirror and ran her hands down her sides.

"Luke's knees are going to buckle when he sees you walk down the aisle," Mabel said.

Alice turned sideways and laid her hand against her flat belly. "I don't know. The crinoline makes my hips and arse look huge."

Mabel lifted the hem of Alice's dress and peered under. "Pretty sure we can take it out. We'll just need to hem it up an inch or two."

"But what would Ma think? She was so happy when I told her I'd be wearing her dress. It won't be the same. And I promised her."

"Your mother would have wanted you to wear whatever makes you happy. And it'll still be her dress. But it's up to you. Personally, I think you'll look beautiful whatever you decide. And just wait till we put your hair up and add a little makeup."

Alice turned so Mabel could undo the buttons in the back. "I'm afraid my makeup will be streaking down my face. You can't even mention the wedding and Da starts crying. I know he's going to start bawling like a baby when he walks me down the aisle. Then I'll start. And you know what happens when I cry. My eyes swell up, my face gets all blotchy, and my nose starts to run faster than McAskill's Brook. I'll be a snotty mess. And all those people staring at me…makes me shudder."

"Your father still misses your mother and knows how much she wanted to see you get married. You worry too much. You'll see, Corliss will rise to the occasion and everything will come off like clockwork. It's going to be a beautiful day."

"I hope so. It's just…well to be honest… I'm scared."

"Is it the … you know…*the Tango*?" Mabel asked.

Alice gave her a bewildered look.

"You know… *the nasty*…the wedding night? Because if–"

"No. It's *not that*. It's…well…it's the whole thing."

Alice stepped out of her dress and sat in front of her mirrored dresser. Mabel walked up behind her and pulled Alice's ponytail loose.

"Did you have doubts? I mean, about whether Stanley was the one?"

Mabel smiled and dropped her head, thinking back to the shack and the night Stanley proposed. She hadn't doubted for a second that he was the man she wanted to spend the rest of her life with. From the morning he surprised her at the brook and they talked on the footbridge, she knew no one else could ever measure up to her gentle coal hauler. Still, she had resisted his proposal, not because of any doubts about him, but because of her shame; a secret shame only she and Stanley ever shared.

Alice looked in the mirror at Mabel's thoughtful expression. "Sooo, *you did have doubts!*"

Mabel knelt beside her. "Alice, every marriage is a leap of faith. Not just in the person you plan to spend your life with, but in yourself. You have to trust your heart. What does yours tell you?"

Alice hesitated.

"You do *love* Luke?" Mabel asked.

"Yes."

"Then, there you have it," Mabel said. "It's only natural to have pre-wedding jitters. Honestly, I'd be surprised if you didn't feel a little nervous. After all, it's the biggest decision you'll ever make."

"I guess."

Mabel lifted Alice's hair up off her neck and held it at the back of her head. "What do you think of a French braid?"

Alice shrugged. "So, do you think Luke is having doubts?" she asked.

Mabel laughed. "Honestly, no. I've never seen him happier. He's like a new man. You can't wipe the grin off his face. He's fixed up the store and is taking his medication. I can't remember the last time he had an episode. And he's going to see about his leg. All the things he didn't care about before you two got together. You bring out the best in him. He's been mad about you from the first time he saw you at the store. But that's not to say that he isn't a little nervous about the actual ceremony. God, he's even got Stanley trying to teach him the two step. Now, there's a sight," she said. She squeezed Alice's shoulders. "So, you okay?"

Alice smiled and nodded. "Thank you."

"Good. Now that we have that settled, what to do with your hair? And has the future Mrs. Toth decided if she'd prefer to walk down the aisle with a flat fanny, or a big bottom?"

Dan turned on his side and looked at the clock on the bedside table. It was almost ten. He was relieved Gladys had already left for work and that he didn't have to wake up to her constant nagging or fend off her nosy intrusions. He held up his throbbing left hand and squeezed his eyes shut, questioning his decision to return home. But then what choice did I have, he thought. Not like I could stay on in Quidi Vidi with no work and the Captain of the Hunky Dory out to kill me. "Fuck," he whispered, cursing himself for being so careless and getting caught screwing the boss's daughter. He leaned back on his pillow, thinking about his predicament and weighing his options. Maybe, I should go to the police and just deny any association with Lenny. Afer all, I have an airtight alibi for when the kid went missing and Lenny isn't around to dispute anything I say. Or, I can do as I planned, get my hands on some quick cash, head west and resume my life as Barry Sheppard.

He lit a cigarette, wondering what his aunt did with the money from the tea and sale, and if she still hid her savings in the shed. "Wouldn't surprise me in the least," he mumbled, thinking she was as dumb as a post. He looked around the room and momentarily felt a tinge of guilt. It was exactly as it was thirty-five years ago when he arrived as an eight-year old orphan with nowhere else to go. Same wallpaper. Same furniture. Same boyhood treasures.

He butted his cigarette, walked to the dusty bookcase and ran his finger over the gilded titles stamped on the spines of the tales he used to devour. *The Last of the Mohicans. Treasure Island. Swiss Family Robinson.* He stopped at *Robinson Crusoe*, easing it from the tightly packed array of classics his uncle would proudly present to him whenever he had managed to scrape together a few extra dollars. He opened the cover and flipped through the pages, stopping at an inky sketch of an unoccupied island dotted with palm trees; their spiky heads bending toward the sand from the powerful, invisible wind.

Dan slowly closed it over and ran his hand over the cover, thinking, like his boyhood hero, he was stuck in a place he had no way out of. "Fucking cops!" he screamed, sending the book flying across the room.

A half hour later, he was putting the shed's floorboards back in place, resigned to the fact that there was no immediate escape. For now, at least, he'd have to put up with the mind-numbing ramblings of his fat-assed aunt and act the doting nephew.

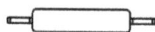

"I'm home. Whoa little one! Slow down."

"How are the roads?" Mabel hollered from the kitchen.

"Greasy." Stanley crouched beside Mary Margaret, pulled a hankie from his pocket and held it to his daughter's wet nose. "Can you blow for Daddy?"

"Good girl," he said, running it back and forth over her upper lip and feeling her forehead. He stood and started to remove his snowy jacket.

Mabel came around the corner cradling a casserole dish. She arched her eyebrows, smiled and held it out to him.

He knew the look. "*What?*"

"Do you mind?"

"Do I have a choice?"

"No."

"Didn't think so," he said. He began re-buttoning his jacket. "Let me guess. Lily?"

"Yes."

"Hey, JC! Want to come with Dad? Check on the horses and go for a drive."

JC put his pencil down and ran to the door. Stanley helped him on with his boots, as Mabel urged his arms through the sleeves of his woolen coat.

"Oh, just a minute," she said, running into the living room and returning with a bag. "Just some mittens and a couple of scarves I picked up for the little ones at the tea and sale. Be careful."

Mabel watched them get in the car, took Mary Margaret by the hand and returned to the kitchen to finish supper. An hour later she began to worry. She knelt on the sofa and pulled back the curtain. "Where are they?" she said, as the wind churned up the gathering snow. Two hours later she was frantic. She fed Mary Margaret, put her to bed and cleared the snow off of the front steps. She then paced back and forth in front of the living room window. The phone startled her. She ran to it, praying it was Stanley.

"Oh, hello, Flora? No, I was awake. Of course. Not like anything will be moving if this keeps up. Yes, I'll see you on Monday. Good night."

Mabel hung up, regretting she had ever hired her unreliable sitter. At least, this time, Flora had a good excuse. Thank goodness for Myrtle, she thought. She smiled thinking of how good Myrtle was to fill in in a pinch and of the special bond that had grown between her neighbour and JC.

She, once again, looked at the clock. It was now going on nine and, apart from the light from the front porch that illuminated the swirling snow, the night was the darkest she could remember. There were no headlights from passing cars on the street below and only a few dim emanations from homes in the distance.

'Damn it, Lily! Why don't you have a phone," she muttered, knowing full well the young widow and mother of three could ill afford such a luxury. She thought of Lily's circumstances and of the town that was largely unkind to her following Father Gregory's murder. How unfair that so many held her responsible for her husband's actions.

Mabel pulled Stanley's grey cardigan from the back of his chair, wrapped it around herself and walked to her wall of photos. She looked at a black and white image of James, thinking of how he had always looked out for her and of a similar stormy night many years ago. She and James had been standing in the window of the store watching the wind whip up the snow. James had been crying. Mabel had tried to ease his fears, assuring him that Luke would come home from the war and that they'd be together again.

Mabel dropped her head, thinking she had no idea at the time that it would be her last conversation with the man who was like a father to her. She kissed her finger tips and placed them on the fading photo. "You've always been my guardian angel. I need you now," she whispered. She then ran upstairs to her bedroom, removed Father Gregory's maniturgium from her dresser and spread it evenly over her bed. She knelt and prayed. "Dear Jesus in heaven, please keep them safe and bring them home to me."

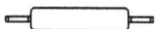

Gladys poked her head into the hallway. "Come get yer bed lunch," she hollered.

Dan strolled in and sat at the table.

"D'ya want marmalade or black current jam?" she asked.

"Marmalade."

Gladys poured Dan's tea. "Must be two feet down by now. I'll have to wear hip waders to get through that snow," she said, hoping her nephew might offer to shovel her front step. "Buses will likely be running late. I'll never get to work on time."

"Don't go."

"*Don't go?* I have to! I don't show up, I don't get paid."

"So you miss a day's pay. You're okay. The house is paid for. And Uncle Norman left you a good sum, *right*?" he asked, hoping she might give him some hint of her worth.

"Still, I gotta keep the heat and lights on. And the cost of groceries is goin through the roof. A ten pound bag of potatoes is almost fifty cents. And I'll be damned if I'll pay what Larry Mendelson's askin for a small brisket. Don't know how some folks manage."

Dan watched her waddle back to the stove. "If it weren't for this damn thing, I'd do it," he said, holding up his bad hand.

Gladys pulled the kitchen curtain aside and peeked out the window. "I'm sure I can shovel a small path to the neighbour's drive. Just hope it don't set off my sciatica."

"At least it's not a wet snow. Shouldn't take ya too long," he said, thinking she could use the exercise.

Gladys let the curtain fall back and returned to the table. "I wasn't goin to tell ya quite yet. Didn't want to get yer hopes up. I ran into Lizzie MacNeil today and she said they have an opening in the Clerk's Office. Accountin department. Notice hasn't been posted yet, but–"

"Ya didn't tell her I was back in town!"

"Of course not. Just asked her if she knew of any work opportunities."

"Good. Busybody would have it all over town."

"Well, if yer gonna be stayin, folks are gonna find out. And ya can't very well get a job without getting out there and lookin. I don't understand why ya just don't go to the police and set things right."

Dan pushed his chair back. "I told you! I don't trust them. I need to talk to McEwan. Find out what he knows."

"But, like you said, you were in Ontario. Just go down to the sta—"

"Goddammit! Enough!" he yelled, slamming his sore hand on the table. Gladys jumped. Dan pinched his forehead and lowered his voice. "You don't know what they're like. Just let me handle it." He smiled at her. "I'm sorry. I'm not myself. My hand is killing me. Cold weather doesn't help."

Gladys reminded herself that he had been through a lot and that his testiness was understandable. "I heard that when ya lose a limb, ya still feel like it's there. Do ya feel like ya still got yer fingers?"

"No. I don't feel like they're there. But sometimes I forget that they're not. Try and do something that used to come natural, then realize I can't."

"Must be awful. If ya don't mind me askin, how'd it happen? I mean, I know it was a fishin accident. Did ya get it caught up in somethin?"

"A pulley drive," he said, thinking he wasn't about to tell her his boss dragged him out of bed and severed his fingers with a cleaver. He closed his eyes, recalling the white bone sticking out of his detached, bloody fingers and the shrill screams of his young bedmate.

"Were ya at sea?"

"Yeah."

"And they just let you go? Didn't offer ya no compensation?"

"No. Just paid me what they owed me and sent me on my way. Was pretty well down to my last nickel after I paid the hospital fees."

Gladys shook her head. "You poor boy. Like I said, life ain't fair. And more's the pity, it's been downright cruel to you."

Mabel raised her head. She thought she heard thumping. She got up off her knees and quickly ran downstairs. She opened the door. JC's head was hanging limply over Stanley's shoulder. Stanley stomped his feet one last time to clear his boots of snow.

"Thank God! I was worried sick!" Mabel said, taking JC from her husband.

"He's pretty tired," Stanley said, entering and slapping at the snow caked to his pant legs.

Mabel carried JC into the living room and began removing his coat and boots. "What happened?" she hollered over her shoulder.

"Lily's pipes were frozen. Couldn't very well leave her without water. Then the car got stuck on Sterling Road. There was no one around to help and no way to get it out."

"You walked from Sterling Road?"

"Had no other choice. Anyway, JC was a trooper. And we're here now."

Mabel brushed JC's wet hair away from his forehead. "Are you hungry, sweetie?"

"He's fine. Lily gave him some of your casserole," Stanley said.

JC's eyes were closed and his head bobbed. Mabel scooped him up. "Soup is on the stove. Might need to heat it up," she said, walking past Stanley with JC in her arms and carrying him up to his room. When she returned downstairs, Stanley was standing at the stove in his long johns, blowing into his hands. Mabel ran her hands up and down his arms. "I didn't know what to do. I swear if you were five minutes longer, I'd have gone looking for you."

"Then I'd be forced to check out every coal shed in town," he said, laughing. "That reminds me, I have to call Gracies first thing in the morning. Lily's down to her last bucket of coal."

Mabel picked her husband's wet pants off the back of the chair and placed them on the radiator, leaving a trail of wet, snowy puddles on the floor. She opened the pantry, pulled out the mop and swished it across the floor. "That poor woman. Life sure hasn't been fair to her. I had a word with the president of the Benevolent Society and he said they'd see what they could do to help. Warned me not to get my hopes up. Said some people are saying she concocted the whole story about her husband abusing her and the kids just to get close to Father Gregory. *Imagine?* They say if it weren't for her, Father Gregory would still be alive. It's all nonsense, of course. I hope her good-for-nothing husband goes to jail for the rest of his days."

Stanley lathered his bread with butter, doubled it up and dunked it in his pot of pea soup. "I wouldn't bet on it. Sam tells me he's appealing his conviction. Has some hotshot lawyer from Halifax." He took a bite and ran his hand over his wet chin. "They're saying it was self-defence. Claim Lily's husband went to see Father Gregory to confront him about what he was up to with his wife, and that Father Gregory came at *him*. Sam said the authorities interviewed the oldest boy and that he denies being abused."

Mabel sat at the table. "He's a child for goodness sakes. Probably terrified. I was a lot older than he is when Johnnie was beating me, and *I* denied it. It's not right…the one person put on this earth to love and protect you, ends up being the one you fear most. Breaks my heart. Anyway, I'm sure the truth will come out and justice will be done. I just wish everyone wasn't so mean to her. She barely leaves the house and her kids are being tormented at school."

Stanley poured his soup into a bowl and joined her at the table. "I was thinking about hiring someone to help out at the office. Fred spends more time working the phones and doing the banking than he does on site. Not the best use of his skills or time. And I'm spending all my time on design."

"Can we afford to?"

"I think so. It wouldn't be full-time. Maybe fifteen…twenty hours a week. So what do you think?"

"If you think we can manage."

"Great. I'll tell Lily tomorrow."

"Lily!" Mabel squealed. She jumped to her feet, ran up behind him and wrapped her arms around his neck. "I love you, Mr. MacIntyre."

He grinned. "Good, cause I'm hoping that as soon as I finish my soup, you're going to take me upstairs and show me just how much."

Mabel smiled and whispered in his ear. "But it's not Friday."

He looked at his watch. "It will be soon."

Stanley stood to put his bowl in the sink. Mabel screamed, sending him stumbling backwards. He slipped on the wet floor, cracked his head against the leg of the table and sent the bowl flying.

Mabel was looking out the window and pointing. "There's…there's…somebody out there," she stammered.

Stanley scrambled to his feet.

Myrtle held the flashlight under her chin.

Mabel put her hand over her heart and shook her head. "Good Lord, why is she always sneaking up and scaring the daylights out of everybody."

Stanley opened the inside door, but couldn't push the screen door forward through the heavy snow. "Go around front," he yelled.

Mabel stood in the entrance. "Everything okay, Myrtle?" she asked, still feeling the aftereffects of her fright.

"I was clearing my front step and locked myself out," Myrtle said. She looked at Stanley in his long underwear and quickly turned her head to the side.

"Well, take off those wet clothes. You can stay here the night," Mabel said.

Myrtle looked at the floor.

Mabel elbowed Stanley. "Go put on some pants."

He was halfway upstairs when he heard Myrtle say she preferred her own bed. He dropped his head, knowing what that meant. Ten minutes later, he was back outside, trudging through the heavy snow with his neighbour in tow. It took several attempts to free Myrtle's front porch window free from its frozen sill. He walked home the way he came; the blowing snow hiding any trace of his recent journey.

Mabel was waiting up for him. She, once again, heard the familiar thumping on the front step and opened the door. "You must be tired?" she asked.

"Exhausted."

"That's too bad."

"And why is that?" Stanley asked.

Mabel nodded to the clock on the mantle. "It's Friday."

Stanley tore off his coat, pulled off his icy pants and took her by the hand.

They were at the top of the stairs when they heard the first whimper. They stopped and looked at Mary Margaret's door. Mabel put her finger to her mouth. "She'll fall back to sleep," she whispered.

They were climbing under the covers when the whimper turned to a wail.

"I love her to death," Stanley said, "but seriously, it's like she knows what we're up to."

Who Took My Smokes

Thursday, Nov. 21

Gladys tapped lightly on the door. "Dan, you awake?"

Fuck not now, he thought. "Yeah."

"I'm off to work."

"All right, see you tonight," he panted, hoping she'd bugger off so he could get back to pleasuring himself.

"I left the latch for the basement door on the counter. Hopin ya can fix it today. We're getting more snow and I don't want it blowin in again."

"Yep."

"And I fixed yer lunch. It's in the fridge. Hash…corned beef."

"Okay."

"And if ya don't mind strippin yer bed and runnin yer sheets through the wash. Just hang em on the radiators. Oh, and don't forget to bank the furnace."

He rolled his eyes. "I won't."

"See ya tonight."

Dan sighed, resigned to the fact that she killed the mood. He pulled his hand from under the covers and reached for his packet of Players. He lit one of his three remaining cigarettes, closed his eyes and leaned back, recalling his dream. He was on top of the captain's daughter, driving into her as she screamed his name and dug her nails into his back. Then, it wasn't his young conquest, but Mabel under his hard, muscular body. He was pleasing her in every way possible, and she was loving it.

He sucked in the harsh smoke, sending billowy, blue circles in the air. Over and over again, he replayed the dreamy vision of Mabel writhing under him and begging him not to stop. He lightly tapped his cigarette in the ashtray and laid back down, grateful Gladys was gone and there'd be no more interruptions.

He was sweating and spent. He took a sip of water and placed his glass back on the night table. "Yep. It's a good day to do the sheets," he laughed, pulling the covers up over his shoulder and rolling on his side. He was almost asleep, then his eyes flashed open. He could smell something. He leaned onto his elbow and looked at the floor. His smoldering cigarette had melted away the braided yarn of the rug, leaving a burn mark and an awful stench. "Fuck," he said, reaching for his glass and dousing it with his tepid water. He sat up. "I need to get outa here. Get some fresh air," he mumbled.

An hour later, he was craving a beer. He scraped the remains of his tasteless hash into the garbage and dumped Gladys' milk money jar onto the counter. He was gathering up the loose change when he noticed the unopened latch. He picked it up, examined it and tossed it back down.

At first, he walked with his head down, but soon grew more confident. If Gladys didn't know her own nephew, maybe no one else would recognize him either. He decided to test his theory, offering a passing hello to an old classmate. It worked, he had no idea who he was. He then greeted several more passers-by whom he knew from his days as a cop. Again, they simply nodded and continued on their way.

It took him almost an hour to get to town. He leaned against the stone fence in front of St. Agnes Church, buoyed by his anonymity. No one had a clue who he was. He smiled, realizing his fears were unfounded. He was a stranger in his own home-town. Then, he spotted Willie.

He stood up. "Hey, Willie!"

The simpleton and one-time contender for the national welter weight title, stopped punching the air. He turned to the stranger calling his name.

Dan waved him over.

Willie approached, bobbing and weaving, and bouncing on his toes.

Dan held his arms up as if to protect himself, then laughed. "Got a big fight comin up?" he asked.

"No. No big fight," Willie said.

"Remember me?"

"No. Did I fight ya?"

"I'd never step in the ring with you. Yer way too good for me," Dan said.

Willie grinned and, once again began jabbing at his invisible opponent.

"Wouldn't have a buck or two to help out an old friend?" Dan asked.

Willie dropped his arms and looked around. "No. No money. Sister takes it." He pointed across the street to the Bank of Nova Scotia. "Puts it in there. No, no money. Sister takes it. All in the bank."

Dan leaned back against the fence as a stern-looking, well-dressed woman walked toward them.

"Willie! Stanley's looking for you," Myrtle said, pointing to Stanley standing outside the pool hall. She nodded to the unfamiliar man who was talking to Willie and crossed the street.

"Myrtle's got money. Lots a money. Rich. Paints pictures. Pretty pictures. Gotta go. Boss is lookin for me. Gotta go."

"See ya, bud," Dan said, watching Myrtle enter Arlies. When he turned back, Stanley was walking toward Willie. Dan put his hood up and his head down.

Willie ran to his boss. Stanley draped his arm over his friend's thin shoulder and guided him back to the car. "Who was that you were talking to?" he asked, turning his head to check for oncoming traffic.

"I dunno. Don't remember. Won't fight me. Said I'm too good," Willie said, grinning from ear to ear.

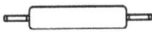

Dan entered The Pithead and sat on a stool at the far end of the bar, careful to keep his damaged hand out of view. He was nursing his fourth beer when Fred Clarke sat beside him.

Fred looked at the bartender and nodded to Dan's foamy, black lager. "I'll have the same." He rubbed his hands together. "Friggin cold out there," he said, throwing his Export A's on the counter and draping his jacket over the back of his stool.

Dan nodded, thinking, like everyone else, his uncle's old fishing buddy had no idea who he was sitting beside.

Fred tried to make small talk, but quickly got the message the stranger sitting next to him had no interest in making a new friend.

"There you are," Fred said, jumping off his stool and greeting Luke at the door. The two decided to take a table near the window. Fred returned to the bar to pay his tab and collect his jacket. He was walking toward Luke, when he suddenly stopped and made his back to the bar. "Hey, Skanky? Did you see my smokes?"

The young bartender turned his attention away from another thirsty customer and shrugged.

"They were right here on the bar."

"Sorry," Skanky said.

Fred patted his jacket, then looked at the introverted stranger who he had sat next to. He was dumping a handful of change on the counter and separating the coins with his index finger. His other hand was in his pocket.

"Hey, buddy? Ya didn't happen to take my smokes by mistake, did ya?"

Dan pushed the exact change toward the bartender and picked up the remaining coins. "Nope."

"Yer sure?"

Dan glared at him.

"What's in yer pocket?"

"Fuck you!"

"Look, just give me back my smokes. No harm done. I'll even give you a couple for the road."

"Told ya. I didn't take yer fuckin smokes."

"Then how about showin me what's in your pocket?"

"You wanna see what's in my fuckin pocket!"

"Yeah! I do!" Fred said.

Luke jumped to his feet, worried fists were going to start flying and that Fred was about to be pummeled by the beast towering over him.

Dan suddenly charged at Fred. He grabbed him by the collar, pulled his gnarly hand from his pocket and shoved it in his face. "There! Satisfied, arsehole!"

Fred recoiled at the gruesome sight and immediately felt ashamed. He looked around the now deadly quiet bar, taking in the familiar, wide-eyed patrons staring back.

"Sorry, bud. Really! I just thought…" Fred stammered. He quickly reached in his pocket and pulled out a twenty dollar bill. "Here, let me buy you a beer."

Dan swiped it out of his hand. "Thanks, I'll buy my own," he said and walked out. He crossed the street, reached in his right pocket and tapped his packet of Export A's against his bad hand. A cigarette popped loose. He bent down, biting it between his teeth. He quickly pulled it out of his mouth. "Well, look at that," he whispered. Stanley was laughing and holding the door open for Dirty Willie and Ten-After-Six. "Boys are havin a night out on the town and the little missus is home all by her lonesome."

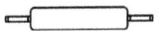

Gladys made her way up the snowy path, anxious for a cup of tea to warm her chilled bones. The house was in darkness. Dan must be out, she thought. She stepped in and shivered, thinking it was almost as cold inside, as it was out. She turned on the light and looked at the dirty dishes and the unopened latch on the counter. She then walked to the radiator and felt the sheets. They were cold and damp. She stood on the landing to the basement, pulled the overhead string to light her way and carefully stepped down the steep stairs. She looked at the snow gathering around the partially closed door, shook her head, then banked the furnace. She was re-entering the kitchen when she heard him in the porch.

"Yer home. Ya musta got off early," Dan said, pulling out a chair and kicking off his boots.

"It's after six."

Dan recognized her tone and knew she was pissed. "Sorry, I meant to get home earlier. Tidy up a bit. I got tied up."

"With McEwan?"

"No. I called the station. He's outa town."

"*Really*?"

"Yeah, *really*."

Gladys could tell he had been drinking. "I thought I saw him on Commercial Street today."

"Don't think so. Unless buddy at the station was just givin me the brush off," Dan said, peeling off his coat.

"Ya might want to leave it on. Ya didn't bank the furnace, like I asked."

"Shit. I knew there was something I forgot."

Gladys picked up the latch. "It wasn't the only thing you fergot."

He gave her an apologetic look. "Tomorrow, I promise."

"So, yer finally leavin the house?"

"Started to get antsy. Needed some fresh air."

"Who d'ya meet up with?"

"No one you'd know. Guy I used to play hockey with," he lied.

"Then I guess it's okay for me to talk to Lizzie about—"

"Not this again," he said, waving his arm over the table.

"Where were ya? I know ya were drinkin?"

"Buddy's place. Ran into him outside Murdoch's store. I needed smokes," he said, tossing his cigarettes on the table. "By the way, I borrowed some of your milk money." He reached in his pocket and passed her the twenty dollar bill he took from Fred. "Here," he said. "Got lucky at cards. Now ya can afford a brisket."

"Keep it. You need it more than me. Just don't go wastin it on liquor."

"Ya sure?" he asked, shoving it back in his pocket.

"Ya can buy me a brisket once ya get work."

"And a dozen roses to boot," he said, winking at her.

They ate supper with their coats on. Dan promised her he'd track down McEwan, clear the air with Captain Dunphy and start looking for work.

Gladys was putting his stiff sheets on the bed when she spotted the splayed book on the floor next to the bookcase. She picked it up. "Yer reading your old favourites?" she said.

"No. Fraid I out grew them. I'm more into detective novels…Dashiell Hammett and Raymond Chandler. Anyway, I meant to put it back. My sore hand started searin and I dropped it. Had to lie down. Sorry."

Gladys slid it back in place. "Yer uncle loved buyin ya these books. Remember him readin them to ya?"

"Yeah. He was a good guy. I sure miss him," Dan said.

"He loved ya like his own," Gladys said. She ran her fingertips over the top of the dusty bookcase, brushed them against her apron and returned to make the bed.

Dan looked down at edge of the burnt rug sticking out from under the bed, hoping she wouldn't see it.

Gladys chopped his pillow with the side of her hand and laid it against the headboard. "There, all set." She was on her way out, but turned back. "I'll likely be at work by the time yer outa bed, so don't forget about the latch. Good night," she said and closed the door.

Dan crawled under the warm sheets, hoping they'd bring him back to Mabel and his dream from the previous night. He tried to re-envision her naked body on top of him, but couldn't concentrate. His mind jumped to the scene in the bar, to his conversation over supper with his pushy aunt, and to the police and what they might know. His instincts as a former cop nagged at him. Gladys had assured him they just wanted to talk to him because he and Lenny spent time together in Dorchester, but there had to be more to it than that. Did Lenny tell them anything before he died? So what if he did, he thought. It'd be my word against that of a dead man. Suspicions were hardly proof. Hell, I'm probably getting worked up over nothing. Maybe I should just get a job for a while, save what I can and move on. What other choice do I have? He had searched high and low for any money Gladys might have had stashed away, but with no luck. And apart from a few pieces of jewelry and some silverware, there wasn't much to hawk. "Fuck," he murmured and lit a cigarette, thinking back to his conversation with Dirty Willie. *Myrtle's got money. Myrtle's rich. Paints pretty pictures."*

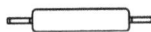

Stanley crept upstairs and quietly crawled in next to his wife.

"How was your night?" she asked.

"Sorry. I didn't mean to wake you."

"You didn't. I'm too excited to sleep."

He snuggled up closer, spooning her. *"Oooh?"*

Mabel laughed. "Don't go getting any ideas. Amour called. They're coming home."

Stanley nuzzled her neck. "That's terrific. When?"

"Not sure. They haven't made the arrangements. Michael's got an interview with the coal company on the twenty-ninth. Might be getting his old job back."

"So they might be moving home for good?"

"Maybe. Michael told Amour not to get her hopes up. He still has to meet with the president and board of directors. Anyway, Amour said they'd be home in time for the wedding and will be staying for Christmas. She'll call as soon as they arrange their flights."

Stanley kept nuzzling her neck. "They're flying?"

"Yes. Wouldn't be me," Mabel said. "I still can't figure out how they keep those contraptions in the air. *Oh*, and don't go spillin the beans to Myrtle. Amour wants to surprise her. Actually, don't tell a soul. You tell one person and the next thing you know you might as well have taken out an ad in The Post. So, did you have fun tonight?"

"Yeah. But Fred had a run in with some guy at the bar." Stanley ran his hand up and down her leg. "I have a favour to ask," he whispered.

"What's that?" Mabel said, smiling to herself.

"Luke's looking for another dance lesson. I'm hoping—"

Mabel elbowed him. "Sorry. I offered. He said I make him too nervous."

"And I don't?" Stanley said. "It's not right, two grown men waltzing around like that."

"You make a very handsome couple," Mabel said, laughing.

Stanley put his hand on her shoulder, rolled her over onto her back and bent down to kiss her.

Mabel grimaced.

"What's wrong?" Stanley asked.

"You smell like a brewery."

"I can fix that," he said, quickly tossing the covers aside and tearing out of bed for the bathroom. He entered the hallway and stopped dead in his tracks. Mary Margaret was coming out of her room and rubbing her eyes. He picked her up and took her back to her room, promising her he'd give her a special treat if she stayed in her own bed. Ten minutes later, he cupped his hands, blew into them and sniffed, satisfied he had replaced the bitter taste of Indian Pale ale with the minty taste of Gleem. He ran back to his room and jumped in bed, next to JC.

"You smell sooo good," Mabel said, snickering.

"*Seriously?*" he said, rolling over onto his side and roughly pulling the covers up over his head.

The Abdominal Snowman

Friday, Nov. 22

Dan pressed the latch in place with the thumb of his bad hand and leaned in, turning the last screw in place. He stepped back to examine his work. It was crooked. He tried flipping the side arm over, but it wouldn't fit in place. Despite the cold, his stumpy hand was burning. He picked up a hammer and tapped the underside of the latch. "Fuck this," he said, tossing the hammer back in the toolbox. He returned to the house and washed his breakfast dishes. He didn't need Gladys coming home and giving him the gears for not cleaning up after himself. He tried to read The Post, but threw it aside. He felt like he was going crazy, like he was back in Dorchester and the walls were closing in on him. He put his coat on and headed for town. He'd steer clear of The Pithead. Maybe, check out Iggies and sucker some poor schmuck into a game of poker. With any luck, he could put the slight-of-hand tricks he perfected in Dorchester to good use and parlay his twenty into ten times as much. He could even use his sore hand to his advantage. No one would question why he kept it off the table.

He walked down Commercial Street, dodging the end-of-the week shoppers streaming in and out of the unusually busy shops; their windows, plastered from top to bottom with hand-painted signs proclaiming amazing discounts on everything from fresh fish to used furniture. He stopped at the same place he spotted Dirty Willie the day before and, once again, leaned against the fence, a popular gathering place for those anxious to catch up on the latest scuttlebutt. He looked to his left, eyeing similarly bored men, dancing on the balls of their feet and blowing into their hands to fend off the numbness that accompanied the raw, wet air. Their wives or girlfriends, he supposed, warmly browsing inside for that special something they'd never find, or could ill afford.

He smiled when he saw her approach. A young boy was walking ahead of her, and she was holding a toddler's hand.

"JC! Wait for mom," Mabel called out.

They stopped within two feet of him. He could hear Mabel tell them to look both ways before crossing the street. The boy's mitten fell from his pocket.

Dan hesitated, then picked it up. He tapped Mabel on the shoulder. "Yer boy dropped his mitten."

"Thank you," Mabel said and smiled.

She doesn't have a clue, Dan thought, feeling a familiar stirring. He closed his eyes, thinking of what it would be like to have his way with her. Would she respond like she did in his dreams.

Mabel took JC's hand. "Okay, let's go."

Dan followed them as far as Mendelsons, wondering how she and Stanley came to be reunited with their son. He pretended to read the weekend flyer taped to the window, and watched Larry Mendelson reach into the pocket of his white meat cutter's jacket and pass a red penny sucker to the boy, and a yellow one to his sister. Mabel smiled, gratefully acknowledging the kind man who was always so generous to his patrons and their children. Don't be fooled, Dan thought. Greedy bastard's only gonna gouge you at the checkout counter. He kept watching, until he lost sight of them, then continued up Commercial Street. He stopped when he noticed the paintings in Arlies' window. He bent down and looked at the childlike initials scrawled in the bottom, right corner. *MM.* He entered and edged his way down the narrow aisles crammed with wooden toys, hand-knit wares and cheap perfume.

"Can I help you?" a young man asked.

"Just looking round. *Oh*, the pictures in the window? They expensive?"

"Smaller ones go for five. Larger ones, for eight. They're pretty popular. We got a few more in the back if ya wanna check em out." The young man turned to his co-worker who was re-stocking shelves with model airplanes and miniature toy soldiers. "That reminds me, Myrtle's comin in after choir practice for her consignment money. If I'm not here, make sure ya tell Lester to set it aside."

Dan wondered if Myrtle, like Gladys and so many others burnt by the Great Crash, didn't trust the banks. He made his way to the back of the store.

Brightly coloured paintings of barns, boats and birds hung on the wall; a good number of exposed nails, confirming their popularity. I should probably get the old hag something for Christmas, he thought. The lobster boat, piled high with traps and sitting low in the water, caught his eye. Gladys would be pleased. It would remind her of Uncle Norman's boat. He looked around, quickly lifted it off the wall and shoved it under his coat. He lingered for a while, picking up the odd trinket and slowly putting them back in place, then headed for the exit.

The young clerk behind the checkout smiled. "See anything ya liked?"

"Sorry, way too expensive for me," Dan said, thinking Arlies could use his skills as a security guard.

Forty minutes later he was sitting on the can in Iggies, examining the crude painting and wondering why anyone would waste good money on such a useless thing. He began tapping his finger over the artist's initials. "So, Miss Myrtle, exactly how rich are ya?" he whispered.

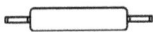

Kenny Ludlow turned at the sound of boots on crusty snow and watched their familiar silhouettes approach. "Bout time," he called out to Tommy Simms and Harley Woodward. He ran to Tommy. "Did ya get it?"

Tommy opened his jacket, exposing almost a full quart of Lamb's Navy rum.

Kenny grabbed it and held it up. "Party time."

The boys began kicking away the hard snow gathered at the base of the Chimney. "What are we gonna use for mix?" Harley asked.

"Frosty," Kenny said, pointing to the necks of a half dozen bottles sticking out of a mound of snow.

They sat huddled together, looking out over the gully below; their breath visible in the crisp night air. Tommy unscrewed the rum and Kenny uncapped a Frosty. They both looked at one another and then at Harley.

"*What?*" Harley asked.

"Did you bring cups?" Kenny asked.

"Darn it!" Harley said.

"Jesus, Harley, ya got a brain like a friggin sieve," Kenny said.

Harley quickly reached in his pocket. "But I brought the smokes."

Kenny grabbed the rum from Tommy, took a large swig and began coughing. "Holy shit, that's strong," he choked. He opened two more Frosties and passed them to his friends. "Drink half of it. Then we can add the hooch."

"Jesus, Kenny, yer smart," Harley said. "I'd never of thought of that."

"So, we're all set? Yer parents won't be home till late?" Kenny asked Tommy.

"Yeah. We're good. They're goin to the Colliery bowlin party in Number Two. It'll be midnight before they stumble in. Gotta warn ya, though, they'll either burst through the door tearing each other's clothes off, or they'll be biffin boots at one another. One minute they're yelling and cursin at each other, the next, they're all lovey-dovey. I ain't never gonna get married. Makes ya all friggin weird in the head."

"But they know we're bunking at your place, right?" Kenny asked.

Tommy took a sip of his drink and pinched his eyes closed. "Yep."

Kenny clinked his bottle against Tommy's, then Harley's. "Here's to a good night," he said.

An hour later they were smoking the last of their cigarettes and sipping straight rum.

"Look at that moon," Tommy said. "It's friggin huge."

"Which one," Harley slurred. He stood to hurl his empty pop bottle into the gully, lost his footing and fell headfirst. He tried to get up, but kept falling back down.

"He's loaded," Kenny laughed.

Harley finally got to his feet and turned around. His face was covered in snow.

"The...the abdominal snowman," Kenny said, pointing and laughing.

"It's *not* ab..dom..in..al snowman," Tommy slurred. "It's ab...abob min...abob...mini...niable."

They were all laughing now. "We're drunk," Harley said, flopping down and waving his arms across the hard snow. "My bodies warm, but my balls are freezin."

"Well get off the friggin ground," Kenny said.

Tommy turned and looked at the stone chimney that was a popular gathering spot for kids up to no good. "Too bad we didn't bring some wood. We coulda built a fire."

Kenny started laughing.

"What's so funny?" Tommy asked.

Kenny was now bent over, struggling to talk.

"*What?*" Tommy repeated.

"I was just thinkin…I was thinkin about…about…Mr. Spenc…Mr. Spencer's…Pon…Pon…Pontiac."

Tommy burst out laughing.

"Remember…remember lookin out the window and seein it burst into flames. Fuck, I thought we were done for," Kenny said.

"And remember the time the witch poured her beet juice over us and cast the spell on us? I was sure my dick was gonna fall off," Tommy said.

"*Seriously?*" Kenny said, still trying to get his laughing under control. "I knew she was fulla crap."

Tommy shoved him. "Bullshit! I remember you askin me how my dick was. Ya wouldn't been askin, if ya weren't scared shitless."

Kenny wiped his eyes. "Okay. Maybe just a little."

Harley rolled onto his side and spewed his frothy, black brew over the hard, glistening surface of crusty, white snow.

"Uh-oh," Tommy said, "He's pissed to the kills. How the hell are we gonna get him home?"

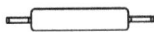

Dan stood outside Iggies, disappointed his visit wasn't as profitable as he had hoped. He only managed to get in one game of poker and spent his meagre winnings on whiskey. He wondered if Gladys was home making supper. She'll probably have another hissy fit if she finds out I had a few drinks, he thought. He needed to kill a couple of hours and hope the old crow would be in bed when he arrived home.

He walked back to the fence, surprised to see a few stores still open. "Greedy bastards extended their hours in the lead up to Christmas so they can suck the last dollar out of every sentimental schmuck," he mumbled. He opened his coat and repositioned Myrtle's painting so it wouldn't slip down to his waist and sat on the cold stone, hoping the buses were still running. He was lighting a smoke, when he saw her in the doorway of Arlies. She tugged on her gloves, stepped out and turned down the street. He wondered if she was heading home. He threw his smoke on the ground. Only one way to find out, he thought, pulling up his hood.

Myrtle took the path to the brook. She stopped partway down the hill, brushed fresh snow off a bench and sat facing the town's Christmas tree.

Dan hid among the trees that formed a natural boundary between Catherine Street and the brook, and glanced back at the empty street and blackened store windows. Did ya pick up your consignment money, he thought.

Myrtle was looking up at the full moon when she heard the crunching snow. She was about to turn, when Dan reached over her shoulder and lunged for her handbag. Myrtle quickly pulled it away and swung it at his head, knocking him off balance. She was scrambling up the path, when he grabbed her leg, pulling her down toward him. He was now on top of her, pushing her face into the snow with his mangled hand to mute her screams. There was a boulder sticking out of the snow. It took several attempts to kick it free of its snowy encasement. It only took one swift blow to crack Myrtle's skull open.

"Jesus," he whispered, dropping the rock, scrambling to his feet and staring down at the white snow turning black. He looked around, grabbed Myrtle by the arms and dragged her up under the trees. He then snatched up her handbag and quickly slid down the icy path to the water's edge. He ran along the side of the brook to the footbridge and looked back up the hill, relieved no one was in sight. "Don't run," he said to himself, slowing his pace to a brisk walk. He crossed the footbridge, climbed the hill, waded in among the alder bushes and spruce trees, and dropped to his knees. He dumped Myrtle's handbag upside down, throwing her lipstick, compact and glasses aside, then shoved her small change purse in his pocket. His damaged hand throbbed as he punched through the icy coating to the softer snow below. He grabbed her glasses and lipstick, tossed them back in her handbag and quickly buried it. A light came on. Dan peered under the limbs of the snowy trees to the property beyond and sat deadly quiet; the only sound, his heart pounding in his ears.

"Hurry up. Go do your business."

Dan didn't move. He could hear the dog scratching at the snow.

"Atta boy. C'mon!"

"Midway! Middie! C'mon, boy! Get in here!"

The Sheltie eagerly sniffed along the other side of the trees, then started barking. His impatient master approached. Dan could see his untied pit boots through the low-hanging, snow-covered boughs. There was a sudden, sharp yelp.

"Stupid dog! It's fuckin freezin out here! Get in the goddamn house!"

Dan heard the door close and waited for the light to go out. "Fuck," he whispered. He sucked in the piercing night air and began trudging through the knee-deep snow, holding his arm out to keep the stiff, icy branches from slapping his face. He finally reached the top of the steep path leading to Park Street, waited for a car to pass, then darted across to the deeper woods on the other side. He laid down and stared up at the moon, waiting for his heart to quiet and praying his aunt would be asleep when he got home. The last thing I need is to have that nosy, old witch peppering me with a ton of questions, he thought.

Kenny pulled on Harley's coat sleeve. "Get up!"

Harley mumbled.

"Christ, Tommy! Give me a hand."

They took hold of Harley's wrists, draped his arms over their shoulders and started down the path to the brook.

Tommy turned his head to the side and threw up.

"Fuck! Neither one of ya can hold yer liquor," Kenny said, thinking he didn't feel great either.

They were at the bottom of the path leading to Commercial Street when Kenny suddenly flung Harley's arm off his shoulder. "I need a piss," he said, climbing up to the edge of the trees.

Tommy tried to hold his rubber-legged friend up on his own, but crumpled under the weight, and fell to his knees. Harley slumped to the ground like a rag doll. "Fuck, Kenny. We're never gonna make it up the hill. We shoulda gone the other way, like I said."

"Yer crazy. No way we coulda drug puke face through the woods. Snows too friggin deep," Kenny said.

"Maybe I should go home and get my toboggan. We can pull him the rest of the way," Tommy suggested.

"For Christ sakes, keep yer voice down. You're gonna get us caught," Kenny whispered.

"I'm sick," Harley mumbled.

Tommy turned quickly toward Harley. "Sssh! Hey, what's that?" he said, crawling across the snow and picking up an overturned frame. He flipped it over and held it up to the moonlight. "I think it's one of the witch's paintings. Ma's gonna love this," he said, putting it inside his jacket.

Kenny watched his warm piss eat a hole into the glistening snow, then gave a quick shake and zipped up. "Ferget the toboggan. It'd take too long. I'll go to the bowlin alley and call my brother to see if he'll come get us." He pointed at the trees. "You and Harley can wait in there." He spotting something sticking out from below the branches and slowly approached. "Jesus Christ!"

"What is it?" Tommy called out from the bottom of the hill.

Kenny ducked under the boughs and knelt beside the body, lying face down in the snow.

"What is it, Kenny?" Tommy asked, again.

Kenny pushed the branches aside and scrambled to his feet "It's...it's—"

"Hey, what's goin on down there!"

Kenny looked up, immediately bringing his arm up to block the blinding light shining in his face. He started to run.

"Hey, you! Get back here!"

Kenny knew it was too late. "We...we... we were just walkin back from the Chimney and I ...I just saw her," he stammered.

Winston MacRae, a foreman at the Machine Shop, pushed him out of the way and rushed to the body. He rolled Myrtle onto her back and felt for a pulse. "Hurry! Go get help!"

Tommy crawled up the hill, looked down at the motionless body and the blood pooling around her head, and barfed.

Winston MacRae glared at Kenny. "Go! Quick! Get an ambulance!"

Kenny tore off, Tommy started to cry, and Harley lay passed out in the snow, oblivious to the fact that, come morning, he'd be locked up next to his two best friends and nursing a wicked hangover.

Stanley turned off the living room light and carried JC upstairs to bed. "One more night in your own bed," he whispered, pulling the blanket up over his shoulder and kissing his forehead.

Mabel was standing outside Mary Margaret's room holding a bottle of Buckley's cough syrup and a spoon. "I'm going to have to call Dr. Cohen."

"It's a *cold*," Stanley said, following her into their bedroom.

"A stubborn one. And I don't like that rattle in her chest. I wish she could bring it up."

"She'll be fine."

"Still, if she's no better by the time she wakes up, I'm taking her first thing in the morning. I'll need to get back and get the house in order. Change the beds. Do a wash. Clean the bathroom. Wax the floors. I certainly never expected Amour and Michael would be arriving so soon." She dropped her arms to her side. "God, I wish there were more hours in the day, or more days in the week. I've never felt so frazzled, with the wedding…and Christmas … not to mention all the orders were taking for the holidays."

Stanley kicked off his slippers. "I can take her."

Mabel smiled. *"Can you?"*

"Why not? One less thing for you to worry about." He dropped his pants, threw them on a chair and began unbuttoning his shirt.

"I thought the kids could sleep in our room. We'll put Mary Margaret back in her crib."

"She won't like it," Stanley said.

"I think she'll be okay as long as she's in with us. Victoria can have her room, and Amour and Michael can stay in JC's." She pulled the bedcovers back. "The bed's not ideal, but—" She stopped and looked at Stanley. "Is that someone at the door?"

"Apparently so."

"At this hour?"

Stanley grabbed his pants. He had one pant leg on and the other partway up, when the knocking got louder. "I'm coming," he yelled, hopping on one foot and urging his other through his twisted pant leg.

He pulled the front door open. "Gordon? What's going on?" he asked, zipping his pants.

"Sorry, I know it's late. Wasn't sure who else to turn to."

Mabel looked down from the hallway above. She could see her husband, but not who he was talking to. She sensed that whoever it was, they weren't bringing good news. She pulled her robe around her and started downstairs.

"Myrtle's in the hospital. It doesn't look good," Captain Dunphy announced.

"Dear God! What happened?" Mabel asked.

"She was attacked. Likely robbed. Don't know a whole lot at this point. Doctors were asking about next of kin. They think someone should be with her in case she passes through the night."

Mabel put one hand over her mouth and the other on the banister rail. "They think she's going to die?" she whispered.

"They said it's a good possibility. Took an awful blow to the head and lost a lot of blood."

"I won't be a minute," Mabel said and disappeared upstairs. She was dressed and back at the door in less than three minutes.

"Gordon will drive you," Stanley said. He held Mabel's coat open as she frantically pulled on her boots. She jumped up, shoved her fists into the arm holes and pulled her coat around her neck. She held up a finger and tore back upstairs. She almost tripped on the way down. She grabbed her purse, leaned in and kissed Stanley's cheek. "Pray for our friend," she said.

Stanley watched Mabel jump in next to Dunphy. She was clutching Margaret Cameron's Bible and Father Gregory's manitigurium.

Lipstick, Lies and the Long Wait

Saturday, Nov. 23

Charlotte Rogers tiptoed across the shiny floor and eased the open Bible off of Mabel's lap.

Mabel opened her eyes and rubbed her stiff neck. "How is she?" she asked, looking at Myrtle's bandaged head, black eyes and blotchy red face.

"Sorry for waking you. I thought your Bible was about to fall on the floor and I didn't want it to startle you. She's holding her own. No change, good or bad," Charlotte said, putting the Bible on a side table.

"Is she in a coma?"

"Yes." Charlotte walked to the side of Myrtle's bed, checked the bottle hanging from her IV pole and wiped away the fluid dripping from her patient's nose. She then leaned in to examine the bruising around Myrtle's ears.

"Why are her eyes black? Did they hit her in the face?"

"No. It's a symptom of the blow to her head. So is her runny nose. Her brain is swollen and she's leaking fluid. The redness on her chin and cheeks is from lying face down in the snow."

"Who would do such a thing?" Mabel asked.

"Gordon told me they have three young boys in custody." She shook her head. "No more than fourteen or fifteen years old. Doctor MacLellan said that if it wasn't for her wig, she would have likely died on the spot. Apparently, it helped cushion the blow and the weaving acted as a natural bandage keeping the scalp from peeling back more. They had to cut it away. It was glued to her head from all the sticky blood."

Mabel thought of the day on the porch when Amour whipped Myrtle's toque off and plopped the wig on her head. Myrtle was so furious her hairless head had been exposed, she threw the wig in Amour's face and stormed off. Mabel smiled, thinking of the unlikely beginnings of a wonderful friendship. She pressed her fingers into the corners of her wet eyes. "My friend, Amour, gave her the wig. She's on her way home from London. She made me promise not to tell Myrtle she was coming. I guess it's Amour who'll be surprised… it won't be a nice one."

Charlotte squatted in front of Mabel's chair and put her hand on her knee. "You're a good friend. And no matter how it looks, I know Myrtle knows you are here. I'm sure of it. Knowing someone is here for her will help her fight. I've seen so many folks come in alone and leave alone, without a single soul to hold their hand, or tell them they were loved. I often think some of them might have made it if they had something…someone to fight for." She stood up. "Breaks my heart. Worst part of my job."

Mabel smiled at the pretty nurse with the big heart. "Gordon's lucky to have you."

"Actually, we're not seeing each other anymore."

"I'm sorry, I didn't know," Mabel said.

"You have nothing to apologize for. We just started to drift apart."

"Are you doing okay?" Mabel asked.

"I'll be fine. It was a mutual decision. It's…well…well we just seemed to have lost…that spark. And with my shift work and his new position as acting chief…let's just say our careers haven't helped. But we're still good friends. He still drives me to work when he can. He dropped me off this morning."

"I always thought you two were such a perfect match. Just assumed you'd get married," Mabel said.

Charlotte walked to Myrtle's bedside, slid her arm around her back and adjusted her pillow. "Ya know, Mabel, I was always a little jealous of you," she said, grinning.

"*Of me?*"

"Yes, you! Gordon often talked about you. Mabel this and Mabel that."

Mabel had always known that the handsome captain liked her. She even sensed he might have a crush on her, but she was still taken aback by Charlotte's revelation. "I can't imagine," Mabel said, suddenly feeling uncomfortable and anxious to change the subject. She began picking at her cuticles. "Will the doctor be by this morning?"

"I'm sure he will. He normally begins his rounds—"

They both turned to the door.

"Is it all right to come in?" Alice asked.

"Of course," Charlotte said. "Congratulations. I hear you and Luke are getting married."

Alice smiled and nodded. "How is she?"

"She's not out of the woods yet. I'll leave you two ladies to get caught up," Charlotte said.

Alice waited for her to leave. "I imagine it won't be long before she and Captain Dunphy walk down the aisle," she whispered to Mabel.

"Actually, Charlotte just told me they broke up."

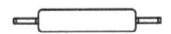

"Dan. Dan," Gladys said, lightly tapping on his door.

He opened his eyes, whipped the covers back and sat naked on the side of his bed.

"Danny!" she repeated, opening his door. She screamed and quickly slammed it shut.

"*What the hell!*" he yelled, quickly pulling on his pants.

"I need you to come to the kitchen."

He flung the door open. "What for?"

"Lizzie MacNeil's here. I thought you could talk to her about the job."

He was ready to kill his aunt. He ran his hand through his hair. "Christ, you told her I was here!" he said harshly.

"Be quiet, she'll hear you," she whispered. "What was I supposed to do? She just popped in and ya left yer coat and boots in the middle of the kitchen. Ain't like she didn't know there was a man in my house. What else was I supposed to tell her? And ya did promise me ya'd look fer work. And it's—"

"Okay! Okay!" he said, holding up his hand to keep her from going on. "Give me a minute to get cleaned up."

He returned to his room and began pacing. "Fuck," he seethed, thinking about the night before and praying Myrtle couldn't identify him. No way, he thought, it was too dark, and it all happened so fast. Hell, for all I know, she's dead. He lit a cigarette, plopped down on his bed and examined his red burning hand. "Goddammit. Twelve lousy bucks! And now this," he murmured, thinking it was only a matter of time before Lizzie told everybody in town that he was back home. He wasn't ready. He needed more time to figure out his plans.

"Dan! Lizzie can't stay long," Gladys hollered from the hallway.

"I'm coming!"

Dan put on a shirt, took a deep breath and entered the kitchen. He stood with his left hand buried in his pants pocket. "Hello, Lizzie," he said, forcing a smile.

She turned to Gladys with her mouth hanging open. "Yer right! He sure *has changed*. But as handsome as ever." She looked back at Dan. "I'da never have known it was you."

"*You* haven't changed a bit," Dan said, thinking she was as hideous as ever, with her drawn on eyebrows, clownish rouge and garish, blue eyeshadow.

"Oh, I'm a little greyer round the temples. But aren't we all." She leaned forward and slapped Gladys' knee. "Nothin a little peroxide can't fix. Anyway, yer aunt tells me yer lookin fer work."

"Yes."

"And ya got a good head fer numbers?"

"I think so."

"He's bein modest, Lizzie. He's very good with numbers," Gladys said.

"So, I heard ya hurt yer hand?" Lizzie said.

Dan removed it from his pocket and held it up.

Lizzie's eyes widened. "Oh, dear. Is it painful?"

"Yes."

Lizzie reached into her purse and put the application on the table. "Well, I can't promise ya anythin. We got quite a few applicants. Most of them women. Frankly, I think it's more of a man's job, given you need to know yer math and all. But I'm not the only one doin the hirin. Just the same, I think yer chances are pretty good. Only thing that might stand in yer way is... well...yer time away. You know, in Dorchester." She looked at Gladys. "But everyone deserves a second chance, *right?*"

Gladys nodded.

"And yer aunt, here. Well, she's got lots of real good connections with her work at the church and the Benevolent Society. I'm sure between the two of us, you'll be given every consideration." She tapped the application with the tip of a bright red fingernail. "Just make sure ya get this to me by end of day, Monday. Hirin committee said absolutely no late applicants."

"Thank you," Dan said.

"Well, I better get a move on," Lizzie said, standing and putting on her elbow-high, red leather gloves.

Gladys followed her into the porch. "Drop by anytime."

Lizzie turned to face her. "*Oh*, I don't suppose ya heard anythin bout the commotion in town last night?"

"No. What happened?" Gladys asked.

"Heard a guy on the bus say a woman was attacked."

"Dear lord! What's this world comin to," Gladys said, shaking her head.

"Ain't *that* the truth! Anyways, I'll be sure to tell ya if I hear anythin else. Catcha later, alligator," Lizzie said, gripping the wooden rail of the back step and balancing her thin, busty frame on her five-inch heels.

Gladys closed the door and spun around, clapping her hands together. Her broad smile quickly faded. Dan was nowhere to be seen.

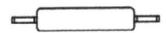

Captain Dunphy barely stepped foot in the station when he was besieged by three angry fathers shouting obscenities and demanding to see their sons.

"Enough!" he finally screamed. "Just let me get in the door for goodness sakes." He nudged past them and looked at the boys' mothers sitting on the bench, holding hands and crying.

"McEwan told me my boy's sick. I wanna see him this minute!" Harley's father shouted.

Dunphy turned around. "He's rum sick. And by the way, since you didn't care to ask, the victim's still hanging on. With any luck, she'll recover and be able to identify her attacker."

"So when can we see them?" Tommy's father asked.

"Give me a minute to check on things," Dunphy said. He disappeared down the hall, took the back steps to the basement and walked along the row of cells. He stopped at the second one. "Jesus, Geezer, you're back? This isn't your home, ya know?" Geezer waved him on.

Dunphy was surprised when he found all three boys in one cell. Harley was passed out in the fetal position on the cot, Kenny was stretched out on the floor with his jacket balled up under his head, and Tommy was sitting with his back against the wall; his head and arms resting on his bent knees.

Dunphy shook the shoulder of his bailiff, sound asleep in a chair with his head titled back against the wall.

"Yeah?" the bailiff said, trying to find his bearings. "Oh, sorry, Captain. Been a long night."

"What the hell were you thinking? They shouldn't be in the same cell."

"Why not?"

Dunphy shook his head.

The bailiff shrugged. "So, ya want me to split em up?"

"Yes. Give them some time alone with their parents," Dunphy said and headed for the stairs."

The bailiff slid the heavy, steel door aside. "Kenny and Tommy, come with me," he ordered.

Tommy opened his red-rimmed eyes. "Are we goin home?"

"Not yet."

"What about Harley?" Kenny asked.

He looked at Harley's green face and the vomit on the floor and gagged. "He's fine where he is."

The boys were quickly reunited with their panic-stricken fathers and weepy mothers. Kenny and Tommy both professed their innocence and begged forgiveness for drinking and lying about their whereabouts. Harley wasn't apologizing for anything. He couldn't sit up, let alone talk.

Dunphy would allow them all the time in the world, thinking it might be one of the last times they could play on their parents' sympathies. He re-read Winston MacRae's troubling statement and threw it on his desk. The evidence was circumstantial, but still compelling. They were found drunk at the scene, Kenny was standing near Myrtle's motionless body, and Tommy was in possession of one of her paintings. Daylight might bring more answers, he thought, hoping McEwan and the team of officers he had scouring the brook would find a clue that would see the boys go home with their heartsick parents. He heard the light tap and looked up.

"Sam?"

"Hi, Gordon."

"You here for one of the boys?"

"Kenny Ludlow. I'm hoping he doesn't need me."

Dunphy leaned back in his chair. "Let's just say, I'm glad you're here."

"Have they been questioned?"

"No. They were drunk as skunks when they were brought in. They're pretty shaken up *and hung over.* Christ, Harley reeks of vomit."

"So, you haven't questioned them or laid any charges, but you won't let them go home? Seems to me they have every right to walk out of here," Sam said.

"They're being held for public intoxication. And to be honest, I figure they're probably safer here than at home. I thought Harley's father was gonna have a conniption fit." Dunphy leaned forward. "Does Mary Catherine know you're representing one of the boys?"

"Not yet. She'll be fine. She knows how I make a living."

"Still, to think her husband is representing the alleged assailant of one of her good friends. I dunno, could make for trouble on the home front."

"Everyone's entitled to a defense. So, I can see my client?"

"Yes. But you might want to start with this." Dunphy picked up Winston MacRae's statement and tossed it across the table.

Sam read the one page statement and tossed it back. "He didn't witness anything. It's all circumstantial."

"Still, Winston heard voices coming from the area at least two or three minutes before he came across Kenny standing next to Myrtle."

"*So?*"

"*So,* why wasn't he screaming for help?"

"Maybe Winston spotted the boys at the same time they came across her," Sam said, worried he'd seen convictions with far less evidence.

"Honestly, Sam, I hope you're right. Jesus, they're kids for Christ sakes. I just hope they didn't get so damned smashed up on booze they did some fool thing that'll ruin the rest of their lives. Hell, if Myrtle dies and they're nailed for it, they'll never see the light of day."

Dunphy's desk sergeant appeared in the doorway. "Hey Chief?"

"What is it?"

"It's a reporter from The Post. Wants to have a word with you."

"Tell him...no comment."

Stanley walked in holding Mary Margaret's hand.

Mabel squatted in front of her and felt her forehead. "She still feels warm. How are you feeling, honey?" Mary Margaret was staring at Myrtle's bruised eyes and bandaged head. Mabel took her daughter's tiny hands in hers. "Myrtle's going to stay here for a little while so the doctors can make her feel better."

"Maggie Mae saw a doctor this morning, too. Didn't you?" Stanley said.

"And did he make you feel better?" Mabel asked. Mary Margaret held up a bandaged finger.

"And he gave her some new medicine for that stubborn cough," Stanley said.

Mabel stood up and kissed him. "Thank you. Where's JC?" Mabel asked.

"I dropped him off at Mary Catherine's. I wasn't sure how he'd react to seeing Myrtle."

"Did you tell him she was in the hospital?"

"Yes. He wanted to come, but I said Myrtle needed her rest. I just told him the doctors were running some tests." He nodded to Myrtle. "How's she doing?"

Mabel filled him in on everything Charlotte and Dr. MacLellan shared with her. "They're relieved she made it through the night and that her breathing is strong, but they're concerned she's still in a coma. They said even if she survives the initial trauma, she might develop meningitis or have clotting."

Stanley nodded. "Amour called this morning. They were diverted to Boston due to bad weather. She said they don't expect to get in to Halifax until tomorrow afternoon at the earliest."

"You didn't tell her, *did you*?"

"No. Didn't see the point. Thought if we waited, we might have better news. Look, if you want to go home, I can stay."

"No. Alice was by earlier. She's coming back later to spell me for a few hours. Luke will drive me home. Besides, sounds like I have an extra day to get the house in order."

Stanley smiled. "It's in tip-top shape."

Mabel gave him a puzzled look.

"I couldn't sleep after you left. Figured I'd put the time to good use. I put the kids in our bed, stripped the others and did a couple of loads of wash."

She squeezed his arm. "Handsome *and* handy."

"*Oh*, and I cleaned the tub, waxed the floors and still found the time to commit a break and enter."

Mabel raised her eyebrows.

"I broke into Mrytle's and drained the pipes. Figured she'd be in here for a while."

"Well then, my busy homemaker and thoughtful husband, I guess I'm gonna have to do something extra special for you." She drummed her fingers against her chin. "Let's see. I could take you dancing?"

Stanley shook his head. "Not what I was hoping for."

"Or cook your favourite meal?"

He shrugged.

"I got it! I'll bake you *your very own pie.*"

He screwed up his face.

"No? Not that either? I can't imagine anything else I could possibly do to properly thank you."

"Let's go, Maggie Mae," Stanley said. He picked her up, leaned into his wife and whispered in her ear.

Mabel started to laugh. "Not possible. Luke won't have it. He doesn't want anybody else but you guiding him across the floor."

"Worth a try," Stanley hollered over his shoulder and disappeared out of sight.

Sam walked along the row of cells looking for Kenny.

Tommy's father jumped off his son's cot and rushed to the cell door. "*Sam? What's going on? When can we take the boys home?"*

"Captain Dunphy wants them to come around a bit more before he questions them."

"Tommy swears they had nothin to do with it. It's true they were drinking at the brook. You know, boys will be boys. They just stumbled across the body. They had nothing to do with it!"

"Then that's what Tommy tells the police."

"Please! Will you represent him?"

"I've already agreed to represent Kenny."

"Can't ya represent all three?"

"I wouldn't recommend it," he said, explaining they should each have their own lawyer in the event they started to turn against one another.

"They'd never do that! They're The Blackheads for God sakes. They're thick as thieves."

"Still, I'm thinking of what's in your son's best interests. I'm sorry," Sam said. He reached in his jacket pocket and handed him a business card. "Call this guy. He's good. If he doesn't take the case, I'll reconsider."

An hour later, Sam left Kenny's cell, confident the kid was telling the truth and that it was just a case of bad timing. He was heading for the front door when he saw Dunphy coming toward him.

"Sam, can you come back at one? McEwan should be back by then with an update of the crime scene. I'd like to start with Kenny. Oh, and I might let Harley go. He had to have been too drunk to be a party to an assault. I'm pretty sure he doesn't remember a thing."

Sam looked at his watch. "Gives me just enough time to go home and grab a quick bite," he said and hurried off.

Mary Catherine heard the car pull up and met her husband at the door. "Who called earlier and why'd you just rush off like that?"

"A client."

"*On the Sabbath?*"

"They're Catholic."

"And you couldn't put them off?"

"No."

Mary Catherine took his coat from him and hung it on a hook in the hallway. "Well, I'm glad you're home. Someone attacked Myrtle last night. She's in the hospital and it doesn't look good."

"I heard."

"Mabel spent the night with her. I'm heading there now. Anyway, Stanley dropped JC off this morning. He's upstairs playing with the kids." she said, reaching for her coat. "Your lunch is in the fridge. And the kids need some fresh air. I told them you'd take them skating on the dam. Make sure you bundle them up."

"I can't," Sam said, suddenly unsure of how his wife was going to take the news.

Mary Catherine gave her husband an exasperated look. "What do you mean, *you can't?*"

"I have to get back to the station by one."

"For goodness sakes! Tell them something came up and you can't make it."

Sam smiled and reached for her hand. "We should talk," he said, ushering her into the kitchen.

Sergeant McEwan sat across from Dunphy, advising that they had completed a thorough search of the crime scene and there was nothing worth reporting. "Assailant likely hit the victim with the boulder found at the scene. Oh, and we found an empty rum bottle and cigarette butts near the chimney where Kenny and Tommy said they were drinking."

"Must have been a botched robbery. Did you question the neighbours in the area?" Dunphy asked.

McEwan nodded. "Nobody saw nothing."

Dunphy put his head down.

"What are ya thinkin?" McEwan asked.

"Ever know a woman go to town without her handbag?"

"No."

"Me neither. And how did Tommy end up with the painting? He said he just found it in the snow. If that's the case, how did it get there?" he said, remembering Charlotte pulling on his arm and pointing to Myrtle's colourful artwork in Arlies' window.

"So, is that it?" McEwan asked, standing to leave.

"Actually, go tell Harley's parents they can take him home. He's in no position to answer any questions. I'd rather he puke at home, than in his cell. Bad enough we got Geezer stinking the place up."

The desk sergeant was back at his door.

"If it's The Post again, give them the same answer," Dunphy said.

"Sorry, it's not The Post."

"What is it then?"

"There's a guy here who wants to have a word with you. Says his name is Dan McInnes."

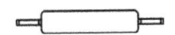

Sam sat across the kitchen table from his wife and offered up all of his lawyerly arguments. Everyone's entitled to a defense. He's a boy. These things happen when you live in a small town and everyone knows one another.

Mary Catherine would have none of it. She was furious. "I can't believe you would agree to this! Myrtle's hanging on for dear life and you're trying to get her assailant off!"

"Alleged assailant. And by the way, he hasn't been charged yet," Sam said sheepishly.

"So that's it! Walk away now before you get in too deep. There's lots of other lawyers around. Sam, you can't do this. I won't allow it! Myrtle's a good friend. And I won't be the only one furious with you. Mabel and Stanley will never speak to you again."

"Of course they—"

"Well, maybe they will, but I won't!" Mary Catherine said sharply. She stood up and glared at him. "It's your choice. Take the case, or take the couch!"

"Please, Mary Catherine! If I knew the kid was guilty, I'd never have agreed to—"

"So can you swear to me… *right here and right now*… he's not?"

"Of course not. It's just that—"

"I rest my case," Mary Catherine said sarcastically and stomped out of the room.

Sam put his elbows on the table and rested his head in his hands. They had fights before, many of them heated, but this was the angriest he'd ever seen his wife. He wondered if he had made a mistake. Maybe he should just advise Kenny's father he has a personal conflict and needs to back away. He'd help him find another lawyer. But who, he thought. Contrary to Mary Catherine's assertion, there weren't that many defense lawyers to pick from, and the government-appointed attorneys were so overwhelmed, they rarely mounted a winning defense, even when their clients were innocent.

Sam put his plate in the sink and poured himself a glass of milk, satisfied he had come to a decision. He'd sit in on the interview with Dunphy. If he had any doubts about the veracity of Kenny's story, he'd recuse himself. He walked back to the porch, put on his coat and looked up from the bottom of the staircase. "Mary Catherine. Mary Catherine! Mary—"

His wife finally appeared at the top of the stairs. "*What is it?*" she asked through clenched teeth.

"I'm heading to the station. I'll be back before two, so you can go to—"

"Oh, go…go piss up a rope!" she hissed and walked away.

"The hospital," he murmured.

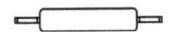

Dunphy could have been knocked over with a feather. He had no idea Dan McInnes was back in town and was shocked to hear he was waiting to see him. His former colleague walked in, clean shaven and wearing a toque. His face was fuller and he was definitely bulkier. Dunphy wasn't even sure he would have recognized him if he passed him on the street.

Dan's heart was pounding, but he knew he had to maintain a cool, even cocky demeanour. "Didn't take you long to move up the ranks," he said, looking around the office he had once hoped to occupy.

"Have a seat," Dunphy said.

Dan kept his hands in the pockets of his unbuttoned coat and casually sat across from Dunphy.

"When did you get back to town?" Dunphy asked.

"Five days ago."

"I assume your aunt told you I wanted to talk to you?"

"Yeah. She mentioned it."

"You took your time coming in?"

"I was under the weather. But I'm here now, aren't I?" Dan reminded himself that the best defence was a good offence. He had to show Dunphy he was not afraid of him. "*So, Gordon?* No pleasantries? No, how are ya, Dan? How'd ya get along in the slammer? *Nooo*, that was never your style, was it? *No, not you*...you just cut straight to the chase."

Dunphy looked at his watch. "Actually, *Dan*, I wasn't expecting to see you, and I'm already running behind. Let's just get this done. Did Gladys tell you why I wanted to talk to you?"

"Yeah. Said something about some guy I spent time with in Dorchester. The guy who kidnapped the MacIntyre boy. I don't get it. I heard the kidnappers are dead, so I'm not sure how I can be of any use. But, I guess, if ya figure I can be of assistance—"

"How well did you know him?" Dunphy asked.

"Who?"

"Lenny...Lenny Slade."

"*Is that who took the boy?* Aunt Gladys couldn't remember his name." Dan tilted his head to the side and turned down his mouth. "Knew him well enough, I guess. Spent a fair amount of time together in the yard. Big buffoon.

We weren't friends or anything." Dan feigned a shudder. "Kinda gave me the willies. He had this sick fascination with little boys."

Dunphy wasn't sure if he was being played, or if McInnes was being truthful. "When was the last time you were in town?"

"Ya mean after you shipped me off to Dorchester?"

"Yes."

"Like I said, five days ago. Went to Newfoundland and did some fishin after I lost my job on the lakes. *Just a minute. What are you getting at?* You're not suggesting I had anything to do with the kidnappin? Christ, check it out, I was in Ontario at the time. I'm sure if you called—"

Dunphy held up his hand. "We already did."

"Then what the fuck is this all about?"

"Skinny thought he saw you at The Pithead a couple of years ago. Shortly after the boy was kidnapped. Kind of strange, don't you think? Skinny claims he saw you around the same time as the MacIntyre boy went missing and your aunt was robbed. And who else, but someone who was close to her, would know she hid her money in her shed?"

Dan shrugged and leaned back in his chair, like he had nothing in the world to be worried about. "Skinny needs his eyes checked. Wasn't me. And talk to Aunt Gladys. She's convinced it was Stanley MacIntyre who robbed her. Said he was hanging around and watchin her house. Christ, I was the one who always told her to put her money in the bank. Besides, if I needed her money, all I woulda had to do was ask. She would have given it to me. But I wasn't back in town, and I certainly didn't steal, *or need* her money. I made a good livin working the docks." He leaned forward. "Listen, Gordon, you know I'm no fan of MacIntyre, but I'd never harm a kid. I actually came down here thinkin you wanted my help. Never thought for a sec, you'd be grillin me. I don't know what ya think I know, or did... but—"

"Lenny Slade claimed he was you."

"*What?*" McInnes said, laughing.

"He brought the kid into the hospital claiming he was Dan McInnes."

"Jesus, Gordon! There gotta be a dozen Dan McInneses in Caledonia alone. So he pulled my name out of a hat."

Dunphy felt McInnes was mocking him. "And then there's the kidnappers. They never looked for a ransom...and the barn fire."

"*What barn fire?*"

"Lenny set fire to Stanley's barn in order to create a distraction and grab the boy. During the Adshade investigation you kept insisting that Stanley set fire to his own barn as a diversion. Strange coincidence, don't you think?"

Dan tilted his head back and looked up at the ceiling. *"You can't be serious?"* He lowered his head to be at eye level with his interrogator. "I know ya never liked me, but I didn't think you thought I was a total idiot. And as far as the kidnappers not askin for ransom, like I told ya, Lenny had a thing for little boys."

Dunphy's desk sergeant was back "Hey, Captain. Sam Friedman's been waiting. He's asking when you might get started. Said he can't stay much longer."

"Tell him, I'll be out in a minute."

"Honestly, Gordon. I remember you tellin me I was on a wild goose chase when I said MacIntyre and Cameron killed Johnnie. Seems to me, you're making the same mistake. I had no idea the kid was kidnapped till I got home. Shit, I was under the impression he fell off a cliff and his body was never found. Hell, I didn't even know Lenny was the kidnapper till you just told me."

Dunphy stood up.

"That it?" Dan asked.

"For now. But, Dan, you should know I'm the least of your worries. Stanley MacIntyre's convinced you were involved. So you better keep your distance."

Dan smiled. "Ain't like I'd be invitin him out for a beer." He stood and took another look around the office. "Whatever happened to Ted?"

"Retired. Ya know, Dan, this could've been your office, if you hadn't been... been—"

"What?" Ambitious?"

"Such an arrogant prick."

Dan felt both relief and excitement as he walked down the hall. Lenny hadn't ratted him out, the cops had absolutely nothing to go on, and he played Dunphy like a fiddle. He looked up to see Sam Friedman sitting on a bench against the far wall, staring at him. He smiled and nodded to him, wondering if the jittery Jew had any idea who he was.

Dunphy walked down the hall. "Is that who I think it was?" Sam asked.

"Yep."

"Jesus," Sam said, "Stanley's gonna kill him."

Dunphy put his hand on Sam's shoulder. "That's what I'm afraid of."

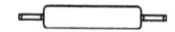

Dan was on his way out of the station when he spotted McEwan with a couple of other guys standing on the side of the building, having a smoke. He hollered and waved to him. McEwan looked, but turned away, unsure who the stranger was yelling to.

"Tubby!" Dan shouted.

McEwan did a double take and ran to his old friend.

"Jesus, Dan. Look at ya. I didn't recognize you. Ya bulked up, buddy," he said, slapping him on the arm. "When did ya get back?"

"Few days ago. So how've ya been?" Dan asked.

"Can't complain." McEwan nodded to the station. "Were ya talkin to Dunphy?"

"Yeah. He hasn't changed much. Had some crazy notion I was involved with the MacIntyre kidnappin. I set him straight. *Fuck*, I thought the kid fell off a cliff, and I wasn't even in the area. He's always had it in for me. So, I see they still got ya workin weekends."

"Got called in. Woman got smacked at the brook last night. Myrtle Munroe? You know, the painter?"

"Never heard of her. Any leads?" Dan asked, relieved McEwan was on the case.

"Picked up three kids at the scene. Idiots had one of her paintings. They better hope she doesn't kick the bucket. Anyway, how long ya in town for?"

Dan shrugged. "Playin it by ear."

"Stayin with yer aunt?"

"Yeah."

"Great. Look, I gotta get back in there or Dunphy will be on me like shit on a hot shovel. We'll catch up over a beer. I'll call ya," McEwan said, taking the stone steps to the imposing, brick building two at a time.

Dan smirked. The day hadn't started out well with Lizzie's unexpected visit, but it was getting better with every passing hour. Dunphy had nothing to go on, and now the encouraging news they had picked up three suspects for attacking Myrtle. He had been worried about losing Myrtle's painting at the scene, thinking he should never have said a word to the clerk. If anyone discovered the painting was missing, he might have exposed himself to suspicion. Dropping the painting at the scene now seemed like a stroke of good luck. This calls for a celebration, he thought. He lit a cigarette and thought of Dunphy's warning to stay clear of MacIntyre. "Fuck you," he muttered. "It's MacIntyre who better watch out." He closed his eyes, picturing Mabel's lovely smile when he handed her the kid's mitten.

Dan walked up the back stairs to Iggies, entered the near empty bar and went directly to the men's room. He urgently unzipped his pants, masturbated and breathlessly whispered her name.

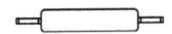

Dunphy threw his jacket over the back of his chair. The clerk at Arlies said Myrtle had stopped in just before the store closed and collected her payment of almost two hundred dollars. He also confirmed she had a beige handbag, and that he watched her open it and put her consignment money in an inside pocket.

If the boys were responsible, they must have ditched her handbag at the scene, he thought. He called for McEwan, instructing him to gather up four other officers and some shovels, and start digging through the snow for the handbag.

Sam appeared in the doorway, anxious to get on with Kenny's interview and back home so Mary Catherine could get to the hospital.

Dunphy brought him up to speed on his visit to Arlies and Myrtle's missing handbag. "Sorry, Sam. I need to delay the interview till McEwan reports back. Shouldn't be more than an hour or two."

Sam looked at his watch, thinking his wife was going to string him up by the balls.

"You know, Sam, if they find her handbag at the scene, your client is in a shitload of trouble."

"And if they don't?" Sam asked.

"I'm not sure."

Sam rubbed his forehead. "If, as you say, Myrtle had her handbag on her at the time of the assault and it's not found at the scene, then I think it just goes to prove the boys didn't do it, and you have an assailant at large."

Dunphy puckered his mouth. "I know it's an odd thing for the acting chief of police to say, but I hope you're right. They're kids for Christ sakes. Still, the circumstantial evidence is pretty worrisome. Winston's time line… Kenny trying to run…the painting."

"As you say, it's all circumstantial," Sam said.

"I know, but still...unsettling. Speaking of which, I'm worried about what Stanley will do when he finds out McInnes is back in town. I got a bad feeling about things. Hopefully he'll give the bastard a wide berth, but I'm not betting on it. I'm going to have a word with him. Wondering if you wouldn't mind doing the same?"

Sam nodded. "Absolutely. God knows this town isn't big enough for the both of them."

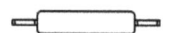

Mabel sat at Myrtle's bedside, squeezing her hand and watching the life-sustaining fluid slowly drip from the bottle and into the thin tubes running into her wrist. "Where *are you*, Myrtle? Can you hear me? I'm worried about you. We all are. You need to wake up and get well. And there's going to be a big surprise waiting—"

"Any change?" Alice asked, taking off her coat and laying it on a chair.

"No."

"Where's Luke?"

"He ducked into Dr. MacLellan's office. Needs to set up an appointment to have his leg X-rayed before the orthopaedic surgeon arrives from Halifax. Said he'd meet you by the entrance in ten minutes." Alice looked at Myrtle. "Doctors tell you anything else?"

"No."

Alice glanced at the door, then pulled her chair close to Mabel. "I know this isn't the best time, but I was hoping to talk to you?"

Mabel leaned over Myrtle and wiped her runny nose. "About the wedding?"

Alice hesitated. "Well...yes. I —"

Mabel jumped to her feet. "Oh my God, Myrtle! You're awake!" She ran into the hall. "She's awake! She's awake!"

An older, heavy-set nurse followed Mabel back to the room and waved her hand in front of Myrtle's face. There was no reaction.

"What's going on?" Mabel asked. "She's awake, *isn't she*?"

"Nope. Still comatose."

"But her eyes are open?" Alice said.

The nurse adjusted Myrtle's pillow. "Involuntary reflex."

Mabel sat down heavily.

Alice laid her hand on Mabel's back. "You're tired?"

"More like disappointed." She looked at Alice and smiled. "You wanted to talk about the wedding?"

"It can wait. Go home and get some rest. I won't leave her side. I promise."

Mabel put her coat on. "I might as well tell you the news. Not like Myrtle's going to find out."

"What news?" Alice asked.

"Amour and Michael are on their way home. Should be here tomorrow."

"Is Victoria coming with them?"

"Of course."

"That's wonderful!"

"With any luck, they'll be staying for good. Michael's got an interview. Might be getting his old job back. Regardless, they'll be here for the wedding and Christmas. Poor, Amour. She wanted to surprise Myrtle."

Alice looked at Myrtle's battered and bruised face. "Maybe Amour's just what she needs."

Mabel smiled. "Anyway, looks like we'll need to set three more places for the reception. Well, I'm off. I'll be back around eight."

"Stay as long as you like. I don't mind," Alice said.

"Shake yourself," Mabel said. "The bride needs her beauty sleep."

Dunphy was at the front desk when he saw the paddy wagon pull up front and his officers get out with their shovels.

"Find anything?" he asked.

McEwan stomped his snowy boots on the mat. "Only a curious crowd."

"We did a pretty wide perimeter, but it's a big area with a lot of trees and snow. Honestly, it's like lookin for a needle in a haystack. The fellas were freezing their balls off. We'd be better off waiting for a good thaw and a downpour." McEwan leaned his shovel against the wall. "If ya want, we can take another crack at it in the morning? It's gotta be there somewhere."

"Or the boys are telling the truth. Let's see what Kenny has to say for himself. Bring him up to the interview room," Dunphy instructed, before heading back to his office.

"They're back," he said to Sam.

"*And?*"

"And nothing yet."

The interview took less than an hour. When Kenny wasn't crying, he was insisting they never had anything to do with the attack, never saw a handbag, and that Tommy found her painting in the snow. He said he had walked up the hill to have a leak, and that's when he noticed something sticking out from under the trees. "When I realized it was a body, I just panicked. I swear, I wouldn't have left her there!" He rubbed his sleeve under his runny nose and his hand over his tear-stained face. "*I did run fer…fer hel…help,*" he cried.

"Kenny, if the handbag is buried somewhere near the crime scene, we're going to find it," Dunphy said, watching for his reaction.

Kenny lifted his head. "We didn't see no handbag. I swear."

Dunphy stood up. "Okay. You can go."

"*You're letting him go?*" McEwan whispered in his boss's ear.

"Yes," Dunphy said firmly

Kenny's father leaned over the table. "You mean we can go *home*?"

"Yes."

"*So that's, it?* He's not being charged?"

"That's it for now," Dunphy said.

Kenny's father put his hand under his son's elbow and helped him to his feet.

"Kenny," Dunphy said. "If we find the handbag, you'll be back here so fast your head will be spinning. And remember, this ain't no joyride you go braggin to your buddies about."

Kenny shook his head and turned back at the door. He tried to compose himself. "Wha…wha…what about Tommy?"

Dunphy smiled. "He'll be in his own bed soon enough."

Sam snapped his briefcase shut and quickly put on his coat. "Thanks, Gordon."

"Don't thank me yet. Things are far from over."

"Keep me posted," Sam said, quickly gathering up his things..

Dunphy turned to McEwan. "Go get Tommy and his father. No point in holding the kid any longer. And I need you to do up a roster. I want the crime scene staked out around the clock. If one of the guys buried Myrtle's handbag at the scene, they'll likely go back for it."

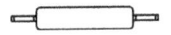

Sam pulled into his yard and shut off the ignition, grateful Gordon didn't go too hard on Kenny. He doubted his wife would be so generous with him. He checked the time and sighed. It was after four. He reached for his briefcase and was about to step out when he saw Mary Catherine standing beside the car with a scowl on her face and her arms folded across her chest.

He opened the door. "Sorry I'm late."

She thrust out her hand. "Give me the damn keys!"

Sam got out and was about to place the keys in her hand when she snatched them from him and elbowed him out of the way.

"I'm sorry. *Mary Catherine?*"

She slammed the door, started the engine and quickly rolled down the window. "Your bed clothes are in the cedar chest in the hall. And don't wait up!"

Sam watched her drive off and slowly made his way up the front steps. When he walked in, Irwin, Ruth and JC were sitting on the stairs, staring at him.

"Hi, kids," Sam said.

Irwin rested his chin in his hand and his elbow on his knee. "Hi, Papa."

Sam hung his coat on the hook, sensing they were watching his every move. He was right. "What's up, guys?"

"Papa, mommy's really mad at you," Ruth said.

Sam brought his hand to his forehead and pinched his temples. "I know."

"What did you do?" Irwin asked.

Sam smiled. "My job." He bent down, scooped Ruth up in his arms and kissed her cheek. "There's nothing to worry about. Everything will be fine. You'll see."

Ruth wrapped her arms around her father's neck. "But, Papa, I heard mommy say she was gonna fuckin kill you."

Mabel was barely inside the door, when Stanley reached for his coat. "Hey! Watch it! You're getting water on my clean floors," he teased.

Mabel jumped back on the mat. "Pardon me!"

"I'm going to get JC. Any change with Myrtle?" he asked.

Mabel told him about her misplaced excitement. "I'm worried about her."

Stanley gave her a peck on the cheek. "You worry about everything. It's still early. She'll come around."

"I hope so. How's Mary Margaret? Is she still running a fever?"

"*Mabel*, she's fine. Been asleep on the couch for the last two hours."

"And no word from Amour?"

"No. Weather likely has everything bottled up. She said she'd keep us posted. Pot roast is in the oven. I'll be back in a jiffy," he said, running out the door.

Mabel looked around her spotless kitchen and headed into the living room to check on Mary Margaret. She felt her daughter's forehead, relieved she didn't feel warm. She arched her back, wishing she could just slide into a hot tub and ease her stiff neck and sore muscles. She smiled when she saw the Electrolux tucked away in the corner and the lemon oil polish on the mantle. "You're a good man," she whispered.

The phone rang. "Oh, hello, Gordon," she said, thinking about her recent conversation with Charlotte and suddenly feeling flush. "No, but he shouldn't be too long. Of course you can. Is everything all right? Yes, I'll be here." Mabel put the receiver down, wondering what Captain Dunphy wanted to talk to her and Stanley about. She peeked at Mary Margaret, still sound asleep, and walked to the hall mirror. She examined her tired eyes, then reached in her purse for a brush to rein in her unruly hair. "What am I doing?" she murmured.

Mabel returned to the kitchen and started peeling carrots. "A little lipstick won't hurt," she said, returning to the mirror and applying it evenly over her lips. She smacked them together and ran her fingers along the corners of her mouth.

She heard a car, the footsteps on the steps and then the knock. "Hello, Gordon."

"How are you?"

"Good. C'mon in. Don't worry about your boots." She pulled out a chair. "Here, have a seat. I was just about to make some tea."

"How's Myrtle?" Dunphy asked.

"She's still in a coma. Charlotte told me you have three boys in custody?"

"We had them in for questioning, but haven't laid charges."

Mabel filled the kettle. "I honestly don't understand how anyone could do such a thing. Boggles the mind."

He nodded. "I agree. So, Stanley's not home yet?"

"No."

"Good."

Mabel suddenly felt her face get hot and hoped it didn't show. She looked up from the stove and gave him a puzzled look. "*Oh?*"

"Probably best I speak to you first."

"About what?"

"I thought you should know—"

JC charged through the door.

"Hello, honey," Mabel said. "Did you have fun with Ruth and Irwin?"

"Yes. I need to pee," he said, kicking off his boots and tearing through the kitchen.

Stanley came in carrying a paper bag. "Hey, Gordon. Didn't expect to find you here."

"Didn't expect to be here."

"Congratulations. Heard they made you acting chief."

"Thanks. I'm sure Chief Peach will be back before long."

"Any leads on Myrtle's attacker?" Stanley asked.

"I was just telling Mabel we had three young guys in for questioning, but haven't charged them. Not yet, anyway."

"Anyone we know?"

"Actually, I'd prefer not to say."

Stanley held up the paper bag. "Well, I hope whoever did it gets the book thrown at them. Care for a drink?"

"Sure."

Stanley looked at his wife. "What's up with Sam?"

"What do you mean?"

"I dunno. Just seemed out of sorts. Said he needed to talk to me about something, but it wasn't a good time and he'd call me later."

Mabel shrugged.

Stanley uncapped the bottle and smiled at his wife. "What's with the lipstick?"

"*What?*"

"You're wearing lipstick?"

"I always wear lipstick."

He laughed. "*You do not!*" He gave her a funny look and made a swirling motion with his finger around his mouth. "It's all over your teeth."

Mabel felt like she could crawl under the sink.

Stanley pulled two glasses from the cupboard. "So, what brings you by?" he asked Gordon.

"Not what, but *who?*"

Stanley screwed up his face and handed him his rum.

"Dan McInnes is back in town," Gordon said.

Stanley looked at Mabel, then back at Gordon. "When?"

"Five days ago."

Stanley downed one rum after the other as Gordon tried to dismiss the circumstantial evidence Stanley was convinced tied McInnes to the kidnapping. "Okay, Gordon, I get he was in Ontario at the time of the kidnapping. I get that Skinny might have been mistaken when he claimed he saw him. I'll even concede someone else might have known Gladys hid her money in her shed and that it was just a weird coincidence the kidnapper said his name was Dan McInnes. I agree, it's all circumstantial. But, this is what I don't get. I don't get why the kidnappers never looked for a ransom."

Gordon knew better than to tell his agitated friend that McInnes claimed Lenny was into young boys. "Look, Lenny depended on his crazy sister. She lost a baby. Lenny was probably—"

"Bullshit!" Stanley said.

It took another hour for Mabel and Gordon to convince Stanley that if he went after McInnes, he'd end up in jail, and that Mabel and the kids would pay the highest price. In the end, Stanley promised them he wouldn't seek McInnes out, but that if he ever came near his home or threatened his family, all bets were off.

Alice and Luke arrived.

"Oh, hello, Captain Dunphy," Alice said.

Mabel put her hand over her mouth. "Oh my God, is it Myrtle?"

"No! Sorry! Mary Catherine is with her. She said she didn't mind staying the night. Anyway, Luke wanted to speak to Stanley. Bad timing?"

"No. Come in. You can stay for supper. Gordon, you're welcome to stay as well?"

"Thanks, but I should go."

"Oh, stay!" Alice said.

"No. I got a few things I need to see to back at the station."

Alice looked disappointed. "Are you sure?"

Mabel looked at the bride-to-be, curious as to why she was pressing the handsome bachelor to stay.

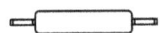

Gladys sat alone eating her supper, worried for her nephew. He had stormed down the hall to his room after Lizzie left, then took off, without so much as a word to her. She was putting his plate in the fridge, when she heard him in the porch. She turned to see him holding a potted plant.

"You shaved!" she said, smiling. "Oh, now *that's* the Danny I remember. And you're so much more handsome. I was thinking the interview committee wouldn't care for your beard. Not everyone's a fan of facial hair, ya know. What do you have there?"

"I couldn't find roses."

"*Roses*? Roses are for pretty young ladies, not ugly, old coots like me." She took the sickly, green plant from him and put it on the window sill. "It's lovely. Thank you."

"Are you hungry?" she asked.

"Famished."

"Great, I made one of yer favourites. Homemade beans in molasses, with bologna and fried potatoes." She put his supper in the frying pan to heat up and wiped her pristine countertop clear of imaginary crumbs, nattering on about his appetite as a boy.

Dan rolled his eyes, wishing she'd shut the fuck up. She was going to drive him mad.

Gladys laughed. "Norman always said you had a hollow leg." She joined him at the table. "So how was your day?"

"Great. Went to see Dunphy. It was just a big misunderstanding."

"I told ya so. Oh, there's the phone," she said, putting her hand on the table and pushing herself up from her chair.

Dan watched her waddle off, opened his flask, took a swig and returned it to his pocket. He picked up the frying pan and flipped it upside down onto his plate. "Fuck," he said, as the watery beans spilled over onto the counter.

Gladys returned. "That was Lizzie. Wanted to tell me that it was Myrtle Munroe who was attacked. She's a local artist. Lizzie says she's barely hangin on."

"That's too bad," Dan said, praying she'd hurry up and die.

"Apparently she was attacked outside her home and her body was dumped at the brook. Hit in the head with a hammer. Lizzie wasn't sure, but she thinks she was also assaulted in a more intimate way, if you know what I mean. What's that?" Gladys said, looking at the brown streaks dripping down her cupboard doors and onto the floor."

"Sorry. Spilt some bean juice," Dan said, hoeing into his bologna.

Gladys got down on her knees with a grunt, bent over and began rubbing the stubborn, sticky streaks marring her shiny white counter.

Dan held a spoonful of beans to his mouth and looked at his aunt. Her flowered frock was pulled taut across her wide ass, and her dimpled legs were bulging at the seams of her thick, beige stockings. He put his spoon down and pushed his plate forward.

"There. That's better," Gladys said, struggling to get up. "What's wrong? Beans too sweet?"

"Lost my appetite."

"Ya sure? Cause I don't mind fixin ya somethin else?"

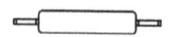

Luke and Alice sat at the table with Mabel and the kids. Stanley stood at the counter, poured himself another rum and ranted about Dan McInnes.

Mabel walked up and placed her hand on his back. "I don't want JC hearing this," she whispered.

Stanley brought his mouth to her ear. "He has no idea what I'm talking about."

"But I do, and I don't want to hear another word. In fact, I don't want to ever hear his name again."

"Sorry, hun," Stanley said. "It's just that I know—"

Mabel held up her hand and shot him a look. "Sit and finish your supper." She returned to the table. "So, Luke? You must be disappointed Mark's not going to make it home for the wedding?"

"He's busy. Between school, work, girls and hockey, I'm not surprised. Besides, now I have my dance partner as my best man," he said, winking at Stanley.

Stanley slapped him on the back. "I'm honoured you asked."

Mabel pushed some mashed potatoes on a spoon with her thumb and held it to her daughter's mouth, then glanced at Alice. "You're quiet. Everything okay?"

"Yes."

Mary Margaret folded her arms and turned her head to the side. Mabel sighed, put the spoon down and picked up her teacup. "You were going to talk to me about the wedding?" she said to Alice.

"Oh, it's nothing. It can wait."

"Is it about the gown? Honestly, we can take the crinoline out in no time."

There was a knock on the front door.

Luke pushed his chair back. "I'll get it."

"Anyone for some rice pudding with raisins?" Mabel asked. JC's hand shot up. Stanley held up his rum, and Alice patted her belly, indicating she was stuffed. Mabel was about to get up when the hands came around her face, covering her eyes. "Who's there?" she asked, laughing.

Michael and Victoria stood behind Amour and held their fingers to their mouths.

"You get one guess," Stanley said.

Mabel started to laugh. "It's a woman. It can't be Mary Catherine, she's at the hospital. And I don't think it's Lily. I have no... *Amour?*"

Amour pulled her hands away and jumped in front of her. "Surprise!"

The kitchen was transformed into a chaotic scene of arms around necks, slaps on the back and fawning over the kids. Questions were asked without complete answers offered, and everybody was laughing and smiling. Mabel stepped back to take it all in.

Amour ran up to her, bounced on her toes, brought her hands together and squealed. "I've never been more excited in my life." She grabbed Mabel by the wrist, dragged her down the hall and picked up the phone. "I saw that Myrtle's drapes were drawn, but it's what, quarter past six? You can tell her you're…you're making chutney and it's all…all runny…and that…that you need her to—"

Mabel took the receiver from Amour and placed it back on the cradle.

"What's wrong?" Amour asked, looking at Stanley and Michael huddled in the kitchen.

"Myrtle's not home. She's in the hospital."

"Is it serious?"

Mabel nodded. "She's in a coma. She was attacked."

Amour put her hand over her mouth. Michael approached his wife and ran his hand down her arm. "I'm so sorry, hun. I know how excited you were to surprise her."

The joyous homecoming and buoyant mood of the happy gathering abruptly turned quiet. Mabel led Amour into the living room and told her what she knew. Stanley, Michael and Sam gathered the luggage off the front step, and Alice and Victoria did their best to occupy JC and Mary Margaret.

Amour stood. "I need to see her."

Michael dropped a large suitcase in the hallway. "*Tonight?*"

"Yes, now!" Amour said firmly.

"I'll go with you," Mabel said.

Twenty minutes later they were walking down the hall to Myrtle's room. Mabel stopped and pulled on Amour's sleeve. "You should know, she doesn't look good."

Amour smiled and nodded. When she entered the room, she burst into tears. Her dear friend was unrecognizable, with her head wrapped in gauze, her racoon-like eyes and her snow-burnt face.

Mary Catherine got up from her chair and hugged Amour.

"Any news?" Mabel whispered.

"No."

Mabel took Mary Catherine by the hand. "Let's give them some time alone." She led her across the hall to the chapel. Mabel looked at the flickering votives and thought of Father Gregory kneeling at the altar, surrounded by an orange glow. She put her head down, thinking about their last conversation and of how mean she was to him.

"Alice told me Amour was coming home. I didn't think it was tonight," Mary Catherine said.

"Neither did I." Mabel squeezed her friend's hand. "It was good of you to come and offer to spend the night."

"Believe me, if I weren't here, I might be in jail."

Mabel raised her eyebrows. "What are you talking about?"

"I'm so damn mad at Sam. Seriously, I could kill him," Mary Catherine said, explaining he was representing one of the boys. "I told him you and Stanley would be furious as well."

"Captain Dunphy was by earlier and told me he let the boys go home," Mabel said.

"So, they haven't been charged?"

"No, but he didn't rule it out."

"Sam better hope they're not. Because I won't stand for him representing anyone who attacked our friend."

Mabel didn't say anything.

"*What*? You agree with me, *don't you*?"

Mabel smiled. "He *is* a defense attorney. I don't know. I mean…I hope whoever did this to Myrtle gets their due. I guess I'm just thinking about what might have happened to Stanley if Sam didn't step up and represent him. It wouldn't be the first time an innocent person was falsely accused. Just don't get ahead of yourself. I think you need to trust Sam to do the right thing." Mabel then told her McInnes was back in town.

"Stanley must be beside himself."

"He is. He promised he wouldn't do anything stupid, but I'm still scared."

"I guess we're in the same boat," Mary Catherine said.

"What do you mean?"

"We're both hoping our husbands don't fuck things up."

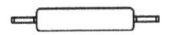

Mabel and Mary Catherine left the hospital, both insisting they would have been happy to stay with Myrtle so that Amour could rest up from her trip.

"She's where she wants to be," Mabel said.

They were pulling onto Brookside Street when Mabel told Mary Catherine to stop the car. "That's Charlotte. We should see if she needs a lift."

Charlotte hopped in the backseat, grateful to get out of the cold and cursing her unreliable brother who promised to pick her up. "Thank you, ladies. You're a lifesaver. I live on Douglas Avenue. Hope it's not too far out of the way."

"Not at all," Mary Catherine said. "So, Charlotte, does Gordon ever talk to you about police business?"

"Not really. But then we don't get much opportunity to talk anymore," she said with a hint of sadness.

"Charlotte and Gordon broke up," Mabel said.

I'm sorry," Mary Catherine said. "I wasn't aware."

"That's all right. Like I told Mabel, we ended things on good terms. We're still friends."

Mary Catherine slowed to turn onto Commercial Street and looked in the rear view mirror. "Then I guess you don't know anything about the investigation into Myrtle's case?"

"I heard they had three boys in custody."

Mabel turned to Charlotte. "Gordon told me they released them."

"When did you see Gordon?" Charlotte asked.

Mabel thought of their awkward conversation in the hospital. "He just popped by for a minute to tell Stanley that Dan McInnes was back in town."

"Oh," Charlotte said, wondering why such news required a personal visit.

Mary Catherine dropped Charlotte off and turned to her quiet passenger, picking at her cuticles. "Looks like the town has a new eligible bachelor."

"I guess so."

"He sure is handsome."

"Do you think?" Mabel asked.

Mary Catherine started to laugh. "You can't be serious. Are you blind? I always figured he and Charlotte would get married. Wonder what happened. You don't suppose he's a little light in the loafers?"

Mabel shook her head. "Why is it that if a man isn't married by the time he's thirty, he must be homosexual? Nobody says the same thing about a woman."

"No," Mary Catherine said with a chuckle. "We just say they're ugly or frigid."

Mary Catherine pulled up to the darkened house.

"Looks like everybody's in bed," Mabel said, stepping out of the car. She held the door open and ducked her head back inside. "Go easy on Sam."

Mary Catherine nodded and waited for her to enter the house, then drove off.

Mabel turned the living room light on and went to her wall of photos to say good night. "James," she whispered, "please keep Stanley from doing something he'll regret." She then tiptoed upstairs and pushed her bedroom door open, the light from the hallway helping her find her way around the unlit room. She looked down at JC curled up on his makeshift bed on the floor and peeked in the crib. Mary Margaret wasn't there. She was sprawled across her side of the bed. Mabel changed into her nightgown and gently repositioned Mary Margaret.

"Did Amour come back with you?" Stanley whispered.

"No. She insisted on staying. Did I wake you?"

"Can't sleep."

"Is it McInnes?" Mabel asked.

"Yes."

"Please try and put him out of your mind."

"You must be tired?" Stanley said.

"Exhausted. I feel like I could sleep through to next week." She leaned across Mary Margret and kissed his cheek. "Thanks for all you did today."

Stanley tugged on the blanket and brought it up over his shoulder. "I'm sure you'll think of a way to show your appreciation," he said.

Mabel laughed. "I'm still thinking." She turned onto her side and was just about to sink into a welcomed slumber.

"Do you feel that?" Stanley asked.

Mabel opened her eyes. "Yes."

Stanley sat up. "But she hasn't wet the bed in weeks."

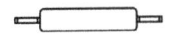

Mary Catherine turned on the hall light and removed her coat. She glanced at her husband on the couch and crept past him on her way upstairs.

"How's Myrtle?"

Mary Catherine stopped and turned around. "The same. Amour is with her now."

"*Amour?*"

"Yes. They all arrived this evening. Michael has an interview with the coal company. I didn't mean to wake you."

Sam was relieved his wife seemed less icy. He sat up. "I'm sorry."

Mary Catherine told him to scooch over and sat on the edge of the couch. "I might have over reacted."

"I don't blame you. It's just that he's a kid."

"I know. Mabel told me they let him go home," Mary Catherine said.

"For now. There's still a chance he might be charged. Look, I honestly believe he's innocent. But, Mary Catherine, I won't represent him if it means it will create friction here at home."

She put her hand on his shoulder. "Mabel reminded me that if it hadn't been for you, Stanley might have been falsely accused and put to death. I'm going to trust you to do what's right."

Sam smiled and put his head down. "Thank you."

Mary Catherine stood. "I'm exhausted. Let's go to bed."

Sam followed her upstairs. "Your daughter has a pit mouth," he said.

Mary Catherine stopped mid-step and looked back at him. "*What?*"

"Your daughter has a pit mouth," Sam said, repeating what Ruth said, word for word.

Mary Catherine dropped her head and covered her eyes. "Oh, no! I didn't mean for her to hear. What did you say to her?"

"I told her I was going to get a cake of Sunlight soap and wash out her goddamn mouth."

Mary Catherine's head shot up.

Sam laughed. "Just kidding."

Amour blew her nose and laughed. "Mabel told me your wig probably saved your life. Remember the day I got drunk and plopped it on your head. God, I was so embarrassed. And then I brought you the cake as a peace offering. I don't know if I ever told you, but I didn't buy it. Mabel made it."

She tucked her hankie in her pocket and took Myrtle's hand. "I need you to get better. I might be moving back home and I need by best friend. I need you to teach me how to make chutney. And you haven't met Michael or Victoria. You'll love them. And I know they'll love you."

An older nurse came through the door to check the IV bottle.

"How long can she stay like this?" Amour asked.

"There's no telling. Could be hours…days. Could be longer. Hopefully, not *too much* longer. She needs to eat."

"She's not in any pain, *though*?"

"No."

"Is it possible…she could die?"

"*Is it possible?* Yes. There's also a good possibility she won't. Right now, it's mostly up to her and the good Lord above."

Amour squeezed Myrtle's hand. "Hear that Myrtle. You have to fight. Fight like you've never fought before."

The nurse placed her hand on Amour's shoulder. "Keep that up, honey. I'm sure she senses you're here. Ya never know, with your encouragement, she might be back on her feet in no time."

Amour smiled and nodded.

"And hopefully, if all goes well, there won't be any permanent brain damage."

The Silver Compact

Sunday, Nov. 24

Gordon was driving to church when he spotted one of his uniformed officers leaning over Commercial Street Bridge and smoking. He quickly pulled over and approached him. "What the hell are you doing?"

The young officer spun around. "Keeping an eye on the crime scene, like McEwan told me."

"Jesus Christ almighty! You're not supposed to be standing out here like a sore thumb. This is supposed to be a stakeout…not a…not a friggin… friggin stick out. Go change, get your ass back here and make yourself less… less visible."

Gordon's flustered subordinate flung his butt onto the ice below and took off.

Alice spotted the handsome captain angrily kicking at the hard snow and tugged on her father's sleeve. "Pull over. That's Captain Dunphy. Maybe he needs help." Corliss pulled off to the side. Alice jumped out and walked toward him. "Car trouble?"

"Oh, hi. No, car is fine."

Alice gave him a look of concern. "You look like you're carrying the weight of the world on your shoulders."

"It's just…just police business. It's nothing, really."

Alice thought he looked as dashing in his Sunday best as he did in his uniform. "You should have an overcoat on. You'll catch your death of cold," she said, resting her hand on his arm. Dunphy smiled, then nodded over her shoulder. Alice turned to see who he was greeting.

Mabel rolled down her window. "Everything okay?" she asked, wondering if the blush on Alice's cheeks was due to the cold air or something else.

"*Oh*, Da and I were driving by and thought Gordon might have car trouble," she said, pointing to her father.

"Car's fine," Gordon said. "Just waiting to meet up with one of my officers."

Mabel smiled and nodded. "We're on our way to see Myrtle."

"I'll drop by later," Alice said.

"Great. We can chat about that matter you wanted to discuss," Mabel said. She rolled her window back up.

Stanley drove into the hospital parking lot and looked at his pensive wife. "You're quiet all of a sudden?"

Mabel shrugged and put on her gloves.

"Anything bothering you?"

"I'm not sure," Mabel said and stepped out.

Amour was struggling to keep her eyes open when they entered Myrtle's room.

Mabel unbuttoned her coat. "Still the same?"

Amour started to cry. "The nurse told me that, even if she lives, she could have brain damage."

Mabel hugged her.

Amour tried to collect herself. "I don't know what to do with myself?"

"I do," Mabel said. "You're going home, crawling into bed and getting some sleep. Stanley will take you home."

Amour was too tired and emotional to resist. She kissed the top of Myrtle's head, and she and Stanley left.

"Well, Myrtle. Looks like I'll be doing my praying here today, instead of in church," Mabel said. She reached for Margaret's Bible, then opened the drawer of the bedside table for Father Gregory's maniturgium. It wasn't there. She looked under the table and bed, then went to the nurses' station. No one she asked recalled seeing it. She returned to Myrtle's room and, again, checked everywhere she had just searched. She sat down heavily, wondering where it could be, assuring herself it would show up. She flipped through the Bible in search of an appropriate passage. *Dear Friend, I pray you may enjoy good health and that all may go well for you, even as your soul is getting along well.* She couldn't concentrate. She marked the page with the Bible's thin, red ribbon, closed it over and ran her hand over the black, pimply cover with its gold-embossed lettering.

The cleaning lady walked in with her mop and bucket. "You didn't happen to come across a white cloth with gold fringes by any chance?" Mabel asked.

"No, dear. Did ya check the drawers?"

"Yes."

The frail, elderly woman shrugged, dipped her grey, stringy mop into the hot water and swooshed it across the floor. "Ya know, dear, whenever I misplace somethin, I pray to St. Anthony."

Despite her growing unease, Mabel smiled. She thought back to Father Cusack explaining its significance. *It's a cloth given to a priest on his ordination that is then buried with his mother. A sign that she has lent her son to God.* Mabel's heart began racing, thinking it was a bad omen and something terrible was going to happen to JC. This is silly, she thought. It will turn up and JC will be just fine. Stanley's right, I worry too much. She then thought of Dan McInnes. Like Stanley, she believed he was behind the kidnapping. She searched at the bottom of her bag for loose change and ran to the pay phone. Her hand was trembling as she tried to insert the dime in the slot. "I need you to check the dresser for the maniturgium. I know. That's what I thought, too. It's not here, I checked. Maybe with all the upset, I forgot I took it home. Yes, I'm fine. Where's JC? Building a snow fort? Out back? Could you check on him? Please, Stanley! Just do it! Yes, I'll wait." Mabel smiled at a nurse watching her bark her orders into the phone. "Good. Keep an eye on him. I told you, I'm fine. Maybe just a little rattled. If you find the maniturgium, call the nurses' station and have them pass on the message. I will."

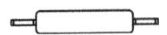

Wally-One-Nut saw Ten-After-Six make his way to the bridge. "Hey, Peter. Having a profitable walk?"

Ten-After-Six raised his head. "Not so much. Found a dime. Heading home."

"Better than a kick in the arse," Walter said. He leaned over the bridge. "Beautiful day. Cold, but at least the sun is shining?"

"Don't like winter," Peter said. "Snow makes it harder to find money."

Walter laughed. "Too bad about Myrtle Munroe."

"Terrible," Peter said. "Lots of rumours making the rounds."

Walter blew into his cupped hands. "Heard they hauled in three young guys, but let them go. Hope they get whoever did it. So, have ya been taking in any of the games at the forum?"

"No."

"Ya should see this young Vince Ryan play. Doesn't look like much, but boy can he skate and handle the puck."

Peter raised his head. "Not a fan of hockey. Find it hard to follow the plays," he said. A glint from the trees along Brookside Street caught his eye.

Walter pulled his collar around his neck. "Well, I'm off. Game's about to get started." He laid his hand on Peter's bent back. "Hope you have better luck on your way home."

Peter walked up Brookside Street, then turned down into the thicket, wondering what shiny object awaited him. He couldn't find anything and was about to leave, when he spotted the tip of a mysterious silver object poking up through the snow. He rubbed the shiny disc on his pant leg and put it in his pocket. He was back on Brookside Street when he heard his name being called. He turned to see one of the town's young constables waving at him. "Hey, Peter. How's it going?"

"Good."

The officer turned and pointed toward town. "Sorry, bud. I'm outa smokes, and all the stores are closed. Wondering if I could bum a couple?"

Peter handed him his packet. "Take four."

"Thanks. I'm on a stakeout and freezing my arse off out here," he said, lighting his cigarette. "So, ya havin any luck today?"

"No. Just a dime and this," he said, showing him his latest find. He pointed to the trees. "Found it in there."

The officer took it from him and opened it up. "It's a ladies compact. Oh well, better than a kick in the arse," he said, slapping Peter on the back. "Thanks again."

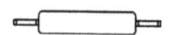

Mabel walked back from the nurses' station, upset that Stanley had not called to say he found the maniturgium. If it wasn't at home, it had to be somewhere in the hospital. Maybe it got mixed up with the laundry. She tried to convince herself it would turn up and that she was being ridiculous to think its disappearance meant something bad would happen to JC. Still, she felt increasingly anxious.

Alice entered. "I brought you a sandwich."

"Thanks," Mabel said curtly. She placed it on Myrtle's beside table.

"Every okay? You seem out of sorts," Alice said, pulling a chair up beside her.

Mabel told her about the missing maniturgium and her fear that it was a bad omen. "I know it doesn't sound rational, but I can't help feeling something really bad is going to happen. Anyway, I'm glad you're here now. I can go home and look for myself." She stood to put her coat on.

Alice dropped her head. "Actually, I was hoping we could have our chat… about the wedding."

Mabel sat back down. "Go on."

Alice smiled at her. "I don't think I can go through with it."

Mabel titled her head. "You mean a big formal wedding, *right?*"

Alice paused. "No. I mean the marriage. I just…well, I just—"

Mabel stood and began pacing. "But Luke is head over heels in love with you. And just a week ago, you assured me you *loved him?*"

"I know. It's just that…sometimes…well sometimes I think I'm getting my concern for him confused with love. I mean I love him, but I'm not sure it's the marrying kind of love."

Mabel sat back down and took Alice's hands in hers. "Alice, you need to be sure. It will break Luke's heart if you don't go through with it," she said, thinking about Luke's struggle with melancholy and what he might do if Alice ended things. "But you also have to do what your heart tells you is right. Obviously, you can't go through with the wedding if you don't love him. That wouldn't be fair to him *or you*. You're sure it's not just nervousness about the wedding, because if it is, you can simply—"

Alice shook her head. "I don't think it's that. It's…oh, hell…I don't know what to think."

Mabel squeezed Alice's hands. "I need to ask you something. And I need you to be truthful."

Alice pulled her hand free, wiped away a tear and nodded.

"Does this have anything to do with Captain Dunphy?" Mabel asked.

"No."

"You're sure?"

"Well, maybe a little."

Mabel leaned back in her chair and closed her eyes.

"It's not what you think. Honestly, Mabel, I started to have doubts about the wedding before I heard Gordon and Charlotte broke up. It's just that... well...when you told me they weren't seeing each other, I started to think about him a lot. Too much. It's not right that I'm thinking about one man when I'm about to marry another. And I tried to share my feelings about the wedding with Luke, but every time I went to talk to him about it, he'd so something really sweet and I'd chicken out."

Mabel thought of Gordon's recent visit and how she had fixed her hair and put on lipstick in anticipation of his arrival. She'd never entertain any thoughts of being unfaithful to her husband. She loved Stanley, like she could no other. Still, she was flattered to learn Gordon was smitten with her, and her ego selfishly got in the way of clear thinking.

Alice blew her nose. "Look, I like Gordon, but I also know I'd never have a chance with him. I don't even think he knows my last name."

"Alice, just because you have had thoughts about Gordon, doesn't mean you don't love Luke. I'm going to let you in on a little secret. The other night when I learned Gordon was coming by the house, I—"

They both jumped at the sound of smashing glass and the jarring clanging of the steel pole hitting the floor.

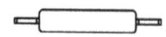

Amour looked out the window and saw Mabel getting out of Luke's car. She ran to the door. "How is she?" she asked, reaching for her coat.

"She came to, but was very agitated. The doctor said it's not uncommon. They've sedated her. Said there's no point in anyone going back tonight."

Amour put her coat back on the hook. "But it's good that she came out of the coma?"

"Yes. They just want to keep her calm. They'll start weaning her off the sedatives in a day or two. Where's JC?" Mabel asked.

"Upstairs with Mary Margaret. Victoria's reading them *Make Way for Ducklings* for the umpteenth time."

Mabel peeked in JC's room. Mary Margaret was curled up on the bed next to Victoria, her new best friend. There was no sign of JC. "Have you seen JC?" she asked Victoria.

"Not for a while."

Mabel checked the other rooms. Again, no JC. She started to panic.

"JC! JC!" she yelled.

She tore downstairs, ducking her head into the living room. "He's not here!" She ran to the back door and began hollering his name.

"I'm sure he's not far. He was here less than an hour ago," Amour said, trying to reassure her.

"It only takes a minute," Mabel snapped, thinking of the day he was snatched out from under her.

Michael came in the front door and immediately saw that Mabel was distraught.

"Michael, JC's missing!" she said frantically.

"He's in the barn with Stanley. They're cleaning the stalls," he said, shooting his wife a worried look.

"Are you sure?" Mabel asked.

Michael laughed and pointed to the door. "Yes. I just left him. He wants some cocoa."

"Thank God," Mabel said. She plopped down on the sofa and put her head in her hand. "I'm sorry. You must think I'm a superstitious fool."

Amour rubbed her back. "Of course not. So, I take it Father Gregory's maniturgium still hasn't shown up?"

"No."

Stanley and JC walked in. "JC wants carnation in his cocoa." He looked at his wife. "What's wrong?"

Mabel crouched beside JC and wrapped her arms around him. "Nothing. All is good," she said, kissing his cheek.

The Change Purse

Monday, Nov. 25

"Dan, dear! I'm off to work," Gladys hollered down the hall. "I left your application on the table. Remember it has to be in today."

"I know."

"And if ya don't mind fixin the latch. It won't close over like it's supposed to."

"Okay," he said, reaching for his smokes. He laid back on his pillow and dragged on his cigarette, thinking he'd have to be out of his mind to take a job working beside garish Lizzie day in and day out. He closed his eyes, picturing her large tits and tight ass, wondering if the old floozy was ever laid. "Fuck, nobody could ever be that desperate," he whispered.

He threw back his bedclothes, stubbed his cigarette and sat on the edge of the bed, thinking that a cushy office job couldn't be any worse than freezing his balls off bouncing around in the middle of the Atlantic. He could buy a car and maybe get a place of his own, away from his bossy aunt. He got dressed, reached in his duffle bag and removed Myrtle's change purse. He needed to get rid of it. He walked into the kitchen, tossed it on the table and began filling the kettle. He turned quickly when he saw the basement door open.

"I thought you left?" he said, glancing at the incriminating evidence, then quickly back at Gladys.

"I figured I better bank the furnace in case you fergot." She picked up the change purse. "*What's this?*"

"I guess the cat's outa the bag. It's your Christmas present."

Gladys turned it over in her hands. "It's beautiful. But ya don't need to be spendin what little ya have on me." She put it back on the table. "I'll pretend

I didn't see it." She tapped the application. "Don't ferget. And don't ferget the latch. Well, I gotta go or I'll miss my bus."

Dan forced a smile and waited for her to leave. He paced around the kitchen, then watched from the living room as Gladys struggled to board the bus. "Fuck," he screamed, cursing himself for being so careless. First I dropped the painting at the scene and now this, he thought. He went back to the kitchen, picked up the application and tossed it back down.

"No more stupid, fuckin mistakes," he muttered.

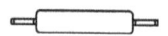

Michael and Mabel dropped Amour off at the hospital.

"Don't forget to ask them to check the laundry for the maniturgium," Mabel said. "And call me about Myrtle."

Amour smiled and waved.

Ten minutes later Mabel entered the store. Corliss was stocking shelves. "Where's Luke?" she asked.

"Gone to the train station. Pickin up something else I'll need to find a place for. Wouldn't be so bad if it was somethin people were gonna buy," he said, shaking his head. "Got this crazy notion to diversify and give Larry Mendelson a run for his money. I worry about the kid. Sometimes I think he's got it so bad, he ain't thinkin straight. Don't have near enough traffic in these parts. But my daughter loves him, so who am I to judge."

Mabel smiled and walked into the bakery. Alice was crimping a pie. She looked up and gave Mabel an apologetic look.

"Mary Mack not in yet?"

"She called. Bus didn't show up. She's on her way."

Mabel hung up her coat. "Come with me," she said, taking Alice by the arm and pulling out a chair. "Have a seat."

Alice sat down and stared down at her lap.

"So, have you made up your mind?"

Alice shook her head.

"Alice, you know…no matter what happens, we'll always be friends. I love you like a sister. I only want the best for you… *and Luke*. But the wedding is less than three weeks away. If you intend to end it, you need to do it sooner rather than later."

"I know. Mabel, I'm so confused. I *do* love him. I'm just not sure I love him in the way...the way you love Stanley. Or the way Da loved Ma. I'm scared I'm making a big mistake."

Mabel thought back to the time when Mary Catherine stood next to her in the bakery, asking how she'd feel if Stanley walked in with another woman. "Okay, so let me ask you this." She pointed to the door. "What if... if you ended things with Luke and he came through *that* door with a pretty, young girl on his arm?"

"I don't know! I wouldn't be here in any event. You know I'd have to quit. I couldn't stay on and face him every day. It would just be too awkward...for the both of us. I imagine Da would find it hard to stay on, too."

Mabel sighed. "I know. It's a huge decision. The biggest of your life. But if you're not sure...you're not sure. You need to follow your heart and not let anyone else, or anything else, cloud your judgement. Not me. Not the bakery. Not your father. I'd miss not having you around, but nothing matters more than your happiness," she said, worried sick about what was going to happen to Luke.

Alice ran her hand under her wet eyes.

"But, Alice, don't wait too much longer before you talk to him." Mabel leaned in and hugged her. "Now, I want you to take the rest of the day off. Maybe go for a walk to the brook. I always find a bit of fresh air helps clear the mind, as well as the lungs. I'll tell Luke...I don't know...you were having menstrual cramps. If he's like every other man on the planet, he'll head for the nearest exit."

Dan dropped his application off at the Clerk's office and went to Iggies hoping for a game of poker. He was surprised when he walked through the door and heard someone call out to him.

McEwan was waving him over. "Hey, bud. Have a seat."

Dan took off his coat, exposing his clubbed fist.

"Jesus, Dan! What happened to your hand?"

Dan recited his rehearsed lie about a fishing accident, telling McEwan he was down on his luck with barely enough money to buy a beer. Their table was soon crowded with empty stubbies, as McEwan droned on about all he did for his demanding, ailing mother.

Dan waited for him to take a breath. "So what's Dunphy like as a boss?" he asked, hoping to ease into the investigation into Myrtle's attack.

"He's acting chief, ya know. Took over after Charlie Peach had a heart attack. Anyway, he's a prick. Told me to assign the guys to keep an eye on the brook. Never told me they were supposed to stay out of sight, and yet he chews me out. Hell, I'm not a fuckin mind reader."

"Why the stakeout at the brook?"

"Figures the kids buried Myrtle's handbag in the area, and they might go back for it. Pretty sure they're not that stupid. Don't matter none to him though. Got us standin out there freezing our asses off all hours of the day and night. Fuckin waste of time and money, if ya ask me."

"So, he *didn't* charge them?"

McEwan held his empty bottle up to the bartender and mouthed *four more*. "No. Let em go home."

"But he still suspects them?"

"Nah, not really. He thinks they were just in the wrong place at the wrong time. Fuckin fool."

"So, you think they're guilty?"

"Your damn right they are. Winston MacRae heard them whispering for two or three minutes before he discovered Kenny standing over her. And Kenny's buddy, Tommy, had her painting shoved under his jacket. Ya know, Dunphy used to play on the same softball team as Kenny's father. Don't tell me he's not playin fuckin favourites."

"So you don't have any other suspects or leads?"

"No. I questioned the neighbours and merchants, and no one saw or heard a thing."

"If I were you, I'd talk to the victim? She must have seen something?"

"Last I heard, she's in a coma. Likely be brain damaged, if she doesn't kick the bucket. Jesus, Dan, it's my day off. Why do you care about any of this shit?"

Dan shrugged. "Old habit, I guess. I always loved police work. I was pretty good at it, too."

McEwan was about to take a sip of beer, but stopped. "Ya were." He laughed and shook his head. "At least till you and Billy Guthro tried to set up Stanley MacIntyre. Still don't know what the fuck ya were thinkin."

Dan drained his beer and stood to leave.

"You're not goin?"

"Yeah. I had enough."

"*Oh, come on?* Look, I'm sorry! Dan! Jesus, I didn't mean to offend you."

"Thanks for the beers," Dan said and walked out.

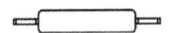

Stanley eased Mary Margret off the bed and put her in her crib, praying she wouldn't wake up. He then checked on JC, sound asleep on the floor. He pulled the covers back and snuggled up to his wife. "Finally, just the two of us," he said. "I've missed you."

Mabel removed his hand from her breast. "Don't even think about it."

"I'll be very quiet. The kids won't hear a thing."

"I barely slept a wink the past two nights. I'm exhausted and my mind's going a mile a minute. I'm worried sick about Luke…*and Myrtle*. Then there's Father Gregory's maniturgium. Amour said they checked the hospital laundry and it's not there either. I know you think I'm crazy, but I'm worried about JC, now that it's missing. And then there's the bakery and Christmas is just around the corner. I need to order supplies and—"

"Let me take your mind off things," he whispered.

"Not a chance."

Stanley sighed. "Would you be tired if I wore a uniform with shiny brass buttons?"

"What?" Mabel said laughing.

Stanley nuzzled her neck. "You know, if I were the town's most eligible bachelor?"

Mabel rolled onto her back. *"What are you talking about?"*

"The lipstick," Stanley said. "You never wear lipstick. Unless, of course, it's a special occasion."

"It was," Mabel said. "The town's most eligible bachelor was dropping by. Honestly, if I didn't know any better, I'd swear you were jealous?"

He ran his hand over her stomach. "I don't have a jealous bone in my body. I know my wife loves me and wants to show me how much. Hell, Gordon's so handsome, I'm thinking about asking him if he'd be my new dance partner."

Mabel turned to face him and laid her hand on his cheek. "I'm afraid of what Luke will do if Alice calls off the wedding. I mean… *seriously worried*."

Stanley flopped onto his back and threw his arm off to the side. "You sure know how to kill the mood. You're also getting a head of yourself. Alice is likely going through what every other bride and groom goes through."

"No. It's more than that. I know it is. She even mentioned that if she cancels the wedding, she'll have to quit working at the bakery. Said it would be too awkward."

Stanley pinched his eyes. "I can see I'm not gonna get any lovin again tonight."

Mabel laid her head on his shoulder and her hand on his chest. "I hate to think I might lose her. The bakery just wouldn't be the same. But, of course, it's Luke I worry most about." She closed her eyes, but couldn't sleep. Thoughts of Myrtle, Luke, and her nagging fear that Father Gregory's missing maniturgium meant something bad was going to happen to JC preyed on her mind. Then there was Lily, living hand-to-mouth and being shunned by so many mean-spirited people.

"Stanley?"

"*What*? I was almost asleep."

"I meant to ask. How is Lily working out?"

"Good. I'm increasing her hours."

At least it was one bright spot, Mabel thought.

Stanley removed his numb arm from under her head and rolled onto his side. "With everything else that's going on in that head of yours, what made you ask that?"

"I dunno. Just thinking about…how much I like her lipstick."

Dirty Politics

Tuesday, Nov. 26

Captain Dunphy stared at the colourful image of the red and blue boat laden with lobster traps, pulling away from the harbour. It didn't add up. If the boys ditched Myrtle's handbag with plans to go back for it at another time, why wouldn't they ditch the painting. It was certainly small enough to fit into a ladies regular-sized handbag.

He put on his coat and headed to town. He stopped outside Arlies and looked at Myrtle's playful artwork in the window. He entered and sought out the young clerk who was the last to see Myrtle before the attack. Dunphy handed him the painting recovered at the scene. "Any other stores selling Myrtle's paintings."

"Not in town."

"I'm trying to find out if someone might have bought it. Maybe they were on their way home and didn't realize they had lost it."

"It's possible, I guess," the clerk said.

"Do you remember selling it?"

"We sell quite a few. But, no, I don't remember selling this one. Maybe one of the other clerks did.

Dunphy showed it to the only other clerk in the store and got the same answer. He returned to the young man, asking that he follow-up with any other clerks and that he check the remaining inventory against their sales records. He left, praying Tommy was telling the truth when he said he found it at the scene.

He was heading back to his office when Mannie Chernin came up from behind and slapped him on the back. "How's my favourite captain?"

"Oh, hi, Mannie. I'm good. *You?*"

"Not bad for an old fella."

"I heard you're running for mayor," Dunphy said.

"Ya heard right. Time to shake things up around here. I'm hoping I can count on your vote…given our mutual interest in law and order n' all."

Dunphy smiled, but didn't bite.

"Here," Mannie said, reaching into his pocket and slapping a pin-back button in Dunphy's palm.

Dunphy turned it over and read the slogan. *ONLY MAN(nie) for MAYOR.* "*Clever,*" he said.

Mannie pointed at Myrtle's painting. "Christmas present, or evidence?"

"Evidence."

"Heard you had three guys in custody and let them go."

"Kids, actually. Not enough to hold them. Pretty sure it was just a case of bad timing."

"Also heard one of the kids had the victim's painting in his possession, and another tried to run?"

"You hear a lot."

"I make it a point. Ya know, Gordon, people are already talking. They're afraid they'll suffer the same fate as Myrtle if they come to town after dark. And a good number of merchants are saying that unless an arrest is made soon, they'll lose out on a lot of business in the lead up to Christmas. Wouldn't want to see that happen now, *would we?* A bit of unsolicited advice, give the town some peace of mind. Bring the unruly gang back in and charge them. Ya never know, you might get lucky. After a few nights locked up, one of them will likely get antsy and rat out whoever struck the blow."

"I'm still not convinced there's enough evidence. Frankly, my gut tells me they're innocent."

Mannie shrugged. "Maybe they are. Still, you should be thinking about the greater good and haul their asses back in. Hell, if you find out they didn't do it, no harm, no foul, ya just drop the charges." He winked. "But not before Christmas."

Dunphy watched the town's crusty, old Crown Prosecutor wave to potential voters and quickly scoot across Commercial Street. What a prick, he thought, as Mannie slapped backs and handed out his buttons.

Mabel entered the store, surprised to see Mary Mack behind the counter. "Good morning. Where's Luke?" she asked.

"Mornin. He drove John to school, and he and Corliss had some runnin round to do."

"Alice in yet?"

"Back there, baking up a storm."

Mabel stopped in the doorway and watched Alice knead her pie crust. "You're hard at it?"

Alice smiled. "Lots of orders coming in."

Mabel hung her coat up, walked up behind her and rested her hand on Alice's back. "You okay?"

"Yes."

"Any closer to a decision?"

"Yes," she said, pushing her fists into the dough.

"Anything you care to share?"

Alice brushed her hands on her apron and looked up from her kneading table. "I'm going to go through with it."

Mabel smiled and hugged her, but was concerned by her phrasing. *Go through with it.* Like she was describing an onerous task and not what should be the happiest day of her life.

"I took your advice and went to the brook. It really helped. I'm sure now. I feel kind of foolish. Like you said, I just had a bad case of pre-wedding jitters."

"As long as you're sure?" Mabel said.

"I am."

"Well, I gotta tell you, you had me a little nervous. I know you've made the right decision. You and Luke were made for one another."

Mabel's initial relief, turned back to worry as the day wore down. Her normally chatty friend was unusually quiet. And despite her best efforts to engage Alice in conversation, she seemed pensive, if not sad. The only time there was a small glimmer of her old self was when Luke arrived and presented her with a single red rose. But it didn't last. The moment he stepped out of the bakery, Alice, once again, seemed lost in her thoughts.

Mabel looked at the clock. "Stanley will be here any minute. Time to hang up our aprons."

Mabel waited at the store window for Stanley to come for her. Luke came out of the storage room and dropped a box at her feet. He grinned and pulled a box cutter from his pocket, ran it down the taped seam and pulled the flaps back. "Look at this," he said, holding up a contraption Mabel had never seen before.

"What is it?"

"A Viewfinder. Going to be the hottest item in town, and nobody else has it, but me," he said proudly. He pulled a round white disc from the box, slid it in place and held it up to the light. "Come see," he said, passing it to her.

"I see a lion."

"Now put your finger here and pull down."

"A zebra."

Luke waited for her reaction. "What do you think?"

"I think JC will love it. Set one aside for me."

"Nope. I'm giving it to him for Christmas."

"Hey, Alice!" he hollered. "Wait till you see this."

Mabel smiled as he disappeared inside the bakery and put her head down. One minute I'm worried the wedding is off, and the next I'm worried it's back on, she thought.

Luke reappeared in the doorway, grinning from ear to ear. "She thinks it's fabulous, like me," he said, taking an exaggerated bow. He didn't see Alice come from behind. She dumped a cup of flour over his head. "Look what my bride did to me," he said, holding his arms off to the side and laughing. He bent over and shook his head from side-to-side. "I'll get you for that," he said.

Mabel grinned at the scraping sound of chairs being pushed across the floor and Alice's squeals. She was still smiling when Stanley pulled in front. He stretched his arm across the seat to help her into the cab. Mabel chuckled, thinking of the playful scene she had just witnessed.

"What's so funny?" he asked.

"Oh, just thinking I worry too much."

The Post

Wednesday, Nov. 27

Captain Dunphy walked in to see The Post on his desk. He picked it up and read the headline below the fold. "Mayoral Candidate Calls for Arrests."

> *Mayoralty candidate, Mannie Chernin, is calling on local police to lay charges against three youths found at the scene of a brutal attack on local artist, Myrtle Munroe, Friday Nov. 22. "I met with the lead officer handling the investigation and he confirmed the release of three teenagers found at the scene of the violent attack on one of our most beloved citizens," Chernin said. He added, "I would never presume to tell the police how to do their job, but as someone who has fought for law and order in this town for over thirty years, I can tell you, that given the severity of the crime and the evidence that I have uncovered, our law enforcement officials should immediately file charges."*
>
> *Mr. Chernin, who emphasized he was speaking as a candidate for mayor and not in his capacity as Crown Prosecutor, said he has heard from a good number of residents and merchants who are growing increasingly concerned about the safety of our streets. "It is a terrible travesty when people are afraid to go down town at night, especially during the busy Christmas season when the stores have extended their hours to accommodate local shoppers. I am calling on Mayor Wareham to immediately get to the bottom of why the police are allowing three potentially dangerous suspects to remain*

at large. The good citizens of our town deserve a mayor who will not shirk his solemn duty to protect the public from future harm."

Mayor Wareham, who is seeking his fourth term in office, said, "My opponent is using a tragic event to try and score political points. It would not be proper for me to interfere or comment on an ongoing police investigation."

Dunphy threw the newspaper aside. "You bastard, Mannie," he muttered.

The desk sergeant stood in the doorway. "Captain?"

"Yes?"

"You have visitors. Mayor Wareham is here with four members of the police commission."

"Which ones?"

His desk sergeant read off the names.

Dunphy nodded. "Just as I thought, they're all members of the merchant's association."

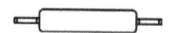

Dan waited for the clerk in Bettens' store to bag the order of the customer ahead of him. He picked up The Post and looked at Mannie Chernin's big grin and fat face. Ya, haven't changed much, he thought. You're still seeking the limelight. He quickly scanned the article, then threw the newspaper on the counter. "A pack of Export A's and the paper."

He headed back to Steele's Hill, put the kettle on and re-read the article. "Pressure's mounting," he whispered. He sipped his tea, thinking it was time to kick it up a notch. He turned to the inside front page and ran his finger down the right-hand column, found the number and went to the phone. "Hi. Yeah, I have some information to report about the attack on that painter. No, I don't want to give my name. Yes, I can hold."

Dan started to have second thoughts and was about to hang up when he heard the voice on the other end. "Oh, hi. Yeah, I'm here. No! No names! Let's just say I'm in a position to have inside information. Mannie Chernin's right. The evidence is overwhelming, and the cops know it. Captain Dunphy's covering things up. *Why?* Cause he's a good friend of the father of one of the suspects. Kenny Ludlow. I know his fellow officers think something's up. Yeah, I got details. Oh, like one of the boys tried to run when he was discovered at the scene. Likely a robbery gone bad. Police believe they buried her handbag in the snow. One of em had a painting belonging to the victim on his person. And here's the kicker, they were heard in the area at least five or six minutes before they were discovered standing next to the body, but they never hollered for help. Yeah, I know. I guess you'll have to ask them. No…no problem. Just happy to do my civic duty."

Dan hung up, satisfied that it would be just a matter of days before public pressure reached a feverish pitch and the kids were picked up. He, once again, cursed himself for stealing the painting, but was satisfied he covered his tracks. Even if his visit to Arlies raised suspicions, the clerk would describe him as a bearded man. He ran his hand over his clean-shaven chin, thinking the chances they'd even discover the painting was stolen were slim to none.

He just had two worrisome matters still nagging at him. The change purse and Myrtle.

Heckles and a Handbag

Thursday, Nov. 28

Dunphy flung the newspaper across his desk and onto the floor, then stepped into the hallway. "Get in here!" he yelled to his desk sergeant. "Tell everyone to be in the interview room in ten." His nervous subordinate bent down to gather up the splayed broadsheet.

"Leave it be!" his boss barked.

Dunphy put the newspaper back together and thought about his meeting with the mayor and members of the police commission. He managed to convince them that they were still in the early stages of the investigation, charges would be premature, and the boys posed no real threat to the public. He knew the latest article in the The Post would result in another visit.

He could hear the rumblings from the overcrowded interview room as he made his way down the hall. They stopped as soon as he soon as he walked in. He held up the front page. "I imagine you all saw this!" He punched at the headline. *"Questions Raised About Police Inaction/Corruption!"* He angrily read from the article.

> *An anonymous source, who claims to have knowledge of the investigation, said the alleged suspects were heard whispering among themselves for five or six minutes before they were discovered near the body, yet they didn't call for help.*

Dunphy tried to level his tone. "It was more like *two* or *three* minutes, but let's not let the facts get in the way of a good story. *Oh*, and how about his one."

The source went on to say that many within the force believe the evidence warrants charges, but that lead investigator and acting Chief of Police, Captain Gordon Dunphy, is refusing to do so because he is a close friend of the father of Kenny Ludlow, one of the alleged suspects.

"Anyone here think that's the case? Didn't think so."

He leaned against the interview table. "I'm your captain, the acting chief and lead on this case. I've made it clear in the past, but I will repeat it again here and now. No one, *and I mean no one*, is to speak to the press about this, or any other ongoing investigation, without my express permission! So can anyone here tell me how The Post became aware of details… albeit misleading details… that I certainly didn't share with them?" He looked around the room. Some had their heads down, some were shrugging, and others were shaking their heads. "*No one?*"

An older officer suggested it might have been Winston MacRae since he was aware of most of the details in the story.

"It wasn't Winston. I spoke to him, and I believe him. *Listen up!* I won't stand for any leaks from this department. And I certainly won't allow Mannie Chernin, the mayor, The Post, or anyone else for that matter, railroad my investigation. As far as I'm concerned, there are still too many unanswered questions and not enough evidence to bring charges. Hopefully, the victim will come around and be in a position to tell us what she knows."

He stood up. "Okay, that's it for now. But, guys, if I hear that any one of you are out there undermining *my investigation*, there'll be hell to pay."

Dunphy waited for the room to clear. He was heading back to his office when the desk sergeant stopped him.

"Sorry, Captain. I just took a call from Mannie Chernin. He said the town's merchants' association is organizing a public meeting for Saturday afternoon and he wanted to make sure your calendar was clear. *Oh, and* The Post called. Asked if you'd care to comment on this morning's article."

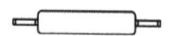

Amour watched the nurse dip her facecloth in the silver basin of soapy water and gently wipe Myrtle's face. "The redness seems to be fading," she said.

The nurse smiled. "Looking much better."

"How much longer do they plan to keep her sedated?"

"Actually, they haven't given her any medication since around six o'clock last night. She needs to eat. We're hoping she won't be so agitated when she wakes."

"Shouldn't she be awake by now?"

"It takes a while for it to pass through her system. Shouldn't be too much longer," she said and left.

Amour picked up a yellowed issue of Chatelaine and turned to the section promising Easy-Peasy Recipes Your Family will Love. The jagged edges along the gutter a clear sign of their popularity with at least one other visitor awaiting a recovery, or sitting vigil. She looked up at the clock, surprised it wasn't even ten o'clock and went to the window.

She pulled the curtain aside and looked out at the heavy, grey sky and at a group of kids hopping across the white clampers floating near shore. "Careful," she whispered as one of the jumpers barely made it onto the icy flow. She went back to her chair and, once again, picked up her tattered magazine. She glanced up, dropped it on the floor and rushed to her friend's side. Myrtle was wide-eyed and staring back at her. Myrtle looked panic-stricken. "Myrtle! It's me! Amour." Myrtle's eyes darted around the room and she tried to sit up. Amour held her down by the shoulders. "Nurse! Nurse! Nur–"

A burly nurse calmly approached Myrtle with a big smile. "Well, hello there. Welcome back," she said, edging Amour out of the way and guiding Myrtle back onto the pillow. "You took a good knock to the noggin. You're in the hospital."

"Am...Amour?" Myrtle said.

Amour took Myrtle's hand in hers and smiled. "Yes, it's me. Amour."

"Amour?" Myrtle said again.

Amour looked at the nurse, worried for her friend.

"She's confused. Hopefully, just the aftereffects of the sedative. Give it time. I'm sure she'll come around. Well, I better go fetch Dr. MacLellan so he can check on sleeping beauty."

Myrtle kept repeating Amour's name and her eyes kept darting around the room. "You're going to be okay," Amour said, wiping away a tear. "Everything is going to be just fine."

Myrtle weakly squeezed Amour's hand. "Amour?"

Gordon couldn't escape the phone. It was only twelve-thirty and, besides fielding a half dozen calls from angry residents, he had spoken to the mayor and the president of the merchants' association. Despite the call from the mayor reminding him he was *acting chief*, the last call was the worst. Kenny's parents called saying they were receiving threats and that they were worried they'd have to pull their son out of school. He sifted through the remaining messages scattered across his desk. There was one from Peter Boyd and Charlotte Rogers.

He dialled the hospital. "Charlotte Rogers, please? It's Gordon Dunphy."

Fifteen minutes later he and Charlotte walked into Myrtle's room.

Both Mabel and Amour were sitting at her bedside.

"You're five minutes too late," Mabel said. "She just nodded off again."

"How does she seem?"

"Confused. Keeps repeating herself," Amour said. "Dr. MacLellan says that it's nothing out of the usual."

"Does she understand what happened to her?"

"Hard to tell. Dr. MacLellan tried to tell her, but she didn't give any indication she remembered anything," Amour said.

Myrtle stirred, then opened her eyes. Again, she looked frightened. Amour patted her arm, telling her everything was all right.

Gordon went to approach Myrtle, but Charlotte took him by the arm and led him to the door. "You need to give it another day or two. I'm sorry I called. It's too soon."

Gordon smiled. "Don't ever apologize for calling me," he whispered. He looked at Amour. "Nice to see you again. Sorry it's under such terrible circumstances." He leaned in and kissed Charlotte's cheek. "I'll check back tomorrow."

Amour and Mabel watched him leave and then the hot flush of hope appear on Charlotte's neck. Mabel smiled, thinking that the spark that Charlotte thought eluded her and the handsome captain was still there, whether they realized it or not.

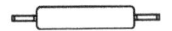

Ten-After-Six was waiting for Dunphy when he returned to the station. "What's up, Peter?"

"Tried callin, but couldn't get through to you. I think I found the handbag you're looking for."

"*Myrtle's?*"

"Yeah, think so."

"Where?"

"In the bushes off Brookside Street. Across from the footbridge. I just left it there."

Dunphy rushed Peter outside to the car. Peter explained that he had found a ladies compact in the area on Sunday and, when he read the article in The Post, he thought he'd go back and check it out.

Dunphy looked at Peter struggling to straighten his back enough to see over the dash. "No one's better at finding things than you are. Hell, you'd make a better cop than most of the guys on the force."

Peter led him through the trees and thick bushes. "There it is," he said. Dunphy picked it up and shook away the loose snow. He opened it up and pulled back the inside zipper. "It's Myrtle's all right," he said, removing the rolled up bills. Something dropped from the bills into the snow. He picked it up. "Must be Myrtle's house key," he said, turning it over in his hand.

"Wow! Never found that much money before," Peter said. He reached in his pocket and handed him the silver compact.

Dunphy told Peter to wait. He looked at his watch, slid down the hill and ran across the footbridge to where the attack took place. He quickly buried Myrtle's handbag in the snow, then retraced his steps. It took almost three minutes. It would have taken at least that long for one of the boys to have buried it and returned to the scene; maybe more, given their inebriated state. He thought back to Winston's MacRae's statement. *Kenny was standing next to the body and Tommy was making his way up the hill.* "Let's go, Peter. I'll drive you home."

"No need. I'm just going back to work," Peter said, heading down the hill to *S&M Design and Construction*.

"Thanks again," Dunphy hollered, then whispered "I think." He slapped Myrtle's handbag against his leg and looked across the brook. Doesn't make sense for them to bury it so far away, he thought. And why wouldn't they have just continued up to Brookside Street and away from the scene. "Damn it," he said, suddenly realizing the answer. They had to go back and get Harley.

"Hey, Captain!"

Dunphy turned as one of the officers assigned to stakeout appeared through the trees. "Is that the victim's purse?" he asked.

"Yes, it's *her* purse."

"Good thing. Wouldn't want to think you were goin all faggoty on us."

Dunphy shot him a look.

"So, I guess that means I don't have to stand out here and freeze my ass off any longer?"

"Go back to your location. The boys don't know we found it."

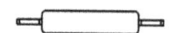

Myrtle opened her eyes, raised her hand and patted the soft, white bandage covering her bald head.

Amour smiled. *"There you are.* How do you feel?"

"Thir…thir…thirsty," she stuttered.

Amour held the glass to her mouth. Myrtle sipped the water, then put her hand on Amour's arm to indicate she had had enough. "Yer…yer…yer home," she said, wiping her chin.

Amour put the glass down, pulled the chair closer and laid her hand on Myrtle's arm. "I wanted to surprise you. You gave us all quite a scare. Do you remember what happened?"

"Nooo."

"You were at the brook and someone hit you on the head."

"Wha..wha. why?"

"Likely a robbery. Does your head hurt?"

Myrtle reached for Amour's hand. "Bah…bah…but…hap…hap…happy to see you. La…la…lucky."

"Yes. You were very lucky. It could have been much worse."

"La…la…Luck…ey."

Amour smiled. "Yes, very lucky."

Myrtle made a fist and pounded on the bed. "Ca…ca…cat."

"*Oh, you mean your cat, Lucky?* I'm sure he's fine. Stanley's been checking on things for you," Amour said, making a mental note to ask about the cats when she got home.

It was a struggle for Myrtle to get her thoughts out, she was tired and becoming increasingly agitated with Amour's questions and non-stop fussing. She pinched her eyes shut and tried to concentrate. "Go…ho…home to ya…ya…your…fam…fam…family."

"I'm not going anywhere. I'm staying right here with you," Amour said. "How about a bit more pudding?"

"I…I…em…sleeeepy."

"Go to sleep. I'll be here when you wake up."

"Nooo," Myrtle said. She pointed to the door. "Fa…fa…fa fuck off."

Amour's mouth fell open and she began to tear up, but quickly reminded herself that Dr. MacLellan said it takes time for the brain to heal and that it would likely be a while before Myrtle was her old self again. She reluctantly put on her coat and kissed Myrtle's forehead. "I'll be back in the morning."

"She's sure? And you're positive Myrtle's consignment payment was up to date? And your inventory shows the store is short a painting? Sounds like it may have been stolen. See anybody who may have raised suspicions, say a couple of young kids, fourteen or fifteen years old? Of course, busy time of year. Thank you. Really appreciate your help." Dunphy hung up and reviewed his notes. The store manager was thinking about buying the painting for her father for Christmas and knew it was still there as late as noon on the day of the attack. Myrtle's consignment payment matched their sales records and their inventory showed they were one painting short. Either there was an accounting error and Myrtle was underpaid, or it was stolen.

Dunphy printed *stolen* on his notepad. He told McEwan about his suspicions and instructed him to verify the boys' whereabouts from noon on Friday, till the time they were discovered at the scene. He was about to head out, when the clerk called back.

"I thought more about what you asked…if there was anybody suspicious in the store. There was a guy in…wouldn't really describe him as *suspicious*…but he did ask about Myrtle's paintings. Left without buying anything. Said they were too expensive."

"Did you ever see him before?" Dunphy asked.

"No."

"What did he look like?"

"Big guy with a beard. Somewhere between six one or two. Wore a toque and a green jacket with a hood. Probably early to mid-forties."

Dunphy hung up. It wasn't much to go on, but at least it was somewhere to start.

The Big Surprise

Friday, Nov. 29

Lily led Michael into Stanley's office.

"Well, this is a surprise," Stanley said, walking from behind his desk and introducing Michael to his new hire.

Lily pulled the door closed behind her.

"I thought you'd be in the middle of your interview by now?" Stanley said.

"It's not for another hour. Had some time to kill and thought I'd tell you about my recent purchase."

Stanley raised his eyebrows.

Michael grinned. "I just bought Amour's Christmas present."

"Must be a pretty special gift?"

"It is. I just bought our old house back. Owner's wife died and he's moving to Springhill to be with his daughter. I made an offer and we shook on it. Of course, it's all conditional on me getting the job. If it all works out, we'll be able to move in after Christmas. And I'm sure you'll be glad to get us out from under your feet."

"You know we love having you. Amour will be over the moon."

"But first I need to get the job."

Stanley nodded. "I'm sure it will all work out."

"Amour will be devastated if it doesn't. She liked London well enough, but I know she missed home and her friends."

"And you?" Stanley asked. "How do you feel about the move? Not like you're moving to a big city. This place can be a pretty sleepy place."

"As long as Amour is happy, I'm happy. And it may not be Boston or London, but it has its charms." Michael nodded toward the door. "So how is your new girl working out?"

Stanley told him of Lily's circumstances. "Turns out it was a win-win situation. I'm helping her get back on her feet, and she's helping me whip this place in shape."

Michael looked at his watch. "I better get a move on. Wish me luck," he said. "And remember, not a word to anyone about the house."

"Your secret's safe with me. Knock em dead," Stanley said.

Michael crossed Brodie Avenue and cut through the alley to Commercial Street. A young man wearing a political button ran up to him and handed him a white poster with bold, black lettering.

Public Safety Meeting, this Saturday, 2pm-4pm, Miners Forum. Everyone Welcome. Vote for Law and Order. Vote Mannie for Mayor.

Michael shoved it in his pocket and entered the British Imperial Coal Company. He was back on the street within the hour. The power poles were plastered with notices, and the street, littered with crumpled up flyers.

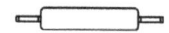

Gordon walked down the crowded hallway carrying Myrtle's handbag. An orderly elbowed his co-worker, whistled and jokingly made catcalls. What the hell, Gordon thought, hanging Myrtle's handbag over the crook of his arm, holding up a limp hand and wiggling his hips. Everyone began to laugh and point in his direction. That's when he spotted Charlotte, wide-eyed with her hand over her mouth. She burst out laughing. He smiled, but despite the levity of the moment, he felt a sudden pang of sadness. He missed her laugh.

Charlotte took him by the arm and shook her head. "I need to take you shopping. Your handbag doesn't match your shoes," she said, quickly ushering him into Myrtle's room.

Amour was in her usual spot, and Myrtle was sitting up and looking alert.

"Hello, Myrtle. Remember me?" Gordon asked.

Myrtle shrugged.

"I have your handbag. Everything's inside…your money, glasses, lipstick and your house key."

"She's having trouble getting her words out," Amour said. "And her memory's a little cloudy. Doctor says she has–" She looked at Charlotte.

"Post traumatic amnesia."

"Myrtle, do you remember anything from the night you were hit on the head?" he asked.

Myrtle looked at Amour. "Hit on the ha..ha..head?"

"Yes. Remember I told you? You were at the brook and someone hit you from behind," Amour said.

Gordon smiled at Amour. "I'll give it a bit more time," he said, picking up her handbag and heading to the door.

Myrtle became very agitated. "She wants her handbag back," Charlotte said.

"But it's evidence?"

Myrtle was now stuttering obscenities.

Charlotte took it from him. "Let her keep it for now. I'll put it in a safe place."

Gordon turned to Myrtle. "Goodbye, Myrtle. Hope you feel better soon."

"Eeeet sha...sha...shit," she sputtered.

Charlotte was about to put Myrtle's handbag on the bedside table when Myrtle grabbed it from her and dumped its contents over her lap. She picked up her silver compact.

Amour smiled. "I gave that to you."

"I...na...na...know...that!" Myrtle snapped.

Gladys hung up the phone. "Dan! That was Lizzie. You have an interview on Tuesday at nine. Dan? Did ya hear me?"

He opened his bedroom door. "Yeah, I heard."

"We need to find something nice for you to wear. Yer uncle's suit coat will be way too small. We should go to Marshall's first thing tomorrow."

"Supper ready?" he asked, brushing past her.

"I'll put it on now," she said, thinking he didn't seem very excited. Gladys poured him a cup of tea and put the bologna on the counter, struggling to cut through the thick coating to the soft, pink meat inside.

Jesus, Dan thought, can't she make anything else. No wonder she's so fat.

"So, we'll go to Marshall's in the morning?"

Dan stirred his tea. "I don't have money for a suit."

"Well, ya need one. It'll be my Christmas present to you. We won't have any surprises under the tree, but then we're not kids anymore. Given your circumstances, it was sweet of you to spend what little ya have on me. I love my change purse. Reminds me of one my mother had."

"What I really need is a car," he said.

Gladys stopped cutting. "*A car?*"

"Yeah, *a car*. Think about it. You wouldn't have to stand out in the cold waiting for the bus. I could drive you to and from work, and when the weather's nice we could go for drives up the coast. Make life a whole lot easier."

"I don't know, I've been getting along fine without a car since your uncle died. And the expense?"

"I'm not talkin about a new car…just an old beater. I could go to Crackies and pick one up for a coupla hundred bucks. I'll pay ya back when I get work," he said.

Gladys slapped a pat of butter into the hot frying pan. "Let me mull it over."

He took a sip of tea, knowing it was just a matter of days before he'd be driving around town.

Gladys cleared the dishes and joined her nephew in the living room. "A car might be nice," she said.

Dan sat up. "So I can check out Crackies?"

"Yes."

He stood up and hugged her. "You wait. Won't be long before ya wonder how ya ever lived without it."

Gladys gathered up her knitting and went to her bedroom. Dan went to the basement, opened the middle door of the furnace and tossed Myrtle's treasured keepsake in among the bright orange flames.

The Meeting

Saturday, Nov. 30

Gordon drove down Commercial Street and turned the corner, surprised there were cars lining both sides of Main Street. Mannie sure knows how to bring out a crowd, he thought, pulling into the first opening he came across. He got out and walked among the steady flow of people heading to the forum.

Mannie was out front with his placard-waving supporters, passing out buttons and encouraging people to vote. He spotted Dunphy and approached. "Glad you could make it."

"Nice crowd," Gordon said.

"A lot of unhappy folks looking to see justice done."

"Justice sometimes takes time."

Mannie smiled. "I'm afraid that's one thing you don't have."

The atmosphere inside was chillier than it was outside. Gordon carefully shuffled his way to centre ice and sat with the mayor and other members of the police commission. "It's freezing in here," he said.

Mayor Wareham leaned in. "Give it a minute. Mannie's about to turn up the heat."

The mayor was right. Mannie quickly revved up the crowd, suggesting gangs of unruly youths were taking over the town, striking fear into the hearts of its law-abiding citizens and putting businesses at risk of shuttering their doors. He pointed to Mayor Wareham. "The police do nothing and the mayor stands idly by. This is my town too, and I won't have it," he said, to the gleeful shouts of his button-wearing cheerleaders.

Gordon had had enough. He got to his feet. "There are no unruly gangs prowling our streets," he said. There was a noisy chorus of boos and calls for him to sit down. He waited for the crowd to quiet and continued, insisting the case was still an open investigation, the evidence did not currently warrant charges, and the boys they had in custody posed no risk to the public. The pro-Mannie crowd would have none of it, shouting out one question after the next without waiting for the answers. Gordon looked to the mayor for help. He got none. Instead, Mayor Wareham simply reassured the crowd he too was concerned and thanked everyone for coming.

Mannie nudged the mayor out of the way. "There you have it, folks. The police refuse to take action to protect you…and the mayor just sits on his hands." He turned at the sound of sticks slapping against the sideboards and looked at the jersey-clad *Miners* impatiently waiting to get on the ice. "I'm getting my cue," he shouted. "I'm glad you came out to show your support for law and order. When it comes time to vote, remember who's on your side. Go *Miners* go!" he hollered, to a wild round of applause.

Gordon waded through the frosty crowd, unaware that Charlotte was sitting in the back with her head down and a heavy heart. He was almost at the exit when he felt the tug on his sleeve. "Be in my chambers in an hour," Mayor Wareham barked.

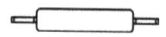

Mary Catherine removed her wedding dress and handed it to Amour. "I really appreciate this."

"I'm happy to help. I thought it was lovely with the crinoline, but I think you're right. It will be even more spectacular once we take it out. Are you getting excited?"

"More nervous than anything."

"I keep telling her that everyone who'll be watching her walk down the aisle loves her, but she won't listen to me," Mabel said.

Amour turned the dress inside out and carefully slid the sharp edges of her scissors along the seam, snipping the taut threads holding the crinoline in place. "Mabel's right. There's nothing to be worried about. You'll make a beautiful bride. It's too bad Myrtle won't be there."

"Any improvement?" Alice asked.

"Yes. She's still frustrated she can't get her words out, but her memory is improving. Said she remembers leaving Arlies and sitting on the bench, but little else after that. It's her short term memory that worries me. She keeps repeating herself and she gets so agitated…so angry."

"Amour, the doctors said that was to be expected," Mabel said.

"I know, but they haven't ruled out the possibility she might stay that way. Sometimes I think they just tell you what you want to hear. Honestly, I love her dearly but she can certainly try your patience. One minute she's her old self and as sweet as can be, and the next, she's telling you to fuck off."

Alice burst out laughing. "I never heard you say that word before."

"I don't say it often, but that doesn't mean I don't think it," Amour said.

Mabel took Alice by the hand and sat her down in front of the mirror. "Amour, I was thinking about a French braid. What do you think?"

"I think it would be lovely."

Amour looked up from the dress and laughed at Mabel's hopeless attempt at making a neat, tight braid. "Watch and learn," she said, abandoning her alterations and edging Mabel to the side.

No one noticed Mary Margaret walk in and pick up the sharp scissors.

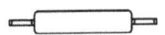

Gordon sat across from the mayor and all but one member of the police commission. From the moment he was ordered to come to the mayor's office he knew he was in trouble, but he never imagined he would be facing the choice of charging the boys or being relieved of his command. He pointed out that the evidence was entirely circumstantial and that he was confident the painting Tommy claimed to have found at the scene was stolen from Arlies, possibly by the guilty party. "We confirmed the boys were either in school or at home with their parents when the painting went missing. I believe Tommy, and I believe Kenny when he said he just came across Myrtle lying in the snow."

"But you have no other suspects?" the mayor said.

"Not yet. Like I said, it's still early. I was given a description of someone asking about Myrtle's paintings the same afternoon I believe it was stolen. I'm sure that if I just had more time I could–"

Mayor Wareham was losing patience. "There's no more time to be had. Mannie's a prosecutor for goodness sakes. If he thinks there is enough evidence for an arrest, then who am I to argue. Then there's the issue of this stakeout you ordered. A waste of time and money, if you ask me. And what about your friendship with the suspect's father."

"We don't hang out together. We played ball together…fifteen years ago. Christ, I played ball or hockey with half the men in town. For God sakes, Mayor, listen to yourself! One minute you're complaining I'm not doing enough and the next I'm doing too much. *Guys*, Mannie needed an issue, so he manufactured one. Do you seriously believe he would have organized a public meeting if he wasn't running for mayor? Of course not! He's playing on people's misplaced fears and using the boys as his path to the mayor's office. Please, I'm begging you not to let him get away with it!"

"Honestly, I don't see what the big deal is. Just arrest the boys. It doesn't mean you can't follow up on other leads," the mayor said impatiently.

Gordon couldn't believe what he was hearing. "No! I swore an oath to impartially carry out my duties free of any —"

The mayor held up his hand. "You leave us no other choice. You are no longer acting chief."

"You can't be serious?"

"We are. Sergeant McEwan has been promoted to the new position of deputy chief. From now on, he's in charge of the investigation and you report to him."

Gordon knew McEwan's first act in his new position would be to arrest the boys. He paused and looked back at the mayor and spoke calmly and slowly. "Your Worship, you know Mannie's already won. Once word gets out the boys have been arrested and I've been dropped, everybody will be singing Mannie's praises, *not yours*." He pointed to the police commissioners. "And as for them, they're not your friends. They're not here to support you, or to see that justice is done. They're here doing Mannie's bidding."

"Careful, Captain Dunphy," the chair of the commission warned.

Gordon smiled. *"Oh, I'm being careful all right.* Careful to carry out my duties according to my conscience. Something I'm afraid you wouldn't know anything about."

Gordon walked out knowing he had sealed his fate. There would be no promotions in his future. He drove home, proud that he had stood his ground, but worried about what was in store, not for himself, but for the boys.

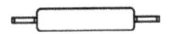

"Oh my God," Mabel screamed, running to Mary Margaret. She took the scissors from her daughter, looked at the long, jagged tear down the bodice of Alice's dress and closed her eyes.

Amour quickly gathered it up and laid it out on the bed. "It's my fault. I should've never left the scissors—"

"It's not *your fault*," Mabel said, tearing up. She whacked Mary Margaret hard on the rear end, grabbed her by the hand and dragged her screaming down the hall.

Alice stood beside Amour. "Ma's dress," she said softly.

Amour brought the frayed edges together. "It looks worse than it is. I'm sure we can make it as good as new."

Alice shook her head. "It's ruined," she said, bursting into tears.

Amour hugged her. "I'm so sorry."

"Ma's dress," Alice repeated, thinking of her dying mother smiling up at her when she told her she and Luke were going to be married. "It's a sign."

"*It's not a sign*," Amour said. "It was an accident."

They could hear Mary Margaret wailing down the hall. Mabel joined them by the bed. "I don't know what to say."

Amour looked at Mabel. "She thinks it's a sign."

"*Of course it's not!*" Mabel said. "Alice, I know how much it means for you to wear your mother's dress. I'll find a way to fix it. I promise."

Alice quickly buttoned her blouse and slipped on her shoes.

"Alice. It's not a sign of anything. Please don't go!" Mabel said.

Alice smiled. "Don't worry. I'll be fine. It's just that…that it belonged to Ma…I miss her."

Stanley charged up the stairs. Mary Margaret was standing in her crib with tears streaming down her tiny, red face. He knew she was being punished for something. "Daddy will be right back," he said and ran to find Mabel. "What's going on?" he asked, wondering why everyone was crying.

Gordon pulled into the yard, got out and smiled.

"This is a welcome surprise. How long have you been here?" he asked Charlotte, sitting on his front step.

"About a half an hour?"

"C'mon in. You must be frozen." He took her coat from her. "Can I get you something? A cup of—"

Charlotte leaned in, surprising him with a hug. "I wanted to apologize," she said.

Gordon put his hands on her shoulders, held her at arm's length and laughed. *"Apologize? For what?"*

"I was at the meeting. I should have spoken up."

Gordon smiled. "It wouldn't have made a lick of difference. It was a pretty tough crowd."

"Mannie's a bastard," she said. "He won't be getting my vote."

"I'm afraid he won't need it. He's hit on a winning issue. The mayor and his cronies are running for cover. I just came from his office. I'm no longer acting chief."

"I'm sorry, Gordon," she said. She followed him into the kitchen and watched him add coal to the stove and fill the kettle.

"They put McEwan in charge. I'm worried about what's going to happen. I know damn well they wouldn't have offered McEwan the position without first getting his word he'd charge the boys. Dumb ass probably already picked them up."

Charlotte got up, took the kettle off the stove and opened the cupboard. "I think this calls for something other than tea," she said, holding up a quart of Four Roses whiskey.

They drank, ate stale saltines topped with pickled herring and lamented the sorry state of politics in the town. "I'm glad you're here. I missed you," Gordon said.

Charlotte smiled. "I missed you, too."

Gordon took her hand in his. "What happened to us?"

"I'm not sure. I think we just let our jobs take over our lives and forgot to have fun," she said, smiling sadly.

Gordon walked around the table, brought Charlotte to her feet and kissed her. "I guess it's true that absence makes the heart grow fonder."

"*Or abstinence*," Charlotte said, laughing.

"*Maybe* a bit of both," he said. He grinned and led her down the hall to the stairs.

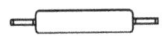

Mabel had no idea of the time, but knew there was no point in staying in bed. She got up, put on her robe and tiptoed across the floor. She stopped and looked down at Mary Margaret. She's so little, she thought. She had never laid a hand on either of her children before. She ran her finger over the scar above her eye, thinking of Johnnie's rage, the blood dripping off her nose and the shattered bowl lying among the limp cabbage leafs on the yellowed, linoleum floor. Of all people, I should have known better, she thought. She kissed her fingertips and lightly touched Mary Margaret's forehead. "I'm sorry. It will never happen again," she whispered.

She crept downstairs, made a cup of tea, took it to the living room and watched the black of night slowly give way to the dull light of an emerging day. Her mind kept flashing from one troubling image to the next. Alice's torn dress, Myrtle's bandaged head, and her daughter's red, wet face as she stood in her crib with her tiny arms stretched out in the hope she'd be picked up and forgiven for whatever made her mommy so angry. She then thought of Father Gregory's missing maniturgium and of how careless she had been with something she had vowed to treasure.

Mabel walked up to the grainy images that brought her comfort when her mind wouldn't settle. She turned on the lamp, touched her mother's face and then the sepia photo of James and Margaret standing in front of the store. "I miss you," she whispered.

"Can't sleep?" Amour asked, looking down from the stairs.

"Afraid not."

"I saw the light was on. What's troubling you?"

Mabel tightened her robe. "Oh, a whole bunch of things. Stanley says I worry too much. Now I'm worried he's right. Come on," Mabel said, heading for the kitchen. "Tea's on. So why are *you* up so early?"

"I had to pee."

Messages, Mufflers and Michael's Surprise

Monday, Dec. 2

Gordon drove up Main Street, thinking about the past two days he had spent with Charlotte. She really was an incredible and beautiful woman. Smart, kind and funny. He closed his eyes, picturing her covering her breasts and running naked from the bathroom. She had jumped under the covers and snuggled up to him for warmth. He could smell the pickled herring and whiskey on her breath. "I missed you," she had whispered. Then, "I love you." He wanted to say that he did too, but the words got caught in his throat. Instead he made love to her for the second time that night.

He parked outside the station and dropped his head, thinking about the one woman he couldn't get put out of his mind. "Enough," he murmured. "Let her go. Let her go."

When he entered the red, brick building, Gordon's colleagues stopped their chatter and walked away with their heads down. The desk sergeant, trapped with nowhere to go, picked up a file, pretending to read something that required his immediate attention.

Gordon knew what he was up to. "Good morning. Any messages?"

"Oh, good morning, Captain. Yes. They're on your desk."

Gordon started down the hall.

"Captain?"

He turned.

"I'm afraid your office has been moved."

"*What?*"

"Sergeant…Deputy Chief McEwan has taken over your office. You're at his old desk."

Gordon smiled. "That didn't take long."

He walked into the much smaller office across from the men's room and threw his coat over a chair. "This will do just fine," he said and picked up his messages. Just as he expected, there were at least a half a dozen calls from the boys' fathers and two from Sam.

McEwan stepped into the doorway. "Since you never did move into the chief's office, I thought you might be more comfortable in mine."

"Never felt it was right to take over a fellow officer's desk when he's just temporarily out of commission," Gordon said.

"Yeah, that's why I took yours."

"That was very generous of you," Gordon said sarcastically.

"Anyway, I hope there are no hard feelings," McEwan said.

Gordon held up his messages. "So, I assume you arrested the boys?"

"Brought them in last night."

Gordon nodded. "When's the bail hearing?"

"Don't know yet."

"And the prosecutor?"

"Mannie said he's looking into it. Said it would be a conflict of interest for him to take the case."

"No kidding," Gordon said.

Sam appeared in the doorway and nudged past McEwan. "Gordon, what's going on? I've been calling. I thought you were going to keep me posted? I can't believe you charged the boys!"

"Sorry, Sam. Just got your messages. I'm afraid you'll have to speak to the lead investigator."

Sam put his briefcase on the floor and gave him a puzzled look. "What do you mean?"

Gordon pointed to McEwan. "The mayor and deputy chief, here, have taken me off the case."

Sam laughed. "*Seriously*, what's going on?"

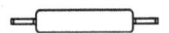

Dan took his time, careful to side-step the rusty mufflers, twisted fenders and discarded carburetors.

"There it is," Crackie said, pointing to a snow-covered black Dodge. "Might not look like much. Has a couple of nicks here and there, but she purrs like a kitten." He banged on the roof to loosen the hard snow sealing the door, yanked on the handle and turned the ignition. It made a loud, grinding sound. He tried several more times. It finally turned over. Crackie got out. "That ain't nothing. Hasn't been started in a while. It's yours for an even two-fifty," he said. He scrapped the windshield clear. "Take it for a run if ya want."

Crackie cleared the path of broken engine parts, as the two-door Club Coupe edged forward.

"I'll have it back in a coupla hours," Dan hollered.

He pulled in front of Woolworths, entered and waited for his aunt to finish up with a customer. "Wanna see our new car?" He pointed to the window. "It's out front. A real beauty. Works great and it's only four hundred dollars."

"Four hundred!" Gladys repeated. "That's a lot more than I was expectin."

"It's a steal. Come see," he said, placing his hand on her back and guiding her to the door. "It started the first try. But here's the thing," he said, screwing up his face. "Crackie said he had a couple of other folks interested in buying it. We gotta act fast or I'm afraid we'll lose out on a great deal."

"It's only got two doors. And it's an awful lota, money."

"I know, but like I said, I'll pay ya back. What time is your lunch break? I'll drive ya home and ya can get your money."

"Twenty minutes. But I don't have that kinda money at home. I keep most of it in the bank...ever since that awful MacIntyre robbed me."

"Great. I'll hang out a bit and go with you."

"Well, ya might as well have a seat at the counter. Order a tea or something. Tell Rosie to add it to my bill."

Dan drank his Iron Brew, willing the clock to tick faster. He didn't notice the young clerk from Arlies sitting to his left, waiting for his take out.

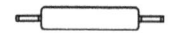

Amour arrived home from the hospital and walked into the kitchen. Stanley, Mabel and Michael were sitting quietly, sipping tea.

Amour looked from one to the other "What's with the glum faces?" she asked.

Stanley pursed his lips. "Michael heard back about the job."

Amour looked at her husband and dropped her shoulders. "*No?*"

Michael got up slowly and hugged her. "Sorry. I know how much you were counting on it."

Amour was devastated, but tried to put on a brave face. "I'm sorry, too. I know you were as set on it as I was. But it's not like *we hate* London. At least we'll be here for the wedding and Christmas," she said, trying not to burst into tears.

Mabel put her hand over her mouth and turned her head to the side.

"I got the *president's* job!" Michael shouted, picking her up and twirling her around.

"*The president's job! But how?*"

"President decided to retire. The board asked if I would take over. I start the second week of January."

"So, we're moving home!" she squealed, no longer able to contain her tears.

"We are! Of course, I'll have to fly back to London and deal with the flat... settle our affairs. And you'll have to enroll Victoria in school and–"

"Look for a new home," Amour said, clapping her hands together.

"That too," Michael said, winking at Stanley.

Mabel hugged Amour. "I'm so happy for you...for all of us. And Myrtle will be over the moon."

Amour put her hand on her forehead. "Oh, my goodness. There's so much to do. Does Victoria Know?"

"Not yet," Michael said.

"Victoria!" Amour hollered.

"She's not here," Michael said. "Luke took the kids to see the Christmas tree."

Stanley went to the cupboard and held up a bottle of rum. "I think a toast is in order. Anyone for a libation?"

The Bus, The Break-in and The Backlash

Tuesday, Dec. 3

Gordon was paying for his gas when he spotted the headline. *Suspects Arrested.* He returned to the car and passed the newspaper to Charlotte. "Mannie's no doubt grinning from ear-to-ear," he said.

"Do you want me to read it to you?" Charlotte asked.

Gordon shrugged and turned the ignition.

> Three Glace Bay youths have been charged with aggravated assault and battery following a violent attack near the Commercial Street Bridge, Nov. 22, that left local artist, Myrtle Munroe, in hospital with significant head injuries. Kenneth P. Ludlow, Thomas A. Simms and Harley G. Woodward, who were questioned by police the night of the assault and released the following day, were taken into custody late Sunday. Acting Chief of Police, Tobias (Tubby) McEwan, said the three youths, who range from fourteen to fifteen years of age, could face additional charges. "As it stands right now, they are potentially looking at anywhere from four to six years." He added, "This was a violent crime that has left a beloved member of our community severely damaged and that has sparked fear throughout the town. We will be bringing the full weight of the law to bear, not just to exact retribution for the victim, but to send a strong message

> to the public that violence of any kind will be met with swift and severe justice."
>
> The acting chief dismissed suggestions the police mishandled the case and that the charges were only laid in response to public pressure resulting from a meeting of concern at the Miners' Forum on Saturday. "Absolutely not. We were simply gathering evidence and doing our due diligence. We're now satisfied we have more than enough evidence to secure a proper conviction."

"Goddammit!" Gordon said, slamming his hand on the wheel. He knows damn well, the painting was likely stolen. Prick should be looking into it. He's hanging the boys out to dry because it's in his own interest. I could string him up by the balls."

"Should I continue?" Charlotte asked.

Gordon turned up Victoria Street. "Go ahead."

> Mayoralty candidate, Mannie Chernin, who organized the meeting of public concern said, "I'm delighted my efforts to protect the citizens of the town resulted in action. My only regret is that it took a public backlash to get the mayor and the police to do what our over-burdened taxpayers pay them to do."
>
> When asked about the sudden change in leadership within the force, which saw Sergeant McEwan named deputy chief, Mayor Wareham said, "That's a matter for the chair of the police commission to address. I've always made it a point to remain at arm's length from day-to-today police operations. It is crucial that our men in blue be able to carry out their duties free of political influence or interference. The last thing we need is for the mayor, or anyone else for that matter, to be telling the police who, or who not, to arrest.
>
> Everette LeBlanc, Chair of the Police Commission, could not be reached for comment.

"What a pile of crap," Gordon said.

"It's not right...what they're doing to you...to the boys. There must be something you can do?" Charlotte said

"Yeah. Quit!"

Charlotte crumpled up the newspaper. "I mean short of that."

Gordon pulled into the hospital entrance. "Tell Myrtle I said hi."

"I'm so sorry, Gordon." She squeezed his arm and kissed his cheek. "So you'll pick me up at four?"

He smiled. "See you then."

Charlotte held the passenger door open and leaned in. "Gordon, we'll get through this."

Gladys beamed when she saw her nephew enter the kitchen. She clapped her hands together and brought them to her mouth. "You're as handsome as Tyrone Power. Come, eat your breakfast, so we can get goin. Best to get there early." She handed him a tea towel. "Put this around yer neck. Don't want to get yolk on your new suit jacket."

Dan took it from her, put it on the table and looked down at his slimy eggs. He pushed the plate aside and lit a cigarette.

"*What's wrong?* Not hungry?"

"I like my eggs cooked," he said.

"Well, at least drink yer tea and eat yer toast. Like your uncle always said, ya need to fuel the mind, as well as the body. Are ya nervous?"

Dan stood and stubbed his cigarette out in his saucer. "No. I'm gonna warm up the car."

Gladys dumped Dan's ashes and took a brush to the stubborn nicotine stain yellowing her good china. She heard the grinding sound of the engine, then the car door slam shut. She pulled the curtain back. Her nephew was kicking the fender.

Dan stormed into the kitchen. "When does the bus come?"

Gladys looked up at the clock, then quickly reached for her boots. "Hopefully, it's running late."

Dan tore out. The *Number Eleven* stopped four houses down. He ran to catch up. The bus started to pull away. He waved and shouted at the driver. The brake lights came on and the door opened. Dan turned. Gladys had her head down, quickly shuffling her large frame down the icy path. "Hurray up! C'mon! Hurray up!" he yelled.

Gladys looked up, then went down hard on her side. She was holding her leg when Dan and the bus driver reached her. "It's my ankle."

"Do you think you can stand?" the bus driver asked.

"I don't think I can get up, let alone stand," she said.

The bus driver looked at Dan. "We'll have to carry her inside."

Dan showed him his hand. The driver ran back to the bus and came back with a sturdy-looking passenger. They were sweating by the time they laid Gladys on the couch.

Gladys looked at her nephew. "Go! You're gonna be late for your interview. *Oh!* Stop in Woolworths and tell them I won't be in."

Dan hopped on the bus and sat next to the stranger who helped him carry Gladys inside. "Thanks for that. Woulda been easier to lift a baby elephant."

"Hope she's all right. You shaved your beard," he said.

"*What?*"

"*Your beard.*" He pointed to Dan's hand. "Aren't you the guy from The Pithead?"

Dan screwed up his face. "*The Pithead?*"

"Yeah. The guy who scared the shit outa Fred Clarke."

Gordon stopped halfway down the steps to the lockup, listening to the boys lament their fate.

"*Guys*, we're gonna be okay. They can't put us away for something we didn't do," Kenny said.

"Yes they can," Harley shouted from his cell. "They do it all the time. I don't know why I'm here. I don't remember a friggin thing."

"God's punishing us for what we did to Mr. Spencer's car," Tommy said.

Kenny tapped his forehead against the bars "*He is not.* Don't be stupid. Look, fellas, Da said we'll be out on bail before ya know it."

"Do ya think they'll let us back in school?" Tommy asked. "Cause I'd rather be shipped off to the big house than spend the rest of my life in the pit."

"Yer not goin to no big house, or *the pit*. We'll be back in school before Christmas break."

"You sure?" Tommy asked.

Despite the fact he hated school, Kenny prayed he was right. "Yeah, I'm sure."

Harley started to cry. "I can't stay here another night."

Gordon put his head down and continued down the grey, stone steps. "Hi, guys." He stopped at each of their cells, handing them chocolate bars and trying to reassure them everything would be all right.

"What's going on?" McEwan asked, surprising Gordon and the boys.

Gordon turned quickly to see his new boss glaring from the steps. "Just checkin on the boys."

McEwan joined Gordon outside of Harley's cell. "The boys are fine. Got a warm place to sleep and three squares a day." He looked at the Almond Joy wrapper at Harley's feet. "Actually, looks like they got it pretty damn good in here."

"You looking for me?" Gordon asked McEwan.

"Yeah. Got a call about a break and enter at the pop factory. Need you and Big Dick to check it out. He's upstairs waiting for you."

Gordon clenched his jaw and followed his new boss to the stairs, cautioning himself not to lose his cool. He took a deep breath. "Look, I know you think it's a long shot, but my gut tells me whoever stole the painting was responsible for the attack. It doesn't make sense the boys would ditch her handbag and not the painting. We need to follow up, assign—"

McEwan stopped and turned sharply. "Let's say you're right and the painting was stolen, it doesn't change a thing. There's plenty of other evidence that points to the boys. For all we know, this mysterious shoplifter you're fixated on, dropped the painting in the area well before the assault."

"But it's worth looking into. Who knows, we might get lucky," Gordon said. He looked back over his shoulder at the boys. "There's too much at stake not to give it our full effort."

McEwan gave him an exasperated look. "What I want, right now, is for you to put your full effort into finding who broke into McKinley's and made off with two crates of Frostie."

"Alice, Mrs. Nickelo said she can make your dress as good as new. Just needs to replace the front panel. Said she's sure she can find a match for the material," Mabel said.

"Thank you."

"Only ten days away," Mabel said. "The hall is going to look spectacular. Amour and Victoria have been making Kleenex flowers, and Mary Catherine has been cutting out red hearts."

Alice put her mixing bowl in the sink. "They shouldn't be going through all that trouble."

"Everything all right?" Mabel asked, sensing something was off.

"Actually, if you don't mind I'd like to go home. I have a bit of a headache."

"Of course. Alice, you don't still believe the incident with the dress was a sign?"

"No."

"Are you having more doubts?"

Alice shook her head and started to cry.

Mabel hugged her. "Then what is it? Is it because you miss your mother?"

"No…well yes. Of course I miss her. But that's not it."

"Then what?" Mabel asked, brushing her thumb under Alice's eye to wipe away a tear. "You can tell me. I'll help you through it."

"I don't know. I'm a horrible person. I did something that's…unforgiveable."

"Whatever it is, I'm sure it's not that bad. Sometimes when you talk things through, it helps you see more clearly. The next thing you know, you're laughing about it. Trust me, there's nothing you could have done said or done that will make me love you any less."

"Don't be so sure," Alice said.

"Then you don't know me. I've seen and done a few things myself. Things I wish—"

"I'm pregnant," Alice blurted, quickly dropping her head.

Mabel walked to the entrance to the store, waved to Corliss and pulled the door shut. "Well then, you're having a baby. What's so bad about that! Plenty of women have babies before they're married. My mother for one. It's nothing to be ashamed of. It's a blessing of love between—"

Alice closed her eyes. "Luke's not the father."

Mabel was stunned. She sat down heavily, wishing she hadn't pried and wondering if Alice's secret lover was her long time crush, Captain Dunphy.

"I know you must think I'm a…a slut. I didn't mean for it to happen. I kept thinking I was late because of all the stress with Ma's passing and my doubts about getting married. Anyway, the other day when you told me to go to the brook and get my thoughts together, I didn't. I had to know. So, I went to see Dr. Cohen. He said I'm likely past three months."

Mabel looked at Alice's belly. "You're hiding it well. Does Luke know?"

"Yes. I told him last night."

"*And?*"

"He's over the moon."

"So, he thinks he's the father?"

"Yes."

Mabel tried to control her tone. "Can I ask who?"

"You swear you won't tell a soul?"

"There is nothing to be gained by spreading the anguish of another," she said flatly.

"Not even Stanley?" Alice pleaded.

Mabel nodded.

"Mark."

Mabel didn't think it was possible that Alice could have shocked her more than she already had, but she was dumbfounded. She leaned back against her chair. "But you told me you didn't care for Mark."

"I don't. I mean...certainly not in the way I do for Luke. Honestly, I don't know how it happened?"

"There's only one way," Mabel said more flippantly than she intended.

"I mean...we only did it once. We were all here in the store, drinking Da's homemade wine. Luke got a little drunk and went upstairs to bed. Then it was just me and Mark. And we drank more and started dancing. Things just got carried away. I feel awful. And I'm sure Mark does too. I know that's why he's not coming home for the wedding. He feels too guilty. Biggest mistake of my life," she said, crying into her hands.

"Were you and Luke sleeping together before you...you and Mark had sex?"

Alice wiped her eyes with the hem of her apron. "No. But we have since. I practically had to force him into bed. After I missed my first period, I thought...well I thought—"

"You better cover your tracks," Mabel said coldly.

"Yes, but—"

"And how long after you slept with Mark was it before you decided to sleep with *your fiancé*?" Mabel asked.

Alice picked up on the dig and immediately regretted sharing her shame with her best friend. "About five weeks."

Mabel walked to the stove, thinking about Luke and what he would do if he knew the woman he adored was pregnant with his brother's child. It would literally kill the emotionally fragile young man who had already experienced so much grief in his short life. She tried to contain her mounting anger at Alice and Mark for their stupid and reckless behaviour. She put a cup of tea in front of the young woman she no longer thought she knew. "So, you weren't sure you wanted to marry Luke, but decided to go through with it because you're pregnant with his brother's baby."

Alice brushed her wet cheeks. "I admit I was having doubts about the wedding. But, like you said, it's only natural to have second thoughts. Honestly, I probably would have gone through with it, even if I wasn't having a baby. Mabel, I know you're disappointed in me. *I am, too.* I've been a fool. But you know how much I care for Luke. He loves me and he'll be a wonderful father. We can make this work. I know we can. Promise me you won't tell a soul."

Mary Mack rushed in, panting. "Goddamn bus. Never even showed up." She threw her shoulder back, wriggled her arm out of her coat sleeve and looked from Alice's tear-stained face to Mabel's stony expression. "Do ya want me to leave?" she asked with a note of concern.

Mabel stood. "No. We're done."

Alice was surprised by the finality of Mabel's words. "I'm so sorry," she said, grabbing Mabel's hand.

Mabel slowly pulled it away. "I'll handle the bread orders this morning. I feel the urge to knead."

Dan had two minutes to spare when he arrived at the Clerk's Office. He was told the interview committee was running behind and it would be another hour. He went to Woolworths to tell them Gladys hurt her ankle and wouldn't be in, then sat at the counter and ordered breakfast. The Post was on the counter. Dan lapped up his eggs, along with the news the boys were arrested, Dunphy was no longer acting chief and McEwan was in charge of the case. The boys are fucked, he thought. He reached for the money he scammed Gladys out of when he overstated the price of the car, then grinned. He pulled his empty hand from his pocket. "Gladys Ferguson told me to put it on her tab," he said to the waitress and left.

He was finally called in for the interview and shown a seat across from Lizzie and the three men who would determine his fate. He didn't waste any time taking control, acknowledging his past sins, taking responsibility for his actions and professing concern for his aging aunt who was so good to others.

"I want to be in a position to care of her, like she and my uncle cared for me when I lost my parents at eight. She's home now and missing work after a terrible fall this morning. As soon as we finish up here, I need to go home to see to her needs." He pulled his damaged hand from his pocket and placed it on the table. "I no longer have the means to do the kind of work most men aspire to, but I'm a hard worker with plenty of administrative experience."

The oldest member of the interview team spoke up. "I knew your Uncle Norman. Gave me my first job, hauling traps. Great man. Very kind."

McInnes pretended to tear up. "Thanks for saying that. I think of him every day. Still read the books he bought me as a kid." He ran his knobby hand under his eyes and cleared his voice. "The classics... Swiss Family Robinson and the like." He glanced at Lizzie. She looked like she was ready to burst into tears.

Ten minutes later he was shaking hands and thanking the committee for the opportunity to put his life back on track.

He was about to leave when Lizzie put her hand on his arm. "I can't say anythin fer sure, but ya did real good," she whispered. "Should be able to tell ya the results in a day or two."

"Thank you, Lizzie. I know I wouldn't have had the interview if it weren't for you."

"Let's hope we'll be working together real soon. Ya definitely got my vote. *Oh*, tell Gladys I hope she feels better and that I'll drop by first chance I get."

"I will," he said, and headed down the stairs. He walked onto Commercial Street feeling like things were finally breaking in his favour. The boys were charged, Dunphy was demoted and, thanks to Lizzie, he was probably a shoe in for the job. He looked at his watch. It was time to celebrate. Gladys would be fine for another hour or two.

Gordon and Richard MacDonald left McKinley's Pop Factory and headed back to the station. Gordon looked at his driver's long legs and massive build. Despite his own six-foot-two frame, he felt small next to Richard, who stood a good six inches taller and outweighed him by well over a hundred and twenty pounds. Everybody felt small in Big Dick's company, especially the department's latest recruit who had the misfortune of sharing his first and last names. Gordon smiled, recalling the day Chief Peach introduced the nervous young man to his new colleagues. *Fellas, we have a new officer joining our ranks. Meet Constable Richard MacDonald, the younger. Henceforth known as Little Dick.*

They were on Commercial Street when Gordon pointed. "Richard, pull over. I'm going to run in Arlies for a bit. I'll catch up with you back at the office." He entered the store and approached the young man setting up a display of *Little Golden Books*. He was hoping for a more detailed description of the suspected shoplifter: a scar, a tattoo, anything. He left feeling discouraged. He was walking up McKeen Street when a car pulled up alongside of him. Gordon peered in the window and opened the door.

"I was on my way to the station to see you. Get in."

"This is a nice surprise. What brings you to town?" Gordon asked.

"You do. I read the paper. Got time for a coffee?" Ted Collins asked.

Gordon brought Ted up to speed on the investigation and the politics that were playing out, insisting he was more and more certain the boys were innocent. He then told him Dan McInnes was back in town. "I'm worried what will happen when he and Stanley cross paths. Stanley promised me he wouldn't do anything stupid, but I don't know, he still thinks McInnes was involved in JC's kidnapping," he said.

"I'm with Stanley on this one," Ted said.

Gordon shrugged. "Maybe he was, but we can't prove it. Just like I can't prove the boys are innocent. Christ, Ted, if it weren't for Mannie those boys would be home right now. They haven't even scheduled a bail hearing. Dollars to doughnuts Mannie's behind the delays. Probably in cahoots with the Crown Attorney. Bastard's got everybody eating out of his hand."

Ted played with his soggy, three-day-old pie. "Mannie's an ass and always will be. As for the police commission, they're a bunch of corrupt assholes. I gotta say, I'm a little surprised by Mayor Wareham. He was always hands off."

Gordon took a sip of his coffee. "He knows he's in trouble. Mannie's got him running scared."

"You actually believe Mannie will get enough votes from the Catholics and Protestants to put him over the top?"

"It's possible. Lots of folks wearing buttons, and they're not all Jewish."

"God forbid. I sold off my pigs and chickens. Thought I'd move back to town. Maybe I'll wait for the outcome of the election. Gordon, I know you're feeling discouraged. I don't blame you. Just don't throw in the towel. Don't let them knock you down. You're better than that." He picked up a spoon and stirred his tea. "Remember the David Greene case?"

Gordon nodded. "Hard one to forget."

Ted smiled sadly. "There's not a day that goes by that I don't think of Isaac hanging in the back of his shop. Don't make the same mistake. Don't roll over… like I did. Ya got to stand your ground. Trust your gut. If you don't, I swear, it will haunt you for the rest of your life." He pushed his pie to the side. "Definitely not Mabel's."

"No one makes pie like Mabel," Gordon said, thinking his friend had lost a lot of weight. "You feeling okay? You're very thin."

Ted patted his flat stomach. "Don't have Muriel to fatten me up."

"Come to supper tonight? Charlotte's coming over after work. She's making cod cakes."

Ted thanked him, but declined, saying he had a few stops to make before heading back to Iona. "By the way, how is Charlotte?" he asked.

"Good."

Ted smiled and shook his head. "I don't know what's taking you so damn long. Why aren't you two married by now?" He playfully wagged his finger at his former sergeant and friend. *"Don't you dare let that girl get away…*or I promise you, that's one thing you'll definitely live to regret."

Dan was up eighty bucks, but suspected he might be getting set up for a hustle. He kept his eyes on the cocky kid who was dealing the cards and laughing off his losses. Dan threw ten dollars onto the pot. "Time to put up or shut up," he said.

The kid smiled. "Go big or stay home," he retorted.

The sixth card was dealt. "Shit or get off the pot," Dan said and laughed.

The young man put another twenty on the table. Dan weighed the odds. There were twelve cards out and three of them were Queens. There was no way the kid was holding another one. Dan threw another twenty in the pot. "Let's see what ya got, kid?"

The young man had two pair, King high.

Dan nodded and showed one of his unexposed cards. He had two pair, fours and Jacks, the Queen of hearts and three of spades, with one card left.

He took his time turning it over. Another four. He laughed. "Sorry, kid," he said, scooping up his winnings and standing to leave.

"*What?* Yer not gonna give me a chance to win my money back?"

Dan drained his beer. "Not tonight." He waved a ten spot in the air. "Anyone here want to give me a lift to Steele's Hill?" he asked.

The house was dark and cold when he pushed open the back door.

"Danny! Dan! Where have you been?" Gladys called from the cold, dark living room.

Dan switched the light on. Gladys was lying on the couch with her coat draped over her. She started to cry.

"Jesus! Ya haven't moved off the couch?"

"I couldn't. I thought you would have been home hours ago?"

He looked at her swollen and discoloured ankle. "It's a sprain for Christ sakes." He turned up his nose. "What the hell is that awful stink?"

Gladys put her hand over her face. "I couldn't get to the toilet," she sobbed.

Mabel waved goodbye to Luke and walked slowly up the front steps. Ironic, she thought, she'd never seen him so happy, and yet she never felt so bad for him. She entered the kitchen and tossed her purse on the table.

"Where is everyone?" she asked, plopping down in a chair.

"Kids are upstairs playing in JC's room. Amour is at the hospital, and I have no idea where Michael is," Stanley said. "You look like hell."

"I feel like it."

"Anything wrong?"

"Nothing a good night's sleep won't cure," she lied.

Mabel checked on the kids and began preparing supper. Stanley took the paring knife from her and told her to put her feet up. He was surprised to see his mostly-teetotalling wife pour herself a stiff drink. "Something's eating at you. It's not the maniturgium again?" he asked.

"Just tired."

Amour came through the front door. "Look who I found."

"Ted! What a wonderful surprise," Stanley said.

Armour took off her coat. "Sweet man stopped by to see Myrtle and offered to take me home."

Mabel was delighted to see Ted, but was immediately shocked at how thin he was.

The men went to the barn to check on the horses, and Amour and Mabel began preparing supper.

"I saw a big improvement in Myrtle. They had her standing for a few minutes. She's not even stuttering that much. Although, she has developed a slight tremor in her right hand. Actually, the only time she got really agitated was when she talked about her mother's change purse. She insists she had it with her the evening she was attacked but, then again, she remembers some things and not others. I have her house key, so I'll take a look for it." She looked at Mabel "You're awfully quiet."

"I didn't sleep well."

"*Again?* I'm sorry. Hopefully we'll be out of your hair before too long. I've been looking at the real estate listings in The Post. I've asked Michael to take me to see some of the more promising ones, but he keeps putting me off. Said we should wait till the new year. I'll get back on him. It's not fair to you and–"

"It's not the sleeping arrangements." Mabel put her knife down and poured herself another drink. "You know we love having you here. Victoria's like a big sister to Mary Margaret and JC. I'm just worried about the wedding and Christmas will be here before we know it. I need to stock up on supplies, and–"

"Let me help. I can pick up supplies…even help with baking. And you shouldn't be so worried about the wedding. *It'll be fine*. I'm so happy for Luke. They make such a handsome couple. I can't wait to hold their babies."

Mabel pinched her eyes shut. If only you knew, she thought.

Amour began wiping the counter. "You know I love Victoria like my own, but I always wondered what it would be like to hold my own baby…my own flesh and blood."

"Honestly, you'd never know she wasn't yours. Stanley and I were just saying how much she reminds us of you. She has your mannerisms. You'd never know she was adopted."

Amour smiled and put her head down. "I know. I can't imagine my life without her. But sometimes… well sometimes I'm jealous of the relationship she has with her father. She's more likely to do things with him than me. I often wonder if it's because we didn't experience the bonding that comes from carrying her in my belly, or nursing her as a baby. I can't imagine how her real mother could give her up. Think about it, you feel the joy of a new life stirring and kicking inside of you…a little person you created, and then you just hand her over for others…complete strangers…to see her through life. I know I could never do it."

"Amour, you *are* her real mother. And under similar circumstances, I believe you'd do the same. What was she to do? She was a child herself, with nowhere to go and no one to turn to. I believe she did the most loving, selfless thing a mother ever could. She sacrificed her own happiness for that of her child."

"I often wonder what she's like…where she lives. If she ever married and has children of her own. If Victoria has a little brother or sister," Amour said.

Mabel pushed down on her knife, slicing her turnip in half. "Unfortunately, that's something we'll never know."

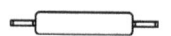

Ted left Mabel and Stanley's with a full belly and greater peace of mind. Stanley assured him he wouldn't go looking for trouble and that he'd steer clear of McInnes. He slowed down and looked up at the big, white house set back off Main Street. The lights were still on. He turned up the driveway, hoping his visit would be welcomed, and not an untimely intrusion.

"Hello, Geraldine."

"Ted, please come in."

"Sorry to stop in so late. Just wondering if Russell might be up for a visit?"

"I'm sure he is." She leaned into his ear. "He's having a good day."

Ted followed her into the living room.

"Ted," Judge Kennedy said, looking up from his reading.

"Don't get up," Ted said, trying to hide his surprise at his friend's appearance. Judge Kennedy's normally rosy, cherub face was now grey and sallow. "I was on my way home and thought I'd stop in and see how you're doing."

"How good of you. Well, as you can see, cancer's winning the war. Making great advances and not wasting any time. But I've still got some fight in me. Not ready to wave the white flag just yet."

Ted smiled. "Horrible disease."

"Yes, but then I don't have to tell you. I've been meaning to call. How are you coping since Muriel passed?"

"I'm doing okay. So I hear you're still working," Ted said.

"On my good days, which are now few and far between. I'm no longer presiding. The powers that be don't think they can take the chance. Figure I might drop dead in the middle of a trial. Pretty much confined to administrative duties...the bullshit stuff nobody likes. But I can't complain, I get to eke out a few more dollars to pay for my funeral. They named my replacement last week. Some hard-nosed, snobby Brit." Judge Kennedy picked his papers up off the table and waved them in the air. "But I haven't kicked the bucket yet. What can I say, I can't help myself. I've always been of the mind that when you quit one thing, you quit another. The next thing you know, you're tits up, regretting you didn't squeeze out every ounce of the things that brought you joy."

Geraldine entered, carrying a tray of tea and fresh-from-the-oven molasses cookies. "Something to warm you up on a cold night," she said, passing a cup to her husband.

Judge Kennedy put his hands out, letting his shaky fingers linger over the back of his wife's veiny hands. "She's always fussing over me...got me spoiled to death," he said to Ted. He waited for her to leave. "Ya know, Ted, I always loved the law. Maybe too much. As I think back now, I regret not spending more time with Geri and the kids. When you're younger, you feel you have all the time in the world. That, if you don't get to it today, you'll get to it tomorrow. Then you discover your kids are no longer kids and you've squandered so many opportunities...lost out on so much. Mind you, Geri never complained. Not once. I sometimes wish she had," he said, putting his head down and showing the first crack in his typically gruff demeanor. He cleared his throat. "Anyway, I'll keep going to the office for as long as I can, but to be honest, I'm at that point when I know I it won't be for much longer. I may be a stubborn son-of-a-bitch, but I'd also like to think I'm a practical man who knows his time has come. I just pray to God I get one more Christmas with Geri and the kids."

Ted bit into his cookie and held the plate out to his friend.

Judge Kennedy waved it away and patted his stomach. "Appetite's not what it used to be. So, I imagine you've been following the antics of our friend, Mannie?"

"I have. In fact, I met with Gordon Dunphy earlier today. He's sure the boys are innocent. Says Mannie's using them for political gain."

"I have no doubt. Mannie's always coveted a career in politics. I'll never forget the first time he showed up in my courtroom. He was still wet behind the ears, but he made mincemeat out of his more experienced opponent. When I congratulated him on his impressive performance, he told me to stay tuned, one day he'd be Attorney General. I guess after two failed attempts at provincial politics, he's prepared to settle for mayor."

"I no longer have a vote, but if I did, it wouldn't be for Mannie. Town is corrupt enough," Ted said.

Judge Kennedy laughed and began coughing. Geraldine appeared in the doorway. "I'm all right, dear," he said, waving her off and running his hankie over his mouth. "Anyway, at least Mannie recused himself. Crown Attorney's assigned the case to a hotshot prosecutor from Pictou. Obviously cut from the same cloth as Mannie. He's petitioned for a three day delay in the bail hearing so he can get up to speed. That tells me he's going to argue the boys shouldn't be released any time soon, if ever."

Ted shook his head. "They're not a risk to the public... and they're not going to bolt."

The two reminisced about old court cases, sports and politics for another hour. Ted looked at the wood-encased Bulova clock sitting on the mantel. "It's getting late. I should let you get back to your reading."

Judge Kennedy picked up his papers. "An appalling treatise from a so-called scholar from Dalhousie. I don't know what's going to become of my profession. A lot of socialist, mumbo-jumbo nonsense, if you ask me."

Ted walked up to Judge Kennedy and held out his hand. "Your honour, as always, it was great seeing you."

Judge Kennedy leaned forward and hugged him. "You were a diligent and honest officer of the law...one of the finest men I've ever known. Take care, my friend."

Ted stopped in the doorway and looked back at the man who had thoughtfully and compassionately presided over the fate of hundreds of men and women during his twenty-five year career on the bench. Judge Kennedy was holding his legal papers in one hand and reaching for his reading glasses with the other. Ted smiled sadly, thinking his friend would soon be out of tomorrows.

"It was good seeing you again, Geraldine," Ted said, reaching for his rubbers.

She smiled. "I'm sure I'll be seeing you again soon."

Ted put his head down, knowing she was referring to her husband's funeral. He touched her arm. "If there is anything I can ever do for you, please call."

Geraldine kissed his cheek. "I will. Thank you for coming and for your kindness." She handed him a paper bag. "I packed up some cookies and a few tea biscuits for you. Eat em up before they go stale. And be careful out there, it's getting nasty."

Ted wiped the snow from his windshield and thought of his long day. He was grateful he took the time to support his friends, just as they had always supported him. But he also felt emotionally drained. He was about to get in his car when he noticed Geraldine watching from the door. He waved a final goodbye.

He turned onto Main Street, leaned forward to see through the blinding snow coming directly at him and realized he almost missed the turnoff to Phalen's Road. He pressed on the brakes. His Ford fishtailed, almost hitting an oncoming truck. "Slow down, old man," he whispered. "Ya got a long way to go. Ya don't want end up dead."

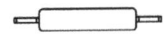

Stanley sat on the edge of the bed and pulled his socks off.

"How did you find Ted?" Mabel asked.

"I thought you were asleep?"

"I only wish," Mabel said.

"He's doing okay. Obviously, missing Muriel. Said he's taking things one day at a time. He's thinking about moving back to town."

"I'm sure that's what Muriel would have wanted."

"You weren't yourself tonight. Sure there's nothing wrong?" he asked.

"I'm fine."

"I asked Ted to come for Christmas dinner. Hope that's all right?"

"Of course."

"Sooo, what would you think if I had the office Christmas party here? If it was just the guys I'd take them to The Pithead, but I can't very well do that since Lily joined us. Wouldn't be fair to leave her out."

Mabel closed her eyes, thinking it was one more thing to add to her plate. "It would have to be after the wedding?"

Stanley unbuckled his belt and dropped his pants to the floor. "Absolutely. In fact, why don't we combine our staff Christmas parties…maybe invite a few other friends? Get it all done in one fell swoop."

Mabel felt like she wanted to burst into tears and turned her back to him. "Okay."

"I think those kids they arrested for Myrtle's attack are John's friends," Stanley said.

"Gordon said he let them go."

"He did, but they brought them back in. They also demoted Gordon and made McEwan acting chief. Ted says it's tied to Myrtle's case and Mannie's the instigator. It's all dirty politics, if you ask me."

"I hope John isn't getting mixed up with a bunch of thugs," Mabel said. "He's a good kid."

Stanley tossed his shirt over a chair, threw the covers back and leaned over and kissed her cheek. "I don't think you need to worry about that. Luke keeps him on a pretty tight leash."

"Not like Mark gives a damn."

"*What?* That's not fair. Mark's away at school."

Mabel angrily pulled the covers over her shoulder. "Mark's never been there for anybody but himself."

Stanley stared at his wife's back, growing more concerned by the minute. He laid down and tilted his head towards her. "I love you. Try and get some sleep."

Mabel tried, but couldn't. She was heartsick for Luke and angry with Alice and Mark. I should have never pried or pushed, she thought. Goddamn you, Alice. How could you betray Luke like that. How can you go through with your vows, knowing they'd be based on a lie.

Mabel looked at her sleeping husband, gently pushed the covers back, crept around JC on the floor and looked out at the moon hanging over the ocean; the image, eerily reminiscent of the time when she was at her lowest, when the thought of another day on earth seemed too much for her to bear. She could picture Luke twisting his cap in his hands and nervously asking her to step away from the edge of the cliff. Neither spoke of that painful moment again, to each other, or any other living soul. He had kept her secret. Now, she would keep one *from* him. She had no choice. If he knew the truth, it would kill him.

Mabel looked to the heavens. Dear Lord, please let him live to be an old man, happily married with lots of children and never the wiser to Alice's betrayal, Mark's betrayal, or mine. And, Lord, please forgive me and give me strength.

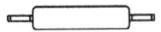

Gordon undid the tight leather strap of his Longines Pilot watch and placed it on the bedside table. "How's Myrtle?" he hollered.

Charlotte turned the water off and ducked her head out of the bathroom. "She's coming along. Only swore once today."

"What about her memory?"

"*What?*" Charlotte hollered back.

"What about her –"

Charlotte appeared in the doorway, wearing a blue bathrobe and smearing a thick, white cream over her cheeks and forehead.

Gordon laughed.

"*What?* A girl's gotta look after her skin."

"Your skin is flawless."

She held up a jar of Noxema and smiled. "*This* helps."

Gordon wanted to grab her and throw her on the bed. "I was wondering if Myrtle remembers anything more about the attack."

"Not much. Amour read her the piece in The Post. She knows the boys. Said they used to call her a witch."

"Yeah, the boys told me. They were just kids," Gordon said.

"They still are. Back in a jiffy," Charlotte said, turning around, kicking her leg back and bouncing on her toes out of the room. She returned a few minutes later with a radiant complexion and dropped her robe to the floor.

"You smell like menthol," he said.

"Is that a good thing?' she asked, straddling his waist.

"Very good."

She leaned down and kissed his neck. "Myrtle did say something about a missing change purse. Said she's positive she had it with her the night of the attack. Apparently it was very old. The only keepsake she had that belonged to her mother." She moved her mouth from his neck to his chest. "She was pretty upset when she realized it wasn't in her handbag." She brushed her lips against his. "Amour's going to see if she might be confused and left it at home."

Gordon suddenly propped himself up on his elbows.

"*Oh, dear.* I can see the wheels spinning," she said.

"If it's not there, it might be where Ten-After-Six found her handbag and we missed it."

Charlotte pressed her fingers against his lips. "Let's just forget about Myrtle and the—"

"Or, maybe her attacker took the change purse, thinking that's where she kept her consignment money."

Charlotte pushed his shoulders down onto the pillow. "Well, there's nothing we can do about it tonight."

They started to kiss, when Gordon moved his head to the side. "But then, why not just leave her handbag. Why take the time to bury it? You'd think they'd just get the hell out of there as fast as they could. It doesn't make sense."

Charlotte lifted her leg, rolled off of him and flopped down on her back. "Oh captain...my captain," she sighed, throwing her arm off to the side.

Doubts, Dick Tracy and a Dead Cat

Wednesday, Dec. 4

"You're picking at your cuticles again," Stanley said. Mabel stopped and laid her hands over her tote.

"Why don't you tell me what's bothering you?" he asked.

"How many times do I have to tell you, I'm fine!" she snapped.

Stanley nodded and turned onto Brookside Street.

"I'm sorry. I just haven't been sleeping well," Mabel said.

"Isn't that usually a sign something's wrong?"

"I'm upset with myself for losing Father Gregory's maniturgium. And, like I told you, I've got a million things to do and too little time to get them done."

"We don't need to have the Christmas party at the house. Why don't I look into renting the Orange Men's hall? We can make it a pot luck."

"No. Amour will help…and Mary Catherine will lend a hand."

"So, what can I take off your plate?"

"I'll think about it," she said, knowing full well there was nothing he could do to ease her worries.

Stanley pulled in front of the store. Mabel opened the door to get out. "I love you," he said. Mabel turned and smiled. "Me too." She watched him drive off, thinking she didn't deserve such a good man. She thought the same when she walked into the bakery and saw Luke doting over Alice.

"Good morning," Luke said.

Mabel hung up her coat. "How is everyone this morning?"

"Never been better," Luke said. "Only nine more days to go. You look tired. Everything okay?"

"Fine," Mabel lied.

Luke held up the teapot. "Got time for a cup, before you start crackin the whip?"

"No," Mabel said, avoiding eye contact with Alice.

Mary Mack came running in. "Goddamn bus. Sorry I'm late."

"Maybe you should consider taking an earlier bus," Mabel said curtly.

Mary Mack had never heard Mabel be so short with her before. She looked at Alice, sitting at the table with her head down. "I'll just go get the supplies," she said.

"No, Alice can get them," Mabel said.

Luke sensed the tension. "I guess I'll just take my tea to the store," he said and left.

Mabel looked at Alice. "Well, what are you waiting for? I'm not running a goddamn teahouse."

Alice burst into tears, grabbed her coat and stormed out.

"Alice! Alice!" Luke yelled, jumping up from behind the store counter. He stuck his head into the bakery. "What the hell just happened?"

Mabel had her head down. She was crying, too.

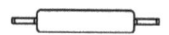

Gordon dropped Charlotte off at the hospital and went directly to Table Head. Mabel's housekeeper answered the door.

"Is Amour here?"

Amour got up from the kitchen table, tightened the belt of her robe and walked to the front door. "Captain Dunphy?"

Gordon told her about his conversation with Charlotte and asked if she had had an opportunity to check for Myrtle's change purse.

"I was just about to get dressed and head over."

The two crossed the field and walked up Myrtle's back steps. "Oh my God," Amour said, stopping and pointing. Lucky, Myrtle's beloved cat was curled up near the door.

Gordon skirted past Amour and bent down.

Amour put her hand over her mouth. "Is it dead?"

"Yes," he said. He looked for a tail to pick it up. "Where's its tail?"

"It's a bob-tail. Poor thing," Amour said.

Gordon put his hand under the cat's rigid torso. "Jesus, it's also missing an ear." He looked for somewhere to put it, then gently laid it at the bottom of the steps. "I'll look after it before I leave."

"It's an outdoor cat. Usually stays in the shed. Myrtle's gonna kill me. I was supposed to check on him."

"It likely died, then froze to death," Gordon said.

"Do you think it was lonely and was waiting for Myrtle to come home?"

Gordon grimaced. "I dunno. I'm not that familiar with cats. I'm more of a dog man."

Amour turned the key and pushed her shoulder against the door. "She said if it's anywhere, it'll be on her dresser."

It wasn't there, or anywhere else they searched, including the living room and kitchen. Gordon opened the cupboard under the sink.

"I doubt you'll find it there," Amour said.

"I'm looking for something to put the cat in," he said.

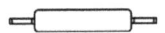

Mabel heard the bell above the door and then the slam. "Luke's gone to check on Alice. I need you to look after the store until he comes back," she said to Mary Mack.

Mary Mack nodded and tiptoed across the floor.

"I'm sorry. I don't know what came over me," Mabel said.

"We all have bad days," her young helper whispered. She dropped a tin bowl on the floor. "Oops."

"Don't worry," Mabel said. "And never mind what I said earlier. You can't help it if the bus is always running late."

"Is Alice all right? I mean...she's been awful quiet lately."

Mabel turned away from her and closed her eyes. "I'm sure it's just all the stress in the lead up to the wedding."

It would be over an hour before Luke returned. He went straight into the bakery and plopped heavily onto a chair.

"How is she?" Mabel asked.

Luke glared at her. "Mabel, I promised Alice I wouldn't speak to you, but I feel I have no choice. You know how much I love you, but I won't put up with you mistreating Alice. She's stressed enough over the wedding. She doesn't need any more piled on."

"I was out of line," Mabel said, wondering exactly what Alice had said to him.

"I know she told you about the baby," he said.

"Yes."

"I don't get it. Why are you mad at her *and not me*? It takes two, ya know!"

"I'm not mad at either of you," Mabel said. "I haven't been sleeping, and I've just been feeling... a little frazzled."

"So, she got pregnant before we tied the knot. What's the big deal? It happens a lot. Hell, you were the one who was always scheming to get us together. Jesus, it's not like it was a one night stand. You know we love each other...that we're committed to one another. Frankly, I expected more of you."

Mabel untied her apron and pulled it over her head. "You're right. I'll go and apologize this minute."

Mabel and Luke walked past Mary Mack sitting behind the store counter. "We'll be back in an hour," Mabel said.

Mary Mac watched them leave. "What the hell," she murmured. "How the heck am I supposed to look after the store and *the bakery*."

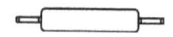

Gordon put the cat in the trunk and drove to the area where Ten-After-Six found Myrtle's handbag. He searched for nearly an hour with no luck. He looked at his watch. He entered the station twenty minutes later. McEwan was there to greet him. "You're late."

"I was on the job," Gordon said, telling him about the missing change purse and repeating his theory that someone other than the boys attacked Myrtle. "If the boys took her change purse, thinking that's where they'd find her money, why bury her handbag? Why not just leave it and get the hell out of there. Likely someone else attacked her, scooped up her handbag, ran across the brook, grabbed the change purse and took off. And why would the boys bury her handbag and keep the painting? They could have easily shoved the painting inside of it."

"They were drunk…probably weren't thinking straight," McEwan said. "As for the change purse, Kenny could have had shoved it in his pocket and tossed it somewhere when he ran to get help. It's probably somewhere along lower Catherine Street."

"You should have the guys scour the area," Gordon suggested.

"Or wait for the next down pour, so we're not all freezing our arses off and wasting a whole of time and money," McEwan retorted sharply. He walked into the hallway and yelled for the desk sergeant to bring Kenny up from lockup and put him in the interview room.

"I'd like to sit in," Gordon said.

"No way. I'll handle it. You're way too… invested," McEwan said.

"You mean in finding the truth?"

"No…in ignoring the evidence to satisfy your bleedin heart. Besides, I'm still waiting for the paperwork on the pop factory. Have it on my desk by noon."

Gordon wanted to kill his new boss, but did as commanded. He finished his notes on the break in and was heading up the hall to put them on McEwan's desk when he saw Kenny being escorted back to his cell. He was running his sleeve under his eyes.

"Keep your chin up. You're gonna be all right. I promise," Gordon said.

"Dunphy!" McEwan yelled.

Gordon spun around.

"In my office. Now!"

Gordon entered what, up to a few days ago, was his office.

"You are not to see or talk to Kenny, or his two accomplices, again! You hear me!" McEwan barked.

"Finished the paperwork you asked for," Gordon said, tossing his notes on McEwan's bare desk. "I'd like to take a couple of vacation days."

"Why, so you can play Dick Tracy?"

Gordon wanted to grab him by the throat. "I've got seniority and plenty of banked time."

"Request denied. Wasn't like you were so generous to me when I looked for the odd weekend off."

"I treated you fairly…the same as all the other guys. You're just being a miserable prick."

"And you're being insubordinate. I could fire you right now, if I had a mind to."

Gordon had had enough. "No need, *chief.* I quit!" he said impulsively and walked out.

"Get back here!" McEwan yelled down the hall.

"Oh, go fuck yourself!"

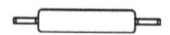

It was only a ten minute drive to Alice's, but the tension in the car made it seem more like an hour. "Call me when you want to be picked up," Luke said coldly and sped off.

I made a mess of things, Mabel thought. She knocked on the door.

Corliss answered. "Someone want to tell me what's goin on?"

"I've upset your daughter. I've come to apologize."

Corliss waved her in. "Fill yer boots. She's upstairs in her room."

Mabel tapped lightly on Alice's bedroom door. "Alice, it's me." Nothing. She put her ear to the door. "Alice," she repeated, "I'm here to apologize. There's no excuse for my rude—"

The door swung open. "You don't need to apologize. I don't blame you for hating me. I hate myself. What I've done is inexcusable."

"Alice, I don't hate you," Mabel said and hugged her.

Alice ran her hand under her puffy eyes. "Did Luke talk to you?"

"Yes."

"I asked him not to."

"He's concerned about you… and none too happy with me."

"I told him you were sharp with me because I'm pregnant. I had to tell him something," she said, plopping down on the bed.

Mabel nodded. "I know. Alice, I won't lie to you. I wish I didn't know. I was awake all night. It's just…well now I feel like I'm part of the deception."

"I'm sorry I told you. I felt so alone. I needed a friend…someone I could trust. It kills me that you think badly of me. But I'm not a bad person," she said, sobbing.

Mabel squeezed her hand. "You made a mistake. A big one. One you'll have to live with for the rest of your life. But you're not a bad person. Far from it."

"Do you think we'll ever be the same…I mean you and me?"

Mabel handed her another tissue." Yes. But you need to promise me something."

Alice dabbed at her eyes.

"You need to promise me you won't give up on Luke. For his sake, as well as the baby's. Even the best of marriages can be trying. And sometimes, in the heat of an argument, things come out. Luke can never know who the father is. It wouldn't only destroy your relationship with Luke, it would destroy Luke's relationship with the baby *and Mark*."

Alice fell into Mabel's arms. "I'll make it work. I promise."

Mabel decided not to call Luke to come get her. She'd walk. She put on her gloves and pulled her collar around her neck, wondering if she and Alice could ever really be the same again; wondering if she was right in urging one friend to hide the truth and betray another. She thought of Luke as a lonely orphan who would stare down at his feet, and as a young man returning from war, sobbing in her arms over the loss of James. And she thought of the night he gave her a little, blue pill, saying it helped him with his melancholy. I had no choice, Mabel thought. "Forgive me, Luke," she whispered. "But better you be deceived and live, than learn the truth and throw yourself off a cliff."

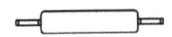

Gordon left the station and went directly to see Sam. "I know the boys are innocent," he said, telling him about finding Myrtle's handbag, her missing change purse and his theory about what happened. "I know Myrtle's painting was stolen, and I'd bet my last dollar whoever took it is the same person who attacked Myrtle."

"You know, Gordon, if this does go to trial, I'll have to call you to testify. Are you sure you want to be sharing your doubts about their guilt with their attorney. I mean, it's great for me and the boys, but not for you. Aren't you in enough hot water as it is?"

"I quit."

"*You quit? When?*"

"Just now."

Sam leaned back in his chair. "Are you sure that was wise?"

"Probably not. But too late now. There's no question the mayor and commission wanted to get rid of me. And you know what they say, you can't fight city hall. And then...McEwan. Miserable prick left me no choice."

"But it's been your life's work. What will you do now?"

"I've got a few dollars saved. I'll find something. Always wanted to be a Mountie...part of a *professional* police service. In the meantime, I thought I could give you a hand. Pro bono, of course."

"I'd never turn down an offer like that," Sam said. "By the way, the bail hearing's been set for nine on Friday. I've agreed to represent all three boys, at least until Tommy and Harley get representation. I referred Tommy's father to another lawyer and he seemed game at first, then backed away. And Harley's father said he hasn't had any luck. Anyway, it's just the bail hearing. I'm sure the Crown's just gonna ask for a minimal surety, and the boys will spend Christmas at home."

"I wouldn't count on that," Gordon cautioned.

Sam laughed. "They're not a risk and *they're not going to flee*."

"Maybe not, but you're forgetting something."

"What's that?" Sam asked.

"You're forgetting Mannie and his cronies are driving this thing. It's not about what's right or fair, it's all politics. Mannie's no doubt pushing his replacement to fight tooth and nail against their release. I hear he's from Pictou County. Any idea who he is?"

"No."

"What about who's presiding?"

"One of the JPs. Not sure who. Judge Kennedy's no longer sitting. I hear he's not doing well."

Gordon stood. "Again, more trouble. Mannie's got them all under his thumb. I better get going. Thought I'd pop in on Myrtle. And with any luck, Charlotte's free for lunch. I gotta break the news I'm unemployed. Better she hears it straight from the horse's mouth."

"Mary Catherine told me you two broke up?"

"We took a break for a while, but we're back together."

"I'm glad. She's a beautiful girl. You're a lucky guy."

"Like you," Gordon said.

"We'll see about that," Sam said, walking Gordon to the door. "Mary Catherine is at the hospital now. She's going to tell Myrtle I'm representing her suspected attackers. Hopefully, Myrtle doesn't fly off the handle and get her all riled up again. I hate sleeping on the couch."

Gordon drove directly to the hospital.

Amour jumped up the moment he entered Myrtle's room and ushered him into the hall. "She's still agitated about her change purse. I didn't want to make it worse by mentioning anything about the cat."

"I won't breathe a word," he said. Ten minutes later, he left with a detailed description of the change purse. He had hoped to have Myrtle draw it, but she became frustrated when she was unable to control the tremor in her hand. He stopped at the nurses' station and was asking for Charlotte when she came around the corner. He led her down the hall. "I need to talk to you," he said.

"Is everything okay?" Charlotte asked, thinking he seemed nervous.

"Yes. Everything's fine." He looked over his shoulder. The other nurses were looking in their direction. "Actually, this isn't the time or place. We'll chat tonight. I'll pick you up at the usual time." He kissed her cheek and started down the corridor. He turned back. "I'll make supper," he hollered.

Charlotte watched him disappear out of sight. When she turned around, her fellow nurses were all smiling. *"What?"* she asked, as a tinge of pink rose up her neck.

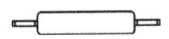

Mabel put on her coat, turned off the light and walked into the store. Luke was flipping the sign on the door, notifying customers Camerons was closed for the day.

"Stanley's just pulling up," Luke said.

Mabel put her hand on his arm. "Are we good?"

Luke smiled. "We're good."

Mabel hugged him.

Stanley was relieved his wife was more engaged on the drive home. He followed her up the front steps. "You must have had a good day. You seem less...less—"

"Testy?" Mabel said.

"I was going to say troubled... but yes...testy works."

Mabel laughed. "Actually, I've been a bitch lately. And you've been very patient with me. I don't deserve you."

Stanley took her coat from her. "No, you deserve better. But looks like you're stuck with me."

Mabel unzipped her boots, thinking of how lucky they were to have found each other and praying Alice and Luke would experience the same kind of joy, long after they were married. She entered the living room. JC was sitting on the floor, drawing. "Is that one of Daddy's horses?" she asked.

"It's a dog," he said. "*See?* He's got a collar."

"*Oh, yes.* I see it now."

"Does he have a name?" Mabel asked.

"Barry."

"*Barry.* Let me guess, he's a Newfoundland dog?"

"No. *He's a shepherd.* He's Barry the shepherd."

Mabel turned to Victoria. "And what are you drawing, young lady?" Victoria handed Mabel her sketch. "It's a change purse," Mabel said.

"Mommy asked me to draw it."

"It's very good. Our friend Myrtle has one that looks just like it."

Amour walked up carrying her tea and looked over Mabel's shoulder. "That's what I was hoping for."

Charlotte hung up her coat and looked at the candles, fine china and crystal wine glasses on the table. Her heart started to pound. Gordon had said he had something to ask her.

"I got supper started. Won't be too much longer. Pour yourself a drink," he said.

"I thought I'd clean up first," she said, thinking he, once again, appeared nervous.

Charlotte closed the bathroom door and did a little dance. "I am the luckiest girl in the world," she whispered. She opened her makeup bag, applied a fresh coat of lipstick and brushed her hair. She spread her fingers apart. They were shaking.

Gordon smiled when she walked into the kitchen. "You look beautiful." He dragged his haddock filets through an egg wash and doused them in flour. His potatoes began to boil over, sending tiny, hissing beads dancing across the top of the coal stove. He went to remove the lid. "Hot! Hot! Hot!" he said, dropping the lid back on top. He nodded to the cupboard. "How about pouring the drinks?"

Charlotte opened the door and looked inside. "I think we polished it off. There's nothing here."

"There's a bottle in the car," he said, rinsing his gooey hands. "Do you mind? It's in the trunk."

Charlotte knew he was up to something. She grabbed the brown bag, returned to the kitchen and put two glasses on the counter.

"Two cubes for me," Gordon said, gently placing his fillets into the scorching cast iron pan. He heard the tinkle of the ice as it hit the glass and then the scream. Charlotte was standing with her hands over her mouth, staring down at Lucky. Lucky was on his back, staring back.

"Jesus!" Gordon shouted, kicking the frozen corpse across the floor. Charlotte was shaking. He sat her down at the table and ran to the car to fetch the other brown bag. "Here, drink this," he said, handing her a glass of whiskey and kneeling beside her. She downed it and began to cough. He waited for her to stop. "Better?" he asked.

"Why would you have a dead cat in your car?" she asked.

"It's Lucky. Myrtle's cat. I forgot about it. I need to get rid of it. You okay?"

She started to laugh. "How could you forget about a dead cat in the trunk of your car?"

"I'm a little scatter-brained lately. I have a lot on my mind. I did something today, and I'm hoping–"

"Yes!" Charlotte said with an exuberance that confused him.

He laughed. "Okay, but I haven't even–"

Charlotte placed her hand on the side of his face and smiled. "Of course. Go on," she said, waiting for him to make the speech he had no doubt rehearsed a million times.

"How would you feel if I joined the Mounties?"

"*The Mounties?*" she asked, trying not to well up.

"Yes. I quit my job today. The Mounties are hiring. And I think I stand a really good chance of getting in. Of course, I'll need to go to Regina for training. I'm hoping you understand that this is something–" He smelled smoke and looked over his shoulder. "Damn it!" he said, getting off his knees and returning to the stove. "I'm sick of all the corruption…all the ugly politics. And McEwan's being an ass." He pushed the pan of blackened fish away from the direct heat. "Anyway, it's a good opportunity to make a fresh start. I always wanted to be a Mountie." He grabbed a tea towel and lifted the lid off his potatoes. "If it all works out, I'd only be away for a few months. So, what do you think?" he asked, turning to see her reaction. He heard the front door close and ran out on the step. "Charlotte! Where are you going? Come back! Charlotte!"

Mannie and the Man in the Camel Hair Coat

Thursday, Dec. 5

Gordon woke with a head-splitting hangover. He remembered combing the streets and pounding on her door. If she was home, she sat in the dark and refused to answer. He got dressed, went to the bathroom and splashed cold water on his face, thinking of her reaction to the news he had quit his job and was looking to join the RCMP. He could understand she might be disappointed in him, but didn't expect that she'd be angry.

He went downstairs and looked down at Lucky lying on the floor. He picked him up and put him on the back step. He was returning to the kitchen when he looked through to the dining room table, untouched from the night before. The special occasion table cloth. The candles. The silverware. He thought of kneeling beside her and her enthusiastic *yes*. "Jesus, she was expecting a proposal," he muttered, cursing himself for being so stupid. But we just got back together, he thought. There was no question he loved being with her, and he certainly missed her after they broke up, but it was way too soon to be planning a wedding. I'm not ready, he thought. And it wouldn't be fair to her when I can't stop thinking about someone else.

He walked to the stove and was about to dump his charred haddock in the garbage when the phone rang. He hesitated, thinking it must be Charlotte, unsure of what he would say. "Oh, hello, Amour. Yes. I can meet you at the hospital. What time? No, thank you. I appreciate it. See you then." He hung up, thinking Charlotte would be working. "I'm going to have to face you sooner or later. Might as well get it over with," he mumbled.

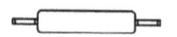

"Danny, dear, can you get me some more hot tea?"

Dan folded over the newspaper, picked up the teapot and entered the living room. He looked at her ankle. "It's not even swollen."

"It's still tender."

"Ya should be using your cane. I gotta go. Got things to do."

"What things?" Gladys asked.

"I gotta fix the car."

Fix the car? Crackie snookered you. Ya should go get our money back."

"It's just the battery. Take me five minutes to get it goin."

Gladys took a sip of tea. "Take ya two minutes to fix the latch. Ya ask me, yer just throwin good money after bad if ya spend another nickel on that old heap."

Dan wanted to put a pillow over her head. "I'm going to town."

He was in the back porch putting on his coat. The phone rang.

"Danny! Can you answer that please?"

"Fuck you," he said under his breath and left.

"Danny!"

Gladys grunted, reached for her cane and limped to the phone. "Lizzie! How nice to hear from you. Really! Oh, that's wonderful! Thank you so much for all your help. Ya just missed him. Oh, I'm fine. Just a minor sprain. I should be back to work on Monday. Not to worry, dear. Yes, Danny's been a huge help. Yes, a good man, for sure. I'd be lost without him. Yes, I'll tell him. Goodbye."

Gladys hung up and hurried to the window. Dan was within sight. She began pounding on the glass and hollering his name.

He heard her, but never looked back.

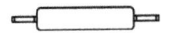

Gordon held Victoria's sketch of Myrtle's change purse. "So, you don't mind if we run an ad in The Post?"

"Off...fer reward. One hund...dred," Myrtle said.

"Are you sure? That's a lot of money," Gordon said.

Myrtle pinched her eyes shut. "Be...belonged to ma...my...mother."

"I understand," he said, turning and smiling at Amour. "Thank you. And thank Victoria for me," he said and left. There was no sign of Charlotte. He was passing the nurses' station when he heard his name. He turned.

"Tell Charlotte we hope she feels better soon," one of her co-workers called out.

"I will," he said, thinking Charlotte must have called in sick. What a mess I made of things, he thought. She never calls in sick.

He drove to town, placed the ad for Myrtle's missing change purse and headed back to his car. He was waiting to cross the street, when he saw Mannie laughing and joking with a man he hadn't seen before. He felt a hand on his shoulder.

"Finally took a day off, I see," Stanley said.

"Actually, I quit."

"*You quit?* Jesus, Gordon, you can't be serious? Ted told me you were having some difficulties, but quit!"

"Who's that guy talking to Mannie?" Gordon asked.

Stanley looked up the street. "No idea. Honestly, Gordon, was that wise? This place will end up going to hell in a hand basket."

"The town will be fine," he said.

"What will you do?"

"Considering the Mounties."

"I hope it works out for you, but, still, I can't help worrying about what's going to happen to the town. Does Ted know?"

"No."

Stanley could tell his friend was distracted. He slapped him on the back. "Good luck with everything." He started to walk away, then turned back. "By the way, Mabel and I are having a Christmas party on the twentieth. Just some folks from work and close friends. Good opportunity for you to take your mind off of things. Bring Charlotte."

Gordon smiled and nodded. "Thanks." He crossed the street. A wet poster, announcing last week's *Meeting of Concern*, hung loosely from the power pole. He tore it off and looked back at Mannie, still deep in conversation with the unfamiliar man in the camel hair coat. He balled up the poster and threw it in the car. He was pulling away, when he noticed someone wave to him. He leaned forward for a closer look. Dan McInnes was sitting on the fence and smiling at him. Christ, Gordon thought, I hope Stanley doesn't see you.

Biscuits, Brisket and the Boys

Friday, Dec. 6

Sam looked over his shoulder at the growing number of spectators. He smiled at Gordon, then at the boys' parents, sitting together on the front bench, directly behind the defence table. He checked the time, wondering what was holding up the JP and Crown Prosecutor.

The prosecutor finally strolled in, like he didn't have a care in the world and draped his camel hair coat over the back of his chair.

Gordon tapped Sam's shoulder and nodded to the tall man in his pinstripe suit and shiny black shoes. "He's a friend of Mannie."

"He looks intimidating," Sam said, feeling his familiar courtroom jitters take hold.

They waited another five minutes for the JP to arrive, but it was Judge Kennedy who came through a side door in the back and slowly made his way to the bench. His large, black robe hung loosely around his neck and off his shoulders. A few spectators began to murmur.

Judge Kennedy banged his gavel. "I might look like death warmed over, but, as you can see, the good Lord has decided he's not ready for me yet. All the same, let's get things rolling just in case he changes his mind. Mr. Schwartz, you are petitioning the court to hold the boys on remand."

"Yes. Thank you. As Your Honour would know, there is an older, female lying in a hospital bed this very minute. In fact, I hear it will be some time before she is released, and that she may suffer life-long damages as a result of the vicious attack on her the night of Friday, November, twenty second." He walked from behind his desk, stood in front of the defence table and stared down at the boys. "The Crown is more than satisfied that there are reasonable grounds to believe that Kenneth Ludlow, aided and abetted by Thomas Simms and Harley Woodward, did unlawfully and willing perpetrate this senseless, vile and cowardly act."

Judge Kennedy held up his hand. "Enough with the histrionics."

"I'm sorry, Your Honour. *Histrionics?*"

"Just cut out the Clarence Darrow act. You can make your case without all the drama."

Schwartz was taken aback by the reprimand and returned to his table. "Your Honour, as someone who has represented the Crown for over fifteen years, I have carefully reviewed the evidence and I agree that there is a very strong likelihood of a conviction on charges of aggravated assault with battery against Kenneth Ludlow and accessory to said charge against the co-accused. In fact, I'm sure of it."

Harley put his head down and started to cry.

"Son. Son, look at me," Judge Kennedy instructed. Harley wiped his eyes and looked up. Judge Kennedy waved dismissively in the direction of the prosecutor. "Never mind him. He's a prosecutor. He thinks it's his job to scare the daylights out of you. Comes in here in his pinstripe suit and acts all high and mighty, making claims he can't back up. So, just ignore whatever he says. I'm the one in charge. Understand?"

Harley nodded.

Judge Kennedy smiled. "Good." He gestured to Schwartz, standing stonily in disbelief. "Continue."

"As I was saying, Your Honour, the evidence is overwhelming. There is a witness who saw them at the scene. Mr. Ludlow attempted to run, and Mr. Simms was found in possession of the victim's property. And while they may be young in years, they are dangerous thugs who are underserving of the court's leniency. I would therefore request the court hold them without bail. Failing that, I would ask that the parents of each of the accused post a bond of no less than twenty thousand dollars."

Sam stood to object.

"Sit down," Judge Kennedy said curtly. He turned to the prosecutor. "Do you understand what their fathers do for a living?" he asked.

"Your Honour, the gravity of the crime and the overwhelming evidence demands that—"

"I didn't think so," Judge Kennedy said. He began to cough. He reached under his robe, spit into his hankie and cleared his throat. "Okay, Mr. Friedman, go ahead."

Sam argued that the evidence was entirely circumstantial, that the painting was likely stolen, and that the thief could be the perpetrator of the assault. "The boys are innocent until proven guilty. Your Honour, they pose no risk to the public and they're not going to attempt to flee. Moreover, Your Honour, the trial could be weeks, even months away, and the boys have already missed several days of school. It would be patently unfair to jeopardize their entire school year by locking them up and interrupting their education." He turned and pointed to the boys' parents sitting behind the defence table. "Your Honour, as you know, their parents could never come up with twenty thousand dollars each. They're not wealthy. They're coal miners who struggle to make ends meet. A bond in the amount requested by the Crown, even a quarter of that amount, might as well be an order of remand."

"Agreed," His Honour said. "There will no remand and no bond."

The prosecutor jumped to his feet. "Your Honour, with all due respect?"

Judge Kennedy held up his hand. "I've sat on this bench for twenty five years. I'd like to think that in my earnest desire to do right by the law, I thoughtfully weighed the implications of the punishments I imposed on those I deemed guilty. But there are things that that have haunted me of late." He smiled and put his head down. "Funny, isn't it...how the closer you come to your day of reckoning, the more you begin to reflect on your time on earth. The choices you've made. The people you've wronged. What truly matters."

No one moved or made a sound.

"Maybe the punishments I dispensed from my lofty perch didn't always fit the crime. Maybe I could have exacted justice without imposing such a heavy price on those who ran afoul of the law. Maybe, if I had been more understanding of the human condition, and less on the letter of the law, I wouldn't have had so many repeat visitors to my courtroom. The rule of law is a human, often flawed invention...the means by which the few decide the fate of the many. And those of us charged with dispensing it fairly, frequently get it wrong. Big shot lawyers come in here...more interested in punishing the accused, than protecting the innocent. More interested in counting another notch on their belt, than in seeing justice is done. And judges like me, go along with it. We forget there is only one true arbiter...

only one judge that truly matters: God our heavenly father. Our laws are written by imperfect men and justice dispensed by imperfect men. And I am one of them."

He looked up at the rapt spectators who would be his last audience, then addressed the boys. "You are young, and you have your whole lives ahead of you. Take it from someone who is old and near death. Remember that before anything else, you are a child of God and subject to His laws before all others. Study your Bible. Love thy neighbour. Treat others as you would want to be treated. And remember, judge not, that ye not be judged."

He picked up his gavel and waved it at the boys. "I am releasing you to the custody of your parents and teachers, with the following assurances. You are to voluntarily present yourselves for arraignment and trial. Foreswear all forms of alcohol. Heed your parents. Go to school and regularly attend your place of worship. Above all, you are to love the Lord. Do I have your word?"

They each nodded. He put his hand to his ear.

"Yes, Your Honour," they shouted in unison.

He banged his gavel. "Dismissed."

Kenny's father stood. "Amen to that!" He began to applaud.

The Crown Prosecutor spun around, glaring at the appreciative spectators standing behind him, also on their feet and clapping. He then angrily snapped his briefcase shut and walked up to Sam. "What is this, some kind of kangaroo court? This is supposed to be a courtroom not a…not a Goddamn revival meeting. Good thing he's dying, or I'd have his ass hauled before a tribunal before the end of the day. See you at the arraignment," he snorted, and charged out.

Judge Kennedy stepped down from his bench. He stopped in the doorway to what was once his chambers, took one long, last look around, then disappeared inside, satisfied that his final act as a judge was one of his finest.

Dan threw his smokes on the kitchen table and removed his jacket.

"Did you get the newspaper?" Gladys hollered from the living room.

"Yes."

"Can ya bring me the ads? And if ya wouldn't mind a splash of hot for my tea?"

Dan removed the section advising readers of the weekend specials promising huge savings to penny-pinching shoppers and grabbed the teapot.

Gladys held out her teacup. "D'ya get the car goin'?"

He tossed the advertisements on the sofa. "Yes."

"Good. We'll need to start it up first thing Monday morning so we don't have to run for the bus again. I don't wanna sprain my other ankle…and you can't be late your first day on the job. Ya excited?"

"Tickled pink," he said sarcastically. He began pouring the steamy brew into her cup, fighting the urge to pour it over her lap.

"Lizzie was such a big help. Ya should buy her some little thing as a special thank you. She likes perfume."

"I'll get right on it," he said. He returned to the kitchen and began flipping through the paper, stopping to read Mannie's latest headline. *Chernin Vows to Repair Town's Crumbling infrastructure.*

> *Local business leaders were among a large crowd of supporters who gathered on Senator's Corner yesterday to hear mayoralty candidate, Mannie Chernin, outline his plans to improve what he described as "the town's deteriorating condition…My number one priority is to create a more pleasurable shopping experience for residents and visitors to our town. If elected, I will immediately install new lighting along Main and Commercial streets, and enhance the downtown core through a new Storefront Beautification Program to be cost-shared with the local merchants' association."*
>
> *Chernin also announced new benches for Queen Elizabeth Park, a new backstop for South Street ballpark, sidewalk repairs and/or extensions in most areas of the town, as well as interior and exterior upgrades to the town hall.*
>
> *When pressed for his response to Hub residents who have been petitioning the town for water and sewer services for their area, Chernin was noncommittal. "Like everyone else, I'd like to see our coloured folks enjoy such amenities. But I won't make false promises for political gain. We need to live within our means. Unfortunately, due to Mayor Wareham's wasteful spending, I'm not yet in a position to establish a firm timeline. I am, however, in favour of establishing a committee, with representation from the Hub District Residents'*

Association, to examine the possibility of moving the town dump to a less-populated location."

"Danny," Gladys hollered. "Larry Mendleson's got a good sale on brisket. Twenty cents a pound."

Dan shook his head, turned the page and stared down. *One Hundred Dollar Reward.* His heart started to pound when he read the description of the rust-coloured, brocade change purse and looked at the remarkably accurate, hand-drawn sketch. He quickly closed the paper.

"Danny! At that price, the briskets will all be gone by the end of the day. Do you think ya could run to Mendlesons? We could have brisket on Sunday."

"Give me a sec. I need to check the fire." He pinched the corner of the incriminating page, shook it free of the rest of the broadsheet and headed for the basement.

"And can you bring me the rest of the paper? I wanna check the obituaries."

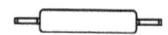

Gordon sat on a bench outside the judge's chambers. He immediately stood when Judge Kennedy walked into the hall. "Your Honour."

"Captain Dunphy. Are you waiting for me?"

"Yes. I wanted to thank you."

"*For what?* The prosecutor didn't stand a chance in there. As soon as I saw him walk down the aisle in his fancy suit and shiny Dacks, I thought of Mannie." He playfully shook his finger at Gordon. "Never trust a man wearing pinstripe."

Gordon laughed. "Can I buy you a coffee?"

"Ya can buy me a tea. Coffee no longer agrees with me."

It was a five minute walk to Woolworths, but Gordon insisted on driving, knowing the short jaunt might prove too much for his ailing companion.

Rosie, a fixture behind Woolworth's counter since the day it opened, passed them two grease-stained menus. "My two favourite customers."

Gordon winked. "You say that to everyone."

She laughed. "Only the big tippers."

Gordon thought of his charred haddock still sitting on the stove. He hadn't eaten in almost twenty four hours and was famished.

Judge Kennedy handed her back the menu. "Just tea for me."

"Same for me," Gordon said.

"What's on your mind, son?" Judge Kennedy asked.

"Well, I did want to thank you. Not just for allowing the boys to go home, but for…for well your lifetime on the bench. Despite what you said this morning, I've always felt you were fair."

"You're too young to remember my early days, before I mellowed."

"I also have a favour to ask." Gordon placed his RCMP application on the counter.

Judge Kennedy put on his glasses. *"What's this?"*

"It's an application for the RCMP. I'm hoping you, Ted and Chief Peach will be my references."

"But why? I talked to Ted…and I know you're upset about all the political bullshit at the office, but you need to ride it out. The department needs you. The town needs you. You can't quit."

"I already did."

Judge Kennedy leaned back on his stool and stared at him.

"I'm sorry, Your Honour. I couldn't take it any longer, and I've always wanted to join the Mounties. A *real* police force."

The two sipped their tea and talked about Myrtle's case, Mannie's antics, and Dan McInnes' return to town. Judge Kennedy picked the application up off the counter and waved it at Gordon. "And what does your young lady think of this?"

"I'm no longer sure I have one," Gordon said.

"I thought you were seeing that pretty nurse from St. Joseph's. The one with the beautiful smile."

Gordon wasn't sure if it was because Judge Kennedy was dying, or because he felt emotionally torn and no longer trusted his own judgement, but he opened up to him in a way he couldn't with anyone else.

Judge Kennedy turned down his mouth. "So you're thirty-six years old. You love spending time with Charlotte, but you think it would be unfair to marry her because you have these thoughts about another woman…a woman you've never had a romantic relationship with and who is happily married?"

Gordon held his cup up to Rosie. "That's pretty much it in a nutshell."

"Did you hear anything I said this morning?"

"Every word."

"Seems to me you missed the part about regretting bad decisions. I wasn't just talking about someone's professional life. In fact, it's even more relevant when it comes to your personal relationships."

Rosie topped up Gordon's tea.

Judge Kennedy held his cup up for a refill and looked at his tormented friend. "Do you want kids?"

"Of course," Gordon said.

"I'll have your babies," Rosie said, batting her eyes and dropping her top dentures.

Judge Kennedy laughed and began coughing. "There, you're all set," he said to Gordon. He picked up his napkin, wiped his eyes, and then his mouth. "Look, Gordon, when I was a young man, I was madly in love with Elsie Ferguson. No other woman measured up. I mean…I thought about her day and night. Like you, I knew I didn't stand a chance of ever making her my wife. And despite the intense feelings I had for Elsie, I married my beautiful bride. I swear to you, I never once felt like I was betraying Gerladine. We've had three great kids, four beautiful grandchildren, and we're still madly in love. Mind you, my youngest boy, Curtis, keeps me awake at night." He shook his head. "Great kid, for sure, but won't settle down. It's like he's got ants in his pants. Keeps jumping from one lousy job, to the next."

Gordon smiled. "He'll come around. He's still young."

"*He's almost twenty-two.* Should have settled on a career long ago. Anyway, take some advice from someone who's gained some insights after nearly seventy years on this earth. Don't turn into a lonely old man who looks back on life realizing you tossed away your best chance at happiness. A good life, is a full life. Yes with a career, but also with a wife and children who love you…despite your flaws. And when I said love thy neighbour, I didn't mean love thy neighbour's wife. Let this couple you're talking about get on with their lives, and you get on with yours. Marry this pretty, young girl of yours and make some babies of your own. You're not getting any younger, ya know."

Gordon smiled.

Judge Kennedy looked down at the application. "I wish I could convince you to reconsider, but I can see that's not going to happen. I'll write you up a letter of reference. You can stop by the house after supper and pick it up."

Rosie approached. "I guess you gentlemen haven't heard the news?"

"What news?" Gordon asked.

She nodded to the end of the counter. "Skinny just told me Chief Peach took a turn for the worse. I guess he didn't make it."

Judge Kennedy dropped his head. "Good, God. What's next?"

Plenty to Hide

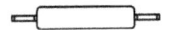

Geraldine Kennedy took her tea biscuits out of the oven, trying not to dwell on the inevitable. She knew the day wouldn't be far off. *Please, God, just one more Christmas with the family.* She lifted the lid and checked on her brisket gently bubbling in the simmering water. She poured a cup of tea, buttered several warm biscuits and put the carton of Crosby's molasses on the tray. She pushed her shoulder against the door. "Supper's going to be another couple of hours. Thought you might like a warm—" The teacup began rattling in its saucer. She quickly put the tray down and brought her trembling hands to her mouth. Judge Kennedy was lying face down over his desk.

"Russell?" she whispered. She struggled to set him upright in his leather chair. "My love," she said, kissing his forehead. "I was just praying for one more Christmas."

She wiped her wet cheeks, laid her hand over his and looked down at her husband's beautiful penmanship. It was an unfinished letter to the superintendent of the RCMP, Nova Scotia Command. She smiled, thinking he was working right up to the moment he took his last breath. She thought of her husband's nightly routine, when he would gather up his files and set them in a neat pile on the corner of his desk. She began gathering up his papers, when she spotted the envelope addressed to *My Darling Wife*. Her hands shook as she opened it.

> *My Beautiful Geri. You are, and always will be, my greatest joy. Nothing in this world made me prouder than to have you on my arm in the day, or share your bed at night. My heart is both light and heavy as I write this, my last love letter. Light, because I know how lucky I've been to have had you in my life for nearly fifty years. If only we could have another fifty. You have been a wonderful wife, and loving mother and grandmother, always putting others before yourself. As I prepare for my final journey, I can only hope that I brought you a fraction of the joy that you brought to me. I am counting my blessings.*

Geraldine pinched her tear-filled eyes, bringing her husband's neatly scribed words into clearer view.

I have written letters to each of our beautiful children and several of my dearest friends. I will leave it to you to find the right time to pass them along. And, please, give our darling grandchildren one last hug from Grampy. Take care, my darling girl. Love Always and for Eternity, Russell.

Mrs. Russell Kennedy fell to her knees, crying. She didn't see the bright beams of the car's headlights flash across the shiny, mahogany panelling in her husband's study, or hear the door open.

"Surprise! Hey, Mom! Dad! *I'm home.* Where are you? Dad! Wait till you hear my news!"

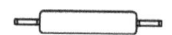

Gordon picked up the receiver and started to dial, but put it back down. Enough was enough. He had already left three messages. He tried to read the paper, but put it aside. He felt out of sorts. He had quit his job, Charlotte wouldn't return his calls and, now, both Chief Peach and his friend, Judge Kennedy, were gone. He poured himself a cup of tea, thinking about the heartbreaking scenes he had just witnessed. First, when he stopped in to pay his condolences to the Peach family and, then, when he showed up at the Kennedys to discover his honour had died less than an hour before. Despite knowing his death was imminent, both mother and son were inconsolable.

He sat sipping his tea and thought about his last conversation with his distinguished friend, hoping he somehow knew that the child that kept him awake at night was about to follow him into the law. He then thought of the advice the good judge offered him. *Don't live to be a lonely old man and miss out on your best chance at happiness.* He re-read the unfinished letter Judge Kennedy was writing at the time of his death.

Dear Sir:

I am writing this letter at the request of Mr. Gordon Dunphy, who until very recently proudly and ably served his town as Captain and Acting Chief of the Glace Bay Police Department.

I have absolutely no doubt that Mr. Dunphy's superb investigative skills, his diligent attention to detail, and his extensive knowledge of the law would make him a valued member of your proud force. Of course, I'm also sure that you are presently sifting through literally thousands of similarly worded recommendations for similarly qualified young men looking to join your ranks. If you believe, as I do, that the true measure of a good officer of the law is, not just his physical strength and mental acuity, but his moral character, then I urge you to look favourably on Mr. Dunphy's request for consideration. As a Judge of the Provincial court for twenty five years, you have my word that you can trust this thoughtful young man's judgement and heart, as much as you could any other man of the law, or any man of the cloth.

And while I write this recommendation at his request, I do so with regret. His voluntary departure from the Glace Bay Police force is a significant blow to local law enforcement in our small town. He is a man of integrity and character. A man that will serve

Gordon ran his finger over the deep blue blot that formed on the page when Judge Kennedy dropped his fountain pen and took his last breath, and thought of his own mortality. The phone rang. He ran to it, hoping it was Charlotte. It was the desk sergeant reminding him to return his uniform at the earliest possible opportunity.

A Funeral, a Fight and a Flat Cap

Wednesday, Dec. 11

Gordon stood on the steps of Holy Cross, surveying the large crowd streaming into the already jam-packed church. He was planning to sit with Ted, but he was nowhere to be seen. He heard the familiar laugh and looked down. Mannie was slapping backs and slipping campaign buttons into the pockets of his captive audience.

Gordon checked the time and entered the church, hoping Ted had arrived early and was already inside. He found a seat at the back, but gave it up to an older gentlemen standing along the wall. He wedged into the spot the grateful mourner vacated and stood below a stained glass image of the Virgin Mary. Several mourners whispered among themselves, glancing in his direction. They likely don't know I quit and are wondering why I'm not in uniform, he thought.

The organist began playing *Be Not Afraid* and the grieving family took their seats in the front. Gordon watched with concern as McEwan assembled his officers and pointed out their assigned spots next to the casket. Big Dick, who towered above his fellow pall bearers, took his place at the back. Little Dick was positioned on the opposite side in front. What the hell are you thinking, Gordon thought.

McEwan gave the order to hoist. The flagged-draped casket, with the black-brimmed police cap resting on top, dipped forward and tilted precariously to one side. They started down the aisle. Chief Peach's cap slid off. Someone quickly put it back in place, but it fell a second time, only to be stepped on and flattened by Big Dick's coffin-bearing partner. Little Dick was now struggling under the uneven weight. He was huffing and puffing, and tiny beads of sweat began dripping down the sides of his red-strained face. A loud chorus of horrified gasps suddenly echoed through the church as his legs gave out, and the casket toppled on its side.

Gordon started to elbow his way through the wide-eyed, stunned mourners, but stopped when several burly men rushed to right the casket and help carry it to its waiting bier.

Mrs. Peach and her daughter were sobbing. Gordon began to choke up. He put his head down, thinking how quickly things change. This time last week, he had a good paying job and a beautiful woman in his bed, Chief Peach was planning to return to duty, and Judge Kennedy was still going to the office. He lifted his head and looked at McEwan, sitting immediately behind the grieving family. He was whispering and chuckling to a fellow officer. You inconsiderate ass, Gordon thought.

The nearly two-hour service, which included speeches from Mayor Wareham and the chairman of the police commission, ended to the strains of *The Strife is O'er*. Gordon waited for the nave to clear and slid into one of the empty pews, hoping to avoid the stares and whispers of the departing mourners. He watched the altar boys in their black, floor-length skirts and snow white surplices efficiently put everything back in order. He wasn't Catholic, or much of a praying man, but he was feeling lost and lonely. He lowered the kneeling pad, got down on his knees and bowed his head. "Dear God. Help me put *my life in order*. Let me find happiness. Show me the way."

Michael needed to arrange for the deed transfer for the South Street property, but dreaded the thought of running into Lizzie MacNeil. He could still remember the first time they met. He was at the bus station, having just arrived from Boston, when she introduced herself and offered to show him around the unfamiliar town. He couldn't shake her after that. She was everywhere he turned, telling everyone she knew, and some she didn't, he was her new beau.

He stopped into Stanley's office and asked that he go with him to the Clerk's Office. "She's just so clingy. You can me help fend her off," Michael explained.

The two walked up the narrow stairway and entered the small room with two wickets. Lizzie was serving a customer. "Thank God," Michael whispered. Stanley grinned and took a seat near the wall. Michael headed to the open wicket.

"Mikie!" Lizzie said, flashing a broad smile. "Get in my line. I won't be a sec."

Michael looked at Stanley. He was holding a magazine up to his face, trying to conceal his amusement.

"I'm in a bit of a hurry," Michael said to Lizzie.

She smiled and nodded to her departing customer. "We're all finished up. I'm all yours."

He hesitated, but felt he had no choice. "Just transferring a property," he said, handing her the paperwork.

"Ya bought back yer old property! Then I guess that means yer back to stay."

"Yes. Amour always loved the place," he said, seizing the opportunity to remind her he was married.

"Is she gonna reopen her fancy bistro?"

Lizzie obviously forgot Michael had said he was in a hurry. She continued to pepper him with questions and took her time attending to the deed transfer. Stanley chuckled and peeked over the top of his two-year old Readers Digest. Two men came out of the back office.

"Dan and I are gonna take our lunch break," McInnes' companion announced to Lizzie.

Stanley stared at the familiar figure glaring back. McInnes grinned and mouthed *fuck you*.

Stanley lunged at him, smashing Dan's head through the frosted glass above the counter and throwing him to the floor. McInnes kicked wildly in Stanley's direction, catching the side of his face and knocking him down. The two rolled around among the crunchy, frosted fragments, tipping over chairs and tables. It took Michael and three other men to finally haul Stanley off of McInnes. By the time the police arrived, the waiting room was in shambles, there was blood everywhere, and Michael had a fat lip.

"Looks like we got a case of two guys who don't like each other much," Big Dick said, putting his pen in his pocket and closing his notebook.

"You're not gonna charge him?" McInnes said.

Big Dick laughed. "If we charged every guy who threw a punch in this town, they'd have to shut down the mines. Ya both look like ya got yer licks in. Ain't no need to tie up the courts." He looked at McInnes. "Of course, if you wanna press charges, that's yer right. You know the drill, just come down to the courthouse and swear out an information. Of course, you'll need a lawyer, and they ain't cheap. It'll cost you a pretty penny."

McInnes wiped his sleeve under his bloody nose and held his clubbed hand against a gash on his neck. "Yer goin to jail, you little prick!" He looked around at the growing number of curious spectators who followed the baton-wielding police into the building and nodded to his co-workers. "Ask them! They saw what happened. He came at me for no reason." He then pointed at Stanley. "Remember, he's the fuckin maniac who tried to kill Dirty Willie. Crazy bastard, always did have a short fuse."

"Go to hell!" Stanley said, as Michael ushered him out and down the stairs.

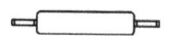

Gordon left Holy Cross Church and stopped by Sam's office, hoping that someone would have contacted him by now regarding the ad in The Post. Charlie met him at the door, advising they still didn't have any leads.

"Do you buy the paper?" Gordon asked.

"Occasionally."

"Same here." He looked around. "Where's Sam?"

"At the courthouse."

Gordon returned to his car and looked down at the crumpled paper on the floor of the passenger seat. He opened it up, placed it on his lap and ran his hand over it to smooth it out. He then went back to Sam's office and pulled Victoria's sketch off the bulletin board. "I need to borrow this," he said.

Two hours later, he tacked up the last of the posters. He was getting in his car when he saw the familiar cobalt jars stacked in the window of Ferguson's Pharmacy. He felt a sudden pang of sadness, thinking of Charlotte standing in the doorway and slathering the thick, white cream over her face.

"Hey, Captain?"

Gordon turned to see the young clerk from Arlies crossing the street.

"Not sure if this is worth anything or not, but that guy who came in the store asking about Myrtle's paintings, I think I saw him. Not positive, but he reminds me of him. Same build. No beard though. I saw him at Woolworth's the other day. Couldn't figure out why he was familiar. Then I saw him again this morning, and it hit me."

"Did you see where he went? Did he go into any of the buildings?"

"No. I was running late. Ran by him on my way to work. It didn't even occur to me till afterwards."

"Did you tell the police?"

The young man looked confused. "Aren't you the police?"

Gordon smiled. "Not to worry." He walked to the nearest pole, ripped the corner off the bottom of the poster he just tacked up and wrote his phone number on the back. "If you see him again, call me right away. If you can't reach me, call this number," he said, jotting down Sam's office number. "Keep an eye on any building he might enter."

"Sure... but like I said, I'm not even positive it's the same guy."

Gordon nodded. "Still, won't hurt to check it out. You might help us figure out who attacked Myrtle." He jumped in his car and headed to the station to return his uniform. He was pulling onto Main Street when he saw Stanley, Sam and Michael standing in front of The Pithead. He pulled over and got out. He looked at Stanley's blood-splattered jacket and Michael's fat lip. "What the hell happened to you two?"

Sam gave him a look of disgust. "Stanley went after McInnes."

"Damn it, Stanley! What the hell were you thinking? You promised me. Hell, you promised Mabel," Gordon said.

Stanley opened the door to the smoky tavern. "He's lucky I didn't kill him. I don't know about you fellas, but I could use a drink."

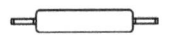

―――◦⊏⊐◦―――

Dan left his supervisor's office, relieved he was given the rest of the day off and not fired outright. He picked his bloody suit jacket off the back of his chair.

Lizzie approached. "What did he say?"

"Told me to take the afternoon off."

"At least ya didn't get sacked." She looked at the bloodstained bandage on his neck. "Maybe ya should have that looked at. Yer still bleedin'."

"It's fine," he said, anxious to get away from her, and the whispers and sideways glances of the rest of his co-workers. He opened the door to the stairway.

Lizzie put her hand on his arm. "I'll testify, ya know. Not right what he did to you. I'll tell em it was self-defence."

"Thanks. Gotta go," Dan said and hurried down the stairs. He threw the door open and blinked into the brilliant sunshine. He'd walk to Iggies. He stopped to light a cigarette, cursing MacIntyre and vowing to make him pay. That's when he spotted the poster and notice of reward. "Fuck," he murmured, quickly tearing it off the pole and shoving it in his pocket. He angrily tossed his cigarette to the ground and looked up and down the street. Every second pole displayed the sketch of Myrtle's change purse. He clenched his teeth and his good hand, trying to stifle a scream. He walked back down Commercial Street and waited for an opportunity to remove the poster on the pole outside Woolworths, praying Gladys hadn't already seen it. He removed three others in the vicinity, tossing them in the town's lone trash receptacle outside The Creamery.

He sat alone in Iggies, grateful for the time to think. He had to plan for Gladys finding out about the change purse and come up with an excuse as to why he had had it in his possession. He'd tell her he found it near the brook. But then, she was expecting it for Christmas and he had tossed it into the coal furnace. He pounded back four whiskeys. He'd tell her he didn't feel right about giving her something he found. Jesus, he thought, she loved it. She'll want to know where it came from and why I no longer have it.

The young man he had cleaned out in seven card stud approached, smiling and waving some cash in the air. "I was hopin ya'd be here. I was lookin for an opportunity to win my money back."

"Not today."

He placed his beer on Dan's table. "Hell, what happened to you?" he asked, pointing to Dan's neck and sitting down.

Dan glared at him. "Are you fuckin deaf or somethin? I said...*not today*."

"C'mon. Just a couple of hands."

Dan lunged across the table, grabbed him by the throat and pushed him back. The kid went arse over kettle. Dan stood, downed the kid's beer and stormed out.

The bartender watched the young card shark scramble to his feet, then turned to the door. "The bastard left without paying," he said.

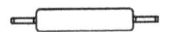

Gordon left The Pithead with a bellyfull of liquid courage. He drove past Charlotte's, but the house was in darkness. He looked at his watch. It was going on four. If she was working the day shift, she'd be finishing up any minute. He raced to the hospital and parked near the door, hoping she'd be among the uniform-clad nurses heading home. A small cluster of employees waited near the entrance for their drive home. Charlotte wasn't among them. He kept his eye on the door, thinking about what he would say. He was still running his lines over in his head when he saw her standing inside the door. He was about to get out of the car and go to her when Dr. MacLellan took her by the elbow and led her out. They were both laughing, like they didn't have a care in the world. Gordon slid back behind the wheel and watched them drive off. "Didn't take you long," he whispered.

He drove home, angry at himself, and Charlotte. He went directly to the bathroom to relieve his full bladder, promising himself he'd become a Mountie. He put the toilet seat up. "Come hell or high water, I gotta get out of this miserable hell hole," he slurred. He was standing over the toilet when he spotted the Noxema bottle and Charlotte's toothbrush on the counter. "Goddammit, Charlotte!" He heard the phone, quickly zipped up and ran downstairs. "Hello. Oh, hi, Charlie," he said flatly.

"I called earlier. Thought you'd wanna know we got almost a dozen bites on the change purse. People have been dropping them off all afternoon. I got a whole drawer full. But they don't look anything like Myrtle's. I keep telling them it's not the right one, but they keep askin me to double check. Crazy, eh?"

"It's getting close to Christmas, and it's a big reward," Gordon said.

"Yeah. Lot of folks desperate for some quick money, I guess. Did ya get to see Sam?"

"Yes."

"Then I guess ya know, Stanley's in a shitload of trouble."

Gordon had barely hung up from speaking with Charlie when the phone rang a second time. It was Mrs. Peach calling to apologize. She advised that she had left the planning for the funeral to Chief McEwan and that it was a great disappointment to her, as it would be to her dear husband, that he was not among the pall bearers. He put the receiver down, went to the kitchen and sifted through the few cans in his pantry. He sat down heavily, drank whiskey straight from the bottle and looked around at his bare walls and secondhand furniture. His mind jumped from one thing to the next. The chief's coffin lying on its side, Judge Kennedy laughing at Rosie when she dropped her top teeth, Mannie glad handing at the funeral, and Stanley sitting across from him in the hazy blue, smoked-filled tavern, describing McInnes' missing fingers and insisting he had to have been the guy that went after Fred Clarke. Gordon looked at his watch, wondering if it was too late to call Charlotte. "What am I thinkin. She's moved on, and I'm too friggin drunk. Forget about her. Forget about everythin!" he muttered. He placed his hand on the table to steady himself and stood up. "Whoa. Get a grip," he said, staggering down the hall. He stumbled upstairs, threw himself down on his unmade bed and passed out.

He didn't hear the phone.

It was Charlotte.

Dan was relieved it was dark. He pulled in front of Woolworths, praying Gladys hadn't seen the posters, or heard about the reward that would tie him to Myrtle's change purse. He watched his aunt waddle toward the door, her cane in one hand and her handbag in the other. "Hurry up," he growled.

Gladys was panting by the time she got in the car. "Lizzie stopped in and told me what happened. I've been callin the house all afternoon, worried sick." She leaned across the seat. "How's yer neck?"

"It's a scratch."

"I hope yer gonna press charges."

"Don't worry."

"Is that blood on yer new suit?"

"Yeah. Mostly his."

"You've been drinkin."

"I had a rough day."

Gladys decided she needed to leave him be.

He decided he needed to keep her on his good side. "How was your day?"

"Same as any other, except for hearin bout what happened to you."

By the time they arrived home, Dan was satisfied Gladys was none the wiser to the reward. It was the next morning he was worried about. She was bound to see or hear about the posters. He hung his suit coat over a kitchen chair and went to the bathroom to check out the gash on his neck. Gladys picked it up to examine the bloodstains and spotted the folded paper sticking out of his pocket. Her hands started to shake as she looked at the image and read the description of the missing change purse. *Her change purse. He must have stolen it.*

She heard him coming down the hall and quickly shoved the poster back in his pocket. "I was just looking at yer new suit coat. Sunlight soap oughta do the trick," she said, trying to control her voice and trembling hands.

Dan noticed the poster sticking out of his pocket and studied his aunt for any sign she read it.

Gladys laid his jacket on the table and reached for the kettle. "Tea?"

Dan gathered up his suit jacket. "Sure. Where's the soap?"

"There's a cake under the bathroom sink."

Dan walked down the hall, furious with himself for, once again, being so careless. He needed to feel her out.

Gladys finished up the supper dishes and took her knitting to the living room.

Dan looked up from his tattered copy of *The Thin Man*. "You're quiet. Anything botherin you?

Gladys stopped mid-purl. "Ankle's still a little sore."

"Want me to get some ice?"

"No. The ice is more painful than the ache."

"So, I guess you heard about the big reward?" He waited for her reaction.

"*Reward?*"

"Yeah, for a change purse. A hundred dollars. Looks just like the one I bought for you."

Gladys pulled a line of yarn from her skein. "Never heard a thing," she said, continuing on with her knitting.

He knew her lack of curiosity meant she had seen the poster. He shook his head. "Can't imagine why anyone would offer a hundred dollars for it. Hell, I paid three for the one I bought you, and I thought the kid I bought it from…Kenny I think his name was…was ripping me off. Anyway, don't want ya to think I'm cheap or anything…I didn't have a whole lot of spare cash lying around…but when I saw it, I thought of you."

Gladys dropped a stitch. "It's not the price of the gift that matters, but the thought that went into it."

"I was thinking I should see if it's the one they're looking for. Probably not the same one, but if it is, it should be turned in. Must mean a lot to whoever lost it, given the size of the reward."

Gladys was beginning to think she jumped to the wrong conclusion. "If it belongs to someone else, they should have it. It'd be the Christian thing to do." She gathered up her knitting. "My old eyes aren't what they used to be. I'm off to bed. Can ya bank the stove before you call it a night?"

Dan smiled and picked up his book. "Sure. Good night." He watched her disappear down the hall, tossed his novel to the side and leaned forward with his elbows on his knees. He dodged one bullet, but knew it wouldn't be long before another came his way. I should never have burnt the goddamn thing, he thought.

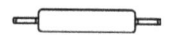

Mabel rinsed the soapy plate and passed it to Amour. "Did you tell Myrtle about Lucky?"

"No."

"Amour, you're going to have to tell her, and the sooner the better."

"I know. She's gonna kill me. She loved that cat. I feel responsible. I promised to check on him. Poor thing, I forgot all about him."

Mabel opened the oven door. "She's not going to kill you." She looked at the time. "Where are those two? Their supper is drying out."

"Obviously, nowhere near a phone," Amour said.

They heard the front door open. "We're home," Stanley said, quickly hanging Michael's coat over his bloody jacket.

"We were beginning to worry," Mabel yelled down the hall. "Come have your supper." She grabbed a dishtowel and reached into the oven to remove her meat pie.

"What the hell happened?" Amour said, touching Michael's swollen lip.

Mabel put the pie down and looked at her husband who was sporting a shiner. "Jesus, Mary and Joseph! What did you two get mixed up in?"

Stanley put a bottle of rum in the middle of the table and told them about the fight with McInnes. His apologies weren't working on Mabel. She was furious. She began pacing and swearing like she did in her younger years. Michael tried to defend Stanley, saying he was taunted, but Mabel shot him a look that stopped him mid-sentence. Stanley kept his head down, knowing it was best to let her vent.

Mabel threw her dishrag into the soapy water. "What's done is done. At least you're okay and nobody was killed. But so help me, God, if I hear you so much as look at that bastard again, you'll have more than a mouse under your eye. You'll be missing some parts you treasure."

Amour dumped a tray of ice cubes onto two dishtowels. "Where did all this take place?" she asked.

Stanley held the icy bundle under his eye. "The Clerk's Office. I had to get survey specs for a property I'm working on. I asked Michael to come along," he lied. "Apparently McInnes got a job there."

Michael elbowed Stanley, urging him to tell her the rest. "There's one more thing," Stanley said sheepishly.

Mabel glared at him.

"McInnes might press charges."

Mabel slammed her fist down, startling Amour and Michael.

"Mabel," Michael said. "It's not as bad as you might think. Sam says—"

"I don't give a damn what Sam says!" Mabel said through clenched teeth. She whacked Stanley on the arm. "You stupid son-of-a-bitch! I told you you'd end up in jail."

"Nobody's going to jail," Stanley said quietly, thinking it was a good possibility he might. "Sam thinks McInnes is full of bluster and that he won't pursue the matter."

"And if he does?" Mabel asked.

"And if he does, Sam says I'll get a slap on the wrist. There were lots of witnesses who saw him strike back. Besides, with his record, he likely doesn't want to step foot in another courtroom. Look, let's not get ahead of ourselves. I'm sure—"

Mabel grabbed him by the chin, turned his head to the side and examined the darkening bruise under his eye. "Wedding's in two days. Fine best man you're gonna make."

The Mending, the Mounties and the Madonna

Thursday, Dec. 12

Amour smiled when she saw Myrtle sitting up in a chair. "Look at you!"

Myrtle pushed her tray table to the side. "I walk…walked down the…ha…hall this morn…morning."

Amour sat beside her. "Fabulous. And your speech is getting better by the day."

"Na…not my…my hand," Myrtle said, holding it up. "Won't be a…able to paint."

"Sure you will. Just give it time."

"How are…my…my cats?"

Amour looked down at the floor. "Myrtle, I'm so sorry. I didn't have the heart to tell you sooner. Lucky died. Captain Dunphy and I found him on your back step. I'm really sorry. I should have checked on him sooner." She glanced at Myrtle and braced herself for one of Myrtle's angry outbursts.

Myrtle reached for her toast and roughly tore a piece off with her teeth. "Had him…nearly…a…eleven…ya….years."

"I know. I'm so sorry. I don't blame you if –"

"He wa…was a cat. Ug…ugly cat. Had…fa…four more lives than…he sha…shoulda. Never…la…liked cats much. But tha…they seem ta…ta…take to me."

"So, you're not mad at me?" Amour asked.

"Ma..maybe...a...little."

Charlotte entered carrying a small box. "Good afternoon, ladies. How are you feeling today, Myrtle?"

"Ca...can't wa...wait to get...the ha...hell out."

"I'm afraid it will be a while yet. I brought in some Christmas decorations. Thought we should make your room more festive," she said, taping a red and white, cardboard candy cane to the wall.

"Charlotte, Mabel wanted me to tell you about her Christmas party. She's hoping you can come," Amour said.

"When?"

"Next Friday at seven."

"I'd love to, if I'm not working." She stepped back to examine the colourful addition to the stark, grey wall. "How's that, Myrtle?"

"Cra...crooked as a da...dog's hind leg."

Charlotte pulled it off and straightened it out. "Better?"

Myrtle titled her head. "No."

Charlotte laughed. "I'll fix it when I come back to check your vitals," she said and left.

Amour looked at Myrtle. "She's a lovely girl. I like her a lot."

"Ya...yes," Myrtle said. "Bew...beautiful skin."

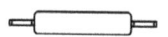

Gordon rolled onto his back. His shirt was damp from sweat. He looked at his watch. It was going on eight. On any other given day, he'd have been at the station for at least an hour. He closed his eyes, recalling snippets of his dream. *He was lying in a coffin that was turned upside down, obviously dead, but also somehow alive. He could hear the panicky voices of those on the outside trying to turn the coffin upright and felt the thud of the heavy box hit the floor. The lid opened and a blinding light shone through a stained-glass window. He was wearing a red tunic, navy breeches and shiny knee-high Strathcona boots. Judge Kennedy put his hand out to help him out. Apart from Ted Collins sitting in the front pew, holding a dead cat and oblivious to his miraculous resurrection, the only other person in the church was Chief Peach. His face was grey and he was punching the inside of his flattened cap. Mannie suddenly appeared, throwing campaign buttons in the air, and pointing and laughing at him in his Red Serge uniform. He wanted to run at Mannie, but couldn't. His feet were stuck to the floor. He turned* and looked into a recess at a statue of the Virgin Mother, cradling her dead son. He lifted one foot, then the other, slowly shuffling toward the stony image. He knelt and prayed for forgiveness. When he lifted eyes to The Madonna, it was Charlotte's solemn face looking back.

Gordon ran his hands over his stubble, quickly sat up and swung his legs over the side of the bed. "Wow," he whispered, thinking about his crazy dream. He went downstairs and put the kettle on, still haunted by the fleeting images that assailed him through the night. He sipped his tea, thinking he rarely remembered his dreams. It must have been the booze, he thought. He placed his teacup in the bare sink and thought of his mother. *An empty sink is a sign of a lonely home,* she had always said. That's when he realized the significance of his dream. There was no family at his funeral.

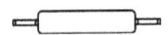

"Mrs. Nickelo did a beautiful job. You'd never know she added a new panel," Mabel said.

Alice followed her up the stairs to Luke's bedroom. "She sure likes to cut things close. I was beginning to think the worst."

Mabel pointed. "There it is."

Alice looked at her mother's wedding gown spread out on the bed. She picked it up and held it to her shoulders. "She's a miracle worker."

"I told you. It's as good as new. Let's see what it looks like on," Mabel said.

Mabel did up the back buttons and looked at the bride-to-be's reflection in the mirror. As much as she tried not to show it, Alice's betrayal gnawed at her, and the much anticipated union of two special friends, was now something she just needed to get through. She forced a smile and patted Alice's shoulders. "You look beautiful."

Alice ran her hand over her belly. "It's a bit tight."

"Good thing the wedding is tomorrow. You're gonna pop soon."

Luke knocked on the door. "Can I come in?"

"Absolutely not!" Mabel hollered.

"I need my wallet. It's on the dresser. Come on, just one little peek?"

Mabel opened the door a crack and handed it to him. "*Now*, go away."

Luke rested his forehead against the door. "Alice, I'm off to meet up with the guys. My last night as a single man. Only fourteen hours to go. I can't wait for you to become my wife. I'll see you at the church."

"Have fun," Alice replied.

Mabel tried not to tear up. Her emotions, driven as much for the love she felt for the young man who was like a brother to her, as they were by the ugly secret she knew would torment her for the rest of her life.

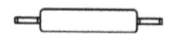

Stanley and Michael made their way to the crowded bar and waited for their bartender to notice them. Luke came up behind them. "He better hurry up, I need to take a leak." Stanley said.

"Me too," Michael said.

"You two go. I got this," Luke said.

Stanley slapped a twenty on the bar. "You're money's no good here. At least not tonight." He hollered to the bartender. "Hey, Skanky! Ten draughts. And don't take any money from this guy. It's his last night as a free man."

Luke grew impatient as the bartender did more talking than pouring and followed his friends into the washroom.

"I never thought we'd see the day," Stanley said to Michael in the next stall. "Mabel said Alice almost called it off?"

"When was this?"

"A couple of weeks ago. I told her it was likely a bit of cold feet, but she said it was more than that. Even said that she and Alice talked about what would happen if she cancelled the wedding. Alice said she'd have to quit working at the bakery cause it would make things too awkward. Anyway, you know Mabel, always finds something to worry about."

Michael joined Stanley at the rust-stained sink. "I gotta admit, I used to worry about him. He was always so...so down. It's like he's a new man."

Stanley chuckled. "Jesus, your eyes look like two piss holes in the snow."

Michael wet a hankie and rubbed his eyes. "It's not the beer. It's the damn smoke. It's thicker than a London fog."

The two headed back to their table.

Stanley looked at Luke's empty chair, then back at the bar. "Where's the guest of honour?" he asked.

Sam shrugged. "Last I saw, he was heading for the can."

Stanley turned to Michael. "Christ! Do you think he heard us?"

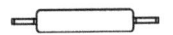

Luke banged on the front door. "Alice! Open up. I need to talk to you! Alice!"

Corliss answered in his loose singlet and baggy boxers. His fake leg was put away for the night and he was leaning on his crutches. "What's going on? Don't think yer supposed to see the bride the night before—"

Luke brushed past him, almost knocking him over.

Alice was looking down from the upstairs landing. "Luke! What are you doing here? What's wrong?"

Luke took the steps two at a time, grabbed her roughly by the arm and dragged her into her room. Alice had never seen him so angry and began to worry he discovered he wasn't the baby's father. "So, I hear you told Mabel you wanted to call it off!"

"What?"

"Don't lie to me! I heard Stanley tell Michael you didn't want to go through with it."

Alice sat on the bed and put her head down.

Luke paced back and forth. "Is it true?"

She raised her head. "I had a touch of cold feet, that's all."

"You're marrying me because you're pregnant. That's it, isn't it?"

Alice shook her head. "No," she said meekly.

Luke glared at her. "You don't sound so sure. Alice, I don't want a marriage based on a lie! If you have any doubts, I need to know, *now*, before it's too late!" He crouched down in front of her, trying to control his emotions. "Just tell me the truth. No matter what you say, I promise…I swear to you…I won't abandon my responsibilities to you…or my child. Alice, do you really love me?"

She brought her eyes up to his. "You know I do."

"Then say it!"

"I love you!"

"And you want to be my wife?"

Alice knew that unless she told him the full truth, their marriage *would be based on a lie*, and that it would be the ultimate betrayal of the man she was sure would lay down his life for her. She also knew her cruel deception would haunt her for the rest of her life; the child growing inside her, a daily reminder of her unworthiness as a wife and mother.

Luke's heart was pounding. He grabbed her by the wrists. "*What?* You're still not sure?"

Alice wiped away a tear. "Yes, I want to marry you!"

"*Yes! You're sure?*"

Alice forced a smiled and nodded. "Yes, I want to marry you," she repeated, feeling she had no other choice.

Luke sighed, leaned over her lap and closed his eyes. Alice ran her hand through his thick, dark hair. "I love you so much," he said.

"I know," Alice said, bringing the back of her hand up to her runny nose and wiping her eyes.

They stayed like that for some time, both quietly thinking of the day to follow and the life they would begin together. One looking forward with excitement and joy; the other, with guilt and shame.

Luke finally raised his head. "I guess I should let the bride get her beauty sleep." He stood up, placed his hand on her belly and kissed her forehead. "I'm sorry for upsetting you. I just needed to be sure. I'll see you tomorrow. It will be the happiest day of my life."

Alice watched him slowly pull the door closed. She could hear his footsteps on the stairs. "Forgive me," she whispered. She then crawled into bed, pulled the covers up over her head and cried herself to sleep.

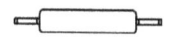

Stanley and Michael drove home, relieved they had seen Luke's car at Alice's.

"Dammit," Stanley said. "I was hoping everyone would be in bed by now. Christ, if Luke calls off the wedding, Mabel's gonna string me up by the balls. As if I wasn't in enough trouble."

"So he overheard you saying she was having second thoughts. Who doesn't?"

"I didn't," Stanley said.

Michael laughed. "Actually, neither did I. Are you going to tell Mabel?"

"What choice do I have?"

"None that I can tell."

Mabel was polishing Stanley's shoes and Amour was ironing. From the moment they entered the kitchen, Mabel knew the night hadn't gone as planned. "You're home early?"

Stanley offered up a guilty smile.

"I know that look," Mabel said. "Tell me."

Stanley explained what had happened. Mabel quietly waited for him to finish. She stopped buffing and placed his shoes on the newspaper by the door. "You had no business repeating our private business in a public washroom, or anywhere else for that matter," she said heavily. "I'm going to bed. I *might* have a wedding to go to tomorrow." She walked away with the same look of disgust on her face as she did the night before, when he told her about his fight with McInnes.

Amour put Michael's shirt on a hanger and hung it on the doorknob. "What were you thinking? Poor, Luke! Hopefully you two didn't ruin everything and destroy his best chance at happiness."

Stanley looked down the hallway. "Hopefully, I didn't ruin my own." He got up, poured himself a drink and took it to the living room, furious with himself for being so stupid.

Amour and Michael tidied up the kitchen. They stopped on their way upstairs. "Mabel was wondering if you spoke to Ted lately," Amour said.

"No. I'll see him tomorrow at Judge Kennedy's funeral."

"Going to be a busy day for you. A funeral and a wedding," Michael said.

Stanley shrugged. "At least we know there'll be a funeral," he said and downed his rum.

He waited for Michael and Amour to finish up in the bathroom, turned off the lights and tiptoed past Mary Margaret's crib. He climbed into bed. "You awake?" he whispered.

Mabel had her back to him. "I'm furious."

He put his hand on her shoulder. "I'm sorry."

Mabel flinched and quickly pulled her shoulder away. "Not another word."

Neither would sleep. Guilt kept them both wide awake until the wee hours of the morning.

Flying Coal, Alfalfa and Tuna

Friday, Dec. 13

Stanley fought with the knot in his tie. He looked at Mabel, sitting at the bottom of the bed, buttoning her blouse. Other than Mabel telling him she spoke to Alice and the wedding was still on, they barely spoke two words to each other since they got up. He turned and pushed the knot up to his neck. "Church hall all set?"

"Yes."

"Great. Well, one thing's for sure, I'm getting my money out of this suit today. This look okay?"

Mabel barely looked at him. "Fine."

He knew it didn't. He loosened his tie, whipped it away from his collar and started over. He tried to lighten the mood. "I hope my dance lessons paid off and Luke doesn't step all over the bride's feet?" Mabel didn't respond. He kept a level tone. "Is this the way it's going to be for the rest of the day?"

"You can only hope," she said, pulling up her half slip.

"Look, I spoke out of turn. I wasn't being malicious. I don't know what else to say, other than I'm sorry."

"You better get a move on. It's disrespectful to be late for a funeral."

Stanley stopped at the bedroom door. "I'll be back in plenty of time to take everyone to Mary Catherine's."

"Do you have the ring," Mabel asked sharply.

He smiled and patted his breast pocket. "Already looked after."

Stanley met up with Gordon and Sam outside of St. Anne's Church. "No sign of Ted?" he asked.

"Not yet," Sam said.

Gordon looked around at the growing crowd. "Not like him to be late. Funny thing, I didn't see him at the chief's funeral either."

"Have you spoken to him lately?" Stanley asked.

Gordon shook his head. "Not since the last time he was in town."

"I hope he's all right," Stanley said, thinking Ted didn't look well the last time he had seen him. "I'll give him a call after the funeral."

Gordon elbowed Sam and nodded toward Mannie greeting mourners gathered near the steps. "He's at it again. Christ, the guy has no conscience."

The three entered the town's largest structure and sat together. Sam looked at Stanley. "I always get nervous when I go to a Catholic Church. Never know what to do."

"Just follow my lead," Stanley said.

The organist began playing *Ave Maria*, giving mourners their cue to stand. Gordon watched as the pall bearers, once again, gathered in the vestibule, hoisted their burdensome load and carried another good friend down the aisle to rest at the feet of the Lord. He put his head down and closed his eyes, recalling the cloudy images of his unsettling dream. Judge Kennedy helping him out of his casket, Chief Peach punching the inside of his flat cap, and Ted Collins sitting alone in the pew reserved for family. He wondered what would become of his town, now that the last two grand bastions of justice were gone, and Mannie was poised to become mayor. *Who's left to root out the corruption and cronyism?* Maybe I made a mistake, he thought. He felt the warmth of a bright light and opened his eyes. The sun was streaming through the windows and shining down upon the solemn face of the Virgin Mother. *Maybe I made two big mistakes*, he thought, and blessed himself.

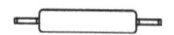

Stanley and Michael dropped Mabel, Amour and the kids off at Mary Catherine's where the bridal party was getting ready and continued to Luke's.

"I'm worried about Ted. Not like him not to show up for his friends' funerals."

"Call him," Michael said.

"I tried. The operator said the phone lines are down from Ironville to Iona."

"Was he planning on coming to the wedding?" Michael asked.

"Yes."

"You're starting to sound like Mabel. I'm sure there's a good explanation why you haven't heard from him."

They arrived at the store. Stanley pointed to the sign on the door. *Closed for the day. Getting Married.* They went upstairs to Luke's apartment.

"Here, let me help with that," Stanley said, taking a cufflink from Luke. "Wow, you look like a guy who's about to get married."

"That's what I was going for," Luke said.

"Sorry about last night."

Luke shrugged. "It's all good. I over reacted. We had a good talk. Michael, how about pouring the drinks," he said, nodding to his dresser.

Stanley whistled when John came in the room. He was wearing a new suit and his shiny hair was plastered in place with what Stanley determined was an overabundance of hair product.

Michael poured three stiff drinks and looked at Luke for his approval to pour a fourth for John. "It won't hurt. We need to toast the groom."

"A small one," Luke cautioned.

The door opened.

"Oh my God! What are you doing here!" Luke said, rushing to hug his surprise visitor.

"Whatcha mean. Couldn't very well miss my big brother's wedding, now, could I," Mark said. He pulled John into a headlock and mussed his hair. "And look at you, all decked out like Dapper Dan in your fancy duds. Easy on the Brylcreem though, bud!" he said, holding up his greasy hand and laughing.

Michael passed him a glass. "You're just in time for the last toast to your brother as a single man."

Mark looked from Stanley's shiner to Michael's fat lip. "What the hell happened to you two?"

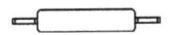

Mabel was alarmed when she saw Alice's swollen eyes.

Alice dropped her hands on her lap. "I look like a mess."

"Your eyes are a little puffy, but we can fix that," Mabel said, thinking it was hopeless.

"It's hopeless," Alice said.

"It is not!" Mabel assured her, quickly sending Mary Catherine for ice.

"I need to pee again," Alice said, running to the bathroom.

Amour gave Mabel a concerned look. "She must have been crying all night," she whispered.

Mabel nodded. "The ice should help."

Mary Catherine returned with the ice. "I don't think this is gonna work. It's hopeless."

Alice overheard her. "I told you!" she said, flopping down on the side of the bed and tearing up again.

"Don't cry," Mabel scolded. She took the ice from Mary Catherine and told Alice to lie down and put it over her eyes. An hour later Mabel was relieved the swelling had subsided, but the ice left red blotches on Alice's frozen cheeks.

"Now I look like a goddamn clown! I can't walk down the aisle looking this."

Amour held up her makeup bag. "I have a fix for that." Amour worked her magic and began braiding Alice blonde mane.

Sam knocked on the door. "Ladies, you better get a move on. It's getting nasty out there."

Mabel pulled the curtain aside. "There must be a half a foot of snow down." She looked at the time. The wedding was a little more than an hour away and she still hadn't dressed the kids.

Everyone was scrambling around when Sam knocked a second time "Corliss is here for Mary Catherine and the kids. Ya better hurry up. Time's a ticking."

"Voila!" Amour said.

Mabel turned around and gasped when she saw the bride. "You look stunning. Now let's get you into your dress."

Mabel, Alice and Amour stood inside the front door, waiting for Sam to shovel a pathway to the car. Mabel looked in the hall mirror, gave her hair another quick brush, then reached into her purse for the cameo brooch James had given her after Margaret had died. She closed her eyes, remembering what he had said when he presented it to her on her wedding day. *Margaret wanted me to wait for a happy occasion.*

Amour watched Mabel pin Margaret's brooch on the high-necked collar of her pale blue suit and knew she was missing her friend. "Remember, too much nostalgia can cast a black shadow over the brightest of days," she whispered.

They were approaching the corner of Park and Brookside streets when the tires starting spinning on a slight incline, creating an icy rut in the hard packed snow. Mabel took the wheel and Sam put the full force of his one hundred and sixty pound frame against the bulk of his two tonne Buick Roadmaster. His feet kept sliding out from under him. He stood up and looked around. There wasn't another car in sight. He'd give it one last go. He spread his legs, dug his rubbers in and pushed as hard as he could, falling forward and banging his forehead on the bumper. He was still lying in the snow, when a truck pulled up.

Kenny Ludlow and his father jumped out. Ten minutes later, with Mabel behind the wheel and coal shovelled under the tires for traction, Kenny, his dad, and Sam began rocking the car forward and back. Mabel gunned the engine, spitting coal and icy debris out from under the hot, spinning tires. The car plowed ahead, swerving from side to side. Mabel didn't stop. She drove straight through the intersection, fishtailing onto Brookside Street. Sam looked at his new, tan coat, splattered with black stains from the flying coal.

"Better not keep the groom waiting any longer," Kenny's father hollered over the howling wind. "We'll follow you the rest of the way."

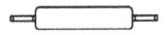

Luke looked at his watch, peeked out at the smaller than expected crowd and started pacing. "I knew it. She had a change of heart."

"Don't get yourself worked up. It's slow going out there," Stanley said, thinking if they didn't arrive in the next few minutes he was going to have to investigate. He walked into the nave, winked at the kids sitting with Michael and Victoria and scanned the guests. There was no sign of Ted. He was about to rejoin Luke and the others, when he saw Sam come through the main door. He ducked his head into the sacristy. "They're here," he said, then rushed up the side aisle.

Mary Catherine was attempting to brush away the stubborn, black stains on her husband's coat.

"We got stuck," Sam said.

Stanley looked at Sam's red forehead.

"What happened to you?"

"My Buick got the best of me."

"Where's the bride and —"

"I told them to wait in the car. I'll need help getting them up the steps. And they're worried about their hair. The wind really picked up."

Stanley put his hand out to help Mabel out of the car. He smiled when he saw she was wearing the familiar pale blue suit she wore on their wedding day. A gust of wind showered them in a mist of fine, white snow. "You look beautiful?" he said.

Mabel couldn't hear him over the wind.

Stanley led her slowly up the treacherous climb, thinking of the day she had tumbled down their front steps and they lost Mary Margaret's twin brother. They reached the top step. He let go of her arm. "There's a surprise waiting for you inside," he shouted, rushing back to the car to help Sam escort the bride inside."

"*What?*" she hollered.

Amour did her best to fix Alice's windblown hair, then took her seat. Mary Catherine handed Mabel and Alice their modest cluster of carnations.

Mabel hugged Alice. "You are a beautiful bride. Oh, and I'm glad you decided to go with the flat ass."

Alice grabbed her hand. "I know Ma's here in spirit, but I'm glad you're by my side."

Mabel smiled. "Ready?"

"Yes."

"Just a sec," Corliss said. He wiped his eyes and blew his nose one last time, then held his arm out to his daughter. "Okay, let's do this," he said.

Mabel nodded to Amour, who in turn signalled for the organist to begin. Mabel followed Mary Catherine down the aisle, smiling at the sound of Corliss's metal leg clanking with every step. She looked at Luke beaming at the sight of his bride, then at his groomsmen. Her stomach dropped when she saw Mark standing next to his brother. Alice can't possibly know either, she thought.

Mabel stood next to Mary Catherine and studied Alice's reaction. The beautiful, blushing bride who had started down the Aisle, was now ashen, and her hands were shaking so much, Mabel thought her bouquet would become a puddle of petals at her feet. She looked out at the guests. Stanley was sitting with Mary Margaret on his lap. He tilted his head toward Mark and winked. If only he knew, Mabel thought.

Mabel put her head down, thinking of the irony of Father Cusack extolling the virtues of love between a man and woman and the sanctity of the marriage vows. She prayed. *Dear God in heaven, forgive me for my part in this deception. Know that I did it out of love. Bless this couple and keep their union whole. Let them be happy…*

Mary Catherine elbowed her. She was trying to stifle a giggle. She gestured for Mabel to look at John. John's hair was sticking up in the back, like Alfalfa from the Little Rascals. Mabel caught his eye, smoothed down the crown of her own hair, indicating he should do the same. He did as urged, but it slowly crept back up. She then looked at Mark. He was grinning from ear to ear, totally unaware of the pain he was inflicting on the bride. Totally unaware, he would soon be a father.

Best man, my ass, Mabel thought.

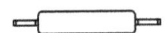

Mabel followed the eager groom and rattled bride up the aisle. Mark came up from behind, put his arm over her shoulder and kissed her cheek. "Surprise, surprise," he said. "How's my favourite girl?"

"Hello, Mark," Mabel said in a tone that made it clear it wasn't a pleasant one.

He gave her a puzzled look. "*What*? What did I do?"

Mabel kept walking. Mark stopped in his tracks and shook his head, wondering if she was pissed because Stanley wasn't the best man.

Mabel hugged Luke and waited for a chance to speak with Alice. She leaned into her and put her hand on her forearm. "Are you all right?"

Alice nodded, but her bottom lip was quivering and her eyes were welling up. Mabel hoped it was the result of Mark's surprise visit and not the wedding itself.

Everyone was gathering around to congratulate the newlyweds.

Stanley put his arm around Mabel's waist. "Nice surprise, eh?"

"When did you find out?"

"When I went to pick up Luke. What's wrong? It was a beautiful wedding."

"Half the quests didn't even show up… Mary Catherine's parents and Sam's. Mary Mack didn't even make it," she said, trying to hide the real reason for her agitation.

"Not like we can control the weather. Ted's not here, either. Actually, I'm worried about him. No one's heard from him in over two weeks, and he wasn't at the funeral this morning. Something's wrong. Look, I hope you don't mind, but I thought I'd take a quick run to Iona."

"*Now!* But the roads are treacherous and you have to give the toast to the bride."

He pointed to Mark. "Best man gives the toast. And the snow has let up." He held up a set of keys. "Besides, I'll have Luke's Plymouth. It can plow through anything. I'll be back in plenty of time to dance with *my bride.* "

Mary Mack burst through the door. She pulled her knit hat off. "Damn! I missed it, didn't I?"

Mabel nodded.

"Goddamn, friggin bus!"

Mabel smiled. "Mary Mack, you're in church."

"Christ, I fergot," she said, quickly covering her mouth.

Stanley kissed Mabel's forehead. "Save me some cake and say goodbye to the kids for me."

"Be careful," Mabel said. She watched him speak to Luke and Alice one last time, then reach for his overcoat.

"Where's Daddy going?" JC asked.

Mabel rubbed the top of his head. "To check on a friend."

Stanley paused near the entrance, looked back at Mabel and mouthed *I love you.*

A sudden blast of frigid, Atlantic air sent a neat stack of church bulletins fluttering to the floor, then the heavy, oak door slammed shut, startling Mabel and the small gathering.

Mark approached, laughing. "Hell, for a moment there, I thought Jesus fell off the cross."

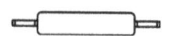

Mabel looked out the window. There was no change from the last two times she had checked. The snow had stopped, but the winds were still high. She turned to the sound of boisterous laughter and shook her head. Mark was getting drunker by the minute.

Michael called the bride and groom into the middle of the floor, started up the gramophone and placed the needle on the spinning vinyl. Mabel held her breath, knowing how nervous Luke was. Despite worrying about Stanley and her growing annoyance at Mark, she found herself smiling. Luke masterfully guided Alice around the room, happily singing along to Bing Cosby's satiny version of Only Forever. Mabel touched her cameo brooch, thinking back to the night at the Bistro when James and Margaret seemed to magically glide across the floor, captivating the attention of everyone in the room. How proud they would be of the man Luke had become, she thought. And how proud Stanley would be knowing his dance lessons paid off.

Mary Catherine pulled a chair up next to Mabel, Amour and the kids. She pointed to John and Victoria doing the jitterbug. "Aren't they adorable?"

Mabel stood up for a better view. "And very good." Mary Margaret slid off her chair and ran around the floor, twisting about and wildly thrashing her arms at her sides.

Mark waited for the music to stop and staggered up to the newlyweds' table. "Hey!" he yelled far too loudly. "Time for my speech. My toast to the happy couple. Stanley was supposed to do this, but he's not here. Imagine, he's out there, in the middle of the storm, checkin on a friend. He's a good guy, Stanley. Love, love, love him. Love his beautiful wife, too. Although she don't seem too happy with me for some reason. Anyway, yer stuck with me. What can I say, my big brother married the girl of his dreams. Alice... sweet, sweet Alice."

Alice put her head down.

"And didn't Luke do a good job on the dance floor? Hell, you'd think he was Gene Kelly or Fred Astaire out there. Ya'd never know he had a gimp leg."

Michael placed some drinks on the table and leaned into Mabel. "Was that supposed to be funny?" he asked.

Mark was undeterred by his failed attempt at humour. "Anyways, I'm happy for him. Most of you probably don't know this, but before Luke came on the scene, I was Alice's boyfriend. Swear to God, it's true. *Right*, Alice?"

Luke put his arm around his wife's shoulder.

"I don't like where this is going," Mabel whispered.

"Neither do I," Michael said. He started to stand, but Amour placed her hand over his and told him to sit back down.

"Anyways, I don't mean to suggest he came between us or anything. We're brothers for Christ sakes, and brothers don't do stuff like that to each other. We're happy for one another. I love my big brother. He's a war hero, ya know. That's how he got the bum leg. Got shot down somewhere..." He pointed to the wall. "I dunno, over there somewhere. And I love his bride. I really, really do. He's a lucky, lucky guy, and he'll be a great husband and father."

Luke whispered in Alice's ear.

"Obviously, she loved him more than his handsomer, younger brother," Mark said, laughing. "And Luke...Luke had a bad case of Alice... right from the get go. Ya could see it a mile away. Hell, I don't think he had any other girlfriend. Not his whole life," he said, making a wide swoop with his arm and stumbling into the table. "Oops," he said, straightening up. "Not a single one. He was always shy around the ladies. In fact, Alice, I think yer gonna be crawlin into bed next to a virgin."

"That's it," Michael said, standing. He hollered to Mark. "Mark! Time for a few more dances before we shut things down."

"Okey dokey. But not till I get a kiss from the bride," he slurred, leaning into Alice.

He hit the floor hard and didn't move a muscle.

Luke had decked him.

Mabel sat uneasily in the back of the car with the kids, trying to hide her mounting concern for their father. The normally ten minute drive from the church hall took over forty minutes and they had to leave the car at the bottom of the driveway and make their way through knee-deep snow. Mabel was angry, exhausted and near panic by the time she settled Mary Margaret and JC into their beds. She went downstairs and sat on the sofa looking out the window for any sign of her husband.

Michael handed her a whiskey. "He's a big boy. I'm sure he's holed up somewhere. Probably worried... you're worried." he said, trying to reassure her, as well as himself.

"He should have been back hours ago," Mabel said.

"If he's not here in the next hour, I'll go look for him. I just need directions on how to get to Ted's."

Amour entered from the kitchen. "Is that necessary? I mean...he's probably going to show up any minute. Next thing you know, we're sending him back out to look for you."

"It's *not necessary*," Mabel said, flatly. "Stanley always says I worry too much."

Amour sat next to her. "He's right, you *are* a worrier."

Michael and Amour tried their best to distract her, talking about the wedding, Mark's shameful behaviour, and a possible budding romance between John and Victoria. It was pointless.

"I know you two must be exhausted. Go on up to bed," Mabel said.

Michael smiled. "We don't mind waiting with you."

"I know, but I think I'd prefer to wait alone."

Michael held his hand out to help Amour to her feet. He then went to the kitchen and came back with the bottle of whiskey. He put it on the table next to Mabel and kissed her cheek. "He's fine. I'm sure of it."

Amour hugged her. "Good night."

"Good night."

Mabel tried to remind herself that it was less than a month ago when she was sitting in the same spot, fearing the worst. It turned out fine. I have to believe it will again, she thought. By the time the clock struck midnight, she was in a full blown panic. She picked up the receiver and dialled the number, hoping the only person she knew could help, would answer. It rang at least a dozen times before she heard the groggy voice on the other end.

"Gordon, it's Mabel…Mabel MacIntyre. I'm so sorry. I didn't know who else to call."

Window Pains

Saturday, Dec. 14

Gordon immediately called the County Police, asking if they received any reports of accidents or abandoned cars from the Glace Bay town limits through to Iona. He paced back and forth waiting for the officer to check and get back to him.

"Sorry bout that. Apparently, there's too many abandoned vehicles to count, and the bridge near the George's River connection is out. A car smashed through the railing and it's closed to all traffic."

"Any idea of the make or model?"

"Sorry. I just got called in. Barely had time to get my coat off. Hold on a sec," he said, putting the phone down. Gordon could hear unintelligible chatter in the background. He waited.

"Ya still there?"

"Yes."

"Okay, apparently the car is still underwater, nose down. Don't know the colour or make. They got a wrecker on the way to see if they can bring it up."

Gordon closed his eyes. "And the driver?"

There was a pause. "Guys say there's no sign of the driver. Figure he's probably still in the vehicle."

Gordon crawled along the Sydney-Glace Bay highway, slowing several times to see if any of the cars on the side of the road might be Luke's. It was almost three-thirty when he stopped at the end of a row of cars near the bridge, and ran toward the officers shining their lights down into the water. A cable was attached to the back axel and the winch engaged. The car barely moved, but you could now see a corner of the back end. It was black. Dunphy put his head down, reminding himself that most cars were black. The wrecking crew had to stop several times to readjust the cable.

Gordon approached an officer holding a flood light. "This is agony. I'm praying it's not a Pontiac."

"We'll know soon enough. Hey, aren't you Dunphy?"

Gordon gave the stranger a bewildered look. "Have we met?"

The officer shook his hand. "Arnie White. *Remember?* A couple months ago, Geezer was on a bender. He wouldn't tell me where he lived. Insisted I take him to your lock-up. Poor bastard. Anyway, do ya think you might know the driver?"

"I hope not."

The order was shouted for the wrecker operator to hoist. Sheets of snowy ice began to crack and break away, as the downed vehicle was released from its watery grave. *Please don't be a Pontiac. Please don't be a Pontiac. Please don't be a Pontiac.* Water streamed from around the doors. The shiny black Pontiac hung mid-air, swaying back and forth, like a huge, prized tuna, proudly hoisted on display.

Gordon sat back on his heels and dropped his head. "Fuck," he murmured.

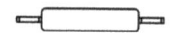

Mabel sat by the window, chewing her nails and picking at her raw cuticles. It was after four and there was still no sign of Stanley, or Gordon.

"Still no word?" Amour asked from the stairs.

"No. I called Gordon. He's out there looking for him. Hopefully, I didn't put him in danger."

"Mabel, I'm sure they're both fine. Did you sleep at all?"

"Could you?" she said harshly.

Amour shook her head. She walked into the living room, unsure of what to do or say. "Can I get you anything? Maybe some tea?"

Mabel looked at the clock. "No."

JC appeared on the stairs, rubbing his eyes. "What's wrong mommy?"

Mabel smiled. "Nothing sweetheart. Mommy just can't sleep. Go back to bed now, *okay?*"

"Where's Daddy?"

"Remember, I told you he was helping a friend?"

"Yes."

"Well, he's still there helping him. Now, go on back up."

"I'm thirsty."

Amour got JC some milk and settled him back in his room. When she returned, Mabel was bent over on the couch, with her hands over her face. Amour sat beside her and rubbed her back. Like Mabel, she was thinking the worst.

"I know something awful has happened. Amour, I was so mean to him lately. I'll never forgive myself if that's the last…the last–" Mabel sobbed. Amour held her and rocked her back and forth like a mother would a child, thinking she could never go on if something should ever happen to Michael.

Gordon sat in his car waiting for the body to be retrieved. He slammed his hand on the steering wheel. "Goddammit!" he screamed, thinking he had lost another friend and, the town, another good man. He thought of what he would say to Mabel. He envisioned her standing in the doorway, then collapsing from anguish. He put his head back, closed his eyes and prayed. He jumped when Arnie rapped on his widow.

"Driver's a male. Likely early forties."

Gordon ran to the small gathering surrounding the body. He blessed himself. It wasn't Stanley. "Thank you, dear Jesus," he said. That's when he saw one of the officers carrying a second victim. A young girl.

The officer placed her on the ground next to her father. "There's another child in the back seat. A…a boy," he choked out.

Everybody talked in whispers as the body of the second child was laid next to what Gordon assumed was his baby sister. He thought of their grieving mother anxiously awaiting word they were okay. The solemn quiet of the heart-breaking scene suddenly gave way to shouts.

The officer who had removed the first child charged toward the bodies. "Cover them up! Goddammit! They're cold! Cover them up!" he screamed hysterically. One of his colleagues tried to stop him, but he broke free, peeled off his coat, tucked it around the lifeless arms of the two young victims and broke down, sobbing.

Arnie looked at Gordon. "He has kids around the same age."

It took another hour for the police to give the okay for Gordon to cross the bridge. He slowly approached the wooden structure and glanced at the wrecker operator, hunched over the back seat, handing soggy packages, wrapped in colourful paper, to his co-worker. Gordon blessed himself a second time, knowing that within hours, a young mother, joyfully anticipating Christmas morning with her husband and children, would have her world shattered. From now on, the wonder and warmth of the holiday season, would bring her nothing but heartache and grief.

Gordon drove slowly along the road to Boisdale, stopping twice to check abandoned vehicles, neither a black Pontiac. The sun was coming up by the time he reached Ted's. He parked at the bottom of the driveway and looked at the high drifts leading to the house. The front steps were covered in snow, the house was in darkness and there was no car in sight. He turned around and headed back to town, hoping that Stanley found his way home, and that he was in bed, curled up beside his wife. He then thought about his own bed, wishing he was in it, and Charlotte was lying next to him.

Michael placed a tray of steamy teacups on the table. It will be easier to spot Luke's car now that the sun is up," he said to Mabel.

She jumped up. "There's Gordon." She pulled the front door open, wrapping Stanley's cardigan around her.

Gordon slogged up the driveway, waved and shook his head from side-to-side.

"Nothing?" Mabel asked.

Gordon stomped his feet on the top step and slapped at the snow covering his pant legs. "Sorry. I got as far as Ted's. No sign of him, or Stanley." He knew not to tell her about the submerged car and the tragic toll the storm had taken on a father, his two small children, and the family left to grieve.

"Where the hell can he be?" Mabel said, returning to the window.

Mabel spent the next hour either checking the time or staring quietly out the window. Her heart started to pound and she sat up. A car rounded the bend and started to slow down. *Please! Please! Please!* It stopped and the passenger door opened.

"Oh, my God. It's him!" she squealed, tearing out of the room. She flung the front door open and ran off the step, struggling to plow forward through the heavy snow and high drifts. She fell headfirst.

Stanley rushed to her side. "Well, you're a sight for sore eyes," he said, helping her to her feet. He laughed and brushed the snow off her face.

"I'm gonna kill you. You scared the day lights out of me," Mabel said, throwing her arms around his neck. Stanley scooped her up and carried her back inside.

JC came downstairs and ran to his father. Amour and Michael hugged Stanley, then each other. Gordon stood back and watched the happy reunion. He put his head down, thinking about the very different scene unfolding in another home overcome by news of an unfathomable tragedy.

"Time for tea," Mabel sad, laughing through her tears.

They gathered around the kitchen table. Stanley explained that he got as far as Ted's. When he realized Ted wasn't home, he tried to cut across to Northside East Bay, but the Burnoit Road was impassable, so he had to turn back. "By then, the bridge was out. I thought I'd turn around and break into Ted's, but the car cut out on me. I got as far as the saw mill and pounded on the nearest door. Thankfully the owners took pity on me." Stanley thought of Clair and the old farm house with the beautiful hardwood floors Fred and Ten-After-Six had laid for the woman who had almost cost him his marriage. He smiled at his wife. "I'm sorry. I knew you'd be worried, but the phones were still out."

"Well, thank goodness you're home now. I just wish we knew where Ted was and that he's okay."

Stanley turned to Michael. "After lunch, we'll take my truck and tow Luke's car back. Maybe pick up a Christmas tree along the way."

Gordon tilted his head. "Wait a sec. I checked out the abandoned cars along the Boisdale Road. I didn't see a black Pontiac."

Stanley wrapped his cold hands around his cup and blew into his tea. "It's a Plymouth."

Gordon smiled at Mabel. "I thought you told me Luke drove a Pontiac?"

Mabel grimaced. "I'm sorry. Is there much of a difference?"

Amour shrugged and the men laughed.

"So, how did the rest of the wedding go? Did I miss anything?" Stanley asked.

Gladys lifted Dan's glass and looked down at the white water stain on the nightstand, vowing to make her nephew restore her beautiful, chestnut heirloom. She was pulling the sheets off the bed when she noticed the black stain on the rug. She bent down to examine it more closely and spotted the magazines under his bed. She reached in, pulled them out and gasped at the covers featuring scantily clad women in various vulgar poses. She opened one, then another, slowly turning each page, tilting her head from side-to-side as she tried to imagine what unspeakable things they were doing to one another. Every page, of every magazine, was as disgusting as the one before, sometimes showing men with men, women with women, and even multiple couples engaged in the most obscene behaviour she had ever seen. Gladys had heard of girly magazines before, but never knew the extent of the depravity contained within their pages. She put her hand over her mouth. "My nephew's a pervert," she whispered.

Gladys heard the car. She quickly shuffled the magazines into a pile and slid them back under Dan's bed. She was carrying his sheets into the kitchen when he came through the door. He put the grocery bag on the table. Brisket's no longer on sale. Greedy Jew hiked the prices just before Christmas."

Gladys dropped the sheets on a chair. "Don't say things like that! It's not Christian."

"Maybe not. But it's true." He reached in his pocket and tossed eighty dollars on the table.

"*What's that?*" Gladys asked.

Dan knew he had no choice but to part with his money. "Turns out the change purse was the one they were looking for. I took twenty out to cover the groceries. It was your change purse, so it's your money."

"Did they wonder where you got it?"

"Yeah. I told them I bought it from Kenny, if that's his real name. Anyway, owner was just happy to get it back."

"I'm glad it's back with its rightful owner, but I don't expect ya to give me the reward."

"Are ya sure?" he asked.

"Yes."

Dan scooped up the four twenties. "If you insist."

"Did ya get a chance to press the assault charges?" she asked.

He threw his coat over the back of a chair. "I'll do it Monday... on my lunch break. I'm gonna lie down for a bit. Give me a holler when supper's ready."

Dan went to his room and locked the door. He got down on his knees and pulled his magazines out from under his bed, anxious to get to the delicious girl who bore a striking resemblance to Mabel. They were out of order. He closed his eyes, distinctly recalling licking the glossy image of Miss Naughty November and putting it on top of the pile. He looked at his closed door. "Maybe Miss November's not the only naughty girl in this house," he whispered, unbuckling his belt and getting into position.

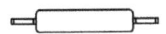

Gordon left Mabel's and Stanley's. He couldn't wait to fall into bed. He was stopped behind traffic when he noticed a clerk in Ferguson's window building a pyramid of Noxema jars and felt the familiar pang of loneliness. When he got home, there was a letter addressed to *Gordon* wedged inside the screen door. He recognized the handwriting. He stepped inside and tore it open.

Dear Gordon. I tried calling. I came by for my things. If you wouldn't mind packing them up and dropping them off at the hospital whenever you get the chance. I hope you get accepted into the Mounties. They'll be lucky to have you. I wish you nothing but the best. Merry Christmas, Charlotte.

Gordon put Charlotte's note back in its envelope and laid it on top of Judge Kennedy unfinished letter. He started to cry. He wasn't sure if it was lack of sleep, the scene at the bridge, the loss of his friends, the finality of Charlotte's letter, or a combination of everything that brought him to tears. He laid down on the couch, but couldn't sleep. He went upstairs, pulled Charlotte's robe from the back of the door, gathered up her slippers and toiletries and casually tossed them into a box. He paused when he picked up her jar of Noxema. He unscrewed the lid, sniffed the familiar scent of menthol and thought of the last time they made love. He put the lid back on, held the jar above the box, then slowly dropped it on top off her robe. "Fuck!" he yelled, kicking the box across the bathroom floor.

He arrived at the hospital a half hour later and was told Charlotte wouldn't be in for another two hours. He placed her box of belongings on the counter.

"Can you make sure Charlotte gets this?" he said to an older nurse jotting notes on her clipboard.

He drove home, stripped down to his underwear and crawled in bed, satisfied he had done all he could.

It was dark when he woke. He was famished. He was making porridge when the phone rang. He charged into the hall. "Hello?"

"Yes. Not to worry. When is it again? Friday at seven. Yes, I'd like to come. Charlotte? I'm not sure. Thanks, Mabel. Yes, I'm glad he's home, too. You're welcome. Goodbye." He put the receiver back on its cradle, wondering if Charlotte got his note and why he hadn't heard from her by now.

Egg Nog, Tinsel and Cleavage

Monday, Dec.16

Mabel separated the tangled mass of tinsel and gave each of the kids a handful. JC, Mary Margaret and Ruth threw it onto the tree. Victoria and Irwin quietly came behind them, pulling the mangled clumps apart and carefully draping the silvery strands on the ends of the boughs.

"I feel like I've been through the wringer. With the wedding... and being down a pair of hands at the bakery...I just want a nice relaxing Christmas," Mabel said.

"When will Alice be back?" Mary Catherine asked.

"She's coming in on Saturday to help with the last minute rush."

Amour attached a hook to a bell. "I told you, I'd help."

Mabel smiled. "You've got enough on your plate with Myrtle, making meals and helping out with the party. Mary Mack and I will get it done."

Amour couldn't hook the bells fast enough for the small hands eager to hang them in a cluster. "I should see if Dr. MacLellan will let Myrtle out so she can come to the party. If she finds it too much, Michael could take her back. I know she's going crazy being cooped up in there. Sweet Charlotte has been decorating her room, but it's hard to make a hospital room festive."

Mary Catherine lifted Ruth up so she could reach a higher branch. "Sam tells me Charlotte and Gordon split up again."

"When?" Mabel asked.

Mary Catherine shrugged. "Not sure."

"That's funny. I just spoke to Gordon and he never mentioned anything. I was so sure they'd make it work this time," Mabel said.

"I wonder if Charlotte broke it off because he quit his job," Mary Catherine said.

"I doubt it," Mabel said.

Mary Catherine ran to the radio and turned it up. "I love this," she said, singing along with *I'll Be Home for Christmas.*" She grabbed Ruth by the hands, swinging her arms from side-to-side. "*Oh*, I meant to tell you. I ran into Lily this morning. She looks fabulous. Said she loves the job."

Mabel smiled and put her head down. "She's a sweet girl…burdened with far too many troubles. Her kids being tormented…the ugly rumours that just won't let up about her and Father Gregory… and that good-for-nothing husband of hers claiming he never laid a hand on her or the kids. I don't know how she gets up in the morning. By the way, Mary Catherine, if you have anything lying around the house that you can spare, I've been collecting some things for under her tree."

Stanley walked in, put a tray of drinks on the coffee table, quickly jumping back as the kids charged in for their frothy, Christmas treats. "Who are you collecting for now?" he asked Mabel.

"Lily."

"She's been a godsend. Worth every penny I pay her and then some," he said, returning to join Michael and Sam in the kitchen.

Stanley looked around for his glass, then poured another eggnog and added his rum. "So, you don't think McInnes will lay charges after all," he said to Sam.

"I don't think so. Pretty sure he would have done it by now. I still can't believe he got a job. A good one at that. So many people looking for work and they hire the likes of that. Speaking of which, anyone hear from Mark?" Sam asked.

Stanley shook his head. "Left the morning after the wedding with his tail between his legs. I still can't believe I missed out on everything. Jesus, he and Luke used to be so tight. I hope they can get past this. But Mark's not such a bad kid. And it's not fair to lump him and McInnes together. He just got drunk and stupid."

Sam laughed. "I know I shouldn't be making light of it, but you should have seen the look on Luke's face when Mark tried to kiss Alice. Hell, I didn't even see Luke throw the punch. Mark just crumbled to the floor, like a house of cards in a wind storm." He tilted his glass toward Stanley. "He'd give you a run for your money."

Michael topped up his drink. "Mark's an ass. Way too big for his britches."

They heard a crash and ran into the living room. Mary Margaret was lying face first into the downed Christmas tree. Stanley straddled the trunk, picked his limp daughter up from among the tinsel, bent boughs and smashed bulbs, and handed her to her worried mother.

"What's wrong with Mary Margaret?" JC asked.

Mabel hugged her baby girl to her chest and kissed her forehead. Mary Margaret threw up. Mabel turned her head to the side, curled her mouth and looked at Stanley. "I think Daddy got his drinks mixed up. She reeks of rum."

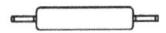

Gordon picked up the receiver, but, once again, put it back down. She must have read my note by now, he thought. He opened another beer, plopped down on a chair and looked at the one brightly wrapped package nestled below the saggy boughs of his pathetic Christmas tree. He raised his bottle in the air. "I did this for you, ya know," he said and took a swig. He put his head back and closed his eyes, picturing Dr. MacLellan snuggled up next to Charlotte with his arm over her shoulder. "At least he's got a good job," he whispered under his breath. He was nodding off when he heard the phone.

"Hello."

"Sorry it's late. I just got off work and the place was crazy. I saw that guy again."

Gordon was glad to hear from the kid from Arlies, but disappointed it wasn't Charlotte. "When?"

"Around five. He was comin outa the Clerk's Office. I tried to see where he was goin, but my boss hollered for me to get back to work."

Gordon hung up. It wasn't much to go on. People were always coming and going out of one of the town's busiest offices. Still, it was the second time the kid saw the suspected shoplifter in the area. At least he knew he was still in town. He looked at his neatly folded uniform on a chair in the hall, thinking he shouldn't put it off much longer. He'd return it in the morning and hopefully have another word with McEwan.

He walked back to the phone and began dialling. "Hello, this is Gordon Dunphy. Yes, I called a few days ago to report a missing person. Ted Collins. I already checked it out. He wasn't there. Yes, I checked the hospitals. It's just not like him. No, he has no immediate family in the area. It's possible, but I doubt it. He would have told one of his friends if he was leaving for an extended period of time. I understand. Still, you have my number, let me know if you hear anything. Great, thanks."

He hung up. "Goddammit, Ted! Where the hell are you?"

"What do you mean you didn't lay the charges?" Gladys asked.

"What's the point! I can't afford a lawyer. Besides, he'd just get a slap on the wrist."

"So yer just gonna let him get away with it?"

"I got no choice," Dan said impatiently.

Gladys heard the knock and answered the door. "Lizzie! What a lovely surprise."

"Not too late I hope." She handed her an envelope. "Just makin the rounds with my Christmas cards. I refuse to pay the outrageous postage. Up to four cents a letter. Anyways, always thought it more special to pass on my greetings in person."

"How kind of you. Take off yer coat and sit for a bit. I was just about to put on a fresh pot. And I made fruit cake."

"Love fruit cake," Lizzie said.

Gladys filled the kettle and almost gasped when she turned around. Her friend was wearing a silky, green blouse that left half of her breasts exposed.

Lizzie applied a fresh coat of scarlet lipstick and smacked her lips together. "Do you like my new holiday blouse?"

"It's...lovely. But ya might want to do it up more," Gladys said, gesturing for her to button up.

Lizzie did as told. "That better?"

"Much."

"Dan home?" Lizzie asked.

"He's in the living room, listenin to Max Ferguson."

Lizzie stopped in the doorway, returned her blouse to its revealing state and ran her hands down her skin-tight, black skirt. She ducked her head into the living room. "Hello, Dan."

Dan stared at her chest and smiled. "Hi, there. You look nice," he said, thinking he should at least try and be charitable.

"My new holiday outfit. You don't look so bad yerself. Joinin us for tea?"

He held up his empty cup. "Just finished one."

Lizzie sat next to him on the couch, making small talk and offering up an eyeful of her best assets. She moved closer, put her hand on his leg and pulled his collar back. "How's that neck of yers comin along?" she asked.

Dan knew the horny, old slut was coming onto him. He grinned. "Neck is fine," he said. He picked up her hand, kissed her palm and pressed it down on his crotch. "This could use some attention."

"Tea's ready," Gladys called from the kitchen.

Lizzie slowly pulled her hand away. "Coming," she called out, redoing her top buttons. She leaned in and whispered, "I could use a drive home."

Dan looked down at his growing excitement. Gladys did tell me I should give her something for helping me get the job, he thought. I'll just keep my eyes closed.

Lizzie's hand shook when she put her teacup on its saucer. She reached for her coat. "I really should get going."

"But you haven't finished your tea...or tried my fruit cake," Gladys said.

"I'll take a piece to go. I hate to run off, but another busy day tomorrow. Can I use yer phone to call a cab?"

"I'm sure Dan won't mind giving you a ride."

"I don't mind at all," Dan said, putting his teacup in the sink.

They drove to the Number Eleven coal heaps. Dan started to have second thoughts, but he was ready to burst. He slammed the car in park. Lizzie wriggled her arms free of her coat and leaned in to kiss him. He quickly put his face between the hollow of her breasts, then reached up and tore her blouse open. Ten minutes later, he zipped up, hoping he hadn't opened a can of worms. "Better get you home," he said, trying not to look at her hideous face.

Lizzie was sliding her arm into the sleeve of her torn blouse. Her face was streaked with black mascara and her mouth smeared with her red, waxy lipstick.

They didn't speak so much as a word to one another, until Dan pulled up to her company house. "Night," he said.

She tried one last time to kiss him.

He turned his head. "Let's not get carried away. I'm not lookin for a wife… *or* a girlfriend."

Lizzie stepped out of the car, watched him drive away and wept.

Ho...Ho...Ho and Off You Go

Friday, Dec. 20

Gordon waited for the desk sergeant to put his sandwich down. "How's it going?" he asked, handing him his uniform.

"Not bad," he said, clapping his hands free of crumbs and licking his fingers clean of egg salad. He tossed Gordon's newly-pressed jacket and creased pants on a chair. "And you?"

"I'm okay. McEwan in?"

"He's in with Big Dick. Shouldn't be much longer."

Gordon walked into the hall and looked up at the black and white portraits of the stern-looking men who had led the force over the years. He put his head down, thinking of the time he had asked Chief Peach why his portrait wasn't among them. He had smiled, saying it was an honour he believed should be reserved for the dead.

Gordon turned back to the desk sergeant and pointed to the wall. "You need to put Chief Peach's photo up there."

He shrugged. "McEwan's lookin into it. Said it wouldn't be right to put his own up, before we put up the chief's."

"Since when did we start hanging photos of acting chiefs?" Gordon asked.

"Since the acting chief decided we should," McEwan said from the hallway. "You here to see me?"

"Yes."

"Make it quick. I gotta a shitload of crap on my desk and an important meeting at eleven."

"The clerk at Arlies tells me he thinks the guy who stole Myrtle's painting is still around. Wondering if you might have a chat with the kid and maybe have the guys keep a look out for him."

"You want me to assign my officers to look for a guy who… maybe…maybe stole a painting. You do know it's Christmas, *right*? Look, I know you want to believe the boys are innocent, but this notion you have that this mysterious thief is somehow tied to the assault is just plain crazy. Face it, the evidence points to Kenny and his pals. Jesus, Gordon, ya gotta let it go. It's not your job anymore."

"No, *it's yours*, but you don't seem to want to do it."

"Oh, I'm doing it all right. And ya know what I'm *not doing*? I'm not wasting the department's lean manpower on a stupid stakeout. Jesus, it's a good thing you quit before I fired you."

Gordon was doing all he could not to pummel him.

"By the way, are you behind all those posters blowin all over the place? The ones offering the big reward?"

"What if I am?"

McEwan shook his head. "We both know Kenny ditched the change purse. But, hell, don't let me stop ya. It's up to you if ya wanna throw good money away on some cockamamie theory. *Oh*, and tell your buddy, MacIntyre, that if he even looks at Dan McInnes again, I'll nail his hide to the wall."

The desk sergeant cupped the receiver. "Hey, Chief. It's Shedden's Studios on the phone. They're running behind. Want to know if you can sit for your portrait at one, instead of eleven?"

McEwan glared at his desk sergeant.

Despite his growing anger, Gordon grinned. "I can see you're busy."

McEwan started to walk away and turned around. "I heard you're applyin to the Mounties. Ya know, Gordon, ya could've asked me for a reference."

"Thanks, but I needed someone who could spell R.C.M.P."

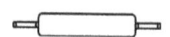

Gladys opened the door and spotted the gold button wedged between the crevice of the seat and backrest. She picked it up and put it in her pocket. Lizzie would be happy to know she didn't have to search for a match, or switch out all of the buttons on her holiday blouse. She waited for her nephew to lock up the house and join her. Dan jumped in and started the car. Gladys was idly chatting away, when another flash of gold near Dan's feet caught her eye. How strange, she thought, stopping mid-sentence.

"*What?*" Dan asked.

"Nothing," she said, thinking back to the previous night. Lizzie had left abruptly and it seemed to take Dan an unusually long time to return home. It's not possible she thought. Lizzie is so much older and, despite her sometimes questionable appearance, she was a God-fearing woman who wouldn't dare participate in such disgraceful behaviour. Still, to lose two buttons.

Dan turned down Highland Street. "You were about to ask me something?"

"Oh, yes. I was just wonderin…how do ya like workin with Lizzie?"

"She's all right?"

"I was thinkin bout invitin her and her sister, Izzie, over for Christmas dinner?"

"Her sister's name is *Izzie*? *You can't be serious*?"

Gladys adjusted her purse on her lap. "Izzie for Isabel… Lizzie for Elizabeth. They had a brother, but he died from consumption when he was nine or ten."

"Let me guess. His name was…Tizzie?" Dan said, shaking his head and chuckling.

"No. Bruce. So, what do you think about inviting them for dinner?"

"You're jokin, *right*?"

"No. Lizzie could use a break. Her sister's not right in the head. And it would be a nice thank you for all—"

Dan started to laugh. "*Lizzie's* not right in the head. How the hell did you two ever become friends? Yer as different as night and day. You do know her reputation round town?"

"She's a kind woman with a good soul. Look what she did for you? Granted, she might not always dress appropriately, but ya shouldn't judge a book by its cover. She does a lot of good work for the Benevolent Society…and not everythin ya hear is true."

Dan thought of Lizzie leaning in for a kiss. "If it's all the same to you, I'd prefer if ya didn't. She can sometimes be a little…I dunno….clingy." He pulled into a spot along Commercial Street.

Gladys felt she needed to test her troubling theory. She pointed. "What's that by your foot?"

Dan looked down. Fuck, he thought. "Looks like some kind of bauble. Likely belonged to whoever used to own the car."

"I think that's one of the buttons from Lizzie's new blouse. Must've popped off," Gladys said, studying his reaction.

Dan picked it up and handed it to her. "Here! Ya can ask her the next time ya see her," he said, slapping it into her hand.

He watched his aunt enter Woolworths, worried she might have put two and two together, then headed to the Clerk's Office. Lizzie was standing at her station. "Good morning," he said, quickly rushing past her. Lizzie never acknowledged his greeting. Dan glanced at her throughout the morning. She was unusually quiet, efficiently dealing with her clients, without her normal, playful banter. Jesus, she's trying to make me feel guilty, he thought. Sorry, you ugly, old witch, ya got what ya asked for. He pulled his adding machine in closer and began tapping in numbers. He turned when he heard the familiar voice.

"Hello, Lizzie. Woolworth's got its Friday special on. Jig's dinner. Want to join me for lunch? We can use my discount." Gladys smiled and waved to her nephew.

The two old friends sat at Woolworth's counter, sharing the latest rumours making the rounds and waiting for Rosie to take their orders. Gladys reached into her purse and uncurled her fingers. Lizzie looked down at the small, golden disc and then up at her friend. "Is that my button? I didn't even realize it was missin." She picked it off Gladys' palm and bent down to put it in her purse. When she sat up, Gladys was holding another gold button under her friend's nose.

"Actually, I found two…*in Dan's car,*" Gladys said, raising her eyebrows. Even under Lizzie's thick, creamy, orange rouge, Gladys could see she was blushing.

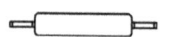

Amour waited at the back entrance of the hospital for Michael to come for her. She looked at the time, wondering what could be keeping her always punctual husband. She promised Mabel she'd be home by four to help with last minute preparations, and she was already a half hour late.

An ambulance pulled up to the bay and the attendants jumped out and quickly removed the stretcher. Amour blessed herself and briefly prayed for a good outcome. Twenty minutes later, she was pacing. "Damn you, Michael," she said and picked up the phone to call Bay Taxi.

She arrived home to a flurry of activity. Mabel was barking out orders like a drill sergeant. The housekeeper was to get the kids bathed and dressed, Stanley was to vacuum and water the tree, and Mary Catherine was to lay out the assorted meats, and day-old sweets Mabel had brought home from the bakery.

"I'm so sorry," Amour said. "I don't know what happened to Michael. He was supposed to pick me up over an hour ago. He said he had to drop by the office, but wouldn't be long. No doubt has his head down reading reports and lost track of time."

"Blame me," Stanley said, entering the kitchen. "I asked him to pick up the libations. On a Friday night, and with all the Christmas parties…place will be a madhouse." He didn't mention that Michael was also going back to the Clerk's Office to complete the deed transfer he never got to finish the day of the encounter with McInnes.

Amour peeled hard boiled eggs. "Dr. MacLellan refused to allow Myrtle to attend the party, but he didn't rule out the possibility she could be discharged for Christmas day. *Oh*, and Charlotte said she's coming." She looked at the time, growing angrier by the minute.

Mabel surveyed the kitchen, did some last minute tidying up and went upstairs to get ready. "No word on Ted?" she asked Stanley.

Stanley sat on the edge of the bed to change his socks "No. Gordon talked to the County Police, but they said there's nothing they can do."

"He had to have gone away," Mabel said.

"Without telling anyone?"

Mabel was pulling her dress over her head when they heard the knock on the front door. "Damn," she said. "It's not even six-thirty yet. You'll have to get it."

Mabel chuckled when she heard the unmistakable voice and then the apology. For the first time Mabel could ever remember, Mary Mack was early.

Amour entered Mabel's room, tilting her head to attach her clip on earring. "I could shoot Michael. He knows he's responsible for the drinks, and the guests are already arriving."

"I'm sure he'll be home soon. By the way, you look lovely," Mabel said.

It was going on seven and a good number of the guests had already arrived, but there was still no sign of Michael. Stanley was beginning to worry he'd run out of booze, if he didn't show up soon. Amour called the coal company, but couldn't get through. Her anger began to turn to concern, as more and more guests arrived, including Luke and Alice who provided a momentary distraction as everyone gathered around to offer their congratulations to the returning honeymooners.

Stanley was examining his near-empty quart of rum, when he heard the loud thumping on the back step. Santa was stomping his shiny black boots on the mat and throwing his large, red sack over his shoulder. Stanley opened the door and laughed. "Get in here. And you better have some libations in that bag of yours."

Charlotte waved good night to Myrtle and put her coat on. She wondered if Gordon would be at the party. He likely wouldn't come if he thought I was going to be there, she thought. He didn't even return my things like I asked.

She was near the exit when Dr. MacLellan charged toward her. He grabbed her by the arm. "Come with me," he said, quickly leading her down the hall. Charlotte looked at the blood-soaked face and the crushed forehead of a man she knew would soon be deceased. He was moaning and trying to talk. She bent over him and clasped his hand. "You're in the hospital. Everything will be fine," she kept repeating, knowing the last thing he was likely to hear, was a lie. The weaker his grip got, the tighter she squeezed. "Stay with me. Stay with me," she pleaded.

Dr. MacLellan roughly jabbed a syringe through his pant leg, into his thigh. "The morphine will ease your pain," he said.

Charlotte wiped away the blood pooling in his eyes and smiled. "My name is Charlotte. And I'm not going anywhere. I'm staying right here with you." He nodded, gasped and began coughing up blood. Charlotte looked up at Dr. MacLellan. He was shaking his head.

Charlotte wondered if her patient knew he was dying and if he was scared. She prayed his suffering would end. Her prayers were quickly answered. His head fell limply to the side. Charlotte continued to hold his hand.

Dr. MacLellan put his hands on her arms. "He's gone."

Charlotte leaned in and kissed the dead man's bloody forehead and fell into Dr. MacLellan's arms sobbing. He led her to a chair, squatted in front of her. "There's nothing more we could have done. He's at peace, now."

"I...I...I know," she said, struggling for air between sobs. "It's still...har...har...hard. Especially at...at...this time of year."

The ambulance attendant approached. "There's another body out back. D.O.A."

"Was it a car accident?" Dr. MacLellan asked.

"No. Another accident at Number Twenty-Six. Tram brakes failed. Jumped the tracks and smashed into the coalface."

"Any idea who the deceased is?"

"No, but the other guy was the director of coal operations. Has six kids. Youngest is four."

Dr. MacLellan took off the deceased's coat and removed a bloody envelope tucked in the inside pocket. He opened it up. "It's a copy of a deed. It's in the name of Michael Donnely."

Gordon was heading to the party when the phone rang. He had his hand on the doorknob, considering whether or not to answer. He had given up hearing from Charlotte. It was six days since he dropped her belongings off at the hospital, and yet she didn't get in touch. He stepped outside, then suddenly realized it might be the County Police calling about Ted. "Hello. *Charlotte!* What's wrong? *What*? You need to slow down. Oh, my God. When? They don't know? Yes, of course. Yes, I understand. I'm on my way."

Gordon hung up, stunned by Charlotte's news. He thought of the happy gathering they were about to disrupt and the latest gut-wrenching scene he was about to witness. He raced down the front steps and sped to the hospital.

Dr. MacLellan and Charlotte were standing out front. Gordon put his head down when the handsome doctor embraced Charlotte, reminding himself that she had called him for help, not to rekindle their relationship. He leaned over the front seat and threw the passenger door open. Charlotte ran to the car, jumped in and hugged him. "Are you all right?" he asked.

"My God, Gordon! Amour must have just left the hospital when they brought him in. I had no idea who he was. I can't stop crying. They have a young daughter. Amour was just telling me how much she adored her father. It's not fair. It's heartbreaking at any time, *but at Christmas*. God, they're in the middle of a party."

Gordon thought of the heart-wrenching scene at the bridge. He looked at her bloodstained coat. "I think you need to remove your coat."

Charlotte immediately undid the buttons and peeled it off her shoulders. "Thank you for doing this. I wasn't sure who else to call."

He reached in his pocket and passed her his hankie. "I'm glad you called. Just sorry it's under these circumstances."

"What am I going to tell Amour?"

"The truth."

"I can't. It was awful. You couldn't even see his face. And he was holding my hand and trying to talk. Then he started spitting up blood."

"Sometimes it's easier to spare the grieving the truth. Tell her he said he loved her."

"I can't do that!"

"Yes, you can. And you have to!"

Charlotte blew her nose. "I'm drawing a blank. I can't remember their daughter's name."

Gordon thought of Amour passing him the sketch of Myrtle's change purse. "It's Victoria."

Charlotte kept repeating her name. "Victoria…Victoria…Victoria."

Gladys put Dan's tea in front of him. "I'd like for you to come to church on Sunday."

"I'm not the church-going type."

"It might do you some good. You could meet people. Maybe a nice, young lady."

Dan laughed. "I'm not looking for a woman in my life."

Gladys closed her eyes. It was a conversation she dreaded, but she also knew she had to at least try and save his troubled soul. "I know you look at those filthy magazines."

Dan dropped his head.

"I'm not a stupid woman. I know you have urges. All men do. That's what a wife is for. You're a good lookin man… and ya've got a good job now. There's lots of pretty, young women hopin to meet a guy like you. Ya should be settlin down and getting a place of yer own. Maybe have some—"

Dan's head shot up. *"Oh, so that's what this is about.* You want me outta here!"

"That's not what I'm sayin. It's just well...well I don't think Lizzie is right for you. She's much older and —"

"*Lizzie?* Have you lost your marbles? I'm not interested in Lizzie! She's grotesque."

"I didn't find just one button in your car. I found two," she said, trying to keep her hands from shaking.

Dan stood up and dumped his tea in the sink. "So, ya found a couple of her buttons. She was pretty much bustin out of her blouse to begin with. I don't know what yer thinkin, but yer crazy if ya think I'd touch that woman. What the hell did you two talk about, *anyway?*"

Gladys began to wonder if he might be telling the truth. "Lizzie said nothing happened. Said you were a gentleman."

"*Then?*"

"Then, I guess I'm mistaken," Gladys said, nervously twisting her wedding ring.

"Yer damn right you are!"

"Still, I want ya to consider comin to church? It's not gonna do you any harm. Actually, ya might enjoy it."

"I'll think about it," he lied.

"And I want you to get rid of that trash under yer bed."

"I'll burn them tonight," he lied again.

Gladys smiled. "And I don't want ya sayin such mean things about Lizzie. Whatever else ya think, she's a good woman. When I told her ya collected the reward for the missin change purse, she was really happy for ya. Said it couldn't have happened to a better person."

Dan stared at his aunt in disbelief. "*You told Lizzie I collected the reward?*"

"Yes?"

"*Why?*"

"Why not?" Gladys asked.

Dan clenched his teeth. "Cause it's none of her goddamn business, *that's why!* Jesus, do you have to tell her everything? She's a friggin news bag...for Christ sakes."

"I saw no harm in it."

Dan gave a dismissive wave and stormed off.

Gladys jumped when he slammed his bedroom door. She sat looking down the hall, wondering why such a small thing had set him off. She put her palm on the table, pushed down and wearily got up from her chair. It must be his unattended urges, she thought. I need to find him a wife.

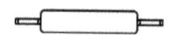

Stanley elbowed his way through the noisy, crowded kitchen and into the living room. "Kids we have a special visitor. Amour, you come, too," he said, waving for her to follow.

Santa swung his sack onto the floor. "Ho…Ho…Ho. Merry Christmas!" he said, in a deep, throaty voice.

The adults made way for all the kids to run to the jolly man in his red suit, and black boots and gloves. Mary Margaret didn't care for the scary, white-bearded stranger. She backed away and wrapped her arms around her father's leg. Amour smiled at Santa and playfully wagged her finger at him. Her late husband was forgiven for being so tardy and for planning such a special surprise.

"Did you know about this?" Amour asked Mabel.

"I swear I had no idea. *And you think I worry too much,*" she said and laughed.

Stanley started digging through Santa's bag in hopes of replenishing his thirsty guests. Fred Clarke tapped him on the shoulder. "Where's Lily and the kids?"

Stanley straightened up. "I thought they were coming with you and Aggie?"

"She said you were picking them up."

"*Me?*" Stanley said, wondering if he forgot.

"Want me to go and check on her?" Fred asked.

"Do you mind?"

Santa handed brightly coloured packages to his eager recipients. Stanley leaned in and whispered in his ear. "Where's the liquor?"

"There's a quart of rum in the trunk of my car."

"*Ted?*" Stanley said.

Ted winked and chuckled. "Saint Nicklaus to you."

Stanley stood up and looked at Amour smiling at the man behind the beard. Like him, she assumed it was Michael. Stanley was relieved Ted was okay, but started to panic. He picked up Mary Margaret and nodded for Mabel to join him in the hall.

"Thank goodness he's home. I was beginning to worry," Mabel said.

"It's Ted," Stanley said.

"Where?" Mabel said, scanning the room.

"*Santa*. It's not Michael. *It's Ted*," he whispered.

"Then where the hell is Michael?" Mabel asked.

Stanley looked into the kitchen at Amour and Victoria laughing at Santa's antics. "I have no idea."

The front door opened. Charlotte walked in with a blotchy, tear-stained face. Gordon followed behind, with an expression Stanley immediately knew spelt trouble.

Fred Clarke drove up to Lily's pitch dark company house. He probably just missed her, and she was already at the party. He was about to pull away, when Lily's neighbour waved from his step. Fred rolled down his window. "Hey, Nipper. How's it goin, bud?"

"Good."

"See yer still hauling on the fags."

Nipper held up his makin. "Not sure what's gonna put me in the grave first, dees or dah wife. She hates em. Makin me freeze me arse off out here. Gonna catch me death a cold."

"I guess I just missed Lily?"

"By bout four hours. Went to the mainland to spend Christmas with her sister."

Fred turned his mouth down. "Didn't know she had a sister?" Nipper shrugged and flicked his butt into the snow. "Merry Christmas," Fred said, rolling his window back up. He drove back to the party, thinking it odd that Lily never mentioned anything about going away for the holidays. She had said she and the kids were looking forward to the party. When he pulled into the yard, Mabel and Stanley were huddled together on the front step with Gordon and another woman he didn't recognize. He was about to approach them, but backed off when Mabel fell into her husband's arms, crying.

Amour was admiring Mary Margaret's new dolly and trying to reassure the frightened toddler that Santa was a good man who loved little boys and girls. She looked up and saw Mabel and Stanley come through the front door, followed by Gordon and Charlotte, and knew something was wrong. Stanley picked up Mary Margaret, and Mabel took Amour by the hand. Amour's heart was pounding. "What is it?" she asked, looking from one grim face to the other.

"Come with me," Mabel said, leading her up the stairs.

"You're scaring me," Amour said.

Mabel had her sit on the bed. "It's Michael. There's been an accident."

Amour gave her a confused look. "But...but he's downstairs. He's—"

"It's Ted. *Ted is Santa.* Amour, I'm so sorry. Michael is gone," she said, immediately struck by the finality of her words.

Amour brought her hand to her mouth and shook her head. *"No!* He's downstairs. He's Santa."

Mabel tried hugging her, but Amour shoved her away and stood up. "No!" she repeated, more defiantly.

"I'm so sorry. He went to the mine and the—"

"No! It's not true. It can't be true," she said and tore out of the room. She ran downstairs, roughly pushed the partygoers out of the way and charged at Santa, angrily ripping off his beard. She held it to her chest, fell to her knees and screamed, *"Noooo!"*

Victoria entered and looked around at the stunned observers. "Mom! Mommy! What's wrong?"

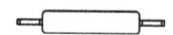

Mabel laid next to Amour and Victoria, listening to their muffled cries, hoping her presence, if not her words, brought them some comfort. She could hear one car door after the other slam shut and the snow crunch under the tires of her departing, heartsick guests. She pinched her eyes shut, the image of Amour sobbing and Victoria calling out for her *daddy* would be forever seared into her mind.

She waited for Amour's breathing to fall into a slow, steady rhythm, then silently cried over her own loss. She loved Michael, not just for the kind man he was, but for the joy he brought to his wife and daughter.

The black room slowly brightened from a light seeping in from the hallway. Mabel lifted her head off her wet pillow and peeked over her shoulder. Mary Catherine was standing in the doorway, holding Mary Margaret's small hand. Mabel gently raised her arm off of Amour's waist, eased herself off the bed and went into the hall.

"How are they?" Mary Catherine asked.

"As expected. They're asleep now."

Mary Catherine offered a sad smile. "God love them." She looked down at Mary Margaret. "Little Miss Muffet, here, wants her mother to read to her."

Mabel knelt down and took Mary Margaret's doll from her. "She's beautiful. Auntie Amour is not feeling well, and Mommy needs to stay with her for a little while. You can sleep in Mommy and Daddy's bed, and Mary Catherine will read you and your new dolly *Smokey the Cowhorse*. Okay?" she said, passing her doll back to her. Mary Margaret put her arms around her mother's neck. Mabel stifled a sob and looked up at Mary Catherine. "They might not fully comprehend, but they know." Mabel stood up. "Who's downstairs?"

"Most have left. Fred and Aggie are on their way out. Sam took the kids and JC back to our place."

Mabel nodded, watched them walk down the hall to her room and returned to the bed and the two broken souls she knew would never again be the same.

Fred held Aggie's coat open for her.

"Not the night we were hoping for," Stanley said.

"I'm so sorry for your loss. I didn't know him, but I hear he was a lovely man," Aggie said, hanging her purse over the crook of her arm and pulling on her gloves.

Stanley lowered his head. "That he was," he said, opening the door. "Fred? I meant to ask, what happened to Lily and the kids?"

"Apparently, they went to the mainland to spend Christmas with her sister."

Stanley shrugged. "I didn't know she had a sister. Anyway, just as well. Thanks for coming," he said, joining the others in the kitchen. Alice and Charlotte were wrapping the uneaten food and pouring the remains of unfinished drinks in the sink. He held up a spent bottle of whiskey. "Ted, I think we could use that bottle of rum of yours."

Gordon pulled Stanley aside and handed him the bloody envelope. "It was in Michael's jacket. A deed."

Stanley carefully folded it over and put it in his pants pocket. He started to cry. "It was supposed to be a surprise for Amour."

It was after ten when Mabel crept downstairs. She placed the vial of tiny blue pills in front of Luke. "They did the trick," she said, thinking back to the bitter anguish she suffered on the night she thought she had lost JC.

Stanley took the rum from Ted and topped up everyone's drinks and raised his glass. "A toast," he said. "To a great man. A great friend and…" His voice began to crack. "And a devoted husband and father. To Michael Donnely."

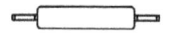

Gordon reached over the seat and squeezed Charlotte's hand. "I'm proud of you. In time, you're words will bring them comfort."

"I lied."

"It was a beautiful lie. Don't you think it's what Michael would have said?" Gordon asked.

Charlotte dropped her head. "I suppose so."

Gordon stopped at the corner of McKeen and Main streets. "I could go left or right?" he asked, praying she would come home with him. He waited for her response.

"Left," she said.

Gordon smiled. They entered the dark house. "Want a drink before bed?" he asked.

"Make it a double. Might help me sleep. I'm going to change," Charlotte said and started up the stairs.

"You can wear one of my shirts."

Charlotte stopped and gave him a puzzled look. "Why wouldn't I wear my nightgown? Did you throw it out?"

"No. I dropped it off at the hospital…like you asked."

"I didn't get it?"

"So, I guess you didn't get my letter either?"

"*What letter?*"

Gordon smiled. "Doesn't matter. Get changed. I'll get our drinks."

Charlotte came downstairs wearing his shirt and wrapped in a blanket. The tree lights were on and Gordon had started a fire. She sat on the sofa with her legs tucked up beside her.

"What do you think of my tree?" Gordon asked, passing her her drink.

"I think it looks…pathetic," she said, laughing. "You need more tinsel…more bells. Maybe some angel hair."

Gordon smiled mischievously. "Or maybe it needs more…*you*."

She felt like her heart was going to burst. "So, tell me about this mysterious letter."

"First, tell me about Dr. MacLellan."

"What about him?"

"I get the sense, you're…I dunno…smitten with him?"

Charlotte grinned, thinking he was jealous. "*Well*...he is very handsome."

Gordon pouted and tilted his head to the side. "Not bad lookin, I guess."

"And he's very sweet and kind. His patients love him."

Gordon shrugged.

"And, of course, he has a fabulous career and buckets of money."

"I suppose he also walks on water," Gordon said.

"Ya gotta admit, he's the perfect catch." She paused and then grinned. "For some other lucky girl."

Gordon scooted closer to her, pulled the blanket over his shoulder and stared at the box under the tree. "The letter. It was an apology."

"*Oh?* For what?"

"For being stupid...a blind ass," he said. He suddenly stood up, picked up the box and handed it to her. "Open it."

"It's not Christmas."

"It's close enough. Go ahead, open it."

Charlotte peeled off the red bow and carefully undid the silver wrapping. "Not a dead cat, I hope?" she said and laughed. She pulled back the flap and looked inside. "*What's this?*"

"Noxema."

"I can see that, but there must be twenty jars."

"Twenty eight, to be exact."

"No wonder I couldn't find it anywhere." She held up the cobalt blue jar, twisting her wrist from side to side. "Why so many?"

He lifted the box from her lap, took out another jar and unscrewed the lid. He put it to his nose, sniffed it and handed it to her. Charlotte gasped when she saw the ring sticking out of the thick, white cream. Her bottom lip began to quiver.

"It was my grandmother's. I'm hoping you'll wear it as my wife?"

Charlotte laid her trembling fingers over her mouth. "But what about the Mounties?"

"I don't know what I was thinking. I'm allergic to horse hair," he said and laughed.

Charlotte threw her arms around his neck. "Of course, I'll marry you!"

Gordon removed the fiery opal, poked his little finger inside the band to remove the creamy substance and playfully dabbed it on the tip of her nose. "A few hours ago, I thought I'd lost you forever. And as gut wrenching as this day has been, I'm happier at this very minute than I've ever been." He slid the ring on her finger and laid his forehead against hers. "I'm getting married and my sexy, beautiful wife is going to have flawless skin for at least another twenty-eight years."

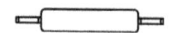

It was going on midnight when Mabel crawled in next to Mary Margaret.

"It was a difficult night," Stanley whispered.

"It's going to be a difficult week and painful Christmas. I dread the thought of tomorrow. I told Alice to close the bakery. I'll take Amour to the morgue. It's going to be awful. Charlotte said to be prepared for the worst."

"I'll go with you," Stanley said.

"No, stay with Victoria and the kids. John said he'd come over and help. Such a sweet boy. He'll be good company for Victoria."

"We'll have to call Michael's brother-in-law and let him know," Mabel said.

"I can do that," Stanley said.

"I don't understand," Mabel said. "Why was Michael in the mine? He hadn't even officially started…and he's…*was*…the president, for goodness sakes."

"He had been hearing rumblings the mine wasn't safe. I guess he wanted to check it out for himself. Apparently they were well founded. I feel like I lost a brother."

Mabel wiped her cheek. "Me too. By the way, where was Ted the past couple of weeks?"

"Ice fishing with his old friend, Clarence. They went to Loch Lomond and got storm stayed."

"I never heard Ted mention that name before?"

"He was the captain of the Sydney Police. He was with Ted the night Ted found JC. Just lost his wife. I guess he needed someone he could relate to."

"But, how did Ted hear about the party?" Mabel asked.

"He didn't. Said that he was sitting home alone, missing Muriel and feeling sorry for himself. They used to always dress up as Mr. and Mrs. Clause, and drop in on friends. I guess he wanted to relive something that would remind him of happier days."

"It's sad they never had children. They would have made great parents, and Ted wouldn't be nearly so lonely. He'd probably be looking forward to Christmas with his grandbabies instead of grieving alone," Mabel said.

"He feels awful about all the confusion."

"It's not his fault. He had no idea what was happening," Mabel said.

Stanley propped himself on his elbow. "I know, but you know Ted."

"I didn't think this night could get any sadder," Mabel said.

"There's one more thing," Stanley said. "Michael bought the old house on South Street. He wanted to surprise Amour. That's why we were at the Clerk's Office the day of my run in with McInnes. It's going to be hard to tell her. Just another painful reminder of what a wonderful man she lost."

Mabel closed her eyes. "Yes, he was a beautiful soul. Amour always loved that house, but I doubt she'd want to live there without him."

"I was thinking the same. Awfully big house for two."

She Friggin Bit Me

Saturday, Dec. 21

Mabel's eyes flashed open. Despite sleeping for less than five hours she felt like she had overslept. She looked at Mary Margaret sprawled on her back and Stanley hanging off his side of the bed. She checked the time and sat up, dreading the day ahead. She walked down the hall and quietly opened the door to Amour's room. Victoria was sleeping, but Amour wasn't beside her.

Mabel was on her way downstairs when she spotted Amour standing before the wall of photos. Just as Amour had comforted her the night they feared something terrible had happened to Stanley, Mabel put her arm over her friend's shoulder.

Amour kept her eyes on the fading pictures. "We all die…some young, some old, some from an agonizing illness, or a tragic turn of events. It's all so random…so unfair. I never really gave it a whole lot of thought before… how tenuous our time together was. I just assumed we'd be together forever. I know this must sound awful, but I'm mad at him." Amour tilted her head back and laughed. "Crazy, *right*?"

Mabel squeezed her shoulder. "No. It's all part of the grieving process."

Amour shook her head. "*Process*…it almost sounds like…like something that has a start and end date. Like one day you'll wake up and puff… just like that, you're over it. I'll never live to see that day."

"It will be hard. And the next few weeks and months will be gruelling. But the heart, like everything else, heals over time," Mabel said.

Amour brushed her cheeks and quickly turned to face her. "Not mine. I hate God for what he did. I hate him, and I will never, ever forgive him," she said angrily. She softened her voice. "I need to see Michael. I need for him to tell me how to breathe. How to move forward without him."

Mabel smiled. "We'll see him soon. But, Amour, as you know, he experienced a severe blow to the head. You need to prepare yourself."

"Charlotte told me he arrived at the hospital just after four. I saw the ambulance pull up. I prayed for whoever was inside…you know, one of those quick throw away prayers you do as a matter of course. Little did I know that it was Michael. He would have known I was there… waiting for him. *God, I was cursing him for being late at the same time as he was dying.* Then, I just hopped in a cab and came home. I always believed that if something terrible ever happened to him, I'd somehow know…somehow sense it. Maybe if I wasn't so angry at him for keeping me waiting, I would have." Amour sucked in her upper lip. "Looks like I'll be waiting for a long time to come. And, right now, that day can't come soon enough."

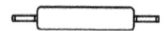

Stanley pulled Victoria's door closed. He'd let her sleep for as long as possible. He hurried downstairs to answer the phone. It was another member of the coal company's board of directors calling to convey their condolences. He hung up and, once again, tried Michael's brother-in-law. Again, no answer. There was a light rap on the door. Fred entered carrying a casserole.

"Thank you, Fred. I'll put it with the other dozen or so. I don't know where we are going to put it… with all of the uneaten food from the party."

"I said the same thing to Aggie, but she said food speeds the healin and ya can never have enough of it. At least Aggie can't," he said and laughed. "God forbid if I drop dead, she'll be as big as a house."

Mary Catherine came from the kitchen and took the casserole from Stanley. "We've taken over Myrtle's fridge."

"So, boss, I know the timin ain't great, but I wanted to tell ya, I had a call from a couple of the guys. They really appreciate the bonus cheques. Wanted me to tell ya it was very generous of you."

"We had a good year. Everybody was a part of it. Everybody should share in it. I hope you're happy with yours?"

"Sure am. But here's the thing...the cheques aren't clearin. Bank claims there's no money in the account. I normally wouldn't bother ya with something like this, especially with what yer all goin through, but being so close to Christmas and all, guys were countin on a few extra bucks to do their shoppin."

"There must be some mistake. There's plenty of money in the account," Stanley said, thinking back to the day he wrote them out. "I must have used my personal cheque book. Unfortunately, there's nothing I can do until the bank opens."

Fred nodded. "Thanks. I'll let the fellas know."

"Wait!" Stanley opened his wallet and handed him all but five dollars. "Talk to the guys and see who needs it the most. And tell them not to worry. I'll fix them up first thing Monday morning."

Fred hesitated at the door. "Boss, ya don't suppose Lily had anything to do with this, do ya?"

"*Lily?*"

"Yeah. After the guys started callin, I got a little suspicious. No one ever heard Lily mention a sister. And she said she was comin to the party."

"Fred, I'm sure it's just a screw up at the bank. Lily would never do anything like that."

"Yeah, yer right. Shoulda kept my big mouth shut."

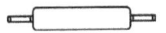

Mabel followed Amour upstairs and settled her into bed. She drew the curtains and went downstairs. John, himself a fatherless child, was sitting next to Victoria on the couch, offering well-meaning, but awkward, words of comfort to his new friend. He gave Mabel a helpless look that made her feel as badly for him, as she did for the young girl he was hoping to console.

Mary Catherine and Alice did their best to make room in the fridge for the latest casserole to arrive.

Stanley wiped Mary Margaret's face. "How did it go?" he asked Mabel.

Mabel shook her head. "It was better than I expected, but still awful," she whispered.

"I finally reached Michael's brother-in-law. He and the twins are devastated. He offered to handle Michael's affairs in London. Notify his co-workers… sell the flat. He's going to call back to speak with Amour."

Mabel nodded and reached for her coat.

"Where are you off to now?" he asked.

"To tell Myrtle about Michael. She never met him, but she's going to be heartbroken for Amour." She hollered into the kitchen. "Mary C! Ready whenever you are."

Mary Catherine joined her and Stanley at the door.

Mabel hugged Stanley. "We shouldn't be too long. Check on Amour from time to time, but don't wake her up if she's sleeping. And do your best to keep Victoria distracted."

Stanley watched them get in the car and drive off.

"Every time I close my eyes I see Michael's face. It's hard to imagine he wasn't killed instantly," Mabel said to Mary Catherine.

They turned onto Sterling Road. "Would have been better if he was."

"I know the folks at the morgue did their best to make him presentable, but he still looked horrific. I had to turn away. I can't imagine how Amour managed to get through it. She was so strong."

"Do you think she's in shock?" Mary Catherine asked.

"I don't know. She was very stoic. I left her alone so she could say her goodbyes and she just came out of the room and said she wanted to go home. Asked if I'd tell Myrtle and apologize to her for not going to visit."

"Do you think Amour will be okay? I mean financially?"

"Yes, I'm sure of it. Michael was very responsible. And they have the flat in London. God, he was a good man." Mabel picked at her nails. "He bought their old property on South Street."

Mary Catherine glanced at Mabel. "Amour never mentioned anything to me about that?"

"She doesn't know. He planned on giving her the deed for Christmas. I can't imagine she'd want to live there. Too many painful reminders of what's been stolen from her."

"But they did have a history there," Mary Catherine said, pulling into the hospital.

They entered Myrtle's room, surprised to see her sitting up in a chair. She quietly took in the sad news without saying a word. She then slowly walked to the cupboard, gathered up her shoes and clothes, and went into the bathroom.

Mary Catherine looked at Mabel. "What's she doing?"

"I think she's making a break for it," Mabel said.

"But she just can't get up and leave!"

Myrtle opened the bathroom door. "Let em a...a...arrest me."

Mabel approached her. "Myrtle, I'm not sure it's wise to leave before—"

Myrtle headed for the corridor. "Are...ya...ya...comin...or not?"

Mabel and Mary Catherine ran behind their quick-footed friend as she whisked past the nurses' station.

"Wait a minute!" one of the nurses called out. She ran up to her escaping patient and grabbed her by the wrist. "Where do you think you're going? Let's go back to your room and...Ouch!" she screamed, shaking her hand in the air. "She friggin bit me!"

Mabel and Myrtle disappeared out of sight.

Mary Catherine stood wide-eyed with her hand over her mouth. "We'll have her back in a couple of hours," she said.

"Keep her," the nurse muttered, bending her head to more closely examine the white indentations of Myrtle's teeth.

Mary Catherine burst out laughing. "Wait up," she hollered, running down the hall.

Charlotte pointed to the display of magazines in the window of MacLeod's Bookstore. "Let's see if they have the latest issue of *Life?*"

Gordon followed her inside and surveyed the packed shelves of new and used books. He could hear Lizzie MacNeil whispering an aisle over. "I'm sorry, Fiona. I can't help it. I'm heartsick. He was such a good lookin man, and we dated for quite a while. There was a time I thought he was the one. Such an awful tragedy."

"Didn't he marry a rich widow? The one that used to own the fancy restaurant?" Fiona asked.

Lizzie took out a hankie and dabbed at her mascara-smeared eyes.

"Oh, now stop that foolishness. No need getting all maudlin on me. I asked ya out, so ya could help me with the last of my shoppin," Fiona said.

Lizzie put her hankie back in her purse. "Yer right." She picked up a mystery novel. "What about this one?"

Fiona turned it over and checked out the price. "*Are ya crazy!* I didn't win the friggin Irish Sweepstakes. Besides, I'm married to the guy, not datin him. Look for somethin under four dollars."

Charlotte paid for her magazine, and she and Gordon stepped out onto the sidewalk. They were about to continue with their Christmas shopping, when Charlotte suddenly stopped and patted her pockets. "Here, hold this," she said, slapping her magazine into Gordon's chest. "I must have left my gloves inside."

Lizzie and Fiona came out.

"Everything in there is way too dear for me," Fiona said. She pointed to the fading poster on the pole. "What I wouldn't do to lay my hands on that right now."

Lizzie pulled her collar around her neck. "Too late fer that. A colleague of mine already claimed it. Do ya wanna grab a cup of tea?"

"Excuse me," Gordon said, approaching Lizzie. "Did you say a colleague of yours collected the reward?"

Lizzie flashed a smile. "Well, hello there. Merry Christmas."

Gordon smiled. "Merry Christmas. Lizzie, who is it you said collected the reward?"

"Dan McInnes."

"He told *you* that?" Gordon asked, thinking Sam or Charlie would have told him if someone turned in the change purse.

"No, not exactly. His aunt did. Gladys Ferguson."

"You're sure?" Gordon asked, puzzled by the news.

"I didn't make it up," Lizzie said, wondering why the former captain of the local police would be so interested.

Charlotte came out of MacLeod's and waved her gloves in the air. "Got em!"

Gordon rushed her to the car. "I need to go see Sam," he said, telling her about his conversation with Lizzie.

He knocked on Sam's door, waited, then turned to Charlotte sitting in the car. She rolled down the window and hollered. "They're probably at Synagogue."

Gordon jumped back in the car, recalling the clerk from Arlies say the guy who might have taken Myrtle's painting was seen outside the Clerk's Office. His mind was racing. He backed the car up. "I think I might know who attacked Myrtle," he said, explaining his theory.

Charlotte shook her head. "Once a cop, always a cop." She licked the tip of her middle finger and flipped the page of her glossy magazine. "Elsie Ferguson died," she said.

Gordon thought the name was familiar. *Elsie Ferguson. Elsie Ferguson.* It suddenly hit him. That's the woman Judge Kennedy had said he had been in love with. He thought back to their last conversation at Woolworths when the judge urged him to marry Charlotte and forget about his fixation on a married woman. He stopped at the end of Sam's driveway and waited for the oncoming traffic to pass. "Was she one of your patients?"

Charlotte started to laugh. *"One of my patients?"*

Gordon looked at her, wondering what was so funny.

She leaned against the passenger door and held the magazine open, showing him the two-page spread declaring *Broadway Stage and Silent Film Star, Dies Suddenly.* "She's a famous actress. *What*, you've never heard of her?"

Gordon smiled, thinking of the judge's clever ruse. "Actually, I have. I hear she left a lot of broken hearts in her wake."

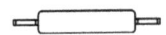

Mabel sat with Myrtle in the backseat. "Myrtle, you shouldn't have bit her."

"Sha...sha...she shouldn't been hol...holdin on...ta me...like that."

Mary Catherine looked in the rear view mirror. "I thought it was hysterical. And we could all use a good laugh right now."

Mabel closed her eyes, thinking of Michael laid out on his cold, metal table, and Amour kissing his caved in forehead. She then looked at Myrtle's head wrapped in white gauze. "Still, they're not going to be too happy with you when we take you back."

"Na...not goin back," Myrtle said firmly.

They entered the house. JC charged at Mrtyle and wrapped his arms around her legs.

"Careful!" Mabel cautioned. "Myrtle has a sore head."

Myrtle smiled and squatted next to JC. "I...ma...missed ma..my big boy," she said, tapping the tip of his nose.

"What's wrong with your head?" he asked, gently touching her forehead.

"Na...nothin time wa...won't heal." Myrtle stood, unbuttoned her coat and laid it on the back of a chair near the entrance to the living room. She then took JC by the hand and followed Mabel and Mary Catherine into the kitchen.

Mabel smiled at the teary-eyed, young woman sitting with John and sipping her Iron Brew. "Victoria, this is Myrtle, your mother's best friend," said Mabel.

Myrtle hugged the grieving child and kissed her cheek. "I na... never met ya...yer...fa...father. Ba...but...he...had to be a goo...good man. I'm...sa...sorry.

Victoria ran the back of her hand under her eyes. "Thank you."

"I saw...ya...your sketch. Va...very good. Ya...you could....ta...teach me a tha...thing or ta...two."

Mabel gasped. Mary Margaret toddled in, dragging a white, linen cloth with gold fringes across the floor. Mabel rushed to her. "Mary Margaret! Where did you find this?" she asked, taking it from her daughter's tiny hand.

Mary Margaret began to cry. Mabel hugged her and brushed her bangs back. "I'm sorry, sweetie. Mommy's not mad at you. I'm happy you found it." It took several minutes for Mabel to reassure the frightened child she did nothing wrong. Mary Margaret took her mother by the hand, led her into the living room and pointed to Myrtle's coat.

"You found it in Myrtle's coat?" Mabel asked.

Mary Margaret shook her head. "Pocket."

Myrtle looked bewildered. "Na...na...never seen...it...be...fore in ma... my la...life."

Mabel smiled. "It doesn't matter. I'm just glad to have it back. I thought I had lost it forever. One of the nurses must have thought it was your scarf and put it with your coat." She closed her eyes and looked up. "Thank you, God," she whispered and blessed herself.

Myrtle swatted Mabel's arm. "Now, ta...take me to her...or...or I'll ba... bite yew."

Amour opened her bleary eyes, then let them fall shut, the image of a head wrapped in a white turban lingering in her dreamy mind. She opened them a second time and slowly propped herself up on her elbow. "*Myrtle?*" she said groggily. "What are you doing here?"

Myrtle smiled and pinched her eyes closed, concentrating on getting her words from her head to her tongue. "Sa...sitting with ma...my friend. You wa...were there for me when my ha...head was broken. Now...I'm ha... here for... ya...your bro...broken heart."

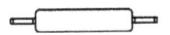

Sam ran to the phone. "Hello."

"Hey, Gordon. No, I just got in. I had a meeting with the Jewish council after Synagogue. What's going on? *What?* No. What's this all about? *Dan McInnes?* Well, he's lying. Charlie would have told me. I have no idea why he'd claim he collected the reward. It must be some kind of mistake. Maybe Lizzie got her wires crossed. Of course, it's worth looking into. Yes, I know. Still be careful about what you say to McEwan. As you know, he and McInnes go way back. The arraignment for the boys won't be until the new year. You're engaged? *When?* Congratulations. When's the wedding? The spring. Yes, it helps to have a steady income. So you've given up on the Mounties? I'm really happy for you. Charlotte's a great girl. Yes, I'd like that. We even have a tree. Mary Catherine made me. Let me know what you hear? Yes, I'll double check with Charlie. Thank you. And Merry Christmas to you."

Mary Catherine came through the door with Irwin and Ruth.

"How is Amour?" he asked.

Mary Catherine told him what she knew of Amour and Mabel's visit to the morgue, and about Myrtle's escape from the hospital. "I promised the nurse I'd take her back in a couple of hours, but Myrtle will have none of it. Says she's misses her own bed and no one's gonna make her go back."

"I just got off the phone with Gordon. He and Charlotte are engaged."

Mary Catherine smiled. "I knew he'd come to his senses."

Ruth pulled on her father's pant leg. "Look what I got, Papa," she said.

Sam squatted beside her. "What's this?" he asked, looking at the tiny, ceramic image of a baby lying in a cradle.

"It's the baby Jesus! I'm gonna put it under the tree," Ruth said proudly.

Sam looked at his wife. *"Seriously?"*

Mary Catherine laid on her best Yiddish accent, hunching her shoulders and making circular motions with her hands. *"What can I say? They were five cents apiece at Mendelsons."*

Sam didn't laugh. His wife took on a more serious demeanour. "Oh, don't be so...so orthodox. What harm will it do? Life's short." She hung up her coat. "By the way, I told Mabel we'd join them for Christmas dinner. She's hoping it will be good for Amour and Victoria to have lots of friends around."

Sam held his arms out at his side and turned his palms upward. "But it's the first day of Hanukkah?"

"So, we take the Menorah with us."

"I really don't have a say in this, *do I?*"

Mary Catherine squeezed his arm and, once again, lathered on the thick accent of a Jewish mother putting her foot down. *"How can you even ask such a thing? Of course, you don't!"* she said and laughed.

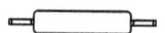

Gordon dropped Charlotte off at his place and drove to the station. He was fairly certain McEwan wouldn't be in, as he was always angling to get the weekends off. Now that he was the boss, Gordon doubted he'd ever work another. He entered the quiet station and waited at the front desk for the duty officer to finally show up, explaining he had left behind a few personal belongings. The duty officer waved him on. Gordon ducked in his old office and picked up an ink well that belonged to his grandfather. He peeked out at the trusting, young officer engrossed in *The War Cry*, slipped into the adjacent room, rifled through a few file folders and found McInnes' department-commissioned, head and shoulders photo. He slipped it in his pocket, then walked past the front desk, waving his ink well in the air. "Got it," he said and left.

He waited at the end of a long line of shoppers filling Arlies' till with money they could ill afford to part with, smiled at the young man behind the counter and showed him Dan McInnes' picture. "Is this the guy who might have stolen Myrtle's painting?"

"Um, not sure. The guy in the store was older, had a beard, and he was… fatter in the face."

"This photo's about fifteen years old. Does he look like the guy you saw coming out of the Clerk's Office?" Gordon pressed.

"Maybe a little. But, like I said, I'm not even sure it's the same guy that was in the store."

Gordon picked a pen up off the counter and handed it to him. "Draw his beard."

"On the photo?"

"Yes."

The hesitant clerk began scratching his pen over the grainy image. He put his pen down and stared at the bearded face.

"What do you think?" Gordon asked.

"Could be." He handed it back to Gordon. "I just can't swear to it."

Gordon stood outside Arlies, looked at the marked up photo and walked toward his car. He stopped at the entrance of Woolworths and peered in, wondering if Gladys Ferguson might be inside boasting to customers about her charitable work with the Benevolent Society with one breath, and spreading her vile gossip with the next. Why would she tell Lizzie McInnes collected the reward, he thought, and pushed the door open.

"Merry Christmas. Welcome to Woolworths. How can I help you?"

Mabel hung up the phone and turned to Stanley who was siphoning water from the Christmas tree. "Glad to have that out of the way. Dr. MacLellan's not pleased Myrtle flew the coop." She laughed. "Said he'd check on her in the morning, as long as Myrtle promised not to bite him." She returned to the living room and began wrapping the more delicate bulbs in newspaper. "We need to tell Amour about the house."

Stanley had his arms stretched the length of the tree, holding it at a tilt. "I'm just not sure it's the right time."

Amour surprised them from the stairway. "What are you doing?"

Mabel looked at Stanley, then at Amour. "We're making room for the… for folks to say their goodbyes to Michael."

"There'll be no wake," Amour said flatly. "Leave the tree where it is."

Stanley righted the tree.

Amour continued down the stairs, took an ornament from the box, removed the newspaper wrapping and placed the metallic blue angel on the bare tree. There'll be a funeral, and then there'll be Christmas, as there always was. Michael would have insisted on it…for Victoria and the kids."

Mabel smiled. "Amour, we can put the tree in the barn and bring it back after the wake. It's really no trouble. The kids will–"

"No," she said harshly. "There will be no wake. And I'd like to have the funeral on Monday."

"Of course," Mabel said. "I'll call father Cusack and look after the arrangements. Did Michael have a favourite hymn or a verse you might like–"

"Not that he mentioned. Like me, he probably thought his funeral was a long way off." "I trust you to pick whatever you think is appropriate."

Stanley returned the tree to its festive state, while Mabel consoled her anguished friend over tea. He could hear Amour's muffled sobs and Mabel's reassuring murmurs. Then he heard the phone. It was Fred Clarke.

"I popped into the office to get a jump on some estimates before the Holidays and found a letter on your desk. Pretty sure it's from Lily. Looks like her handwriting," Fred said.

"Open it," Stanley said.

"I dunno, boss. It don't sound good."

"What does it say," Stanley said, his concern mounting.

Fred cleared his throat. *"I'm sorry. I had no choice. I did it for my kids. I promise to pay you back. Please, give me time to put things right. Lily."*

Stanley ran his hand through his hair. She couldn't possibly have cleared out his account. She'd never do such a thing. He hired her, and he and Mabel both looked out for her and her kids.

"Boss? You there?"

"Yeah, I'm here."

"I guess that explains the rubber cheques."

Stanley's heart began to pound and his mind race. "There's got to be another explanation."

"Can't imagin what that could be. Sorry, boss. I know this is the last thing ya need on your plate right now. Let me know if me and Aggie can help out in any way."

Stanley smiled at Mabel and Amour as they walked past him on their way upstairs. "Thanks, Fred," he said, slowly placing the receiver back on its cradle.

Mabel looked down from the stairway. Her husband was staring down at the phone. "Everything all right?" she asked.

Stanley looked up. "Oh, it's nothing. Just a little glitch at the office. Good night."

A Funeral, a Shoe Box and the Finger

Monday, Dec. 23

Mabel and Stanley tiptoed around the kitchen, hoping not to wake Amour and the kids, and dreading the day ahead. The funeral was at eleven. Mabel prayed for a good turnout. Neither Amour nor Michael had lived in town for any length of time, and apart from a handful of her former co-workers at the bistro, and Michael's colleagues at the coal company, their family and friends were few in number. Stanley had more than the funeral on his mind; he was concerned about his bank account and the survival of his business. He looked at the clock, wishing it would tick faster.

"I have to go to town for nine," he said.

Mabel put down her knife. *"Today?"*

"Yes."

"What for?"

"I have an appointment with a potential client," he lied.

"Call and cancel. I need you here. For goodness sakes, we're burying Michael in a few hours."

Stanley knew not to argue. She'd be livid enough when she found out they were both played for fools. He took his coffee to the table and tried to comprehend Lily's deception, and how she pulled it off. He wondered if he should call Gordon for advice, but decided to wait until after he spoke with the bank.

Mabel put a carton of molasses next to his plate of homemade bread. Michael's death was taking a toll on him, she thought. He's looking for a diversion from the heaviness of the day. She squeezed his hand. "I jumped too soon. Keep your appointment. There's not that much left to do and Mary Catherine will be here shortly. But shave and wash up before you go, so we're not all scrambling for the bathroom at once. Your suit is hanging on the back of the closet door."

Stanley stood and kissed her forehead. "I'm not really hungry." He left to get washed and dressed for the sad formalities to follow.

He leaned over the basin, dipped his safety razor in the hot, soapy water and ran it along his jaw line. "Goddammit," he muttered, holding the razor head with one hand and twisting the handle with the other. He dropped the dull blade on the side of the sink, replaced it with a new one and started over. He hated the daily routine of shaving almost as much as Mabel hated his stubble. It was a simple enough task that he knew pleased his wife, yet, on this morning, it seemed particularly burdensome. He swished the blade around in the hair-speckled, foamy water, feeling guilty about complaining about something so small. What Michael wouldn't have given to be standing here next to him, performing *his* morning ritual.

Stanley placed his hands on the sink, leaned forward and started to sob.

JC barged through the door. "I need to pee! What's wrong, Daddy?"

Stanley bent down, pulled his son into his chest and kissed his cheek. "Daddy…daddy was just thinking about how big you're getting. You're growing up so fast. Pretty soon, I'm gonna have to teach you how to shave."

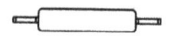

Gordon eased the knot up to his throat and considered the result. "Look okay?" he said, turning to face Charlotte.

She yawned and stretched her arms wide, casting off the remnants of a deep sleep. "Very handsome. What time is it?"

"It's not quite nine," Gordon said, easing his foot into his shiny black shoe. "I need to go to town. I'm hoping Gladys Ferguson is working. I'll be back before eleven. Seems like all I do these days, is go to funerals." He leaned down and kissed her.

"I'll be ready. Good luck," Charlotte said, rolling onto her side.

Gordon entered Woolworths and approached the lunch counter.

Rosie put her coffee pot down. "Well, now! Look at *you*! Ya here to whisk me away?"

"C'mon, Rosie, you know I'm spoken for."

"So am I, but it'll only take a sec to pack my bags," she said and winked.

"Not today, I'm afraid." He looked around the store. "Gladys Ferguson in?"

Rosie leaned into him and whispered. "I hear she's a lousy lay." She laughed and pointed. "Doin what she does best, foldin mens pants and causin turmoil."

Gordon approached Gladys from behind. "Good morning, Mrs. Ferguson."

Gladys spun around. "Captain Dunphy!" She touched his wrist. "What am I thinkin. Mister Dunphy. I read in The Post they let ya go."

He smiled. "Actually, I quit."

Gladys smoothed her hand over her neat stack of Gabardines. "So what can I do for ya? Lookin for a nice pair of dress slacks, or maybe a good deal on dungarees?"

"Neither. I ran into Lizzie MacNeil on Saturday. She claims you told her Dan turned in the missing change purse. The one with the reward."

Gladys sunny demeanour suddenly changed. She hesitated, wondering why it was a matter of interest to the former officer. "*Oh?*"

"Did your nephew tell you he collected the reward?"

"What's this about? And why are *you* askin?"

"It's...it's just that I heard the reward *hasn't* been collected? Any idea why Dan would tell you otherwise?"

Gladys wondered what kind of trouble her nephew might have gotten himself into. She pressed her hands together to keep them from shaking. "This old brain of mine sometimes gets confused. I'm probably mistaken."

Gordon knew she was covering for McInnes. He reached in his pocket and unfolded the poster. "Ever see this change purse? It belonged to Myrtle Munroe. Was stolen the night she was attacked."

Gladys barely glanced at it. "No. Not that I can recall."

"*You're sure?*"

She paused. "Yes. I'm sure."

Gordon put the poster back in his pocket. "No worries. I was just walking by and thought I'd stop in and ask. I'm sure it's just a big misunderstanding. Thanks. Oh, and Merry Christmas."

"Merry Christmas," Gladys said flatly, returning to her folding.

Gordon went to his car, sat and waited. He'd bet his last dollar she'd come out any minute and head straight for the Clerk's Office.

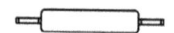

Lizzie plunked the open shoe box on Dan's desk.

He looked up at her, then fingered the bills in the box. "My Christmas bonus?" he said, wondering what she was up to.

"Yer the only one in the office who hasn't contributed to the Turkey and Toy Drive. Figure with yer reward money, yer good for at least a five."

Dan patted his pockets. "I don't have any cash on me."

Lizzie shook the box. "Change will do."

"I'll get you tomorrow."

"Tomorrow's too late. We're doin the shoppin after work."

"Then, I'm sorry. It'll have to wait till next year." He picked up his pencil and ran it along the top of his ruler.

Lizzie grabbed the box and turned toward her wicket. "Yer aunt's here," she said coldly.

Dan looked over his shoulder. Gladys was at the door, frantically waving him over. He angrily pushed his chair back and approached. "What is it? I'm working!" he hissed.

"Gordon Dunphy came by the store. He was askin about the reward ya collected fer–"

Dan quickly looked around. "Keep your voice down," he whispered harshly, feeling panic set in. "*When?*"

"About fifteen minutes ago. Lizzie told him ya collected the reward, but he claims no one turned in the purse. He said it belonged to Myrtle Munroe." She leaned in and lowered her voice. "The woman who was attacked. Wondered why you said ya collected the money if ya–"

"He doesn't know what the hell he's takin about! Jesus, I showed you the reward money," he snapped. He wanted to kill her *and* Lizzie. "Like I told ya, I bought it from a kid who was hawkin stuff on the side of the road. Same kid Dunphy had in custody and let go. Little punk's been re-arrested for the attack. What the hell did ya tell him?"

Gladys smiled nervously at Lizzie. "Nothin. Danny, ya didn't do nothin–"

"Of course not! Look, I gotta get back to work."

"But–"

He glared at her. "Jesus Christ almighty! Are ya tryin to get me fired? Go back to work!"

Dan returned to his desk. His heart was pounding like a jackhammer. He picked up his pencil and snapped it in two. "Fuck," he muttered, thinking it wouldn't be long before Dunphy, or possibly the police, paid him a visit. He knew the chance of them believing his line about buying the change purse from Kenny was slim to none, and, even if they did, how would he explain the lie about collecting the reward money. And his aunt was bound to ask where the purse was. *Think. Think.*

Gordon watched Gladys leave the Clerk's Office. The normally gregarious gossip brushed past shoppers on the busy street and headed directly back to her station at Woolworths. He was sure his visit rattled her and that her stack of neatly folded Gabardines would soon be a jumbled mess. He was also sure he was closing in on the person responsible for Myrtle's attack. He looked at his watch and started the car. He still had time to pay McEwan a visit and get Charlotte in time for Michael's funeral.

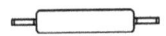

Stanley spoke to the teller who confirmed his account reported a balance of four dollars and thirty-two cents, with more than a dozen uncashed cheques still outstanding. He wasn't surprised, but still felt like he had just been kicked in the gut. He waited at the counter for the teller to return with the bank manager.

"Mr. MacIntyre," the manager said, extending his hand. "I hear there's a problem with your account. Come with me and we'll see what we can do."

Stanley looked at the stamped cheque made out to *cash* and totalling sixteen thousand, five hundred dollars. He immediately recognized the signature. It was his. He closed his eyes, recalling the day Michael dropped in on him and they went to the Clerk's Office. He had been signing the bonus cheques. He must have signed one without including the recipient's name.

The young teller whose initials verified the transaction was summoned to join them. She nervously smiled at her boss. "Is there a problem?"

She confirmed she thought it was a large amount of money, but knew Lily worked for *S&M Design and Construction,* and that she had been given authority from the company to look after the banking. She turned to Stanley. "When I questioned Lily about the large amount of money, she said you were opening a new office on the mainland and needed the money right away in order to settle a property transaction. She told me the seller demanded the money in cash and that you were back at the office waiting to head out and conclude the deal. I'm sorry. I didn't think she'd–" She started to sob.

"It's not your fault," Stanley said, cursing himself for being so careless and trusting.

The bank manager picked up the receiver and began dialling.

"What are you doing?" Stanley asked.

"I'm calling the police."

Stanley thought back to Fred reading Lily's note. *I had no choice. I did it for the kids.* "Hang up," he said.

"*What?*"

"I said, hang up."

The manager looked stunned. "But this is a substantial theft! It needs to be reported."

"I was the one robbed. It's my call."

The manager hesitated, then slowly put the receiver back on its cradle.

Stanley stood to leave. He turned at the door. "I trust any business I do at this bank is confidential and that it will remain so."

The manager nodded.

"Thank you. Oh, and I believe there is sufficient funds in my personal account to cover any uncashed cheques. If you wouldn't mind transferring the money into my business account so the cheques can be processed."

The manager looked at his tearful teller, then back at Stanley. "Of course."

Stanley smiled. "Merry Christmas," he said and left.

He walked to his car, thinking of Michael and the shattered family he left behind. "It's only money," he whispered.

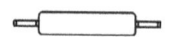

McEwan grinned and leaned back in his chair with his hands behind his head. He'd humour him for ten minutes.

Gordon told him about his conversations with the clerk from Arlies.

"You've got nothing. The kid can't even swear McInnes is the same guy he saw in the store. You've never liked Dan. Did Stanley MacIntyre put you up to this?"

Gordon tried to control his anger. "There's more," he said, telling him about Lizzie's claim that McInnes collected the reward. "He's lying. No one collected the reward. And when I showed Gladys the poster and asked about McInnes' false claim of collecting the reward, she became visibly nervous and immediately trotted off to see her nephew. *Why*?"

McEwan leaned forward. "I thought you gave up on police work?"

"Maybe so, but I didn't give up on the boys," Gordon said.

McEwan's snarky attitude turned to worry. If Dunphy was right, and McInnes was responsible for the attack, he would have egg all over his face, and Dunphy would be vindicated. He wondered what the implications would be once it became public he bowed to public pressure and rushed the charges against the boys. *Would he be demoted. Would Dunphy look for his old job back.* He thought back to the day he met Dan at Iggies, when his old friend and former colleague showed a particular interest in the investigation. He knew he had no choice. He had to at least consider the possibility McInnes was involved.

"Big Dick and I will have a chat with him," McEwan said.

"Great! I'll go with you."

"No way! This is *police business*," McEwan said, thinking that if Dunphy's theory proved correct, he needed to be seen to have made the arrest.

"I've been helping Sam with the boys' defence. I know the case. It only makes sense that I—"

McEwan got to his feet. "Ferget it!"

Gordon knew it was useless to try and change McEwan's mind. "I wouldn't wait too long. He knows I've been asking questions. I wouldn't be surprised if he gets skiddish and takes off."

"No need to embarrass the guy in front of his co-workers, especially if this is all just a big misunderstanding."

"I'd strongly suggest you do it as soon as possible. At least put one of the guys outside his office…in case he decides to bolt."

"Ya always were one to squander precious resources. Don't worry. I got this under control."

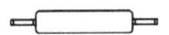

Mabel held Myrtle by the arm and followed Stanley, Amour and the kids up the steps of St. Leo's church. The choir director approached her, advising the organist had come down with a bug and there would no musical accompaniment.

Family and friends settled into the front pews for the final goodbye. Victoria held her mother's hand and rested her head on her shoulder. Mabel sat next to Myrtle, with Mary Margaret on her lap.

Myrtle suddenly stood. "La...let me by," she said.

Mabel turned her knees to the side to let her pass. "Where are you going?"

Myrtle didn't answer. She walked up to the side of the altar, had a brief word with the choir director, pulled out the organist's bench and sat down.

Stanley, Luke, Ted, Gordon, Sam and John carried the body of a beloved father, husband and friend to the front of the church, as Myrtle's beautiful, clear, stutter-free voice stood out from the rest of the choir.

> *Abide in Thee! In that deep love of Thine*
> *My Jesus, Lord, thou Lamb of God divine.*
> *Down, closer down, as living branch with tree,*
> *I would abide, My Lord, my Christ in Thee.*

Despite being unfamiliar with the deceased, Father Cusack spoke as if he had known Michael for years, lauding him for his devotion to his wife and child, and for his dedication to his duties and to God.

He walked away from the pulpit and looked out at the gathering. "As we conclude this Mass of Resurrection and make plans for the holy season, many of us with heavy hearts, remember what we are celebrating. We are celebrating the birth of Jesus. A man of flesh and blood. A man, who through the ultimate and infinite power of our Holy Father, suffered, died and was buried. God gave us his only son to take on the sins of man... so that Michael Joseph Donnelly... and all of mankind...would have their sins absolved and ascend into heaven to sit at His side. Like Jesus, who rose from the dead... Michael has been resurrected, and he is happy in the arms of Our Lord. Yes, let us mourn his earthly passing and give comfort to Michael's family, but let us also give thanks for the power and glory of God Almighty... and Our Lord, Jesus Christ."

Father Cusack nodded to Myrtle and sat off to the side.

Amazing Grace, How sweet the sound
That saved a wretch like me
I once was lost, but now am found
T'was blind, but now I see....

He returned to the front of the altar. "May God bless and abide in you. And may you praise and honour his Holy name. For He is our light. Our saviour. Our salvation."

Dan anxiously watched his fellow workers get ready to leave for the office's annual Christmas lunch. It would be just him and one other junior employee left to man the wickets and handle the phones. He waited for the last person to disappear behind the door, quickly grabbed his things and hurried down the stairs. He stopped at the bottom, slowly pushed the door open and casually stepped out onto the sidewalk.

His hand shook as he tried to get the key into the ignition. "Stay calm," he muttered, edging into traffic. He was on Main Street, when the cars in front began pulling off to one side. He started to panic, thinking it might be a police check. "Thank God," he said, when he saw the approaching hearse, followed by a long line of cars with their headlights on. Unlike the vehicles in front, he pulled out as soon as the hearse passed. He didn't see the woman wearing a white, gauze turban sitting in the back of an oncoming car. She was holding her middle finger up against the window, cursing him for his breach of funeral protocol.

Dan tore into the house and began frantically throwing his clothes into his duffle bag. He then pulled a suitcase from Gladys' closet, tossing in anything of value he could find, including her silverware, a few cherished pieces of jewelry and her dead husband's gold tie clip.

He was back in the car within minutes, hoping to be on the mainland before dark. He knew the police wouldn't be far behind. If Dunphy didn't already sic them on him, Lizzie probably did. He reached over and picked up a handful of bills, letting them drop back into the shoe box. It wasn't much, but it would cover a few nights in a motel.

Despite the frigid air, he stood on the deck of the ferry. He was relieved to be off the island, but realized he had no choice, he had to ditch the car. He'd drive as far as Antigonish and hop a bus.

He parked a distance away from the bus station, entered the near empty depot and checked out the display board. The next bus west was departing in roughly a half hour. He purchased a ticket for New Glasgow and stood behind a pillar with his eyes on the entrance.

A woman walked in with her children, went to the wicket, then settled onto a bench. Her young son began bouncing a small, blue ball. It got away from him and rolled in McInnes' direction. He put his foot over it, laughing as the child and his mother looked under the benches for the little, rubber orb. McInnes rolled his foot back and forth over it, then thrust his foot forward, sending it in the direction of the grateful child.

The boy's mother smiled and mouthed *thank you*.

McInnes approached her. "Where ya headin?" he asked.

"Amherst."

"*Really?* Me, too," he lied, thinking the police would be looking for a single, white male, not a man with a family. "If you want to travel with me, I'll charge you half what you paid for your tickets."

"Aren't *you* getting the bus?"

"No." He held up his damaged hand. "Gotta earn a livin. Hang around here and there, hoping to pick up the odd fare." He nodded to the ticket agent and winked. "He gets his cut."

"But I already purchased my tickets."

"He'll give you your money back. And we can leave now. No hour long wait. No milk route. You'll get there by eight at the latest."

She hesitated, then looked at her daughter curled up on the bench with her eyes closed. "How much for the four of us?"

"I'm feeling generous. Eight dollars all in."

"But that's barely enough to cover the gas."

"Like I said, I'm feelin generous. Hopefully, I'll pick up a return fair. By the way, I'm Barry...Barry Sheppard."

"I'm Lily...and these are my children—"

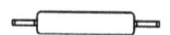

⊏⎯⎯⎯⎯⊐

Mabel closed the door and thanked the dozen or more strangers who had unexpectedly arrived back at the house following the funeral. She turned to Stanley. "*Who were those people?*"

Stanley was pouring fresh rounds for the close friends who remained. "I have no idea. But they were certainly hungry."

Ten-After-Six arched his neck. "They're members of R.I.P.P."

"*Rip?*" Mabel said.

"Yeah, R.I.P.P., the Rest in Peace Party. They're hearse chasers. They love funeral sandwiches."

Stanley laughed.

Mabel gave her husband a piercing stare. "I've never heard of such a thing. And it's *not* funny."

Ten-After-Six sifted through the dwindling array of assorted sandwiches and piled a half dozen or more on his plate. "They *are* good," he said, joining the others in the living room.

"I'm surprised nobody came from the coal company," Mabel said to Stanley.

"I told them not to."

"*Why?*"

"Cause they're bastards, that's why. Two of them pulled me aside when I was leaving the church. Wanted to make sure I understood Michael hadn't officially started, and that Amour has no claim on the company. Couldn't even wait till he was laid to rest."

"I'm not surprised," Mabel said.

Stanley leaned in, kissed her cheek and picked up his tray. "Better serve the *li..ba..tions*," he said, thinking of Michael and how he'd playfully mimic Amour's reference to her alcoholic concoctions.

Despite their own heartbreak, Mabel and Stanley tried their best to lighten the heavy mood.

Amour leaned over and put her hand on Myrtle's leg. "You sang beautifully today. Not a sign of your stutter."

"Ga…ga…gonna have to sing ev…everything…fra…from now on."

Amour smiled and stood. "I'm sorry. It's been a long day. If you don't mind, I'm going to lie down for a while."

Mabel and Victoria stood at the bottom of the stairs and watched her slowly mount the stairs. "Did you want to lie down with your mother?" Mabel asked.

"No," Victoria said, falling into Mabel's arms and sobbing. "I want to curl up and die."

Ted got to his feet. "I'm a little tired myself." He put his hand out to Myrtle. "Shall I escort the songbird home?"

The others took their cue.

Myrtle watched Luke help Alice on with her coat. "Ya...yer getting the... the new wife spread," she said, pointing to Alice's belly.

Luke laughed. "You coming?" he called to John.

John looked at Mabel. "If it's okay, I thought I'd stay for a bit."

"Of course. Stay as long as you like," she said, knowing the young man wasn't ready to say good night to the girl who had caught his eye and tugged at his heart.

Stanley entered the kitchen and began drying the dishes. Mabel unplugged the sink and swished her dishrag around the soapy water. "I love you," she said.

Stanley was surprised by her unexpected pronouncement. He put his arm around her shoulder and pulled her close. "I love you, too."

"Then promise me you won't die before me" she said.

"Sorry, you know I can't." He hesitated. "Actually, I have something to tell you, and I'm hoping you won't kill me."

Now it was Mabel who was surprised. "What's that?"

"Lily left town. She cleaned me out."

Gladys stood in the doorway of Woolworths and watched her neighbours board the bus to Steele's Hill. She checked the time. It was well after five and her nephew still hadn't come for her. She saw Lizzie walk past and quickly ran after her. "Lizzie!' she said, panting. "Yer late closin the office tonight. Is Dan still there?"

Lizzie looked angry. "He left at lunch time. No one saw hide nor hair of him since. He disappeared along with the money for the Turkey and Toy Drive. Sorry, Gladys, yer nephew's not a good man," she said, and continued on her way.

Gladys put her hand over her mouth. The bus started to pull away. Gladys waved her hands in the air. "Stop!" she said, hurrying across the slushy street. She stopped as the bus sped up and bumped its way over the Commercial Street Bridge.

An hour later, Bay Taxi pulled up to her small, tidy bungalow. Gladys rummaged at the bottom of her purse for her key and held the door open for the officers who had been awaiting her arrival. She flicked the light switch and started to cry. Her home was in a shambles. Cupboard doors were hanging open and her cutlery, littered the counter and the floor.

McEwan rushed to the phone to give the orders for a province-wide alert. "A forty-four year old... white male of stocky build. Dark brown hair, but balding. He's driving a...." he turned to Gladys for help. "A black car. We think it's a Dodge. Officers should approach with caution." He hung up, cursing himself for blowing any chance he had of being installed as permanent chief of the Glace Bay Police Department.

When he returned to the kitchen, Gladys' short, stout body was pressed against Big Dick's massive frame. "I gave him all I could," she sobbed. "Loved him like my own. I never thought he would do anybody any harm."

Big Dick rested his huge hands on her shoulders. "I'm sure you did all you could."

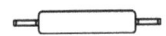

Lily sat uneasily in the front with her sleepy daughter on her lap. She was beginning to think she made a big mistake. Why would her driver be carrying luggage if he was simply picking up fares?

McInnes glanced at the pretty, young woman sitting next to him. "All set?"

Lily nodded and looked at the tote at her feet. She silently prayed he wasn't going to rob her and steal any hope she had of making a fresh start.

It was dark and snowing when they neared New Glasgow. The traffic came to a standstill. McInnes prayed it was an accident.

"What's goin on?" Lily asked.

"Not sure."

A police car passed on the outside. Lily felt sick. She was a fool to think Stanley wouldn't call the police. She looked back over her shoulder at her two young children leaning against the doors with their heads resting on their balled up jackets.

McInnes got out to look ahead. "Fuck," he muttered, jumping back in the car. Remember, play it cool, he reminded himself.

"Is it an accident?" Lily nervously asked.

"No. A police check."

"Turn around!" she demanded.

"*What?*" he asked, thinking she seemed rattled.

"You need to turn around!"

McInnes wondered what she had to fear. He looked back at the line of bumper-to-bumper cars stretching a good quarter mile. *"Why*? What did you do?"

"Please! Just turn around. I'll pay double!"

McInnes pulled on his mouth and watched his teary, nervous passenger use her foot to edge her tote closer to her seat. He knew she was hiding something. "What's in the bag?"

"Please, I'm begging you!"

McInnes started to laugh. *If it wasn't for bad luck, I'd have no luck at all. His fucking decoy was also running from the cops.* "I can't! They have a car up ahead ready to pounce on anyone who tries to avoid the checkpoint. Just be calm. From now on, you're Mrs. Barry Sheppard, and we're on our way to Amherst to spend Christmas with your family."

"You won't turn me in?"

"I hate the fuckin cops. But if we get through this thing, the cost of your fare just went up. Way up!"

They were one car back from the checkpoint.

McInnes turned to Lily. "Pinch her."

"*What?*"

"Pinch your kid! Pinch hard!"

Lily looked at him in disbelief. McInnes reached over and did what she refused to. The startled toddler began to wail.

He rolled down the window. "Evening officer."

The officer shone his flashlight in the car. "Where ya comin from?"

"Antigonish."

"And heading?"

"Amherst. Gonna spend Christmas with the wife's family. Hope the roads are clear up ahead. Got a sick kid. Runnin a high fever."

"Can I see your licence?"

McInnes turned to Lily. "Hun, you packed my wallet?"

Lily was trying to console her red-faced, screeching daughter. "I thought you did."

McInnes concealed his stumpy hand and smiled at the officer. "Sorry about the racket." He reached across to Lily's feet and began rifling through her bag. He pinched the child a second time. "It's gotta be in here somewhere," he yelled above the screaming child. The kids in the back were sitting with their knees up to their chins and their hands over their ears.

"Don't worry about it," the officer said, feeling badly for the child and her anxious mother. "Roads are greasy up ahead. Drive slow."

McInnes slid back behind the wheel. "Thanks. Merry Christmas."

"Merry Christmas," the officer said, indicating for him to proceed.

They were about ten miles down the road when McInnes suddenly pulled over and grabbed her tote. Lily tried to take it from him. He pushed her hard against the passenger door, reached in and withdrew the thick, white envelope. "Well lookie here," he said, grinning and fanning the fat wad of crisp hundreds and fifties. "What did you do, rob a bank?"

Lily started to cry.

"Please! It's all I have! I'm just tryin to start over. I'm a good person. I did if for my kids."

McInnes shoved the envelope in the inside pocket of his coat. "Who's in Amherst?"

"A cousin."

"Well, Mrs. Barry Sheppard, there's been a change of plans," he said, chuckling. "Looks like we got plenty of money to take that honeymoon we never had." He winked. "Ever been to Halifax?"

Gordon slammed down the phone. "Goddamn idiot," he yelled.

Charlotte rushed out of the kitchen. "What's wrong?"

Gordon told her that McInnes skipped town and that Gladys confirmed her nephew had Myrtle's change purse. "I knew it! I told McEwan to have him watched. God knows where the hell he is now," he seethed. "I need to let Sam know... and *Myrtle*. And I better tell Stanley."

He called Sam. "I told you McEwan would fuck this up... Yeah, they issued a bulletin for his arrest.... He had at least a five hour head start. And get this, Big Dick tells me McEwan didn't even tell mainland police to be on the look out for a guy missing half his hand. Just gave a general description and said he drove a black car. Jesus, everybody drives a black car. Idiot! Who the hell knows where he is now. Yeah, you're right. It may not be the outcome we hoped for, but at least the boys can look forward to a happy Christmas."

Charlotte waited for him to finish. "Gordon, the cat!"

"What cat?"

"The dead one."

"*Lucky?*"

"Yes, *Lucky*. He's still on your back step."

"I'm sorry. With everything else on my mind, I forgot. I'll take care of him later."

Charlotte shook her head in disgust. "Poor thing's probably been thawing on and off for the past two weeks."

Gordon gave an apologetic shrug and called Myrtle. She seemed grateful for the update on her attack, but otherwise unconcerned about the fate of her assailant. Stanley, on the other hand, had a different reaction. He was furious the police let him get away, once again insisting he was behind JC's kidnapping.

Gordon no sooner hung up from sharing the news with Stanley, when the phone rang.

Charlotte listened to the one-sided conversation. "Who was that?"

"Mayor Wareham."

"What did he want?"

"Wants me to stop by his office in the morning."

"Did he say why?"

"Said Judge Kennedy's wife stopped by to see him. Apparently she found a letter the Judge had left for him. He thought I'd be interested in its contents."

"Does he know you were right about the boys?"

"Yes."

"And?"

"Just said it was good to finally get to the bottom of things."

Mabel sat on the couch, nursing her drink and waiting for Stanley to return from taking John home. The house was quiet and the room dark, the only light, an orange glow from the crackling fire. She heard the truck pull up and knew her husband would check on the horses one last time. He finally came through the door and sat beside her for one of the few quiet moments they had together in weeks.

Mabel handed him a scotch. "I still can't fathom how Lily could do such a thing."

Stanley clinked his class against hers. "As they say, no good deed goes unpunished. Can you believe McInnes attacked Myrtle?"

"Yes, *but please*...let's not talk about him. He's such a...loathsome...creature."

Stanley nudged in closer. "I just hope the police find him, lock him up and throw away the key."

Mabel pinched her forehead. "There you go again."

"Sorry, I can't help myself," Stanley said. "Anyway, I'm glad the police are looking for *him*...and *not* Lily." He squeezed Mabel's hand." Thank you for agreeing not to report her."

"Don't get me wrong. I feel hurt...betrayed. But I'd never see her go to jail. Bad enough the kids' father's in jail. No point in their mother joining him. And let's face it, it's a lot easier to rebuild a business than it is a family. We'll be all right. The bakery's doing okay. At least I think it is. Mary Mac said she couldn't keep up on her own and had to send customers to McFadgens. Hopefully they'll come back."

"I had to dip into our personal account to cover the bonuses for the boys and a few other outstanding cheques. Not sure there's much left for Christmas."

""We'll manage. But the business will be fine, *right*?"

"I'll need to take out a loan to cover payroll and new inventory. But, we should be okay. It'll just take time to get back on an even footing. By the way, I told the guys what happened."

Mabel leaned forward to see his expression. "What do *they* think?"

"They think I should have reported her. Said we're nuts."

Mabel laughed. "Amour and Mary Catherine think the same. I told them they should put themselves in her shoes. Honestly, I think if I were in her predicament...being shunned by all the so-called do gooders...with her kids being constantly tormented, I might have done the same."

Stanley put his arm over her shoulder. "No, you wouldn't of."

"*How do you know?*"

"Just do. You're tougher than most. You'd find a way to cope...short of larceny."

"There's a little larceny in all of us," Mabel said. She took a sip of her drink, thinking how easy her life was compared to what Amour, Lily and so many others had to deal with. "I wonder where she is, and if she and the kids are okay. Despite what she's done, I'm still worried for her."

Stanley took her drink from her and placed it on the table. "You worry too much," he said, leaning over her and easing her down on the couch.

McInnes rolled off Lily and sat naked on the side of the bed. He lit a cigarette, twisted his body around and glared at his unresponsive bedmate. Lily pulled the sheet up from her waist and held it at her neck, hoping her kids were asleep and unaware of her latest shame. She started to cry.

"Hey, didn't do much for me either!" McInnes said. "Woulda been better if I shoved my dick into the pocket of a fur coat. Yer gonna have to do better than that… or I'm outta here… and you and your three brats will be on your own without a penny to your name. *Oh*, and it won't be long before the cops come lookin for you."

Lily curled into the fetal position. She had already committed an unforgiveable sin. My soul is already damned to hell, she thought. *Can I commit another? Can I kill the wolf in sheep's clothing who did unspeakable things to me while my children slept two feet away?*

She closed her eyes, thinking of her three babies and what would happen to them without her. Would they be torn apart and sent to live with other families, never growing up together…never knowing each other.

Lily blessed herself and silently prayed. *God forgive me and give me strength. Help me through this storm. Help me keep my children safe. Help me find a clear path.* Her eyes flashed open. She suddenly realized why her life was a series of one misery after the next. *God's punishing me for being a bad mother. He's punishing me for giving up my baby girl.*

Off By One

Tuesday, Dec. 24

Mayor Wareham passed Gordon Judge Kennedy's letter. Gordon unfolded it, but hesitated.

"Go ahead, read it," the mayor instructed.

> *Dear Stuart:*
> *I hope this finds you in good health and that I'm not dead yet. I want to live to cast a vote against you. I'd rather vote for a scoundrel and know what I'm getting, than a spineless weasel who doesn't have the guts to put up a fight.*

Gordon stopped and gave the mayor a look that questioned why he should continue.

"Keep going," the mayor said firmly.

> *We've been friends since grade three and my family and I have always supported you with our votes and a generous campaign contribution. No more. Rest assured, even if I'm not here to cast a ballot, my family won't be supporting you. How you could kow-tow to the likes of Mannie and his corrupt cronies is beyond me. You're better than that. The Stuart I knew, or thought I knew, would stand his ground and take his licks. What rankles me the most, is what I see happening within the police department. We both know that even if Chief Peach returns, he will be retiring soon. Gordon Dunphy would have been the natural choice to replace him, but, sadly, I am*

about to write a letter of reference for him to join the Mounties. I hold you as responsible for this sorry state of affairs, as I do Mannie.

With that said, I hope you enjoy the Holidays with your family. We are expecting Curtis to arrive on the twentieth, with the others arriving home on Christmas Eve. Looking forward to seeing everyone and holding my grandbabies one last time.
Sincerely,
Russell.

P.S. I wrote to the Attorney General and lodged a complaint against Mannie for violating the ethical standards of a Crown Prosecutor.

Gordon folded the letter and handed it back to the mayor. "He was a wonderful man. Definitely no shrinking violet."

"No, but I was. And he was right. I put politics before principle," Mayor Wareham said. He stood, walked to the window and looked out. "I miss the crotchety, old bastard," he said wistfully. He turned back to Gordon. "I met with the police commission last night, after I learned about the latest developments. Needless to say, they're also feeling a little sheepish. We'd like you to reconsider your decision to join the Mounties. The job of chief is yours, if you'll take it."

Gordon dropped his head. "What about Chief McEwan?"

"You mean *Sergeant* McEwan. I'm afraid he'd be your problem."

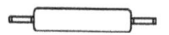

Stanley placed the boxes at Mabel's feet. "I think that's the last of it."

Mabel began peeking inside. "Is Amour's here? Oh, there it is." She reached in, pulled out Amour's unwrapped Christmas presents and put her hand to her mouth.

"*What is it?*" Stanley asked.

Mabel held up a gold name plate. *Michael Donnely, President.* "It's Amour's Christmas gift for Michael."

Stanley took it from her and put it back in the box. "I think we've done enough for the night. It's late and I'm exhausted."

She brushed away a tear. "You go. I still have to do the stockings, and I want to get a start on the vegetables. God knows where I'm going to put everyone."

She started counting on her fingers, stopped, then started again. "I don't know. I think there'll be sixteen of us. We'll need to borrow Myrtle's chairs."

Stanley stepped around the clutter. "Where are the stockings?"

"Go to bed," Mabel said.

"Not without you."

Mabel sighed. "Suit yourself." She pointed to the back of Stanley's favourite chair. "They're under your cardigan."

It was almost midnight when they fell into bed. Two hours later Mabel was still wide awake, thinking about the chaotic day to follow and all that was left to do. She closed her eyes, praying the excited squeals of the little ones would help dampen the heavy sadness that accompanied their fresh loss.

"Mommy! Wake up! Santa was here."

Mabel opened her heavy lids. JC was crawling onto the bed and Stanley was standing in the still dark room, pulling on his pants. She checked the time. It wasn't even five. *"He was! How do you know?"* she asked.

"I peeked downstairs," he said, bouncing on his hands and knees.

Stanley picked him up and put him on the floor. "But your sister's still asleep and we need to wait for her. Let's get you dressed, and you and Dad will go check on the horses," he said, shooing him out the door.

Mabel dropped her head on the pillow, closed her eyes and, once again, mentally counted her dinner guests. She rubbed her forehead, realizing her number was off by one. She had included Michael.

Pit Socks, a Menorah and a Blue Angel

Wednesday, Dec.25

Stanley removed the bulging pit socks from their hooks. "Stockings before presents," he said, playfully wagging his finger.

"An apple," JC pouted, coveting his sister's orange.

"Keep digging," his father scolded. He spotted Victoria sitting on the stairs and peeking through the rails. He smiled. "There's one here for you, too," he said.

Victoria got up slowly and joined them. He handed her her stocking.

"Stanley!" Mabel called from the kitchen. "I can't find my Corningware dish. I need it for the turnips. The one with the little blue flowers?"

"Is it the one I brought to Lily's a few weeks back?"

"That's one more thing we need to borrow from Myrtle," she hollered back.

Amour was the last up. Mabel hugged her when she walked into the kitchen. "We'll get through this together," she said. "Come, I could use your help."

Luke, Alice, Corliss and John were the first to arrive. Mabel was grateful for the noisy chatter, even the odd squabble, as Mary Margaret fought for her time with the Viewfinder Luke had given brother. She lifted a pot lid and stepped back from the escaping steam. She glanced at Amour, spooning Myrtle's chutney into a bowl. "How are you doing?" she asked.

Amour smiled. "I'm trying not to burst into tears. Michael would have been in his element."

Mabel whipped her dishcloth off her shoulder and tossed it on the counter. "Come with me," she said, taking Amour by the wrist. She led her upstairs and sat her down on the bed. "Now cry! Bawl your eyes out! Swear! Hit the pillow! Hit me! Don't hold anything back."

"It won't help!" Amour angrily snapped.

"Believe me it will. Cry until your eyes hurt!"

Amour shook her head. "It doesn't work that way."

Mabel opened the top drawer of Stanley's dresser. She closed her eyes when she saw the blood-splattered envelope. She quickly removed the deed and sat next to Amour on the bed. "Stanley and I have been trying to find the right time to give this to you."

Amour looked at the buff-coloured paper in Mabel's hand. "What is it?"

"It's your Christmas gift…from Michael."

Amour's hands were trembling when she unfolded it. She burst into tears and buried her face into Mabel's chest.

"He loved you so much. He's watching over you. And he knows you miss him. But he also wants you and Victoria to be happy," Mabel said.

They held each other, swayed back and forth on the edge of the bed and cried.

Amour finally sat up and brushed her wet cheeks. "I think it worked. My eyes are sore," she said and laughed.

Mabel got her a tissue. "Michael would understand if you decided to sell it."

Amour blew her nose. "Why would I sell it? I've always loved that house! And I love that Michael bought it for me."

Mabel was surprised. "But it's so big."

Amour walked to the mirror. "Big and beautiful, with a spectacular view of the ocean. My patrons would love it."

"You're opening another bistro?"

Amour smiled. "Actually, I've been thinking about it ever since Michael got the job. I kept my eyes open for a suitable location when I was checking the listings for a place to live, but didn't see anything worthwhile. Now I have the perfect spot. I think it would make a spectacular inn. And it's about time this town had a decent place to eat. The food at Woolworths is godawful. So, what do you think?"

"I think it's wonderful. Michael would be proud of you," Mabel said.

There was a light rap on the door.

"Come in," Mabel said.

Stanley slowly opened the door and stuck his head in. "Hey, hun. Ted and Myrtle are here, and Mary Catherine just called. They're on their way. Need me to do anything with the turkey?"

"We'll be down shortly," Mabel said. They both did their best to conceal the evidence they had been crying. Mabel held her hand out to Amour. "Ready?"

They stopped midway down the stairs and looked out at the chaotic scene below. The adults were chatting loudly and dodging the noisy, run-amok kids, energized by the excitement of the special day, sugar cookies and rock candy.

"Here we go," Mabel laughed.

Amour joined her daughter and the attentive young man sitting beside her. "What's this?' she asked, pointing to the box on Victoria's lap.

"Myrtle gave me water colours."

Amour smiled at Myrtle. "How sweet."

Myrtle reached under the tree. "Ga..got sa...something for you, too," she said, handing her friend a package wrapped in a repurposed grocery bag.

Amour broke the tape and pulled back the stiff paper. It was a back-on view of a man walking into a clear blue sky. He was wearing a long coat and holding a fedora. Amour ran her fingers over it.

"Sta...Stanley sha...showed me a pic...ture," Myrtle said, thinking it might have been a mistake to give it to her so soon. "I'm sa...sorry if—"

Amour looked up at her friend. Her eyes were pooling, but she was smiling. "I love it. It's wonderful. It's...beautiful. And I know exactly where I'm going to hang it," she said, sharing her news about Michael's gift and her plans to open an inn. "I'm going to call it Michael's Manor. *Oh*, and I got something for you," Amour said. She ran upstairs and quickly returned with a box. She handed it to Myrtle. "Sorry it's not wrapped."

Myrtle opened the box and smiled. "Tha...thank you."

"I always thought it was more your colour. What do you think?"

"I ha..hope to get to wa...wa...wear it soon." Myrtle placed the wig on top of her bandaged head.

Victoria and John started to laugh. Myrtle then whipped it off her own head and plunked it on Mary Margaret, who, to the delight of her amused admirers, refused to take it off.

Sam called everyone to attention and placed the menorah near the darkened widow, explaining the significance of the Festival of Lights. "Please join me for the blessing."

Mabel held Mary Margaret, and Stanley picked up JC. "What's he saying, Daddy?" JC asked.

"He's speaking Yiddish. A Jewish language," Stanley whispered.

"I wanna be a Jew," JC said. Stanley stifled a laugh and grinned at Mabel.

Sam lit the shammus and the lone candle on the right, and repeated the blessing in English. "Blessed are You, Lord our God, King of the Universe, who has sanctified us with His commandments and commanded us to kindle the Chanukah light...Amen." Sam lifted his head and put his arm around Mary Catherine. They smiled at one another, then turned to the gathering. "I think this is an ideal time to share our happy news. Ruth and Irwin will soon have a little brother or sister to play with," Sam said, grinning.

The crowed room erupted with handshakes, hugs and well wishes.

Luke looked at Alice and raised his eyebrows. Alice put her hand over her growing belly and nodded. "Mary Catherine! You and Alice will both be pushing strollers. I'm going to be a daddy," he shouted proudly.

"That means I'm going to be a grandfather!" Corliss said, slapping Luke on the back.

The room was, once again, abuzz.

Mabel stood back, watching the clamorous event unfold with a mixture of joy and worry. Luke was holding Mary Margaret's hand over Alice's belly, explaining that there was a little person growing inside. She looked up at Alice. Alice smiled, nodded gently and closed her eyes. It was a reassuring smile, Mabel thought. The warm smile of a woman who feels a a new life stirring within her and who will move heaven and earth to see their child is surrounded by love. Mabel tilted her head back, then placed her hand on her own belly, trying to recall her last period.

Stanley interrupted her thoughts. "Can we eat now? I'm starving," he whispered.

Mabel assigned everyone their elbow-to-elbow seats around the mismatched, uneven tables that stretched from the hallway to the far wall of the living room.

Stanley picked up Mary Margaret to put her in the highchair she had insisted she had outgrown. She would have none of it. She kicked and screamed until her frustrated father eventually gave in to his rebellious two-year-old. "She can sit on my lap," he finally conceded and put her down. He rubbed his hands together. "Let's eat!"

There was a knock on the door, then it opened. "Room for one more?" Mark pulled off his toque and offered Luke an apologetic smile.

"Mark!" John screamed. He pushed his chair back into the tree, knocking an ornament to the floor. Luke threw his napkin on the table and joined his younger brothers in the doorway; the magic of Christmas and his proud announcement he was going to be a father, dulling the hurt of Mark's embarrassing wedding toast.

Mabel looked for Alice's reaction.

Alice shrugged.

"Of course, there's room. It's Christmas," Mabel said, insisting Mark take her spot around the crowded table.

John made his way back to his chair. He was about to sit down when he noticed the metallic blue angel at his feet. He picked it up and placed it on the table between Victoria and her mother. Amour looked up at him.

"It's Michael," John said, smiling. "Michael the archangel."

Victoria squeezed her mother's hand. "Mom, he's with us. He'll always be with us."

There wasn't a dry eye to be seen as everyone took in a moment that was both heartwarming and heart wrenching.

Amour lifted her glass. "To my darling, Michael," she said.

The adults raised their glasses. "To Michael."

Mabel sat on the arm of Stanley's favourite chair with her plate on her lap and smiled as platters of sliced turkey, ham, perogies, and potato latkes, along with bowls of steamy root vegetables, chutney and Myrtle's pickled beets were passed from family to friend, and from young to old. She thought about how lucky they were to have one another, to share in each other's joyous moments and to help each other through times of sorrow. She looked at Stanley, leaning across Mary Margaret, still in Myrtle's wig, and picking onions out of JC's stuffing, and reminded herself of how truly blessed she was. She then thought of Lily, hoping she and her children were safe and warm, and finding some comfort in the love of family on this special day.

"Okay, everybody," Mabel said. "Dig in before it gets cold."

Life Goes On

January 23, 1949

Stanley threw The Post on the table. "I'm home!" Mary Margaret ran to him. He pulled his hankie from his pocket and ran it under her runny nose.

Mabel walked into the kitchen carrying a load of laundry on her hip. "Did you get the paper?"

He pointed to the table, then felt Mary Margaret's forehead. "Her nose is running again. Is she feeling okay?"

Mabel dropped her basket of bed sheets on the floor. "It's always runny. You worry too much. It's just a cold." She opened the paper to the society pages. "There it is!" she said.

Stanley took off his coat and looked over his wife's shoulder at the grainy photo. "And to think the boys almost went to jail." He sat to take off his boots. "Read it to me."

Mabel put on her glasses.

"Local artist, Myrtle Munroe; Chief of Police, Gordon Dunphy; his Worship, Mayor Stuart Wareham; and defence lawyer, Samuel Friedman, were among the dignitaries attending a reception, Monday, Jan. 17, Glace Bay Town Hall, to thank Winston McRae, Kenneth Ludlow, Harley Woodward, and Thomas Simms for their assistance in requesting help after Miss Munroe was left near death after an attack at Renwick Brook, late last year. Miss Munroe is seen in the above photo presenting each of the boys, along with Peter Boyd, who was instrumental in assisting with the police investigation, with a jar of her homemade beets and a cheque for twenty-five dollars. A Canada-wide warrant in connection with the still unresolved crime has

been issued for the arrest of Daniel Alphonse McInnes, a former sergeant with the Glace Bay Police Department."

Mabel folded in the arms of her glasses and laid them on the table. "Poor, Peter. You can't even see his face. If you didn't read the article, you'd never know it was him."

Stanley laughed. "Yes you would. Everyone recognizes the top of his head."

Mabel gave him a disapproving look and picked up her wicker basket. "Don't forget we're going to Amour's for supper. Oh, and I said we'd pick up John. You better get upstairs and shave. Amour hates to be kept waiting."

Stanley smiled and nodded. He picked up Mabel's glasses, rested the arms against his temples and peered down his nose at the sports section. "Yes!" he said, pumping his fist in the air. Vince Ryan had scored four goals to lead the Glace Bay Miners to a six to five victory over the Sydney Steelers. He closed the paper over and started to get up, when he noticed the headline above the fold. *Defeated Mayoralty Candidate Sanctioned by AG for Breach of Ethics.*

He smiled and tapped the headline with his finger. "What goes around, comes around," he said.

McInnes was in a good mood. He had a pocket full of cash, a healthy stash of whiskey and smokes, and he got to sleep next to a warm, if not willing body. Apart from Lily's noisy brats, life was good and getting better. He didn't need to work, there was no sign of the police, and he was free of Gladys. He chuckled to himself, wondering what MacInytre would think if he knew he was living high off the hog on his dime. What a fateful turn of events that I just happened upon the one person who screwed the prick over, he thought.

Lily's six-year old son leaned over the front seat. "Where are we going?"

Lily put her head down. "Mr. Sheppard is taking us to a motel," she said flatly.

McInnes turned his head and looked at the boy. "Your mother's got a job cleaning rooms. And the best part, we get to stay there for free. But ya better be good while she's gone, or I'll feed you to the wolves."

Lily shot him a look. "Please, there's no need to scare the children."

"He knows I'm jokin. Don't ya, buddy?"

The child returned to the back seat, but was back within minutes. "I gotta pee!"

"Yer gonna have to hold it. We're almost there." McInnes pointed. "See, there's the sign for Roachville. Ya know why they call it Roachville?"

The boy shook his head from side-to-side.

"Cause it's full of giant cockroaches. Huge, crusty, black bugs that can swallow a grown man in a couple of bites."

Lily looked at the tears pooling in her son's terrified eyes. "Please! He's just a boy!" she pleaded.

McInnes glared at her. "Oh, for fuck sakes, calm down! And put something on that cheek of yours. The yellow's showin through. Last thing *you* need is for someone to sic the cops on us." He glanced back at the frightened child. "And you! Stop snivelling like a little girl and sit back," he snapped.

Lily reached in her purse and felt the sharp edge of the knife she took from the diner. Tonight, she thought. She closed her eyes, picturing him mounting her and grunting like a pig. She'd surprise him by responding this time. And, just when he was in the throes of climax, she'd stab him in the neck. She prayed she'd find the courage to go through with it. *I have to*, she thought. *I have to do it for my kids.*

"We're here!" McInnes announced. He looked at Lily. "Our new home. It's perfect. No one will ever look for you here. It's smack dab in the middle of fuck knows where… and who the fuck cares."

Till Next Time...

POSTSCRIPTS

Gladys Ferguson finally decided that, with her nephew on the loose, her money was safer in the bank. She removed almost two thousand dollars in crisp bills wedged between the pages of the gold-stamped spines crammed together on the shelves of her dusty bookcase.

....

Chief Gordon Dunphy, accompanied by his wife, Charlotte Dunphy, presided over a ceremony where Mrs. Jerome Peach unveiled the head and shoulders portrait of her late husband. Unlike the dour expressions of his predecessors, the corners of Chief Peach's mouth were curled slightly upward.

....

Lucky was finally given a beautiful send off, fittingly laid to rest in a salt cod box (he loved fish) and buried behind Myrtle's shed, on the shores of the Atlantic. Myrtle, now a redhead, sang *Some Sweet Day, By and By* and gave a hilarious eulogy that left Amour and the small gathering in stitches. There was no hint of a stutter.

....

After a second theft from the pop factory, Big Dick determined it was an inside job. The owner's fourteen-year-old son was discovered by the chimney overlooking the brook, selling Frostie and Iron Brew to his buddies for five cents apiece.

....

Mary Mack ran her gloved-hand over the shiny fender of her 1941 Chrysler Town and Country, surprised to see the bus stop out front. It was actually on time. "You can screw off. I'm done waiting for you and your damn bus," she yelled to the driver. She jumped in and turned the key. There was a click. Then another and another. An hour later she charged into the bakery. "Sorry I'm late. Goddamn car wouldn't start."